THE REVOLUTIONARY

LIBERATE THE CAPTIVES

by

KRISTEN HOGREFE

Write Integrity Press

The Revolutionary
© 2018 Kristen Hogrefe

ISBN: 978-1-944120-58-0

All quoted Scripture passages are taken from the KING JAMES VERSION (KJV): KING JAMES VERSION, public domain.

Cover by Kelli Sorg
Some other illustrations: © Can Stock Photo / gearstd

Published by Write Integrity Press
PO Box 702852
Dallas, TX 75370
Find out more about the author, **Kristen Hogrefe,** at her website, **www.KristenHogrefe.com** or on her author page
at **www.WriteIntegrity.com**

Printed in the United States of America.

"Spirit, that made those heroes dare
To die, and leave their children free,
Bid Time and Nature gently spare
The shaft we raise to them and thee."

Ralph Waldo Emerson, "Concord Hymn"

PART ONE THE RUNNER

Chapter 1

Thursday, 2.12.2150
Warren Satellite

The February wind cuts through my skin as I shiver in the roll call line. On my left, Gath edges closer to shield me from the brunt of the cruel gust.

The coal mines have stained his skin even darker, and his shoulders now bow from the daily toil and unseen weight he bears, a weight I understand.

Three months have passed since our train dumped us in Warren Satellite, a place where prisoners die like rabbits and no one cares. The ride had been shorter than either of us expected. Luther sentenced us both to Baytown, the infamous western satellite where my brother Darius served. Instead, we had landed here, a forsaken coal mining camp. Neither of us knows why.

A few prisoners to my right, an older man crumples in the soot-stained snow. A Wasp stings him with a whip until the snow turns red, and still, he doesn't rise. The Wasp relents and walks away with a grunt. He'll remove the frozen body in the morning.

Last year, I had only heard of Wasps and wondered what they were. Now, I know and wish I didn't. This cruel breed of Gages oversees the satellites and makes life torture for prisoners.

I focus on Harris, the Commanding Wasp who runs the compound. His black boots burn a path in the snow as he inspects the line. Midnight rolls mean only one thing, and I wince for the poor soul slated as tonight's victim. And hope it won't be me.

"My pets, you look pathetic." Harris's voice drips like poisoned honey. "Why are you ungrateful for the care I provide? Which of you has betrayed me?"

My breath catches. What does he mean? Has someone escaped?

On the execution wall, a spotlight convulses. Its operator swings it to blind us and then to focus on the prisoner strapped in the platform chair.

My legs tremble. Although I've witnessed dozens of executions in the last three months, I hate chair killings the most, probably because I've felt the terror of this machine myself.

The model at Warren is older, cruder than the one Gage Eliab had used on me. Its harsh metal frame bulges from overuse, and the wires fringe on either side. Eliab hadn't been joking when he said the satellites served as testing centers for the chairs made to re-program personalities.

Only in Warren, Harris prefers the red lever, which fries prisoners until they resemble burnt toast. Once, he allowed the subject to live, but the resulting Frankenstein lasted but a day in the mines.

The prisoner's head sags from abuse, and bruises cover his face. What has he done?

"Rabbit 12035 has a secret he's not sharing," Harris resumes.

10

"He was presumed dead from a mining accident two months ago, and then yesterday, we found him alive in an abandoned part of the mine.

"But he won't tell us where he's been and how he's survived on his own. Those of you in the front row, you shared a bunkhouse with him. What do you know?"

I gulp. At least I'm in the second row. The man in front of me stiffens, and the woman next to him shakes in terror as Harris begins cracking his whip in front of them. It catches the man's ear. He flinches but remains erect, even as the blood drips onto his shoulder and down his arm.

No one steps forward or says anything. Even if someone knew, he wouldn't say. Harris may call us stupid rabbits, but our unspoken code is to live and die together. There's not much else we can do.

"Very well." Harris holsters his whip and snaps his finger above his head. The Wasp on the execution wall moves to the controls, and the air vibrates as the chair buzzes to life.

The prisoner's groans grow to screams.

I close my eyes to block out the sight, if not the sound. Unwanted tears freeze on my cheeks. How can Gath and I survive here much longer? With each passing day and execution, hope dwindles. If Foxworth had given Darius the drive, then the Brotherhood should have access to the virus I planted. They should be able to find us, even though someone detoured our train and changed our names to Nevada Ingram and Phil Jonas.

But I've almost forgotten I have a name. To Harris, I'm Rabbit 12017, and Gath is 12018.

What I would give to hear Luther call me Cotton! But would he even recognize me? The coal mines have stained my once snow-blonde hair a streaked black, and it's grown to touch my shoulders. At least it helps keep my neck warm.

Has everyone forgotten about us? Darius had promised to come for me. And where's Dad?

The wrenching cries on the wall stop, and I dare to look again. The prisoner, now a hideous gray, slumps in the chair, propped up only by his constraints. His chest heaves as if every breath is agony.

Another Wasp hands Harris a loudspeaker. He spits angrily into it. Gone is his pet-friendly facade. "This is your last chance to speak!" He addresses the prisoner first and then us.

But nothing anyone says can save the man from his fate. The compound remains eerily silent, except for the wind slapping the Warren flagpole which bears the ASU emblem.

"Have it your way," he says at last. "This place is overrun with vermin as it is."

Again, he snaps his finger. I whisper a prayer the end might be mercifully short.

The Wasp yanks the level to full power. I bite my lip but keep my head erect, averting my eyes to Gath's face.

His lips barely move, but I can read them. *Fraternitas Veritas.*

My lips quiver with doubt. If only I could know that somewhere, Darius, Dad, and my other brothers would one day come for us.

Chapter 2

Friday, 2.13.2150
Warren Satellite

I jolt awake, hitting my head on the low ceiling of my bunk bed. The barracks are still dark. The shot was either a nightmare or the start of a new terror initiative.

The bed below rumbles. I peer over the edge and whisper, "Are you awake?"

"Yeah, did you hear that?" Gath's voice croaks.

"It sounded close."

The tube lights flicker on, striking us with their sudden harshness. A Wasp flings the door open and marches down the aisle, striking anyone still in bed with his whip.

I jump to the floor and join the inspection line at the foot of the bunks.

"Straight to the lamp house with you," he barks. "There will be no pellets for you this morning, thanks to your insubordination."

Insubordination? What is he talking about?

My empty stomach gnaws on itself. As tasteless as breakfast

is, it takes off the edge. The Wasps likely have a science behind our calorie counts to maximize our productivity but gradually starve us to death.

I glance pitifully at Gath, now a gaunt giant. With no breakfast, I hope we won't get too dizzy and pass out during the 12-hour work shift.

I follow his slumped figure down the barrack stairs and to the lamp house where we store the day's equipment.

Gath slings a heavy shovel and pick ax over his shoulders and then grabs a methane-gas-detecting lamp that probably doesn't work. But he's a tunneller who searches for new seams and extends the track deeper into the mine. That means he's one of the crew members most likely to encounter dangerous flammable gases like firedamp.

Each day, he carries his equipment on the long trek to the mine, along with most of the other stronger prisoners. They tell us that they used to leave the tools at the mine, but the Wasps changed that rule when equipment started to go missing.

I'm a runner as are most of the other women and weaker, smaller prisoners. We're basically human mules who pull and sometimes load the coal carts. The only benefit is that I have no equipment to haul except a headlamp because my cart and attached shovel wait for me back at the mine.

I look at Gath. "Do you want me to carry something today?" Even as I say the words, my parched throat tightens. Surely, we will at least receive our water rations?

Gath forces a sad smile and shakes his head. "No, Nevada, save your strength."

I want to protest but don't. He never dares to call me Portia and rarely uses the name from my papers. Even that name, foreign

14

though it is, reminds me that I'm human, not a number.

I blink back salty tears, ashamed to admit how emotionally starved I am.

We form a jagged line during the pre-dawn march, shuffling close to stay warm in the below-freezing temperatures.

Every day, at least one prisoner collapses during the march, and the Wasps leave him behind. Frozen corpses dot the path, their bodies entombed in mounds of snow. Probably in the summer, their bones will become visible.

Will mine soon be among them? Our sentences have no bearing on our treatment. My twenty-year sentence is a joke. The average life expectancy is a year or less, though some of the hardier men survive longer.

We reach the gaping entrance of the mine and assemble into our crews, awaiting the day's orders. Usually, the Wasps don't micromanage, so I stay as close to Gath as I can, hoping that I'll be able to claim the track nearest him. With no food, I need my friend's presence to sustain me.

Gath is always watching out for me, trying to protect me. Darius's words from last October were a prophecy: *If your world's about to end, you want that man by your side.*

I hope that in some small way, I help him. But when he looks at me with his sad, silver eyes, I feel even more guilt. He seems to live for me, and most days, I can only think of my empty stomach and lost dreams.

The Wasps unload the frozen water buckets, and we'll have to wait until noon before they'll thaw enough for us to drink. Only when the temperature climbs closer to the freezing point will the workers be able to break off the ice in the buckets with their pick axes so we can reach the water below it.

"Get to work!" A Wasp shouts, and we scurry into the mines away from his crew's crackling whips.

The Wasps hate to enter the mines, so as long as we reach the day's quota, we get a break from their whips and words. The heavy air, soot, and danger of firedamp keep them away.

I hated the mines until I realized they were the only place to escape our taskmasters.

I claim a cart and catch Gath's attention as he gathers track supplies from a pile outside the mine's entrance. "Hop in." A ride is one of the few things I can offer him.

"Save your strength …"

"Hop in. I'm not taking no for an answer."

He smiles his thanks and first loads the new track equipment, his shovel, pickax, and lamp. Then, he climbs inside. After switching on my headlamp, I move to the front and tie the harness around my shoulders and waist. Compared to coal, Gath is a light load.

Five minutes later, my breath comes harder, but I'm not as cold. The mines tend to be warmer than the outdoors. Gath says it's because they keep the average temperature of the area, which at least is warmer than our current late winter temperatures.

"Drop me off at the new track," he says. We leave most of the other prisoners behind as I haul him deeper inside the mine.

We pass a crew with a pile of fresh coal, and I promise to be back to load it in a few minutes.

One prisoner acknowledges me with a nod. "Get the pile at the end of the line first. We'll be working here a while."

"Okay." I squint as I tug the cart farther down the line. We reach the coal pile, and Gath taps on my shoulder.

"But we haven't reached the track you laid yesterday."

"This is far enough." Gath climbs out and places a hand on my shoulder. I'm already huffing hard. "We're going to make it, Nevada."

Why he bothers with our fake names this deep in the caves is a mystery to me. Maybe it's just practice so he doesn't slip later.

I force a smile and catch my breath. "If you say so, Phil."

He unloads his equipment. "Be careful. I thought I saw another opening beyond where the miners left off yesterday and hope it's not a structural weakness. Holler if you need help. I'll be a few dozen yards beyond you."

I nod as he hunches to crawl deeper into the mine. The ceiling height is barely over five feet, perfect for me, but confining for the giant who used to stand over six and a half feet tall.

Turning to my cart, I slide out my small shovel stored inside and begin scooping the coal. It's lonely work, but I've grown used to the strange sounds in the mines. A thud here and a clatter there no longer frighten me.

After three months at Warren, the eerie mine seems like welcome company.

As I scoop the last shovelful, a scraping noise echoes in the confined space. I shine my headlamp around me, wondering if Gath has returned, but don't see my friend.

The sound grows louder and seems to be coming from a narrow corner beyond where I've cleared the coal.

Gripping my shovel, I step toward the noise. Did the crew leave someone behind yesterday? Prisoners collapse in the mines all the time and are left behind to die. Or worse, they get trapped and no one finds them until it's too late.

From the corner, light flashes. My heart quickens, and I crawl toward it. Someone must be trapped.

Now on all fours, I call out, "Hello, is anyone there? Can you hear me?"

No one answers, and I pause. If there were a cave-in yesterday, the area could still be unstable, and I could become the next lost miner.

I scoot my shovel to the left and shuffle back the way I came when my knee scratches something rough like wood. Before I can inspect the surface further, the floor gives way, and I tumble into a den of darkness.

With a groan, I hit the bottom of the hole, and my shovel clatters on the gritty floor. My hard hat bounces off my head, and the light shatters. Though my left shoulder throbs from taking the brunt of my fall, I don't think anything is broken.

I panic. Will Gath notice that I'm gone? He was right. There was a structural weakness, and I should've stayed away from it.

Now, I'm not sure which way is out. I spew pebbles from my mouth. "Help!" My call echoes dimly off the walls, but the expanse swallows it.

Fear makes me shiver. If I get lost in the cave, no one will find me.

I try to stand, but the roof is too shallow. Finding my shovel, I use it to poke the space in front of me and begin crawling in the pitch blackness. The light flashes once again. I'm either seeing things, or there's someone else trapped, too.

The person ignores my calls for help, and the light doesn't return. In search of it, I measure the minutes out loud so that if I have to turn around, I can find the place I started.

My cries for help punctuate my count but receive no answer. Fifteen minutes later, I'm about to give up when the space broadens. Soon, the ceiling grows high enough for me to stand, and

I grope the wall while using my shovel to test the floor in front of me. The last thing I need is to fall into a pit.

In the distance, a dim light glows. Maybe I'm not lost. Perhaps I've connected with another crew.

But the space remains silent of pickaxes and shovels, of cursing and crude jokes. If there is a prisoner crew ahead, I would hear them.

Then what is this? The light shines like a lone lamppost, but as I draw closer, the post takes on arms and legs. It's a man. He's wiry and muscular like a mule.

I freeze. Has he been waiting for me, or worse, luring me somewhere?

We stare at each other. The man's face is hard, unsmiling, but there's a spark in his dark eyes.

He reaches for a latch, and a crude door opens. "Follow me."

My hand hurts from gripping the shovel so hard. Can I even trust this man? But somewhere behind the door, there's a light shining, and its rays are warm and inviting compared to the dark void behind me.

The man crouches to clear the door and disappears inside. I follow him but stop short at the threshold.

It's the portal to another world, the likes of which I haven't seen in three months.

Before me, a bronze staircase spirals down into a long great room with carved marble floors and glistening pearl-colored walls. Different levels host milky white couches and polished maple furniture. Floor to ceiling bookcases boast leather editions, and a glistening black, grand piano graces one of the lower levels.

From the center of the ceiling hangs a sparkling glass chandelier which catches the light like a prism.

19

Perhaps more overwhelming than the sights are the smells, fragrant with coffee and a seasoned breakfast medley.

My knees buckle, and I grip the railing. An arm reaches for me and tugs me inside. In the moment, I had forgotten about the man, who now stands to my left on the platform. He closes the door and beckons me to follow him down the staircase.

The glowing lights and aroma make me feel faint. Somehow, the cold, dank mines have cloaked my misery, but in this beautiful place, it becomes raw. I glance at my scant clothing that hangs loosely about my emaciated frame. My hands and face—and probably every other inch of bare skin—are stained with coal dust.

I feel dirty, ashamed, like a pig from a sty suddenly invited to enter a mansion.

Terror fills me. The only reason a pig would enter a mansion would be for slaughter, to become the main course for dinner.

Dinner. The idea of food undoes the knots in my stomach. At least maybe the lord of the home will fatten the pig before killing it.

The man silently leads me to a long table and pulls out a chair. I hesitate. The fabric is the same creamy white, and I'm so dirty.

The man nods to me. "Sit."

"But—" I blush with shame.

"It's a chair. You're our guest."

I bite my lip and collapse onto it. The man treats me with dignity, like a human being. I've almost forgotten how that feels.

Despite the deep lines—or are those scars?—on his face, I guess he's young enough to be Darius's peer. He wears his brown hair cropped tight like a Gage would.

He turns to the wall and opens a small box to press a button. "Tea and breakfast in chamber 12," he says.

The button must be part of an intercom system like the ones in Crystal.

"Make yourself comfortable. Breakfast is on its way. If you need anything, press this button."

He taps the button again. With a terse nod, he takes a few stairs to another landing and disappears.

He's no sooner left than a dark-haired woman, perhaps in her late twenties, arrives. She's dressed in a trim black uniform and carries a silver tray with a steaming bowl, a teapot, and a porcelain cup.

She sets the bowl before me, and I try not to hide my disappointment. I had been hoping for a real breakfast—but this gruel is the same dull color as the mush in the Warren mess hall. I guess my malnourished body needs to be treated like a baby.

At least this food resembles oatmeal. The subtle cinnamon fragrance suggests it might even taste good.

She pours tea, and the spicy fragrance tempts my muscles to relax. "Sugar?" The rich color of the tea matches her creamy bronzed skin.

"Yes—please." My lips tremble.

The woman's chocolate-brown eyes warm in sympathy behind black-framed glasses. "Is there something else I can get for you?" Her voice is deep for a woman but holds an almost musical accent—though tainted with a mournful quality.

I shake my head dumbly, squinting so I don't cry. All this kindness unhinges me.

The mystery beauty disappears without another word.

With each bite of the food, my guilt grows. Somewhere, Gath is slaving in the mine on an empty stomach.

I stare at the last spoonful. How can I be this greedy? I should save some for later—for him—but there was so little in the first place. The portions were small to match my stomach size.

Swallowing hard, I replace the spoon. I won't take the final bite, though refusing it won't do either of us any good. It might ease my conscience, though.

I sip the tea. It's scalding, but my parched throat doesn't care.

A feeling of warmth relaxes my muscles and makes my eyes struggle to stay open. Was the food drugged?

My heart races. There's something both deceptive and soothing about the spicy tea flavor that lingers on my lips, but I'm too exhausted to resist.

I fold my arms on the table, bury my head in them, and succumb to the arms of sleep.

Chapter 3

Friday, 2.13.2150
Warren Underground

I dream of Luther. He runs next to me on the track, his black eyes glistening with approval at my running pace. We detour into the forest, down the same deer trail I used to follow Foxworth.

The trees clear, and I anticipate the overgrown graveyard where Foxworth and Dad wait to greet me. Instead, I see rubble and burning embers. The winged woman that guards the entrance to Foxworth's tunnel is split in two, broken. Smoke billows from the tunnel's entrance, and I rush toward it in a panic. Two people are trapped inside.

But Luther pulls me back. I try to break free to help the men in the tunnel.

And then I awaken in a cold sweat.

I half expect Lydia to be sitting on the side of my bed, telling me that the last three months have been a nightmare, that I've been going through my routine at the Crystal Globe but haven't remembered any of it—just as she did the day I snapped out of my personality coma over five months ago.

But my old roommate isn't here, though my bed is as soft and billowy as the one in my old dorm room. A silky, satin sheet rests over me.

I blush to find that all my outer clothes are gone and tug the sheet more tightly to my chest. The room is small but ornate. The queenly bed boasts a dark wood frame with a matching bureau beside it.

Neatly folded on the bureau are some clothes. Beyond the bureau is an open door. From it, steam and scented soap waft into my room.

I yank the sheet after me as I scoop up the clothes and peek around the door. A porcelain tub brims with bubbles next to a short towel stand.

Before me is a mirror. I hardly recognize the girl who stares back at me. Coal dust cakes her skin, which is raw and cracked. Sullied, once-blonde hair hangs limply around her taut face, composed of two blue eyes that are now too big for the protruding cheekbones.

I shut the door and drape the sheet over the mirror to pretend the strange girl isn't me.

The heated water relaxes my muscles but can't completely undo the strain I feel. I'm still a prisoner, and if the last three months have taught me anything, they've taught me that nothing comes free.

I soak no longer than I dare and don the clothes, which are nearly identical to my prisoner's uniform, only clean and less threadbare.

But even that sumptuous bath can't erase all the stains on my skin and hair. Maybe they'll have to grow out.

A sense of urgency makes me try the door handle of my room. At least it's unlocked. I don't know how long I've slept or been in this strange place. If I'm missed in the mines and rediscovered, I'll be the prisoner on the wall tonight.

Am I going back? Or am I staying? I'm not sure which thought scares me more. Gath will be so worried if I don't return, but maybe if I stay, I can find a way to help him escape, too.

My steps grow bolder as I leave the empty hallway behind and weave through a small network of rooms.

I follow a strange melody that now fills the air until at last, the halls give way to one of the elevated platforms I saw when I first entered.

All are empty, except one, the one with the grand piano.

Concealed behind it, someone with a head of manicured hair, once dark but now speckled with white, sways in the seat.

The melody is in a minor key that beckons me with its tale of pain, of rage, of revenge. His fingers trickle down a scale and slow as the requiem fades.

As the composer releases a last tragic chord, I reach the level and stop on the opposite end of the piano.

It's as if the music possessed me, brought me here without my consent. If such a melody can control me this way, how much more power can its creator have?

I tremble as the musician stands. He's not so forceful in stature as my father, though he is perhaps his age, but there's something about his presence that equally intimidates.

A neatly trimmed gray goatee frames his face, a fierce composition of a narrow nose, critical eyes, and furrowed brows.

He's dressed in black, though a different sort than my own. His must be made of satin or some silky blend. The only spot of

25

color is an immaculate red handkerchief which peeks out his vest pocket.

"You are Portia Abernathy or Nevada Ingram?" He steps toward me, and I stiffen for inspection.

"How—How do you know my name?"

His eyes flash coldly. "Answer the question."

"Yes." I grit my teeth as he surveys me like all the guards do—like a piece of merchandise. Perhaps I've traded one taskmaster for another.

"And you witnessed an execution last night?"

"Yes."

With a grunt, he stops circling me and steps toward a long mahogany table to pour himself a tumbler of brown liquid.

"As you are aware, a man was executed last night. That man happened to be my runner. The fool was caught, but he had the decency to honor his vow of silence."

I wait for him to finish sipping his glass, wondering what any of this has to do with me.

"It's taken me longer than I expected to find you, but then, you haven't been a priority. I only entertain paying customers."

My breath catches. Did Darius contact this man?

He sets his glass down and paces the floor. There's something unsatisfied about him. His restlessness makes me uneasy.

"However, the timing provides a chance to change that. Although you're a sorry substitute, I might consider you on certain terms."

"Excuse me, but what do you mean—and why am I here?" I try to sound civil, despite his insulting tone.

He pinches the air in front of me. "Rule number one: Do not speak unless I require it. Your kind is cheap. My patience is not."

26

My face flushes, but I hold my tongue. Insults are the only compliments Wasps pay, and I'm accustomed, though not immune, to them.

"You are a guest in the Excivis." He pauses for effect, as if his self-made domain should impress me.

But bullies and braggers never do.

With a frown, he continues. "My network spans manmade tunnels, underground pipelines, and a once renowned cavern system. I control this underworld and any who enter it. I have the power to release prisoners and enslave free men. I own more wealth than the ASU has ever seen. I work for no one. I employ desperados and mercenaries. I have many names and many residences.

"This—" He waves his hand around me, "is only one of my apartments, but enough about me for now. We're here because someone has been asking for you, someone whose name might be familiar to you."

I gulp and hope it's a friend and not an enemy. But surely Eliab has other bones to break than mine. Yet the idea of Darius contacting a man like this one to ask for help worries me nearly as much.

"He's been sending code searching for the whereabouts of Portia Abernathy for three months now." The man laughs.

I don't even know this man's name, and his familiarity with mine grates on my nerves.

"But he's a desperate man and will agree to any terms." He gives me another probing look as if to reconsider whether I'm worth his time.

My frustration boils over. "Who are you, and who are you even talking about?"

27

He glares at me. "Can you listen, or are you as dim as the other rabbits at Warren?"

Rabbits. I've traded a Wasp for a madman, neither of which respect human life.

I whirl toward the stairs. "I'm sorry I'm wasting your time. Clearly, you're wasting mine."

"And where will you go? Back to dig your own grave or perhaps die in a cave?" His voice lilts.

I grip the rail, angry that he is right, angry that I still care enough about living to endure this impossible man's mockery.

Narrowing my eyes, I wait for him to continue. He arches an eye and strides toward me. "Well? Do you crave my patience, or should I send you back to your other cave friends?"

My eyes burn, and I swallow hard. "What do you want with me?"

"No, my dear, the question is rather: what do *you* want with me?"

There's a chair in the corner, an unfriendly leather specimen, but I sink into it. I'm tired of his games yet have no choice but to endure them.

He pulls an adjacent chair to sit in front of me. Leaning forward, he rubs his hands together and studies me with piercing hazel eyes.

"Three months ago, you helped a man named Abe plant a virus in the ASU's intel system that enabled him to eavesdrop on their technology and communication. This same Abe is the one who's been asking about you."

Abe. My pulse quickens. That's the name Darius assumed after escaping Baytown.

"You see, what you failed to plan was a lock to prevent other hackers from accessing the virus. My men tapped in and easily hijacked it. My team added our own security code, thereby locking out your organization—or so-called Brotherhood."

His words sink in. I don't understand how viruses work, but one thing is clear: This man is the reason Gath and I have been rotting in a satellite, the reason my brother Darius hasn't found us.

"But even a virus has its limitations," he continues. "It doesn't have ears unless a Translation is in progress. It can't tell us what happens outside the confines of a communications interface. And that's where you come in."

I flinch. "Me?"

"My late runner bridged the conduit, providing insight into the workings of Crystal. And he was good at it too. It's a pity that a simple prisoner rescue mission at your satellite cost him his life."

There are so many questions I want to ask, but I clamp my mouth shut hoping to avoid another lecture.

"I said earlier that I only consider paying customers, which is why I've ignored Abe's request. He offered money, but currency is cheap. However, as I traced your story back to Crystal, I began to see you might serve some value. In the meantime, my runner found you."

I gasp. "Do you mean—not—not your late runner?"

He nods. "Yes, you were the prisoner he was working to rescue. Only, he made a clumsy mistake before he had the chance. But not all his work was in vain, for here you are."

My lip trembles, to think the man on the wall died because of me.

"And now, you will become his successor."

I narrow my eyes. Working for this impossible man is the last thing I want to do. "And what makes you think I'll agree to that?"

The man's lips curl into a checkmate grin. "Because I offer you freedom and a chance to help your Brotherhood."

My throat goes dry. *Freedom.* Three months in a satellite has seemed like a lifetime.

"But you must agree to my terms."

"I'm listening."

He cracks a smile. "Ah, so you can learn. Good. But you've also shown your insolence."

The man stands and shoves his chair aside. I rise as well and warily watch as he extends a hand toward me.

When I shake it, he grips mine with such force that I wince. "My terms are simple: do what I say without question. You will serve as my runner and perform any operation assigned to you. In return, I will grant you access to the technology your Brotherhood originally stole."

I gasp as the strain on my hand becomes nearly unbearable.

"But first, you must prove yourself capable. Convince the tunneller working with you to destroy his seam. It's too close to one of my trapdoors."

He pauses as his face transforms into a menacing glower. "And never question me again."

Before I can pull away, his hand races up my arm and twists. I cry out in pain as he wrenches my shoulder from its socket.

The searing agony makes the room blur, and I grab my dislocated shoulder with my right hand to support it.

I stagger to my knees as unbidden tears fall. Another figure enters the room. I think it's the man who led me here.

I lift my tear-filled eyes to beg for mercy. But a hard fist in my face is the only answer I receive.

And I black out.

Chapter 4

Friday, 2.13.2150
Warren Satellite

"Portia, Portia!"

I must be dreaming again. No one uses that name anymore.

But surely no dream can be this painful.

I groan and force open a swollen eye. A headlamp shines nearby, and I wince, preferring darkness to its throbbing glare.

A man frantically claws at the ground around me, and then my aching body registers that I can't move.

I'm buried in a cave-in.

"Talk to me, Portia." His raspy deep voice shudders, much like my body does.

"Gath?" I whisper.

"I'm going to get you out. Hold tight."

I wish I could laugh, but the sound comes out more like a sob. "I'm not going anywhere."

"Just talk to me—and keep talking."

"There was a man …" I close my eyes as his cruel face flashes

31

in my memory.

"Keep your eyes on me!" Gath orders, his voice stern.

"It hurts. He hit me."

Gath's warm breath blows on my skin. "What are you talking about? No one hit you."

"He took me to his underworld, called it—" I pause to remember. "He called it the Excivis."

Gath stops digging, and I crack open my good eye. The shadow from his headlamp makes his sunken and ashy cheeks look even paler. His eyes blink in shock, then narrow as he resumes yanking at the rocks around me with renewed vigor.

"You don't believe me?" My voice rasps.

"You're trapped in a cave-in," he repeats. "You hit your head."

"Cave-ins don't give people black eyes."

He bites his cracked lower lip. "They could if a rock struck you just right."

"Gath, you have to believe me. He said to tell the tunneller— you—not to dig any further, that you're too close to discovering one of his trap doors. He said that you have to stop digging for him to ever take me back. He said—" The dust from the cave-in clogs my throat, making me cough till my voice sounds like a dying man's.

"Shh! Save your breath."

I wheeze. "But you told me to keep talking."

A few minutes later, he removes the last large rock around my shoulders. "Can you move, or are you pinned?"

I wiggle in the tight space, but nothing seems caught. That horrid man cocooned me under this rubble but didn't pin me. I suppose he expects a thank you.

"No, I don't think anything's stuck," I say. "But my left—"

Before I can finish, Gath reaches under my arms but releases me when I scream at his touch.

I swallow a cry and tremble to explain. "It's my left arm. He dislocated it."

Confusion and rage that cloud Gath's face soften into pity. "Portia, I have to pull you out." He wipes bloody hands on his sooty shirt. "I can't risk using the shovel in case more rocks fall on you, and I can't move any of the bigger rocks by myself."

I nod that I understand and brace myself as he reaches for me again.

Perhaps this is my punishment. Because of me, the last runner died. He didn't have any anesthetic to numb the pain. Why should I?

I wish I wouldn't scream, but I can't help myself.

The noise attracts other miners, and through tear-sodden lashes, I vaguely make out several figures as Gath lays me down to rest outside the staged cave-in.

He's about to inspect my arm when a spotlight engulfs the tiny space, and a Wasp's shrill whistle pierces the air.

Oh, no. They're always furious when an accident demands their attention inside the mine.

The Wasp appears on a cart and jumps down, kicking Gath away from me. "What's the meaning of this?"

Gath quickly recovers from the blow. "There was a cave-in. I found her trapped and uncovered her."

"Why all the ruckus?" The chunks of rock and coal crackle under his boots like broken bones. The Wasp dangles his whip in front of me. "Get up, girl."

But my legs prickle from lack of circulation, and when I move

33

them too quickly, they lock in place. I fall onto the rocky ground and groan.

He shoves a boot in my stomach. "I said, get up!"

Gath reaches to help me, but the Wasp unleashes his whip on him. "There's nothing wrong with this girl. She's just lazy." He slides the whip onto a loop in his belt and retrieves a revolver.

"For the last time, get up."

Leveraging my weight onto my one good arm, I inch-worm to my knees and then shakily rise to my feet.

Almost in disappointment, he seats the revolver in its holster. And then his eyes fall on my arm, hanging limply by my side.

The Wasp curses at me as he swiftly draws the weapon again. "Useless, that's what you are." He aims at my forehead.

"No, wait!" Gath lunges in front of the barrel, holding up his hands. "It's just dislocated. I can fix it. She'll be fine and pulling her cart in no time."

I hold my breath, half expecting a bullet to blow through Gath's chest and into mine. He blocks my view of the Wasp.

"You have two minutes," he hisses, and Gath instantly faces me.

His voice is calm but commanding. "This won't hurt—as much—if you relax and trust me. Now, lie down."

He helps me settle onto the jagged ground, and I recline on my back.

"I'm going to take your arm and place my foot in your arm socket." His tone reminds me of a Healer's. "Then, I'll apply pressure while angling your arm away from your body, but I won't yank."

I keep nodding. If I say anything, I won't be able to choke down the pain.

34

He gently pulls my arm at a forty-five-degree angle, but my spasming muscles don't want to budge.

"Relax," he coaxes. "It might take some time."

"One minute!" The Wasp reminds us we don't have that luxury. I grit my teeth as Gath applies stronger pressure.

Pop! It's faint, but I hear—and feel the ball and socket return to place. I gasp in relief as unbidden tears run like rivers down my cheeks. Gath grabs my waist and helps me to my feet.

He gives the Wasp a tense smile. "She'll be good as new."

The man snarls and returns to his cart where a small, older man serves as mule. The other miners who came to investigate slink into the shadows as the Wasp again blows his whistle. "I'd better not see any decrease in production, or you all can blame tomorrow's empty stomachs on her carelessness."

Hopeless stares and a few curses fill the void after the Wasp disappears. Some miners glare at me, but most shake their heads in pity.

Maybe my arm is relocated, but my muscles still scream in agony. My hand and arm swell to twice their normal size, and there are no drugs to help decrease the throbbing.

"Give it an hour, maybe two," Gath says. "The swelling will go down."

"Not if I'm shoveling coal," I mutter, limping toward my cart and shovel. Making one load, let alone my daily quota, seems impossible. Maybe Gath should have let him shoot me.

"You're not going to be shoveling coal."

Gath jumps in front of me, and for the first time, I see where the whip cut a gash in his cheek and imprinted a snakelike welt running down his neck.

Bloody hands and all, he shovels the adjacent coal pile into my load.

I feel guilty. "No, Gath, this is my work. You've done more than enough. Go back to your seam before you get in trouble."

He pauses long enough to wink through tired eyes. "Seam? What seam? It was a dead end anyway."

Chapter 5

Friday, 2.13.2150
Warren Satellite

My mattress, no matter how paper-thin, lumpy and lice-infected, welcomes my aching body after a dinner of soggy pellets.

The mush isn't really pellets, but that's what Harris calls it. I think it's better not to guess what the mush is made of. It certainly tastes nothing like the oatmeal I enjoyed this morning.

I try not to think about what I had for breakfast and what wonders a hot bath might do for my aching arm.

Not that anyone could even guess I'd had a bath. Coal dust smears my skin, and my hair may never see the light of blonde again.

At least my crew will live to see another day. We managed to meet quota, or I should say, all but one of us did.

Although I still had to haul the cart, Gath shoveled my coal for me all day. In between loads, he tried to find another seam, but he failed. And the Wasp was anything but happy when he learned Gath's promising seam from yesterday turned into a waste of time.

Of course, it was a perfectly good seam. I'm not sure Gath believed all of my story about the world I stumbled into, but he must have believed enough of it to risk his neck for a chance to save mine.

I tried to apologize after his beating this afternoon, but he wouldn't let me. I feel so guilty I can't even look him in the eye.

I study the cracks and rat holes in the ceiling above me, listening to Gath's labored breathing below. The Wasp on duty hasn't shut off the lights, so a few other prisoners quietly play a game with some rock dice. Most, like me, stare vacantly into space.

Why did that man order me a bath and a better prisoner's uniform if he planned to get me killed? Was it just to torture me with what I can't have?

I think Gath noticed my clothes were different, but no one else did. We prisoners tend to avoid eye contact. There are other women here, but most are men.

And when men are treated like animals, they sometimes behave like them.

I've fared better than the other women, probably thanks to Gath. His body language from day one has kept the other male prisoners from getting friendly with me.

But now, he's broken, nothing but a shadow of his former self. I worry I might outlive him, that I'll be the reason he gets killed.

That would make two lives I have on my conscience.

I can only hope that the man I met today, horrible though he is, might be our ticket to freedom. Though I hate the idea of working for the monster, if I can save Gath, I have to try. For now, I have to at least keep up his spirit.

I roll on my stomach and press my lips close to the cracked wood of my bunk rail. When I pull back the mangled mattress and squint between the flats, I can see his lashes flutter.

Just above a whisper, I spin a new rhyme for him.

Some day
I'll find a way
To take you back where we
belong, to do right by you my
Brother.

He cracks open an eye as a weary smile crawls into his cheeks. "I thought you'd forgotten tonight."

I relax against the frame and press a hopeful grin onto my lips. "Nope, I didn't forget."

In our early days at Warren, Gath had heard me spinning rhymes on my bunk to calm myself. He'd asked me to share one every night since—said it's our way of remembering who we are. I promised I would.

Gath closes his lashes again and murmurs. "My sister, we'll find a way."

A stray tear falls as I reach to replace the mattress, pausing just long enough to trace a fingernail over the two words I'd lightly scrawled there over time.

Portia. Gath.

I study our names every night to remind myself who we are. No one can change that. Closing my eyes, I mouth the names to myself and hope for a way out tomorrow.

Our door jerks open, slamming into the battered wall. I remain perfectly still and squeeze my eyes tighter. *Please, let someone other than Gath and me be the butt of the Wasp's jokes tonight.*

But the Wasp isn't alone. Heavy footsteps, at least half a dozen, cross the threshold. The Wasp barks out orders for a roll call line, and I have no choice but to climb down, careful not to use my bad arm.

Gath hobbles into line next to me right before the Wasp reaches us for inspection.

"I have some new friends for you, my darlings." He spins ninety degrees on his shiny, polished boots and bows mockingly towards the new arrivals.

They're a fierce bunch, seven in all. They look like thugs with rag beanie caps and thick chests.

They've been starved less than we have, but there's a hunger in their eyes that makes me shrink farther behind Gath's frame. He puffs out his bruised, boney chest to block me from their view.

Oh, Darius, I take back any doubts I once had about this man. I love him like a brother.

"Meet Baytown Pipeline Crew 56," the Wasp says. "They'll be staying with us for a few weeks to complete an extension. I expect you'll offer your best hospitality."

I scan the anxious faces of my bunkmates. All of us know there are no empty beds. Some of the women are doubled up as it is.

Beside me, Gath's breath catches as the pipeliners file into the long room. The leader, a swarthy man with sun-bleached hair, leads the way.

The Wasp returns to the exit and flicks off the main overhead light. "Sleep sweet."

With that, he's gone. As soon as he closes the door, Gath pulls me toward our bunk and motions for me to climb beside him. He's volunteering to share with me. I'd rather my bed be with him than any of those pipeliners.

I know he only wants to protect me.

I crawl into his chest, wishing we actually had blankets. Then

40

I would have something to hide underneath.

Footsteps approach. I close my eyes and pretend I'm invisible.

"Hoarding the goods for yourself, huh?" The voice rasps.

Gath stiffens but doesn't get up. "The top bunk is yours."

"I wasn't talking about the bunk." His voice drawls with an accent belonging to one of our more southern squares.

I shrink farther into Gath's chest, but his protruding ribs poke my back.

He takes a deep breath and puts a protective arm over my shoulder. "The top bunk is yours," he repeats.

The pipeliner snorts, and I hope he's going away. I exhale and squint open my eyes, just as he reaches down and yanks me from the bed.

I roll onto the floor and cry out as my left arm hits the concrete.

Gath leaps over me and barrels into the man, sending them both tumbling. Although he had the advantage of momentum, that's soon gone. The pipeliner has been much better fed than Gath.

He pins Gath on the floor and pounds his face with thick fists.

"No!" I scream and jump to my feet, ignoring my arm. I leap on the man's back and yank out his hair in fistfuls.

He curses and claws at me with his arm, like a crab trying to scratch its back. I wrap my legs around his chest and don't let go. He finally gets a good grip on my thigh and wrenches me off, throwing me to the ground.

I elbow my way to Gath's prostrate body. The other prisoners sit upright on their bunks and clutch the metal frames, watching as if behind bars. No one makes a move to help us.

The pipeliner towers over us as his jeering mates crowd around.

"Bully!" I spit at him and dodge a kick. "Only cowards pick

41

fights with starved men."

"Listen to the little avenging angel!" The pipeliner roars in fresh laughter, but his hand rubs the raw spots on his head.

I position myself in front of Gath's face, bloodied and bruised. "Prisoners here stick together, die together. We don't kill each other."

He steps closer, a sneer on his lips. "Who said anything about killing …" He snatches at me, and I fall next to Gath to miss his hand.

The humor suddenly leaves his eyes, which darken like frozen midnight. "Well, boys, would you look at that."

His gaze darts past me to Gath with menacing recognition. "We've found ourselves a traitor."

Murmurs ripple through the room, and I shake my head, confused.

The pipeliner circles like a vulture. "I didn't recognize you at first, old man, but I could never forget the most notorious Wasp of Baytown."

Gath doesn't say a word, so I speak for him. "Liar! All of us here are prisoners."

"You need a girl to defend you?" he sneers, kicking Gath in the side.

I jump on his boot and bite his leg. He curses again and shakes me off like a mongrel.

"Give her what she's got coming, Rig!" Another pipeliner goads.

The door to the barrack suddenly swings open, sending a gust of bitter-cold air inside. The Wasp flicks on the light and cracks his whip.

"Filthy rabbits, quiet down!" He lashes the closest pipeliners until they cower like women. "Get in your bunks. If I hear as much as a squeak from this barrack, all of you will spend the night outside and freeze."

Immediately, the crew disperses into bunks, empty and occupied. I help Gath limp to our bottom bunk as the Wasp extinguishes the light and slams the door.

Rig climbs above us, whispering oaths under his breath. "Enjoy your sleep while you can, old man. You know what you've got coming."

I peek at Gath. He gives me a sad stare but doesn't affirm or deny the pipeliner's words.

"It's not—" I start to say, but he shakes his head.

"Go to sleep, sister," he whispers and closes his eyes.

I don't see the pipeliner crew or Gath for very long the next morning. Wasps escort the pipeliners to their worksite right after breakfast. Their angry eyes and scowls disappear along with them, but their words linger.

The whole barrack had heard Rig's accusation, and no one sat too close to Gath or me in the mess hall.

It's all nonsense. It has to be. Gath may have been a Gage with the Crystal Globe, but he wasn't a heinous Baytown Wasp.

I wish he would defend himself. He's always standing up for me. Why doesn't he do the same for himself?

Without even asking, I carry his shovel and pickax the next morning, but he takes them from me as soon as we reach the mines. It's a good thing, too, because a Wasp ferrets him and some of the other miners away to a different tunnel.

He's demoted from tunneller to a mangy miner because of me.

Hauling my cart, I follow today's crew to where we left off yesterday. Only today, there is no Gath to help me shovel.

The swelling in my arm has gone down, but the soreness remains. I grit my teeth and bear it. If Gath can work in his condition, I can work in mine.

The day passes tediously. Every tumbling rock, every distant echo makes me jolt straighter. At any turn, I expect to see the runner from yesterday, beckoning me below.

But he doesn't seek me out. Perhaps in some way, I failed or displeased the underlord, and now, he's content to watch me rot.

The thought sickens me. I hate that I care what he thinks. The man dislocated my arm and nearly got me killed. And yet, he dangles the carrot of freedom in front of my face, and I'm willing to sell my soul to eat it.

That evening, I drag my feet along the path, following the chain of prisoners in front of me. I miss Gath and hope he's somewhere farther back in the line. The thought of facing a night in the barracks without him terrifies me.

The barb-wire gate creaks open as the Wasps whip us into an inspection line under the glaring compound lights. That's right. It's Saturday night. The Wasps do a final check after the day's work so Harris can file his headcount reports Sunday.

There's no point doing one in the morning. At least one person doesn't return each night.

Harris's office door opens, and two trainees salute as he marches down the steps to inspect the line.

In his arms is Peppermint.

Yes, it's ludicrous, but that's her name, the name of Harris's overfed rabbit.

44

I'm not sure if the albino is a tribute to his twisted sense of humor, but he treats it with all the care and affection he withholds from us. Peppermint's white coat shines with brushed brilliance.

Harris wears her like an arm muff, and the amazing thing is, she just sits there. I've never seen a rabbit remain still the way Peppermint does.

Maybe even she's frightened of her master's moods.

He clucks his tongue and strokes Peppermint. "You look disgraceful, pets. How can I give a good report about you?"

I tune out the speech. He gives one every week, and they're sappy, sarcastic wastes of words.

I crane my neck to find Gath, and in doing so, meet the cold stare of Rig, who shoves past a frail man to claim the spot to my left.

It's too late to slip away, because the Wasps have started down our line, whipping anyone who's not perfectly straight.

Rig checks me in the shoulder. "Where's your friend?"

"Go away," I mutter and hope the Wasp won't hear us. The last thing I want is to draw attention to myself.

"He's not here to protect you, huh?" he mocks. "Maybe had an accident in the mine? He'd be lucky if he did with what he's got coming."

I ignore him and strain my eyes to find Gath. He has to be here.

I scan the last line of prisoners who straggle through the gate. The very last one is Gath. He's dragging his left foot, but he's alive.

Rig sees him just as I do. "Unlucky scum."

"Leave him alone. We're all unlucky to be here."

"You don't know who he is, do you?"

I don't reply but hold my breath as a Wasp passes in front of me. I keep my eyes down in silent submission and hope to escape the lash.

But Rig's stance is defiant, and the Wasp strikes his face to make him drop his gaze.

Fool.

As the Wasp walks away, Rig wipes the bloody gash with the back of his hand. "I'll die before I quit killing their kind, *his* kind."

He didn't mean the Wasp inspecting our line. He meant Gath. "He's not one of them."

Rig sneers. "Is that what he told you?"

"He didn't have to tell me. You've got the wrong man. Lay off him."

Rig snorts but turns his attention to Harris, who might as well be rehearsing a soliloquy on a stage. No one's listening, least of all, Rig or me.

He lowers his voice in mock seriousness. "I'll strike a deal with you, darling. The day you deliver that precious rabbit to us for dinner is the day I'll leave your friend alone."

I stare at the albino as my heart sinks. Rig will never let Gath be, and he knows there's nothing I can do to stop him.

Chapter 6

Monday, 3.2.2150
Warren Satellite

I wake to the crackling discharge of Harris's revolver. At least today, it sounds from another barrack.

For the last two weeks, his new terror initiative has left a prisoner shot dead in his bunk.

But why? Do the Wasps not have enough rations to feed us? That can't be the reason. We barely eat as it is.

Gath nudges me off the bed to join the inspection line. I marvel we're both still alive. Although the soreness in my arm has subsided and he's somewhat recovered from his own injuries, this new sickness grips my heart with dread. One day, one of us might be the target.

Mercifully, the pipeline crew has been moved to another bunkhouse, one with more vacancies, thanks to this new initiative. But there's a growing number of empty beds in our own barrack, and I fear the group might be transferred back.

We march to the mess hall, accept the dirty bowls of pellets, and slide onto the hard benches. There's no longer a gap between Gath, the other prisoners, and me. We all huddle close, a survival instinct.

A mouthy prisoner on my left dares to whisper between spoonfuls. "It was my bunkhouse today," he says. "And I heard what the Wasps said to each other as they dragged the poor soul away."

I swallow the tasteless gruel, waiting for him to go on.

"Orders arrive every day with a random prisoner's name. The Wasp accidentally dropped the slip after he shot today's victim." He pauses for effect. "There was a Merlin Falcon on the paper, so it came from the top."

My breath catches. This man must know about Eliab or at least, his Crystal Gages.

"I've noticed something else," says the seasoned prisoner. "Everyone who's been shot came from Crystal. I don't think these shootings are random. They're sending a message. They're hunting somebody."

Hunting. I glance at Gath. His jaw twitches. Is Eliab hunting for us? Who mixed up our papers from Baytown to Warren anyway?

I mechanically spoon the rest of my breakfast to my mouth and close my eyes, trying to remember every last detail of that horrible court scene.

The features of Luther's face are growing fuzzy, and the thought makes me want to cry. I may never see him again.

I force myself to focus. He had sat in his Court Citizen garb on the judgment seat, banging his gavel with grim determination. "The Court hereby sentences Portia Abernathy to twenty years at the Baytown Satellite."

With his own lips, he pronounced my sentence to Baytown. Then, Eliab hijacked both Gath and me. I rehearse Luther's rescue in my mind as I've done a hundred times.

I was still reeling from the chair's effects when he lifted me in his arms and carried me to the prisoner train.

He said he didn't want me to die. What did he do next?

I squint harder, trying to rake over the scene with fresh eyes. There was a guard who cuffed Gath, and Luther said something to him. What was it?

I can't remember his exact words, but Luther handed him a folder, a file of some kind.

That's right, he said to give it to the Gage in charge of the transport.

In charge of transport.

Had that file contained our satellite destination orders?

If so, Luther knows where we are. But why has he forgotten us? Why has everyone forgotten about us?

Another thought strikes me. Maybe he wanted to hide us here, a place where Eliab wouldn't look for us. But now, these random shootings are targeting Crystal prisoners. If Eliab wants to find us, it's only a matter of time before he will.

I shove my garbled theories aside as everyone at the table rises and returns the now-empty bowls to the mess tub. I have to worry about surviving another day.

No longer do I hope for a rescue from the bipolar underlord who hasn't tried contacting me. The memories of the hot bath and warm food torment me now. I wish he hadn't bothered to invite me to his lair because then I wouldn't dwell on how utterly wretched my existence is.

We march through the thawing snow to the mine, and as is the new normal, Gath parts ways to work with his new mining crew while I follow my assigned one into the main tunnel, hauling my cart behind me.

My knees nearly buckle at the first step, as the strap rubs against the raw skin of my protruding ribs. I'm not much more than a breathing skeleton.

The work crew marches ahead of me, even though a few men cast pitying glances my way.

I'm panting and drenched in sweat when I reach the work site but mechanically pull out my shovel and begin scooping the loose chunks. I'm not usually this drained so early in the morning. I must be feverish.

My cart is half full when a single miner appears from deeper within the tunnel. He waves me over, and I shuffle toward him to see what he wants.

"Get your cart, idiot," he says. "We need you to clear the coal from a new tunnel before we can move forward. It's tight, but you'll fit."

These days, there's not much I won't fit through.

I slip into my harness and groan as the cart lumbers behind me. It's heavier now. I gasp for breath. "Let me empty this first."

He shakes his head. "It's not even half full, and we've got a quota to meet. Get moving."

I want to protest, but I recognize him as one of the crew captains. I jerk forward and follow him into deeper darkness. The walls narrow like a siphon, and at last, the track stops.

He hunches down and points farther into the hole. "You have to go on foot from here with your shovel. Clear out the coal, and when you're done, you can go back to your regular crew."

I nod, and he disappears the way we came.

Goosebumps ripple up and down my arms as I enter the tiny, dark space. It's lonely and damp.

It's a good place to die.

Tired tears trail down my cheeks, and I squint to hold them back. Somewhere, Gath's arms are aching, too. If only I could see his face or hear his voice, I could go on, knowing I'm not alone.

But right now, I am. My will to live begins to fade, but Jael's memory suddenly pricks my darkening thoughts.

My classmate was timid but resourceful. How did she manage to bribe someone to let her make cupcakes anyway? I smile, imagining how that conversation must have gone.

And then she sat bravely as a peer through my trial and dared to cast the one vote that kept me alive. Who knows what that choice has cost her.

I owe her my life. She wouldn't want me to quit.

I fill my shovel and crawl toward my cart. I've no sooner dumped the load than the walls begin to shake, and the tunnel roars with an explosion.

I fall to the ground and huddle close to the wall, shielding my head with the shovel as loose rocks and dirt fall from the ceiling.

The rumbling continues, even after the initial ear-splitting shock dissipates.

There's crashing, very close, and I hug my knees to my chest in a fetal position. A cloud of dust and dirt envelopes me.

No, no, no! Not a cave-in. This horrible little corner will become my tomb if I don't find a way to escape, but I'm too petrified to move.

The echo of the explosion still rings in my ears.

Firedamp. A tunneller, or someone else from the mining crew, must have struck a small pocket of the flammable gas and caught some coal dust on fire. I've only heard an explosion that loud once before.

The poor soul. Or maybe not. Would I rather be blown to bits or suffocate in a claustrophobic hole?

At least my headlamp still works. When the rocks stop falling, I uncurl my body and assess the damage.

Twenty feet away, the entire ceiling has given way, forming a massive wall of rubble where the track used to be.

When I begin to climb it, the unstable rock shifts its weight, sending me tumbling back to the floor. I realize if I try again, I might become pinned.

"Help!" I shout, but my voice bounces off the walls, mocking me. No one's going to hear me. No one's going to miss one emaciated girl.

I fall to my knees as I remember the only other person I've seen take that posture. His knees had sunk deep in snow as he prayed for the desperate condition of his men, the desperate cause for which he was fighting.

George Washington's prayer pricked my soul in that Simulation encounter, and it strikes a flame inside me today.

Professor Mortimer said there was no God. The Codex defined God as the naïve notion of ignorant men who call upon a supreme being in a final plea of desperation.

A final, desperate plea—That's all I can muster myself.

And yet, did Washington's God forsake him? His underdog rebels had won victory against all odds and established the previous civilization.

My knees hit the ground. There is no snow here, only rocks and dirt. There is no wind, only the lonely echo of my panting breath off the tomblike walls.

"God." I choke even as I say the word. Who am I to call on him? Do I even believe in him?

I swallow and try again. "God, if you are there, help me. Please, help me."

I have none of Washington's eloquence, just a hopeless prayer. I hang my head and let the tears fall.

There's a quiet stillness when I rise. Perhaps it is but the eerie aftermath of the quaking. Perhaps it is the quelling heartbeat in my own chest. Perhaps it is a hush of hope.

I wipe my face and begin again to inspect the walls of my prison.

There are some cracks, which might let oxygen into my confined space, but that leaves the option of starving to death. That won't take long in my condition.

I keep moving, feeling along the edges of the cave-in for any loose rocks or openings that I could squeeze through.

My foot catches on something. I trip but catch myself. Circling back, I cautiously feel with my feet for the obstacle in my path.

And that's when my shoe strikes wood.

Falling to my knees, I wipe away the dirt and rocks above the wooden panel and then find the handle I'd tripped on seconds ago.

It's a panel. Rather, it's a small square with a crude handle and something like hinges. A door.

And I suspect I know where it leads.

Trembling, I yank at the handle, which springs open to reveal a narrow, dark tunnel. My headlamp shines on a metal ladder leading downward.

Gripping the first rung, I lower my legs until they touch the second rung and then the next. I give one last glance at the mining cave-in and my cart before pulling the door down. If anyone finds my cart, he will think me dead, buried under the pile of rubble.

I shiver in the confined tunnel and grip the railing tightly. Perhaps that is what the underlord wants.

Gath will think me dead, too—or realize I found another way out. But he can't know one way or the other. The thought makes my gut twist.

I descend quietly, feeling for each rung and testing it before applying my full weight. If I'm wrong and this tunnel is a dead-end, I don't want to end up broken in several places and die in a mud pit.

A warm glow reaches me, and I shake with relief. Yes, there's a light at the end of this tunnel, but I wonder what life awaits me. Surely it must be better than the one I'm leaving.

The tunnel drops me off in a sterile hallway that connects to one of the shafts, like the one I'd entered before. Stepping out, I peer into the main room. I'm on one of the upper levels. Below me are the larger platforms.

There's the piano level where the man dislocated my arm. Lower still is the long table where I ate my first meal.

They're all empty.

"I see you've found your way back." The voice makes me jump. I face the runner who first introduced me to this strange world.

"Yes," I say. "There was a cave-in, and I found a door."

The man nods. "You made good time."

I squint at his meaning. "You—you were expecting me?"

"Nothing happens by accident around here. Personally, I wasn't sure you were going to make it, but he never seemed to doubt."

"Doubt? Doubt what?" Heat rises in my cheeks. "You don't

mean that you staged that explosion?"

He grins but doesn't answer.

"But how could you know that I wouldn't—die in it?"

He motions to a staircase and beckons me to follow. "The fit find a way to survive. If you're cut out for service, you'll outlive the odds."

I stalk after him as anger courses through my veins. "But he dislocated my arm! He nearly got me killed—and you slugged me in the face."

His eyes flash a warning. "Consider it training, but you've only passed the first two tests." He pauses and lowers his voice. "And never, *never* question his methods. It's insubordination."

I choke on the angry retort rising in my throat. I've only traded one slave master for another.

When we reach the dining area, the runner pulls out a chair for me. Like the first time, he orders service and disappears.

And like a mongrel that returns to its own vomit, I devour the portion given me. It's smaller than the first time, a tiny bowl of steaming oatmeal, lightly seasoned with cinnamon. But then, I'm more starved than I was before. Though I want more, I've eaten all my stomach can handle.

I'm instantly tired again, but this time, I stand and force myself to pace the floor. Soon, I'm gripping the back of the chair to keep from falling over, but I'm awake when the runner comes back.

Much to his astonishment, I think.

"Aren't you tired?" he asks.

Any fool can see that I'm fighting sleep like a two-year-old. "May I speak with him?"

The runner seems surprised by the question. "Lord Osb—the

master is not here right now. You need to rest and bathe before you can see him."

I smirk to myself. *Lord Osb*. The man nearly slipped and gave me the master's name, though I don't know why he should be secretive. There aren't many choices for finishing it. Osbert? Osborn?

He frowns. "Follow me to your quarters." I stumble like a baby after him down a labyrinth of halls. Maybe there aren't so many in reality, but to a drugged doll like me, they seem like a myriad.

He opens a door and nudges me inside before shutting it behind me. The room is the same one I used before, complete with bed and bathroom.

Maybe a hot bath will revive me, but I nearly fall asleep in the steaming porcelain tub. My hair is still sudsy when I crawl out. If I've survived a dislocation and explosion, I can't let myself drown in a bathtub.

I slip into the clean clothes provided and dimly note that they're a gray uniform, not charcoal like my prison clothes. With hair sloppily wrapped in a towel, I tumble onto the bed and stop fighting.

A knocking sound wakes me. The satiny sheets coil around me in a once familiar way. I used to always unmake my bed, thanks to my spindly spine. But after spending the last months in a death labor camp, I hardly think about my back anymore. The rest of my aching body competes for attention, and pain is normal, a mere reminder I'm still living.

I finger the luxurious softness between my calloused hands. I don't belong to this world, a world that reminds me of Crystal. I never have.

But I don't want to return to the satellite.

I slide off the bed in search of my boots, but they're gone. In their place sit a pair of slipper-like shoes, soft on top with a rubber sole. Surely Lord Osb. can't send me to the mine wearing these.

And yet, this place has strange manners. Most hosts don't dislocate guests' arms.

There's no one outside my room, but as I open the door, a slip of paper wafts to the floor from where someone had stuck it in the frame.

Wait in the piano room.

That's all it says, but it makes me shudder. The last time I was there … I try not to think about what happened. After closing the door to my room, I wind my way through the hallways.

Lord Osb. is waiting for me there and sits with impatient rigidity on the piano bench. "Have you made your choice?"

He speaks as though our previous conversation ended maybe five minutes ago, and nothing has happened in between.

I take a deep breath and nod. "What would you like me to do?"

His lips hint at a smile. "You will do whatever I ask."

I swallow my fear. "I will serve as runner, but you will have to—to teach me."

"You must prove yourself trainable." He speaks curtly as if to a disobedient child. "Come with me. We have much to do in a month."

He rises and steps lightly down carpeted stairs which lead to one of the lower levels. The velvet carpet gives way to concrete floors and functional workspaces. More workers appear, all dressed in the same gray uniform as I am.

Double doors to my right reveal an enormous kitchen. I nearly keel over from the aromas. There's a cleaning area, first aid station, extensive workshop, weaponry cabinets, and countless other staging centers, the purposes of which I can't even begin to guess.

We finally stop in front of a room primed with stools and counters, assembled in front of a row of mirrors.

"Sit." He points to a swiveling leather chair as a gangly man with a well-trimmed mustache strides our way.

He greets my new master with a reverential bow. "My lord, how may I serve you?"

"Patrick, I need your assistance with this creature."

I cringe at the word but, after glancing in the mirror, decide it suits my appearance. I'm but a shadow of the girl I once was.

"We have to start on her appearance now if we have a chance of making her presentable when her assignment begins."

The man surveys me critically but nods as if the task is not quite impossible. "What is to be her role?"

"Runner—Crystal Runner."

Patrick touches my hair as if he were deciding how to groom a dog. But a dog isn't much different than a rabbit. Both are animals. Both serve owners or are served to owners. At least a dog is a step in the right direction up the food chain.

"She's a blonde?" Patrick presses his fingers between my hair in search of a root color.

Lord Osb. clucks his tongue. "Oh, yes, but I want her to stay dark. It will help her cover and keep people in Crystal from recognizing her."

Patrick's expression deepens as if he wants to ask how anyone as drab as me could once have lived in Crystal. "Should I go ahead and dye it now?"

"It's up to you," Lord Osb. says. "You can wait until later this month if you think her hair's not ready for the treatment."

"Actually, the dye might help seal the damaged hair," Patrick says. "I'd rather not dye it right after a wash, but that can't be helped this time. I'll touch up the color again before she leaves for assignment. Do you want it short or long?" He pinches off my split ends.

Lord Osb. frowns. "How did you wear it in Crystal?"

"Short," I say and press my hair higher above my cheeks. "The short layers fell here, and the longer layers touched my chin."

"Then keep the length, but give her layers." He frowns. "We've got to revive some life into that mane."

"Her hair will look better in an hour," Patrick promises.

"Take as long as you need. I have another appointment, and then the day is wasted." Lord Osb. says. "We'll also need to do dermal treatments, but those can wait until she's put on some weight and any swelling goes down."

Dermal treatments? Swelling? I glance at Patrick who ignores my wide eyes.

"When you're done, drop her off at the kitchen. She's starting a strict eating regimen to gain weight. No one wants to hire a pile of bones. "

"Yes, sir."

Patrick goes to work on my scalp with a washing and conditioning regimen that leaves my roots smarting. I start to relax when he pulls out his scissors and snips away.

Head cocked down and eyes closed, I try not to worry about all my unanswered questions, all my fears, not the least is what Gath must be thinking right now.

Although I've lost track of time, I guess the day is growing late and the prisoners have reached the compound. Gath has noted my empty seat in the mess hall, and now, he finds my bunk barren too.

How would I feel if I were him? My best and only friend— dead or missing?

I'd be in agony.

Chapter 7

Tuesday, 3.3.2150
The Excivis

The kitchen lady must have drugged my meal because I don't remember getting to my room last night.

This morning, there's no knock on the door but a new alarm clock on my nightstand. It's thin and silver, and I almost break it trying to make it stop beeping.

I'm still wearing my uniform from yesterday, but a replacement hangs on the bathroom door. I wash my face and suddenly notice my hair.

It's still thin from malnutrition, but what's there is silky soft and jet black with long layers that start at my chin. I run my fingers through it to convince myself it's really my own and not a wig.

Yes, Patrick is an artist, but I miss my blonde hair. He dyed my eyebrows to match, but the black reminds me of coal dust and makes my skin look ghostly in contrast.

When I reach the dining table, the runner who first found me is there along with Lord Osb. Both seem startled. A waiter silently pulls out a chair for me and then begins serving the meal.

I lower my gaze to my bowl and feel color creep into my cheeks. Patrick's handiwork must make me more attractive for them to stare that way.

"She needs sunlight," Lord Osb. says before taking a bite of his sausage.

I change my mind. No, I'm still not pretty. I'm scary like a specter.

"When do I begin her exercises?" The runner stabs his fork into a mound of scrambled eggs as I accept a bowl of oatmeal from the waiter. There's no sausage or eggs for me, but I do get a piece of toast today, as well as a cup of milk and an invitation for tea.

"This afternoon. See what she can handle in her current condition. I'll go over more of her rigorous health and training schedule later, but the bottom line is she must eat and rest every three hours. This morning, she'll follow some of the women to learn the duties she'll perform as a maid. After the noon meal and a rest period, you'll introduce her physical regimen. After dinner, send her to me in the study."

Again, I feel like a dog that needs training. I spoon my oatmeal in silent submission. At least they feed the dog.

After breakfast, Lord Osb. disappears without even speaking to me, and his runner motions for me to follow.

He steps to push open the double kitchen doors when my need for humanity kicks in.

"Excuse me," I say, "but what do I call you?"

He stops and stares.

"I don't know anyone here," I hurry to explain, "and …"

"You can call me Orbit." There's no offer of friendship, but I don't expect it from the man ordered to punch me in the face.

"Thanks," I say and trail him into the kitchen where the mystery woman with the tropical coloring runs steaming water over a mound of dishes.

She acknowledges Orbit with a grim nod. He explains that I'm her responsibility for the first part of the day.

"She can help me with the dishes, and then we'll start on the rooms."

"Fine. Make sure she eats and rests every three hours."

"I can manage that." She points from me to the sink of breakfast dishes.

I roll up my sleeves and plunge into the pile. Washing dishes is so much easier than shoveling coal.

She peels potatoes and chucks them into a pot sized to feed an army. I wonder how many people operate in this underworld.

"I'm sorry, but I don't remember your name," I say. I'm not sure why names have become important to me. They just have.

"I never told you my name."

"Well, my name is—"

She shakes her peeler at me. "Don't say your real name. You may only tell your given name."

"Given name?"

"Have you got one yet?"

I don't know what she means and shake my head.

"You'll get one eventually."

"So, what's your given name?"

"You can call me Deidra."

It's rehearsed, spoken the same way Orbit said his. I wonder what mine will be. I never liked Nevada and suppose anything will be better than Rabbit 12017.

"How did you come to be here?" I scrub a pan stained with

bacon grease.

"None of your business," she snaps. The gentle glimmer from the first time we met has since disappeared. But then, I hadn't been her charge—her problem—at that time.

I flinch, and her expression softens a little. She would be even more beautiful if she didn't pull her dark hair back in such an ugly, tight bun. Behind the glasses, her face features defined cheekbones and bold brows, though fine wear lines trace her forehead. Her warm brown skin color belongs to a tropical princess—not a kitchen servant.

She takes a deep breath. "It's just—no one asks anyone that question. You're thankful to be alive and to be here. Don't ask questions you don't need to know. For that matter, don't ask ones you do. Watch and learn. It's safer that way."

Safer. Now there's a need I understand. I've felt anything but safe the last several months, ever since I left Chrysoprase, the square I used to call home.

But the idea of *home* can't be bound by any pinpoint destination. If it were, I would have none. Home is where my dad and Darius are, where Gath is, where Luther is. I miss them all.

When I finish the dishes, Deidra shows me how to polish silverware and set a formal table. I didn't know such rules of refinery existed. Frankly, who cares.

I wouldn't if my new occupation didn't depend on it.

Three hours later, she sets broth and biscuits before me, and like clockwork, my body tells me it's time to sleep again.

She helps me to my room. "Why are you drugging me?" I mumble.

Her eyes widen as she pushes open my door. "We're not drugging you. You're malnourished—probably anemic, too. Your body is getting used to absorbing good food again, and now that you can rest, that's what your body wants." She kindly helps me out of my new boots and swings my legs onto the bed. "Get some sleep. Orbit will collect you next. I'll see you tomorrow."

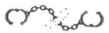

I really hate alarm clocks. Orbit arrives the minute after mine goes off. I lose track of all the hallways and tunnels we take before emerging through a final door that opens into an old concrete drainage pipe.

The day is cold but clear. The sun glares overhead, and I wince. I'm not used to seeing it.

"Wear these." Orbit hands me a pair of sunglasses which fit perfectly.

"Thanks."

He unslings the bag he's been carrying over his shoulder and zips it open while I inspect the strange outdoor arena.

I don't know what else to call it. It's a fraction of the track I used to run in Crystal, but it has a definite outer circle. Around the outer rim is a dense shield of trees, which probably conceal the unlikely area from outside eyes. Inside the circle are posts, old stumps, and half-rotted, giant tires—I can't imagine what machine they once propelled.

An obstacle course? I open my mouth to ask but stop mid-breath, remembering Deidra's words.

Orbit unzips his jacket for more flexibility, revealing a holster on his hip that holds extra magazines. I can't see the handgun but guess it's in the small of his back. I wonder if he'll teach me to shoot and if my Taser skills will transfer to a real gun.

65

"First, we stretch. I know you have muscles, but you've been abusing them."

As if strapping myself to a coal cart was my idea.

Abused though my muscles are, they remember the basic stretches Luther taught me. I lower myself to the ground and begin a rep without Orbit even instructing me to do so. We stretch in silence. He seems to understand that I've done this before.

I silently bless Luther. Somehow, he knew I would have to run to survive. If he hadn't taught me and stretched my muscles and sore back to the breaking point, the satellite would have broken me.

Of course, he didn't know I'd end up a satellite runner. Funny, even Lord Osb. calls his spies *runners*. The irony is not lost on me, the girl who once couldn't run to save her life.

As I finish, Orbit shimmies up one of the tall poles and hooks a rope and carabiner to a chain at the top. He slides down the rope and returns to me. "Okay, watch and learn. I want to see how much strength you have, but I won't kill you on day one. Now, here's how the obstacle course works." He points to the old tires first.

"Let me guess, I have to jump them."

He smirks. "No, you have to flip them."

I blink. "But they're twice my size."

"I'm going to make a soldier out of you, girl."

Soldier. I thought I was supposed to be a spy disguised as a servant. My role becomes increasingly fuzzy.

I step toward the giant tire. The tread is thicker than the length of my hand. I squat with my knees and reach beneath the rubber until I feel dirt. Then, I try to lift but back off the second my shoulder begins to burn. The muscles still haven't fully healed from the dislocation.

Orbit laughs as I rub my shoulder. "You won't budge it today, but you'll flip it by the end of the month."

"Easy for you to say," I mutter. "You don't have a bum shoulder."

His expression darkens. "Don't I? He went easy on you, girl." Before I realize what he's doing, he tears off his jacket and shirt, revealing a chest streaked with scars—I don't want to think about what could have made such a horrible zig-zag pattern. But it's his shoulder that catches my eye.

It's covered in scar tissue.

"Touch it," he dares me.

"I—"

"Touch it!"

I hold my breath and reach to feel it. Below the discolored skin and scarring is metal. I jerk my hand away, but he grabs it and presses it hard into his shoulder.

"Never question his methods." He spits the threat into my ear. "They may seem cruel, but there are far crueler taskmasters to serve."

"I'm—I'm sorry!" I gasp, trying to pull away.

"I'm not." He releases me and turns to the tire. With a fierce cry, he flips it on his first try and then flips the second, third, and fourth tires as well.

I tremble under the open sky. Orbit reminds me of a word I once read in a book of Roman history: a gladiator. They were mutilated fighters who did their masters' bidding for the amusement of the masses.

I look at my hands, already scarred from the coal mines, and fear what else I will have to become to survive.

67

Chapter 8

Tuesday, 3.3.2150
The Excivis

When I wake from my second nap, Deidra is sitting in a chair next to me, studying my face. Beneath her hardened layers, she has a soft spirit.

I had fallen asleep in the same filthy uniform caked with the dirt from Orbit's training.

"I'm sorry," I say, embarrassed at all the earth I've tracked into the bed. "I should've changed before—"

"No need to apologize." She stands. "Orbit works his trainees hard. Your bath is ready, and I'll strip your bed once you get out of it."

I hurriedly stand, wincing at the stiffness that's already taken residence in my limbs. "I can do it later."

She frowns and points at the bathroom. "Bath."

"But I don't want to make extra work for you."

Her hands go to her hips. "If you're not out of those clothes in one minute, I'm stripping them off you myself. I've done it before, you know."

I blush but feel relief as I retreat to the bathroom. At least Orbit wasn't the one responsible for leaving me in nothing but my undergarments during my first visit.

The hot bath seeps through my tired muscles, and I relax under a thick layer of bubbles.

Deidra appears at the door, her arms gripping the bundle of dirty sheets. "You've got half an hour to get dressed and come down to dinner. I've laid out your evening wear. Don't be late. There's no tolerance for tardiness here."

"Yes, ma'am. Thank you." I feel like I'm in school.

She actually smiles and then just as quickly, disappears.

Although the bubbles are the most luxurious thing I've ever felt, I wash quickly so I can dry and dress for dinner.

With a towel wrapped around me, I peek into my room to make sure no one else is there and hurriedly close the door which Deidra had left open.

After living in the barracks, I'm surprised how important modesty is to me. But then, I never worried about bathing there. We didn't have any shower facilities, and even if we did, the pipes would have been frozen.

Then, I notice something shimmery on my bed. It's a dress, but not just any dress. Apparently, *evening wear* means a floor-length, champagne-colored gown as smooth as satin.

Dress in hand, I return to the bathroom. The fabric glides over my body, and I shiver at its touch. I've never worn something this regal. Yet it stirs conflicting emotions inside me.

Anger. Do they think they can change who I am with hair dye and pretty clothes? I press my fingernail to the foggy mirror and trace my name. *Portia.* Externals won't change that.

Fear. This is neither the uniform of a maid or a gladiator, of which I have imagined myself both today. This can only be the attire of a spy who must learn to be comfortable wearing any disguise to do her job.

Shame. I'm wearing a party dress, and what is Gath wearing? Rags.

My gaze darts from my reflection in the mirror to the door behind me. I could run away now. With some trial and error, I could find my way to the trap door and return to the mine. If I could get to Gath ...

I suck in a deep breath and look away from my reflection. I don't even know where to begin searching for Gath in the mines. And even if I found him in line during the night march to the barracks, we wouldn't make it a hundred feet past those Wasps.

Running the other direction—out through the drainage pipe and into the woods—would make me a coward. I can't run away and leave Gath behind. Staying here is the only chance I have to help him.

Water drips from my still-wet hair onto my shoulders and brings my reality into focus. I grab a towel and find a hair dryer to keep from getting the dress wet.

I'm grateful Deidra also left a fuzzy sweater for me to wear. It covers my skinny, bruised arms and might hide the tremors that unpredictably shake my frame.

When I reach the dining level, Orbit and Lord Osb. are already there, wearing suits. Either dinner tonight is formal, or it's another part of my training.

Orbit mechanically pulls out a chair for me as a waiter silently serves an appetizer of broth for me and heavier soup for the others. Isn't attending what I should be doing?

Well, Deidra can teach me. Right now, I have to focus on Lord Osb.

"Orbit tells me you have a natural aim and ability with guns," he says after a spoonful.

I glance at Orbit. Did he really say something nice about me? I return my attention to Lord Osb. who seems to be waiting for my reply. "I trained with a Taser during my undergraduate work, but I need to get better with the recoil of a real gun."

He nods with cautious approval. "He also says you've trained physically before."

"Not his way," I say. My body will be black and blue tomorrow, even though Orbit told me several times he was "taking it easy" on me.

"Yes, he also says you're weak."

So much for a compliment. Orbit's shadowy eyes survey me critically but with something else—maybe approval?

Maybe it's this ridiculous dress.

"That's to be expected in your condition," Lord Osb. continues. "But Orbit says he can teach you as you grow stronger. If you complete his training within the month, you'll begin your assignment."

If. The word terrifies me. If I fail, then what? Will he send me back to the mine? Will he kill me? I know better than to ask. Somehow, I must become strong enough to flip those stupid tires.

I choke down the broth and nod dumbly.

The waiter appears again to clear the bowls and refill the glasses. The two men drink something red, perhaps wine, while the waiter brings me a glass of orange juice.

Lord Osb. sips his as the server sets steaming bowls before us. The rich fragrance makes my stomach lurch.

The man removes my cover to reveal a small portion of brown rice and shredded chicken. I don't envy the heavier red meat and creamy potatoes he serves the men. I dare to hope my stomach can handle my own portion.

It very much wants to.

Lord Osb. cuts into his tender meat. "There is a woman in Crystal, a notable representative in the Dome, who placed an advertisement in the work assignment system for a catering maid."

I chew slowly. If I have food in my mouth, I can't ask all the questions cluttering my mind.

"In your semester at Crystal, did you meet any representatives?"

I gulp down the food. "Once, briefly. My professor took a group of us to the Dome to do an observation."

"Does the name Madame Alexis mean anything to you?"

"Why, yes," I say. "She was one of the Tooler representatives we saw. She seemed a friend of the people."

Orbit sputters. "The people have no friends in politics."

Lord Osb. ignores him. "Would she recognize you?"

"I don't think she even noticed me. I'm small, and there was a group of us."

"Not that it will matter." He takes another bite. "When Patrick finishes his artistry, no one will recognize you."

I slide a strand of black hair behind my ear. What does he mean? My hair is already black as midnight.

Maybe he'll give me glasses like Deidra's. Are hers real, or what identity is she hiding?

He slices another piece of beef on his plate. "Once the work committee approves your assignment, you'll travel to her home to begin. Her steward will contact us to arrange the final details."

73

"But how can I receive a work assignment in Crystal if I didn't graduate from that square?" As soon as I speak, I realize my mistake.

Lord Osb. shakes his head and narrows his eyes at me. "Have you still not learned the first rule of being a servant? Do not speak unless spoken to. Until you learn, you won't be ready."

I blush and lower my eyes to my half-eaten meal. Whose servant does he consider me? His or Madame Alexis's?

"Where was I?" He dabs at his mouth with a silk napkin. "Oh, yes. Although Portia Abernathy did not graduate from Crystal, *you* did. You were living in Crystal, boarding to attend school there. The headmaster had known your father, a traveling Healer, who had cured his daughter. After your parents' tragic death in a fire, the headmaster allowed you to finish in Crystal's education system instead of transferring you to your only living relative, a grandfather, in Jasper. However, following your graduation, your grandfather became seriously ill, so the work committee postponed your service so that you could travel to Jasper and care for your ill grandfather. Your postponement has expired, and your grandfather's health has improved, so you must now take up a work assignment."

Lord Osb. must read the question in my eyes. "Since you're technically a graduate of Crystal, you must return there to complete your first work assignment before you can request a transfer to Jasper."

He pauses to smirk at me. "After all, rules are rules. But thanks to the influence of this generous headmaster, your work assignment will include the condition that once a month, you must have a long weekend in order to travel and attend to your grandfather."

Lord Osb. is the last man I would want for a *grandfather*, but I follow his logic. Each month, I must return to the Excivis ... but for what purpose? To give a detailed report of my work?

The waiter clears our entrees and places small crystal bowls before us, filled with pudding and adorned with fruit.

I nibble at the fruit, and although the pudding is a simple vanilla flavor, I can't stomach it. Or perhaps I can't stomach the blank slate obedience my cruel master demands.

Lord Osb. dismisses the waiter and studies me again. "Now, do you have any questions for me?"

I nearly drop the spoon I'd been using to rearrange my pudding. Any questions? I have a hundred. Yet of all the important ones, I choose the one that reveals my desperate sense to find belonging, even in this underworld. "What should I call you?"

Lord Osb. nods approvingly. "Very good. You are thinking like a servant now. My name is Lord Antonio Osborne, commander of the Excivis and its inhabitants, captain of its forces, and judge of its refugees. You may call me Lord Osborne."

He motions to the attendant to refill his cup. "On the subject of names, we need to discuss yours. Neither Portia Abernathy nor Nevada Ingram will do because both are condemned satellite prisoners and dead for all respective purposes. You will be called Sage Colby."

My heart sinks. Sage? Like the plant?

"Do you know what *Sage* is?" he asks.

"It's a bush?" I offer, trying not to sound disappointed.

"It's the nickname for the Nevada flower and a nod to your satellite name." He smiles at his own cleverness, but the lines of his mouth quickly grow somber. "Colby is for coal-black, which is now the color of your hair. I hope it will remind you of your origins. I picked the Sage flower from the coal-mines, and it can easily return there if it is ever disloyal to me."

Wonderful. I'm to be a desert flower plucked from ashes. "Yes, sir," I say quietly.

"Tomorrow, you'll resume your meal, rest, and training programs with Deidra and Orbit, who will report on your progress over dinner."

Orbit glances at my untouched pudding. "A question, sir—with your permission."

"Go ahead," Lord Osborne says.

"Is she—I mean, are there any physical—limitations I need to know about?" Orbit chooses his words carefully and doesn't look at me. "We've had certain difficulties with prisoners before."

"You mean with processing food?" Lord Osborne shows no discomfort. "I don't think there's a danger of refeeding syndrome. Some of our other rescues were at Warren longer and had been starved more. Deidra confirmed her digestive tract is functioning and expelling properly. Other concerns won't affect her training."

I blush. Are they really talking about my bodily functions at dinner?

Orbit nods and scrapes another spoonful of pudding.

"I'm optimistic she'll be rehabbed and ready for her assignment in a month." Lord Osborne turns his attention back to me. "If you're done, you're dismissed. Deidra will find you in the morning."

Legs trembling, I rise and push back my chair. I'd rather not hear any more of their impersonal conversations about me. "Good night."

Back in my room, I place the satin dress on a hanger and slip into a warm, cotton nightdress Deidra left on my pillow. I'm embarrassed to know how closely she's been watching me, but my heart warms at her little acts of thoughtfulness.

Another surprise waits on the nightstand. Next to the alarm clock is a small notebook and pencil. I wonder if writing out my thoughts is Deidra's idea or part of Lord Osborne's "rehabbing" plan for me.

Heat rushes to my face. If Osborne's behind it, he can forget it. My thoughts are the only private possessions I still have.

They're also a curse sometimes. Though my head pounds from fatigue, my mind won't shut off. I keep replaying my new name and what Lord Osborne had said about it. If that's the case, everyone's name must have significance.

Orbit. It means the path of a satellite or planet around the sun, a name that seems fitting for his role as a runner.

And Deidra—what does her name mean? Does it signify some secret role she plays? Or perhaps, it holds a clue to her past and why she hides behind dark glasses.

I shiver and reach to pull the thick comforter over me. But as my fingers touch its plush softness, I recoil. Gath's sleeping on a hard, thin mattress, while here I am, in a warm nightgown with the plushest comforter on the planet.

Sister, it's okay. I'm happy for you. That's what he would tell me.

I finger the fabric and tug it to my chin. "Gath," I whisper, "I haven't forgotten."

Nibbling my lip, I form tonight's verse and reluctantly reach for the notebook. My rhymes won't mean anything to Osborne, and Deidra might just think I'm crazy.

But I'm going to keep my promise to Gath. I'll keep making one for him every night.

Deidra,
Shrouded beauty,
Kind heart in this cruel place.
Her dark brown eyes hold secrets and
sadness.

Chapter 9

Monday, 3.30.2150
The Excivis

For the first time since arriving almost a month ago, I wake before my alarm. Orbit had said yesterday that I had to pass his exercises—all of them—today. I know what he means, and I don't see how I can.

I roll to my side, and something crunches. My notebook. I must have fallen asleep writing last night.

Retrieving it from under my hip, I smooth its rough edges and flip through the dozens of entries. Each one recounts a story, a sob, a situation I'll tell Gath one day.

3.6
Osborne,
What makes him tick?
Can a heart be stone hard?
He broods and lectures and glowers.
Timebomb.

3.17
Brother,
Where are you? Did
you send for me, or why
am I here? He won't let me ask.
Silence.

3.22
Shredded
hands, muscles, nerves—
Orbit's trying to kill me.
Run farther. Don't flinch. Lift harder.
Bruises.

3.25
Who knew
food is an art?
More rules than I can count,
Fancy wares and airs… who cares?
Just eat.

3.30
That tire,
I'll conquer it
or fail. Orbit says I
have to find my motivation.

_____.

I never finished the last line. My motivation—shouldn't that be obvious? I want so many things, and yet, I can't put them into words.

After setting the notebook on the nightstand, I fling off my sheets. There's no use postponing the inevitable.

I run through my pre-breakfast routine of stretches and then strip for a quick bath. At least the girl in the mirror no longer scares me.

My skin shines from good health. I'm wiry, but the reason is toned muscle, not starvation. Blonde roots peek out from my otherwise black hair. I'll need another appointment with Patrick if I can pass Orbit's regimen.

After donning my uniform, I wrap my hair into a tight bun following Deidra's example and start down the hall.

The only thing left to do is eat a good breakfast and hope Orbit won't make me lose it.

"Try again." Orbit crosses his arms over a sweat-stained shirt that clings to his rippling chest.

Though my shirt is equally as drenched, there's not as much muscle underneath it. My hands are raw from gripping the underside of the course rubber tire. Stupid tire.

I put my palms on my hips and glare at him, panting to catch my breath. Isn't it enough that I scaled his obstacle course and cut my fingers to shreds on the rope? Isn't it enough that I ran my three miles at a clipping pace? Isn't it enough that I shot the failure drill with what he described as "remarkable accuracy"?

Why do I have to lift this useless tire?

A month living in the Excivis has taught me how to vent inside my head, but Orbit is smart enough to guess my thoughts.

"You just don't want it badly enough," he taunts. He steps toward the tire and kicks it. "This tire represents everything that's holding you back from achieving what you want most. What do you want, Sage? How badly do you want it?"

I want to punch him in the nose. No, that won't do.

I want to survive another day. Well, that goes without saying.

Beyond that? My mind draws a blank.

He walks around the tire toward me. "You're stuck in reactive mode. Something happens, and you respond to it. You've got to flip your switch. Be the one causing something to happen, and let others do the reacting."

Orbit invades my personal space and grabs my arm before I can step aside. "All you see is the tire. You've got to look past the tire at what you really want."

I jerk away, but he doesn't let go. Instead, he clasps my neck like a cat would a kitten's scruff and shoves me to my knees, forcing my head inside the tire.

"What do you want most, Sage Colby?"

I grit my teeth. "Let me go!"

He tightens his grip on my hair and neck. "That's reactive. What do you really want?"

The rotting tire smell makes me gag, and I clench my eyes shut to block out angry tears. "I want my family."

"Family?" he scoffs and shakes me. "They're probably dead. Think bigger."

I hate him. I really do. I would trade any big ideal for my small, simple home.

"The Brotherhood," I say at last.

"That's better but weak. Focus."

"I want the Brotherhood to—to give freedom back to the people." I'm practically shouting now. If I'm angry, maybe I can't cry.

He suddenly releases me and doubles over, laughing. "Oh, wow, you really have no idea what you want."

I punch him in the nose.

He staggers for a moment and then firms up his feet, blocking the rest of my wild blows. Before I can blink, he twists my hands behind me and stuffs my head back inside the tire.

He curses. "I ought to thrash you."

"You asked me what I wanted," I retort between coughing fits.

He yanks me out of the tire and tosses me to the ground. I land on my back and stare as he towers above me. Blood trickles from his nose. Even monsters bleed.

But there's approval in his eye. "That's a start. Now, get up. You flip the tire, and you can punch me again."

He snorts and starts to walk away. "But I don't think you've found your real motivation."

I stare at the tire. I picture Professor Mortimer, Felix, Eliab, and even my weaselly adviser Lucius, thinking maybe hatred will give me another charge. But I've spent that negative energy on my one punch to Orbit's face.

I try again. I think of Luther but can't sort my feelings. It's been four months now. Maybe in Crystal, four months feels like four weeks, but for me, they've been a lifetime. Has something happened to him? Do I haunt his dreams the way he haunts mine?

Then there's Darius, my brother on a mission to fight the Dome's abuses. But hasn't he failed? Didn't he promise to come for me, too?

My thoughts turn to Dad. All my life, he's been protecting and loving me, even when I don't understand his ways. And though perhaps he doesn't know where I am, I have no doubt he'll never stop searching for me. Maybe he's looking for me right now.

I want a world that doesn't divide little girls from their fathers. I want a world where families can be free to live and die without the Dome dictating where and how.

But my hope can't hinge on what others are doing for me—or on a dream world that may never exist. It has to hinge on what I can give. Right now, that's not a lot, but my little is the only chance Gath has.

Until I free him or die trying, I will be strong.

I glare at the tire, stuff my arms under its rim, and roar. It's a gladiator's cry, not a girl's.

I flip the tire and fall to the ground, gripping my stomach. I hope I haven't pulled something. That would spell the end of my training.

Orbit runs over and yanks me to my feet. He shakes me. "You found *it*?"

I punch him again.

He sways for only a second—and I imagine it's more from the surprise than from the blow. Scowling, he flexes his face and lurches toward me.

I step aside and shake my sore knuckles at him. "You said I could punch you if ..."

"Whatever." He rubs his jaw, but there's a glint in his eyes. Something tells me he'll pay me back later.

We return to Osborne's underworld earlier than usual. However, Orbit doesn't dismiss me to my room. Rather, he steers me to Patrick's grooming station.

The man grimaces when I sit in his leather chair. "Couldn't

you have at least hosed her down before bringing her in?"

Orbit snorts. "My job was to make her strong. Your job is to make her pretty. Of the two, I think you have more raw material to work with."

"Highly doubtful." Patrick sniffs. "You had a whole month. I have a few hours." He shoos me off the chair. "At least wash your face. The bathroom is over there."

"Yes, sir." I retreat behind the bathroom door.

When I return, Orbit is staring at a tray on a counter with his arms crossed. "Is that necessary?"

"I could say the same for your methods," Patrick returns icily.

"Aren't glasses enough?" He picks up a pair that looks very much like Deidra's.

"Do you wish to question the master?" Patrick challenges him.

"Of course not." Orbit notices me and drops the glasses back on the tray. "Good luck, kid. See you at dinner."

Good luck? Orbit obviously hasn't had Patrick wash his hair before. The experience is heavenly, though I could do without the pungent odor of the dye.

"Sit down." Patrick motions to the chair while mixing the hair dye.

I want to pinch my nose. "Don't you need to wash it first?"

"It will last longer if your hair is dirty—which clearly, it is."

Disappointed, I do as I'm told and don't complain. After applying the dye, he secures my hair in a plastic cap.

"There, that will need a good half hour at least." He washes his hands. "Now, lean back in the chair, and we'll get started on your dermal treatments."

"Dermal treatments?" I ask, but he isn't listening. Dermal means skin, so maybe he's going to give me a facial massage. I'd heard of those in Crystal and they sounded relaxing. I lean into the chair as Patrick lowers a lever and close my eyes.

A bright, warm light warms my face, and something that sounds like a prep table rolls nearby.

"Now I don't want to hear one peep from you." There's a warning in his voice I don't understand.

"What do you mean?" I squint and then stiffen. Patrick leans over me with a long needle pointed at my cheek.

I jerk sideways and ram my elbow into his cart. "What is that?"

"I said ..."

"Sage Colby!" Lord Osborne's voice roars from the doorway.

Patrick and I both jump nearly out of our skin. He straightens immediately and glares at me. "I was just getting ready to start the dermal treatments."

I grip the edge of the chair. "What is he talking about? What's going on?"

Eyes flashing, Lord Osborne marches over to me. "Orbit told me you performed well today. We'll talk about your assignment tomorrow—as long as you cooperate."

I gulp and lean back in the chair, casting a frightened look at Patrick. He rolls his shoulders and approaches me again.

"Please, just tell me what you're doing," I whisper.

"Dermal treatments," he mutters. "I'm going to inject a natural solution to enhance areas of your face."

"Huh?"

Osborne crosses his arms and studies me. "We can't have anyone recognize you in Crystal. With facial contouring, the chances of that happening are much lower."

Patrick nods. "There's only one downside."

My breath catches. "Is it—permanent?"

He snorts. "No, but it will last six months to a year, and I can repeat it as needed."

I involuntarily shiver. "So what's the side effect?"

Osborne places a hard hand on my shoulder as if reminding me I'm in no position to ask questions. "There is no side effect, except a little discomfort."

My gaze darts to Patrick who approaches me again with the needle. I bite my lip as I mouth a silent, "Please."

He sighs impatiently. "The only effect I meant is that you'll actually look—prettier—than you already are." He mumbles. "But Orbit was right. You don't need much help."

Patrick gives me one last warning look before moving closer. "Now hold still and try to relax."

I squeeze my eyes shut and try not to flinch when the needle pricks my skin, causing my eyes to tear.

I hold back the angry flood wanting to break. Lord Osborne seems bent on destroying all facets of my identity.

I am
Portia. He can
change my hair and face but
not my blood. It pumps hot and hard.
Rebel.

Chapter 10

Tuesday, 3.31.2150
The Excivis

"Come on, Sage. Open the door." Deidra twists and yanks on the handle, but it doesn't budge.

I sit on the bed with legs crossed and my back to the door. "Go away."

"You didn't come to breakfast or lunch. You need to eat."

"I'm not hungry."

"You have to let me in so I can help you pack for your assignment. Besides, you have your debriefing meeting with Lord Osborne after dinner."

"I still have an hour."

Deidra taps on the frame again. "I can get a key, but then Lord Osborne might find out."

"I don't care if he does."

"Sage …" Her voice trails off. "Please, I want to help you. Let me help you."

I choke back a harsh reply. It's not Deidra's fault I've been treated this way. I slide off the bed only long enough to unlock the door and then climb back on and face the wall.

Deidra slips quietly inside and closes the door behind her. Her strong hands squeeze my shoulders. "Let me see."

"No, I look ridiculous."

She wraps her arms around my side the way my mother might have—if she hadn't died of fever when I was five. My sister Candace used to cradle me this way until she hung herself just after my seventh birthday.

Unbidden sobs wrack my frame.

"Hey, you're going to be fine." Deidra pets my hair. "You looked beautiful before, and you look beautiful now. The fillers don't last forever."

I sniff. "You've had them, too?"

She gives me a wry smile. "Many times, my dear. Now go wash your face and then come back here so we can get you ready for dinner and your trip tomorrow."

I swallow, feeling somewhat ashamed, but Deidra doesn't scold me. Maybe she knows how I feel.

There's a light tap on the bathroom door, which cracks open. "Put this on," Deidra says, handing me a dress.

"Thanks." The beige tweed fabric touches my knee and hugs my waist, while a high neckline suggests no-nonsense. I feel like a schoolgirl in the dress, even though I never had something this nice to wear in my preparatory years.

When I emerge from the bathroom, Deidra's bending over a small suitcase on my bed, folding clothes and stuffing other items inside. She knows better than I do what I'll need.

She nods at me in approval. "That fits nicely and will be your traveling outfit tomorrow. You might as well wear it tonight, too.

There's a blue sweater in your closet along with a coat, and you'll want tights with your boots."

"Yes, ma'am."

Deidra rolls her eyes. "Don't ma'am me. Now come sit while I finish packing."

I stretch out on my stomach. "What can you tell me about my assignment?"

"Lord Osborne will cover all that with you tonight." Her face seems paler, and the brown eyes behind the glasses, more tired.

I gently rub my face, but there's no trace of pain from yesterday's injections. I shouldn't take out my frustration on Deidra. "I'm sorry for being difficult. You've taught me so much that I'll need for this—this new role I'm supposed to play."

"I've taught you little." She sighs. "You already know how to work hard, and you don't complain. You'll do fine as a catering maid. It's just—oh, never mind."

I pat the comforter next to me. "What else do I need to know? Have you been on an assignment like this?" I hesitate. "The last time a friend helped train me, I had no idea what road lay ahead— and that following it meant losing him."

"Him?" Her eyes glisten.

I lower my head. "Yes, he was my best friend."

"Just your best friend?"

I ball my fists. "I didn't have a chance to find out if he felt something more."

Deidra smiles sadly and sits beside me. "I was once like you, angry about the injustice done to me." She pauses to brush my cheek with her hand. "But it's not a fair world."

"What happened?" I whisper.

"I earned my name." The lines on her face deepen. "According to Lord Osborne, there's an old legend about a woman named Deidra—pronounced Deirdre then—who died of a broken heart."

As she studies me, a strange grace softens her sorrow. "Having you here reminded me of something, though. It reminded me that even though my dreams failed, there are new dreams bound up in young hearts."

I reach for her hand, and she squeezes it. Her words fill me with both dread and courage.

She stands and rests a hand on my shoulder. "I hope your story has a happier ending than mine."

Deidra clears her throat. "That's enough nonsense for now. I need to finish packing your suitcase, and you need to go to dinner." She shoos me off the bed.

"I'm going." I stuff my arms in the first sweater I can find and then hurry down the hallway toward the dining room.

When I reach the table, only my place is set. The waiter brings two courses: steaming soup and a fish filet. My diet has steadily increased, but tonight's serving feels like a feast.

I've no sooner finished when a man appears. His dark green uniform with gold stripes on the shoulder fills me with sudden terror until I realize it's Orbit. He's a precise replica of a Crystal Gage.

He smirks at my gaping mouth. "What? You didn't recognize me?"

"You're—you look like a Gage," I accuse him.

"I could have you whipped for insulting my office," he barks sternly, just as Eliab might have spewed the words.

"Are—are you?" I whisper.

He stands straighter, a glint in his eyes. "We both have new assignments to fill. You look different yourself."

92

I press my hands to my cheeks as they grow warm. "Yeah."

"You look good—better than good."

I bite my lip to keep my anger in check, though there's no concealing it from Orbit.

He pulls my hands from my face. "I've seen that look before. You'd better lose the attitude before we meet Osborne."

"But he had no right …"

Orbit tweaks my chin. "He has every right. We work for him."

I drop my gaze and nod like a misbehaving child. There's no point in arguing.

He motions for me to follow him. He hasn't taken me this deep into the Excivis before. We descend a staircase before reaching two solid metal doors. There's a box to the right of the door, similar to the keypads in Crystal, but this one is different. There are no numbers to enter, only a thumb-size glass panel.

As Orbit inserts his thumb and the doors swing open, something tells me Lord Osborne has access to even more advanced technology than the Crystal Globe University. Hadn't my adviser Lucius said that it would be a few years before finger scans replaced the access codes?

My stomach twists as we enter the sterile room where panels and unfamiliar instruments line the walls and desk stations. If he powers such technology, then why hasn't he been using it to help the people?

At the end of the mechanical room is a partially opened door, through which I glimpse the red cushioned back of a couch and a screen that starts at the ceiling and stops midway to the floor. It rivals the one in my Simulation classroom.

Lord Osborne stands before a control panel and enters something into it. The screen gradually changes from a dull gray to an opaque blue color.

My skin grows cold. No doubt I'm standing before a Translator. Did Lord Osborne steal this technology from the Dome, just like he hijacked the virus from Darius?

With metallic pen in hand, he gestures for us to be seated on a sofa. "Welcome, runners." His eyes sweep across my face to Orbit's uniform. He bobs his head in approval. "Let's talk about your assignments."

Two dark brown folders wait on a glass-top coffee table next to the sofa. When Orbit reaches for one, I do the same.

"Tomorrow morning, show Sage how to find the pipeliner outpost, and then go to Jasper's trading post. Both your train tickets are in your folder for safekeeping."

Jasper. Finally, I have a reference point for where I am. After that fateful train ride with Gath, I'd lost all sense of location.

Jasper is the square to the left of Crystal but reportedly quite affluent. I've heard it's a place of recreation and amusement, but of course, I'd never visited. Poor girls from 'Prase didn't belong there.

They still don't.

Lord Osborne points his pen at me. "The people in Jasper are friendly, flirty. You'll be asked by strangers, and likely spies, what business brings you to or takes you from Jasper.

"Your response must be consistent: You've been caring for an elderly, sick grandfather in an outer cube and now must work to help support him. You've accepted a position as a maid in Crystal.

"They will ask more. Jaspers are busybodies, but you must not chat idly with them, or you will tell them more than you should."

I nod. "What's my grandfather's name?"

He flashes his eyes sternly, and I blush at my mistake. "He

does not have a name except *grandfather*. Do you understand?"

"Yes, sir," I say meekly.

"You and Orbit will both board the same train but must act like strangers. He is, after all, a newly commissioned Crystal Gage, and you are a servant girl."

Newly commissioned. The Brotherhood's last insider was Gath. I never dreamed other mercenaries penetrated the Crystal Gage ranks.

"You must not try to contact or find Orbit, even if you run into trouble. You are strangers, and no commoner ever expresses familiarity with a Gage."

"Yes, sir."

The screen behind him fades to a duller blue, and he presses something on the panel to awaken the color to its lighter state. "You have been to the Crystal platform before, correct?"

"Yes, sir."

"Have you ever been to the marketplace?"

"No, sir."

Lord Osborne uses his thumb to press a notch on his pen, which flashes a red beam. He points it at my folder. "Open it."

The folder has two pockets. The first holds fake identification papers for Sage Colby. The other side contains two letters. One is typed on embossed letterhead from the office of Madame Alexis. It's addressed to a cube in Jasper.

The red dot circles the letter and then moves to my chest. "Guard this with your life. It contains your work assignment to Madame Alexis's home. It also contains your own fictitious address, which you must memorize.

"Present this paper to the steward, who will file it in the household records. Under no circumstances can it fall into other

95

hands. If that were to happen, someone could trace it to a cottage in the Jasper woods where a recovering agent lives. You would jeopardize both your lives."

I wonder if I'll end up recovering in a cottage someday.

"You may, however, let the train conductor look at this letter to convince him you have an official summons. He can give you directions to the Crystal marketplace. Alexis's estate lies beyond it in an elite suburban cube. You'll also need to show it to the guard who monitors the cube."

I blink in confusion. We had no such guards in 'Prase.

Lord Osborne taps something on his control panel, and Orbit leans closer to explain. "Wealthy cubes are often gated with guard houses."

I thumb past the work assignment letter to the second. It's handwritten in a slanted style I can barely read. I scan to the bottom signature which reads M. Colby. Is that supposed to be my grandfather?

As if reading my thoughts, Lord Osborne glances at the letter. "That's a thank-you note from your grandfather to Madame Alexis for agreeing to your monthly visit. It will add a personal touch. Give it to the steward along with the assignment letter for keeping."

An image suddenly flashes on the screen. It's an overgrown meadow with a faded red barn in the background.

"Now tell me: What do you see?" Lord Osborne asks.

"I see a meadow, maybe a farmhouse," I say.

His red bead runs angry circles around the screen. "Describe it in clear, vivid details."

I sit straighter on the sofa and study the image so intently that I barely notice a blue glow creeping into the room. "There's a broken wooden fence along a pebbled road," I say. "Beyond the fence is a meadow, overrun with grass and wildflowers. Three large oak trees surround a faded red barn. The roof has caved in, and the door is slightly ajar."

"That's better, but you missed something. Look at the fence."

I squint at the screen, which seems to move as if with a breeze. This is no longer a picture. It's a Translation, a window into a different place.

I glance at my feet. I'm standing on the pebbled dirt road.

Orbit stands to my left, smirking like a know-it-all. "What do you see now, Sage?"

I run my fingers along the jagged wood fence, overgrown with an azalea bush. Hidden on the inside of the fence, beneath a cluster of pre-spring blooms, rests a rusted, metal box.

"What is it?" I ask Orbit.

"It's what people once called a mailbox," he says.

"What was it for?"

"Mail." He laughs. "It's where all your friends' and family's letters would come, where you would receive your bills and your paychecks."

"Would it be similar to the official communications we received at school or Dad received if he didn't pay enough to the cube enforcer?"

"Exactly." He taps the folder still in my hands. "It would be the place where you would receive a work assignment like this one."

I try to grasp the idea of a personal summons that would come right to my own home but can't. "That summons is official knowledge on the public record."

"Back in the day, it wasn't," Orbit says. "With a mailbox, the summons was private. It was your own business, and no one read it before you did."

Back in the day. "Do you mean in the United States?"

He grins secretively. "You Revisionary candidates aren't the only ones who know about the past."

I finger the mailbox as if carefully inspecting it, but my mind swirls. Orbit knows more about me than I realized.

"Memorize the number on the mailbox: 45 Brighton Lane." He points to the barely visible lettering on the side. "You'll need to find this place and check the mailbox weekly for communications from myself or Lord Osborne. And under no circumstances can anyone catch you checking it."

I study the empty lane. There's a forest on the other side of the dirt road with no houses in sight. "Where is this place in relation to my assignment?"

"On your way between the market and Alexis's cube, there's a fork in the road," Orbit says. "One side will lead you to the estates where Madame Alexis lives, and the other will lead you here. Most people don't even bother with this road, though I suspect some local children use it for playing. You'll have to be careful that they aren't around when you enter the lane. Most children are innocent, but even innocent talk costs lives."

The same breeze that whisked us into the scene signals our exit from it. I'm back on the sofa, but there's a chair across from me that wasn't there before.

"Thank you, Orbit," Lord Osborne says. "We've already talked about your assignment, so you may go now. Collect Sage at 0500 tomorrow morning to start for the outpost."

Orbit bobs his head in understanding and exits the room. I fidget with my skirt on the sofa while Lord Osborne focuses on his panel. His fingers run nimbly over it, much the way Mortimer's did, except Mortimer's were boney.

Osborne's are muscular.

The room again begins to glow, and I glance around, determined not to let Osborne's Translation destination startle me again.

But this time, I remain on the sofa. This time, someone translates to us.

A sob chokes my throat. Seated in the chair an arm's reach away is Darius.

Chapter 11

Tuesday, 3.31.2150

The Excivis

He's close enough to touch, though I know he's only an image. But somewhere, he's real and very much alive.

My brother's brown hair shimmers burnt red in the lighting as if to match the fire that floods his veins.

But is the flame going out? Crow's feet etch his eyes, and the creases in his forehead appear deeper than before.

Darius's confused gaze darts between Lord Osborne and me without a flicker of recognition. "What's the meaning of this, Osborne?" he demands. "Who is she?"

My chest tightens as Lord Osborne's lips twist into a smirk. "She is your sister."

My brother searches my face with desperate hope. "Portia, is that you?"

I gulp. "Darius—Yes."

"Her name is Sage Colby," Lord Osborne cuts me off. "I don't have time for a reunion. I arranged this meeting to confirm our terms."

Darius squints angrily. "I haven't seen my sister in four months, and I hardly recognize her. What did you do to her?"

"I saved her neck." Osborne snaps. "You should be grateful."

Darius folds his arms. "You sure took your time—and some liberties—fulfilling your part of the bargain."

Bargain?

"I had to make sure she was worth it." Lord Osborne's voice is cool as if he's discussing a beverage for the evening meal. "I had my doubts. But that brings us to our terms, and how this arrangement will work."

Darius frowns. "I said I'd pay for you to rescue her, not keep her."

"Your money has no value to me." Osborne sniffs in disdain. "She does. I rescued her—and that will have to be good enough for you. But she's paying her own way as the new addition to my Crystal network."

Lord Osborne pauses to study Darius with a dominating smile. "Besides, don't you want access to that virus? Your sister's service is the only way you can have your cake and eat it—unless you'd like to tell me about the Pelagic Project? Now there's something else I might consider as payment."

Darius's eyes widen, then narrow to slits. "I don't know what you're talking about."

Lord Osborne snorts. "My dear boy, if I can hijack your virus and spy on the CGA, don't you think I can tap into your quaint little Morse wires?"

I want to ask what *pelagic* means and why it could possibly interest Osborne, but Darius presses his lips firmly together. He studies my face—I suppose for scars. He has no idea what I've been through.

Or perhaps he does. He was once a Baytown prisoner. I wonder again how he escaped and how he knows Lord Osborne. Are those two stories related?

My employer waits a moment longer, but Darius doesn't offer any clue about the project he alluded to. "Very well, then, I'll take what I can get. Sage will begin her assignment tomorrow as a catering maid in the household of a Dome representative. As such, she'll join my network of eyes and ears inside Crystal. She'll communicate with me through a receiver my team has concealed inside a deserted barn and through a mailbox drop-off. I'll even give you the box's location so you can message her there in an emergency—just don't abuse it."

Darius scribbles while Osborne gives him the map coordinates.

"In exchange for her service, you'll have access to the virus you planted in the Dome's computers, along with limited use of the receiver at your disposal today." Lord Osborne offers Darius a lofty smile. "You may begin again to build the intelligence for your idealistic Brotherhood."

Darius scoffs. "Is that what you think we are? Some kind of rose-colored rebellion?"

Lord Osborne smiles patronizingly. "My boy, your plans for revolution are as desperate as those belonging to the long-ago rebels of this land."

"But they won," I whisper.

"And how do you know that?" Lord Osborne asks.

"I was a Revisionary candidate. If we can learn from the past, we can change the future."

"A dreamer, just like your brother!" He laughs. "You two

bleeding hearts can have your fun, as long as you pay your dues."

"And what are you requiring of Portia?" Darius demands. "My instructions were…"

"I give the instructions." Lord Osborne's tone changes from sudsy to steel. "You may have initiated this bargain, but I'm the one who sets the terms. Your sister is alive and well. Is she not?

Darius again tries to read my expression, but I drop my gaze. "Frankly, it's hard to tell," he says. "She's changed."

"I think you'll prefer her now to the creature I plucked from the mines." Lord Osborne's voice rises in pitch. "She's gained fifteen pounds, eaten excellent meals, and received rigorous training. Her assignment, if she doesn't blow it, will provide a respectable livelihood for her."

"For what purpose?" Darius presses.

A taunting smile plays at Lord Osborne's lips. "That, Abe, is between Sage and me unless you change your mind and tell me more about …"

"I want regular communications with her," Darius interrupts.

"She'll return to the Excivis once a month. At that time, you may have a brief interchange like this one."

His tone implies our meeting is finished. Although I'm not supposed to ask questions, I blurt out the one threatening to boil over. "Darius, how's Dad?"

I feel Lord Osborne's annoyance that I've spoken out of turn but glue my eyes on Darius's face which grows tenser.

He sets his jaw. "Portia, we haven't heard from him since the explosion."

My throat tightens, but the words race off my tongue. "What do you mean?"

Darius looks down. "He went with Foxworth to help you

escape."

"What? Were they both there when the explosion ...?" My voice cracks. "You can't mean that both he and Foxworth are ..."

"Enough of this nonsense," Lord Osborne mutters. "All your training dissolves under emotion. It's disgraceful."

I blink back hot tears. "Darius, surely ..."

His face blurs, and his last words come through garbled. "I'm sorry."

The screen goes blank.

I'm still reeling from the shock when Lord Osborne claims the seat opposite of me, the seat Darius appeared to have occupied moments ago. "We need to discuss my final fee."

This man has no heart. My dad's missing, presumed dead, and he only wants to talk business.

"Sage Colby." He speaks my name the way an annoyed headmaster might in school. "You can't allow personal feelings to blur your judgment."

I squint back the rising emotion and steady my voice. "With all due respect, my dad's missing."

"Your dad's dead."

"You don't know that."

He shakes his head. "Sage Colby is an orphan. Her parents died in a fire. Remember your place is here, not in your past."

"Okay, my parents are dead," I repeat with a locked jaw, then take a deep breath. *But my dad is still alive. He has to be.*

Lord Osborne folds his hands and leans forward. "Now, listen carefully. As Madame Alexis's catering maid, you'll serve guests from the Dome and other men of power. Among them will be Crystal's Commanding Gage, Eliab Benge."

I recoil in my seat. Eliab? Eliab Benge? Though I've never

heard his last name, I'm sure he's one and the same. Gages must use their first names only to protect the identities of their families.

Lord Osborne watches me closely. "You know him?"

"Yes," I say. "He was partly responsible for sending me here."

"Then you'll like this task. Find out all you can concerning his latest assignment. My sources say he has plans to visit the satellites. I don't know why, but these travels will make him vulnerable to attack and provide an opportunity I've been waiting for. Find out anything you can regarding his movements and plans. When he attends an event, eavesdrop on the conversations."

I nod, not trusting my voice, not daring to tell Lord Osborne that Eliab might be hunting for me.

"There's also another Gage I want you to find," Lord Osborne continues. "He disappeared over the last few months. He's either on special assignment somewhere, or he might be dead. If he is alive, I want to know. Both he and Eliab did me great wrong. I'd like to return the favor."

Another Gage. My heart pounds to the words. Surely, he can't mean …

"His name is Gage Gath Aden."

I must have stopped breathing because Lord Osborne snaps his fingers in agitation. "Focus, Sage. Did you hear me? Repeat what I said."

"His name is Gage Gath Aden," I say in a monotone.

"Good. See what you can learn about his whereabouts."

I swallow and nod.

He rises and turns to the control panel. "Now, before you leave, I want you to watch closely how I operate this Translator. The receiver you'll find in the barn is somewhat simpler. If you can manage the Translator, you can operate it."

Focusing on his movements helps clear my head of questions. I don't bother to tell him that I already know how to program a Simulation, which is more complicated than a Translation.

After we translate briefly to and from the barn location, he taps on the screen. "This device is special because it has the capabilities to serve as both Translator and what we call a Simulator. Actually, any Translator can be a Simulator if programmed with the date software. When you program Translations, choose present time, or you could mistakenly enter today's date for a previous year and miss the session."

As he swipes his finger to shut down the equipment, I blurt, "May I stay a while and practice—just to make sure I'm comfortable operating it?"

He glances at me in surprise. "It's self-explanatory."

"Yes, I know, but I want to make sure I'm competent. Sometimes, stress makes people forget."

His eyes flash approval. "That's true, but I don't want you translating anywhere. Although our receivers are well concealed, you might accidentally transmit to one of the Dome's receivers and compromise your entire mission. As long as you pick a date from the past for practice, that will be fine."

Lord Osborne steps aside so I can operate the panel. "To shut it down, tap the square at the bottom left of the screen and follow the prompts. Now, I have other matters to attend to this evening."

He collects his jacket and pauses to give me one last stern warning. "Make sure you're ready for Orbit to collect you at 0500 tomorrow morning. Also, don't try anything clever with this machine. Every Translation and Simulation gets recorded in the log."

"Yes, sir."

"I'll look forward to your first update."

When he leaves, I turn my attention to the equipment. Now's my chance to find out what happened to Dad. If I translate to four months ago …

But even as the desire fills me, I know Lord Osborne won't approve. And he'll know, thanks to the recording feature.

I close my eyes and remember the last time I had seen Dad. It was that night in the cave. I asked when we'd meet again.

Hopefully under a freer sky. He had said.

Dad wouldn't want me wasting tears on him. He'd want me to work toward making that freedom a reality. Isn't that what he's been doing all along?

The Simulator waits for my command. It's my tool, my chance to figure out the next step. Maybe I can learn something that will help me know what I'm supposed to do.

I select the North American continent and narrow the dates to the 1700s, thinking back to my last Simulation. It was the winter of 1776.

I shudder at the memory of the blood-stained snow and dying soldier. No sooner had I grabbed his flag than the Simulation ended, and Eliab had pounced.

I don't want to visit another winter nightmare. There's a cluster of spring dates, one right after the other, in the preceding year 1775. I wonder how these events may have set in motion the ones I witnessed before.

I select the morning of April 19, hoping to explore my surroundings before too many people are awake.

After entering a duration of thirty minutes, I pause. I've never gone into a Simulation without someone else to administer it. What if something goes wrong?

"Relax," I tell myself. Mortimer had said Simulations can't last over 24 hours, and before then, Orbit would be looking for me.

I take a deep breath, press the *engage* button and dart to the sofa, placed within the Simulation range. The room blurs, and I hold my breath.

Chapter 12

Tuesday, 3.31.2150
Simulation

A foggy haze surrounds me, and there's a trace of something burnt in the air. Maybe someone's cooking breakfast.

I shiver in the morning's coolness. Beneath me, an old, slotted-back wooden chair creaks, the only sound in an atmosphere thick with suspense. Beyond me, stone fences etch a rolling field which slopes downward, perhaps to a river.

A wood-framed house rests behind me, but I'm not about to invite myself inside. I rock back and forth, unsure where to go. The expanse is eerily quiet but far from still.

Something moves to my right, and I freeze. Is it an animal? I can't see well enough to know. Choosing this early hour was not the smartest decision.

No, it's not an animal—or I should say, they aren't animals. They are the silent outlines of men, but there is something strange about them. Long rods extend beyond their shoulders.

My pulse surges. No, those aren't rods. The American history book I had flipped through in the archives showed pictures of men holding those things. A caption had called them muskets. Jutting out from their ends are bayonets.

I have a front row seat of a fight about to break loose.

"What are you doing out there?" A woman hisses from the house behind me. "Do you want to get shot?"

I clutch the chair and swing my neck. Her matronly silhouette outlines the door where she holds a small bundle, a baby. The darkness conceals most of her face, as I hope it does mine.

"What's going on?" I whisper back, tucking my legs beneath the chair. The framework of her long gown makes me conscious I'm not dressed for the day's customs.

"The regulars are here, that's what." She points toward the field. "And our men are readying to protect their homes and families." The ire in her voice makes my spine tingle.

"Regulars?" I ask.

Her voice catches. "Why, the British soldiers. Word is that they torched Concord."

I had smelled something burnt and wish it could be as simple as toast. But Concord must be a place, maybe a town.

She shifts the baby in her arms. "Now, there's a group of them on the west side of the river, by the North Bridge, over yonder. Militiamen are gathering on the high ground overlooking the bridge. There will be a scuffle, for sure, and it will probably head this way." Again, she points into the pre-dawn darkness. "Hurry home, child! This is no place for you."

Child. She must think I'm a youth because of my size. But the first glimmer of sunlight cracks through the haze. She won't mistake me for a child much longer.

"Get along, girl, or join us inside the manse! Trouble will be breaking loose soon enough." The baby whimpers, diverting her attention.

I wave my thanks and jump to my feet, but instead of retreating behind the house, I dart for the closest tree in the direction of the bridge.

The thick tree's two lower branches, like arms, give my clamoring hands something to climb. As I scale higher, I catch my first view of the bridge and the red-coated soldiers on the farther side.

I can see the bridge clearly now. It's maybe 100 yards away. The small company of men the woman had called regulars pace nervously as the countrymen's numbers grow on the hill behind them.

Compared to the red uniforms of the soldiers, the rebels appear to be ordinary farmers or tradesmen. Though rough and worn, they stand proud.

The sight of them makes my heart ache. How much they remind me of men like Red and Randolph. How much they remind me of my brothers.

The April breeze teases my hair as my body grows stiff from waiting—for what, I'm not even sure. The same gentle wind flips the cocked hats of the militiamen.

The smell of smoke grows stronger, and I twist my head to see a plume rising from the direction behind me. There's a stirring from the militia's ranks. They notice the growing smoke cloud, too.

There's murmuring, and then, they begin to descend from the high ground. The rebels march toward the bridge in a regimented manner that makes the redcoats even more nervous, so nervous, in fact, that they move to the east side of the bridge.

The side closer to me.

As they retreat, some tear up planks on the bridge, which riles the approaching rebels even more.

The British must want to stall their advance, and I can understand why. The militiamen number in the hundreds, and I've counted just under one hundred who wear red coats.[i]

The rebels stop at the western edge of the bridge. One man in a brown waistcoat clutches a pole tightly as its square flag flaps in the wind. The design is entirely different from the one in my last Simulation.

This one has a red background with a man holding out a sword. There's some kind of inscription on a banner, but it's too far away to read.

I hold my breath and wonder if this standoff will ever end. There's murmuring.

And then, a single shot rings out.

I blink and grip the branch, straining my eyes. Who pulled the trigger? The regulars or the rebels?

But I can't tell, and now, it makes no difference. A tree is not the safest place to be in a gunfight.

I tumble to the ground and take cover behind a small outbuilding near the old house. Somewhere inside, children cry.

I don't know how long I keep my head down, but finally, I cock open one eye, then another.

Down the dirt road that stretches alongside the house, the outnumbered regulars retreat. My heart surges, and I push myself up. Shots still linger, but they are not as rapid as before. In fact, they're rather one-sided.

After the last of the regulars disappear, the woman and her young children press open the door. Her white knuckles drop an apron she's been using to dry one of the children's tears. She recognizes one of the men and lets out a cry, then takes off running.

The children stare at me curiously.

I understand why. My dress stops below my knee, and their mama's is to her ankles.

Hastily, I grab the apron and slip it over my head. At least it's floor-length and will help hide my bare calves as I try to get a closer look at the river's edge.

A few bodies lie still where they've fallen, but a cheer rises from the militiamen. They've won the battle of the bridge.

A cheer starts to rise in my own throat until I see the flagman kneel beside his companion, face down in the dirt. His grey coat splotches with red.

No victory comes without a cost.

I spy a bucket and grab it, dunking it in the river. Then, without thinking, I hurry to the wounded man. Perhaps he isn't …

The flagman sees the hope in my eyes and shakes his head.

I bite my lip. This is the second time I've watched someone die in a Simulation. I tell myself that this isn't real life.

But it was. And one day, it may be again.

The flagman rises from his knees. "I'll take that drink, if you don't mind."

"Of course." I drop the bucket, but at least it doesn't spill.

He scoops and drinks a handful, savors the coolness for a moment, and then wipes his whiskered mouth. The edges of his jaw grow hard as he studies his friend's prostrate form. "He died to leave his children free. He will not have died in vain."

I glance at his flag. "What does it say—your flag?"

"Vince aut Morire. It means *Conquer or Die*."[ii]

"Brave words," I whisper.

115

"True words," he replies. "And we rebels won't stop until we do."

With that, he reaches down to turn his comrade onto his back and pay his final respects. My heart aches for him. I shift my focus to the dead man's face, now locked in a death-stare skyward.

And cry out in horror. It's my dad.

Chapter 13

Wednesday, 4.1.2150
Excivis

My alarm clock wakes me at 0400 hours. Deidra must have set it to make sure I eat breakfast before Orbit meets me.

Good thing she did. I was in no state of mind to remember it after last night's Simulation.

Gunpowder, blood, and sweat—Their pungent odors were so raw from the scene that I can practically smell them, even now.

I stagger to the bathroom and crank on the bathtub's spigot. I wish it were a shower with hard, pelting droplets that could scrub away the memory.

The mind plays such cruel tricks. That man wasn't my father, and yet, my fears intruded into the scene and transposed Dad's face onto the dead man's.

It was too horrible for words.

Yet war is horrible. How many fathers will fall in our own rebellion? Is mine among the first?

Revolution means death, sacrifice, and suffering. Is the cost worth it? I'm not sure anymore.

After a quick bath, I don the tweed dress again and find the stockings and lace-up leather boots Deidra laid out for me. My small, hardbacked suitcase waits packed by the door, once again thanks to Deidra. I must have walked past it last night—amazingly, I didn't trip.

Half past four, I slip down the hallway in search of breakfast, wondering if there will be any this morning.

There is. Someone placed a simple spread of dry cereal and fruit on the table. I'm too nervous to eat much and wrap an apple in a napkin for later.

Orbit arrives shortly after I return to my room. He's wearing a long black trench coat, which mostly conceals his Gage uniform. He grips a gray duffle bag as I slip my arms into my coat.

"Ready?"

I nod, reaching for my suitcase, and follow him through the hallways, down the familiar route to our training arena. We emerge into the cold, spring morning. A blanket of icy dew chills the ground, and our breath puffs like smoke.

"Pay close attention," Orbit says. "Next month, you'll have to find your way on your own."

He leads me past our obstacle course and into the woods, following an indiscernible trail. Barren branches swipe at our faces and arms for the good part of an hour.

At last, I glimpse a clearing through the trees. A distant train whistle confirms we've reached the tracks.

A decrepit outpost sags at the edge of the woods. It must be the one Lord Osborne had mentioned. Orbit walks to the back of it and then spins on his heels. I copy his movements, not sure why he turned around.

A dozen paces behind the outpost is a giant oak. "Climb it." Orbit gestures to a thick branch.

I set down my suitcase and reach for the branch. This tree reminds me of the rope course and pole climbing he had me practice at the arena. I wonder what else those exercises may have prepared me for.

About fifteen feet up, I pause at a nook where several branches meet.

"Look down," he says. "You should see a crevice. Pull out the box."

Sure enough, someone stuffed a small box in an opening in the wood. I unlatch the box's top and find a round, glass object with an arrow on its face.

"What is it?" I ask.

"It's a compass," Orbit says. "Now, aim it so that the arrow points the way we came. What does it show?"

"It's on the notch to the right of the W."

"Remember that. When you come back, retrieve the compass, and follow that arrow west-northwest. It will take you back the way we came."

I return the compass to its case and hide it inside the wooden crevice before climbing down.

"But how will I find this outpost again?" I ask. "It looks deserted. I don't expect the train will stop here."

Orbit shakes his head but points down the track. "About twelve miles down is the Jasper station for Cube 645—where we're headed today. You'll purchase a ticket to that station. When you disembark, follow the tracks north until you find this place. Be absolutely sure no one is following you."

"Twelve miles?" I repeat. "That's almost a half marathon."

Orbit grins. "Why do you think I've been having you run three to five miles every day? If you can run that, you manage twelve in under three hours."

A train whistle blows again, but this time, it sounds closer. Orbit motions for me to return to the outpost's cover. "But don't worry. Today, we're not walking that far."

"But ...?"

He holds a finger to his lips and strains his eyes in the direction of the train. Then, he waves for me to follow him to the other side of the track.

"There's a cargo station about a mile down from here. Unfortunately, no passenger trains go there, but this morning's cargo train just left and will be passing here shortly. It's still picking up speed and will be slow enough for us to catch a ride." His voice is low and intense. "There's a ladder on the caboose that we can use to swing ourselves aboard. Now, we only have one shot at this. Follow me, and don't get left behind."

I'm shivering but not from the morning air. Orbit didn't teach me how to catch a moving train.

He grips his bag in his right hand, keeping his left free to grab the train's rail. I follow his example, thankful my suitcase is small.

The train is chugging steadily when it reaches us, but the cargo carrier was not designed for speed.

We wait until the engine car passes before darting from the woods. Orbit swings himself on board with all the ease of a monkey.

Though I'm not as fast, I catch the caboose. Orbit watches without offering a hand. I wish he would at least take the suitcase, but then I remember our drills. If he helps me, I've failed my test.

Gritting my teeth, I grab the ladder. The force yanks my

weaker left arm, but I don't let go until I've swung myself on board.

Silently, Orbit motions for me to follow him. Between the last two cargo cars is a small space and ledge where we can rest and wait, mostly concealed from view.

I relax and set down my suitcase, but he gives me a warning frown. "Don't get too comfortable," he says. "We'll reach the small Jasper trading post platform in about fifteen minutes, and we have to jump off before then."

"Jump off?" The train has picked up considerable speed.

"This cargo train isn't stopping there, and someone at the station would spot us."

Maybe a twelve-mile walk would have been the better choice. Jumping off a moving train is crazier than catching one.

"It's still early," Orbit says, glancing at the dawn sky. "The sun won't have burned off the fog when we get there. We'll jump at the bend before the platform, and no one will notice.

"Remember, once we reach the outpost, we're strangers. Don't talk to me or even look at me. I'm a Gage, and you're a maid."

Orbit slips his hand into a deep pocket and hands me a ticket. "Give this to the stationmaster, and he'll show you on board."

I accept it and slip it into a zippered pocket, then pull my coat tighter about me. The train generates its own wind, and my legs already feel numb.

Only fifteen minutes. But I almost dread the outpost more than the cold. From there, I'm on my own.

We ride in silence as the scenery flashes past us like a blurred mural. The sun glows through the haze and creeps up on the horizon.

"Get ready," Orbit says as the bend approaches. "Though it's not stopping, the train will slow past the station, which helps us."

I stomp my feet to warm them, but I can feel my neck flushing. I hope Orbit can't tell how nervous I am.

The train curves at a bend, and Orbit grasps the ladder rail, lowering himself to the last rung.

"Follow my lead," he says and then jumps. He trips on the landing and spirals to the ground before bolting to his feet. He waves at me to hurry.

I circle around the ladder and grip the rail. The ground rolls like waves, and I suddenly feel sick.

The whistle blows. The train will reach the outpost soon. Orbit is running behind the train, waving furiously at me.

I take a deep breath and let go. My knees buckle on impact. I drop my suitcase and roll into the fall. The ground is hard but patched with grass.

I'm sore but not injured. I'm more worried that I've ruined my stockings or torn my dress.

Orbit lifts me to my feet. His hard hands brush me off like a paper doll.

"That was close," he mutters and pulls me toward the tree line. "Fix your hair, and then we need to hurry."

I run fingers through my hair to straighten it and smooth my skirt. There's a grass stain near the hem I hope no one will notice.

He retrieves my bag and thrusts it into my hands. "Stay close until the forest ends at the edge of town. Then, wait until I disappear around the farthest outbuilding before following me."

"What is that building?"

"It's a hostel, so we won't look suspicious appearing from behind it. Follow the dirt road straight. You can't miss the platform."

He is ever my instructor, giving his student the last few tips before the exam.

"Orbit." I hesitate. He's been nothing but harsh with me, and yet, I wish he didn't have to leave. "Thanks."

He grins. "Don't thank me yet. You can thank me if you survive." His face grows sober. "Remember your motivation, whatever it is. You can flip any tire with the right focus."

That stupid tire. He would bring it up.

We reach the forest's edge, and I duck behind the last tree while he strides toward the hostel and then disappears around front.

The train whistles as steam gushes in the distance. Our passenger train is preparing to leave. And I have to be on it.

I emerge from behind the tree and follow Orbit's path. Rounding the hostel, I catch my first glimpse of the Jasper outpost. There's a total of five buildings with the station platform just beyond them.

A creaking noise to my left startles me. An old man rocks in a rickety chair. He smokes his pipe and squints at me from underneath bushy eyebrows.

I hurry toward the platform. Orbit is just walking away from a small booth. That must be the stationmaster's post.

I step behind an older woman in line and try not to look at the cluster of people milling about, waiting for the train.

Even in a small outpost like this one, there's something different about them. Their clothes, though worn, are shades of colors. In 'Prase, we poor cube dwellers wore mostly grays and browns, plain and simple hand-me-downs.

But then, Jaspers enjoy their pleasures. Perhaps their apparel is one way they express their privilege.

Their wandering eyes also make me uncomfortable. They all stare at each other as if summing up themselves in a comparison game. Back home, we kept our curiosity to ourselves. Eye contact with the wrong person could get you in trouble.

The older woman ahead of me arches her brows. "Where'd you find that ugly thing?"

I glance down at my tweed dress, a mix of gray, beige, and blue colors. It's the nicest dress I've ever worn, aside from my uniforms in Crystal and the evening wear Lord Osborne occasionally required.

"I'm heading to my job," I say.

"Eh? And where's that?" she asks.

"In Crystal."

"That's a long way to be going for work." Her words drip with suspicion. Hadn't Lord Osborne warned me about Jaspers?

I simply smile and don't respond, though she waits expectantly for an answer.

"Next!" the stationmaster calls, saving me from more questions. The woman grudgingly turns toward him and hands him her ticket.

After I submit my own, I hurry on board the train. The nosy Jasper catches my eye and pats an empty seat next to her in the first passenger car.

I force another fake smile and move to the next car. I'm relieved to find Orbit, even though he only frowns at me. He taps his nose, and at first, I don't understand what he means.

Does he mean glasses?

I didn't pack any, but maybe Deidra did. There's an empty seat next to a dozing woman and baby, and I quickly claim it. Pulling my suitcase onto my lap, I unzip the outer pocket and suddenly remember my assignment folder. Where had I put that—or had I left it on my bed stand? The thought sickens me.

To my relief, the folder is the first thing I find. *Bless you, Deidra!* She must have sneaked in while I was sleeping to make sure I had everything.

There aren't any glasses in the outer pocket, but I find a pair carefully packed between some stockings in the main compartment.

I slip them on my nose and zip the bag before lowering it between my feet. The mother and baby are still sleeping, ignorant of the girl now wearing dark-rimmed plastic glasses.

The ride to the platform at Crystal must be at least two hours. Maybe I can sleep myself. It's a sure way to avoid conversation.

I close my eyes and, what feels like seconds later, awake to the train's whistle and a crying baby. The sun now shines brightly overhead. Orbit is poised on the edge of his seat, ready to leave the moment the train stops.

We must be here.

I stare out the window as the familiar Crystal platform appears. Six months ago, I had arrived here, expecting to change the world as a Revisionary candidate.

Now, I'm an escaped satellite convict, a wanted member of the Brotherhood, a spy of the Excivis.

I'm a Rogue, but I still want to change the world.

Chapter 14

Wednesday, 4.1.2150
Crystal

"You're from Jasper, but your work orders are for Crystal?" The stationmaster stares with confusion between my passport and the embossed letter.

I hurry to explain. "My grandfather lives in Jasper, and I've been taking care of him on a leave of absence, but my official residence is in Crystal."

He returns my papers. "I see."

"I was hoping you could point me in the direction of the marketplace." I smile sweetly. "After my parents died, I was raised in a boarding house in a different cube and am not familiar with this area."

His eyes soften. "Well now, I'm sorry to hear about your parents. The marketplace is straight down the main road in the opposite direction of the university. You can't miss it. The address for your orders will be in a real nice cube beyond it. Be sure you present your papers to the guard there. You need permission to enter those residences."

"Thank you." I grip my suitcase. Behind me, several students disembark and jostle each other on their way to the university entrance. My heart pounds as I scan their faces, but Luther, Lydia, and Jael aren't among them.

Shoving my fake glasses further up my nose, I follow another group of civilians down the platform, across the track, and toward the marketplace.

A blend of ripe fruit, poultry, and fish blast my nose and cause my stomach to churn as the open-air marketplace appears. I should have eaten breakfast. Remembering the apple, I reach into the top outer pocket to retrieve it, only to find it smashed and bruised. Maybe that's why Deidra packed my glasses between cushiony clothes. Oh well. I take a mushy bite and toss the rest in some tall grass.

The wooden stalls filled with vendors' wares and fragrant foods astonish me. My cube back home never offered such variety and luxury. We lived from hand to mouth on the food rations that were never enough. Crystal's double standards stretch farther than the technology privileges in the university.

I press through the growing throngs until I'm past the market and again on a well-maintained dirt road. I hope it leads to Madame Alexis's estate.

A gray vehicle passes, but the windows are too dark to see through. It's the first vehicle I've seen since my ride in one last fall. Perhaps Madame Alexis herself or another Dome representative is inside. No civilian would ever dream of owning such a mechanical miracle.

As Orbit had said, there's a fork in the road. One branch continues in the same manicured fashion, while the other offers pot-holes and overgrown weeds. I can't be late for my first day of work, but the first chance I have, I'll come back and explore the second.

Rooftops peek over the trees, and a small outbuilding appears. Quickening my step, I clutch my bag more tightly and march with confidence toward the guardhouse.

A man in a blue uniform greets me with a stern nod.

"Hello," I say and set down my bag. "I'm here to report for my work assignment at Madame Alexis's estate." I unzip my outer compartment and hand him my work assignment orders.

He glances from the paper to my face. "Ms. Colby?"

"Yes."

He takes the paper and steps into his guardhouse. When he reemerges a minute later, he returns the letter to me, along with a small card.

"This is your temporary working pass for the community. At the end of your probationary period, your employer will issue you a permanent one. Keep it with you at all times when you leave the community. You'll need to show it to the guard on duty when you reenter."

"Thank you." I tuck it carefully into my coat pocket.

The guard points down the road. "You'll want the fifth residence on the left."

I retrieve my suitcase and continue straight. I've crossed so many hurdles today, and yet, the one before me seems the tallest order.

Lies can protect us. But only the truth can free us.

Dad's words rush in without warning. How long will I have to depend on fake identities to survive? When will I be able to be myself again?

I count five houses and stop in front of a cropped lawn. A pebbled driveway winds around the side of the three-story *mansion*.

That word in the dictionary has never meant much until now, but surely this place can be nothing else. A wrap-around porch graces the lowest story, and balconies adorn the other two. Brick accents climb the corners like pillars, stopping below the trussed roofline.

A primrose garden hugs the front path toward the entrance where a tall archway frames a pair of thick wooden doors.

Would I have lived in such a place if I had earned that Revisionary Dome seat?

I shake off the thought. I don't need a mansion to be happy. I just want a home. For now, though, I'll settle for serving in what might as well be a king's palace.

I stop at the threshold, ready with folder in hand, and pound the brass knocker five times. Any less and the keeper of this place might not even hear me.

A stately man answers the door. There's no other word to describe him. His harshly pressed black suit and stiff white collar boast meticulous attention to detail. His thinning gray hair combs over his head without a strand in the wrong place, while a perfectly trimmed mustache tweaks the corners of his mouth.

"How may I help you?" Though civil, his tone drips with suspicion.

"My name is Sage Colby, and I'm reporting for my work assignment." I hand him the letter and hold my breath.

He glares at me. "Impertinent girl! The servant's door is around back."

"Oh, I'm—so sorry!" I gasp. "I—I didn't know."

"What do they teach in school these days?" He mutters and retreats inside, slamming the door behind him.

I stare after him but quickly collect myself. He still has my letter, and it's my only ticket to making this position work.

Careful not to step on any roses, I circle the house in search of the back entrance. After the porch ends, there's a small overhang above a simple, brown door.

My mouth goes dry as I timidly knock. I've no sooner done so than the door bursts open, and a thick woman nearly collides into me.

She stops short, and the wooden bucket in her hand splashes my skirt. We both jump.

The woman gasps. "Bless me, I'm sorry!"

"No, I'm the one who's sorry," I say, wiping the water off my skirt. At least the woolly fabric wicks it away.

She sets the half-empty bucket on the ground and dries her hands on a stained apron. "What brings you here, dearie?"

"My name is Sage Colby, and I'm reporting for my work assignment." My words gush like a broken pipe. "I'm afraid I've made a poor start, though. I went to the front door first, and now I've made you spill your bucket."

I bite my lip. Lord Osborne would be mortified at my speech.

"Well now, it's all right. Your first assignment, I expect?"

I nod weakly.

"Mr. Chambers can seem a bit cross, but he's a fine steward and will treat you decent. Come inside, and set yourself down. You look completely done in. I'll get you some tea, and then we'll call for Mr. Chambers."

I follow her obediently. The bustling woman motions for me to sit on a wooden bench by a long table that fills the center of the room. Beyond it is a large, open kitchen.

There are two of everything: sinks, stoves, refrigerators, and wide prep tables. I can only imagine all the pots and pans filling the cabinets.

She returns moments later with a steaming cup of tea. "There you are. Now, drink that, and you'll feel better."

"Thank you."

"Goodness, I haven't even introduced myself. I'm Mrs. Gates, the cook. My mister is the head gardener."

"The primroses are beautiful."

She beams with pride. "You should see the greenhouse! Some say he's the best gardener in Crystal."

I gulp down the bitter tea. At least it revives my parched throat and helps soothe my nerves.

"And what's your name again?" She leans against the table as if wanting to sit but with thoughts too busy to actually relax.

"Sage Colby."

"A good, strong name." She nods approvingly. "Names can tell you a lot about a person. You have a hard-working name."

Lord Osborne saw to that. "Yes, I'm here to fill the catering maid position."

"That's a mercy! Poor Rhona is about to go crazy working by herself." She pushes off against the table and glances at the clock. "I have to get busy with lunch, but I'll ring for Mr. Chambers. You wait right here, and don't mind me."

She moves toward the wall and pushes one of several buttons. I watch curiously, having never seen anything like it. Then, she disappears out the door to reclaim her bucket. Mr. Chambers still hasn't come when she reappears with a mound of scrubbed potatoes.

I'm fidgety. What if he doesn't acknowledge me? What if my mistake has cost me the job?

The wood bench makes my back ache, and I've sat too long already. "Can I help you peel those?"

Mrs. Gates bobs her head. "Yes, if you'd like, that would be nice. Bennie usually helps, but she's off today." She pauses. "The other peelers are in the drawer by the sink, and you can help yourself to an apron."

I retrieve both and claim my station by the bucket while she moves on to something else. "I'm sure Mr. Chambers will be here soon."

"I'm sure." I say the words more confidently than I feel. "I'd rather be busy while I wait."

I work in silence as she quarters two thawed chickens before dressing them for baking. I've nearly finished the potatoes when someone clears his throat behind me.

"Ah, Mr. Chambers," Mrs. Gates says. "This is Sage Colby. She's come to fill the catering maid position and has been helping me with some meal chores while waiting for you."

I quickly wipe my hands and offer a brave smile, which he only partially returns. However, his expression doesn't seem as severe as it first did.

He glances with approval at my apron. "Yes, I examined your letter, which checks out fine. I'm willing to overlook your blunder if you prove yourself during your thirty days' probation. There is something I'd like to discuss with you—in my office."

Mrs. Gates nods at me. "I can finish the potatoes. Thanks for your help."

"You're welcome." I hang up my apron and follow Mr. Chambers, leaving my suitcase behind.

He leads me to a private room off the kitchen, a narrow, cramped place with room for two or maybe three people.

Although he takes his seat at a desk, he doesn't motion for me to sit.

"Miss Colby, is it true that you need a weekend off each month?"

My throat constricts. "Yes, sir."

"You realize that's a highly unusual request for a first assignment."

"I'm sorry, sir."

"I trust you have a good reason for it because the work committee has approved the exception on your assignment."

"Thank you, sir." I want to rush and explain about my grandfather but remember Lord Osborne's training. Speak only when spoken to. Answer only when necessary.

Mr. Chambers seems to respect my silence. "I'll submit your orders as filled. However, due to your exception, you won't have any other free time privileges, except the regular off hours allotted to the staff each day. For you, that will be from 0900 to 1100 hours between morning meals and after the evening meal, except on special event nights."

"Very good, sir."

"Some days, you may need to use your morning break to run marketplace errands for Mrs. Gates. As long as you return with her items when she needs them, you may spend the rest of that time however you want."

I nod, waiting expectantly.

Again, he seems pleased with my silence. "As long as you follow staff rules, you'll enjoy free room and board. After the last maid—" He clears his throat. "Now that she's gone, you'll share a room with Rhona. She's our other catering maid and will teach you the house procedures.

"Madame Alexis is out, so you don't have any responsibilities for the noon meal. After the servants eat, Rhona will show you to your room and then explain your tasks this evening."

"Yes, sir."

"There's one final instruction." Mr. Chambers taps his fingers on the desk ledge as if to let off nervous energy. "As I understand, this is your first assignment. Working for a Dome representative brings privilege, but it also brings increased expectations."

He stares hard at me. "You must professionally represent this household."

"Yes, sir," I say, though I don't understand the point he's trying to make.

He continues. "Dome representatives often host meetings and gatherings where they mingle business in a relaxed setting." He pauses as if considering his words carefully. "Sometimes, Crystalites unwind too much and forget their place. They can be demanding on catering maids, especially when they're pretty."

I blush but hold his gaze. His voice is deadly serious. "As evening gatherings wear on, you must keep your eyes low. Servants are forbidden to mix business with pleasure."

"I understand, sir."

"Do you?" He fires the question at me, then sighs. "I hope so. That was the last girl's mistake."

Chapter 15

Wednesday, 4.1.2150
Crystal

"This is your room, the one you'll be sharing with me." Rhona twists the knob and swings open the door. For effect, she waves a long, skinny arm across the humble entranceway as if welcoming me to some grand place.

"Thanks," I say and step inside. There's not much to "our room" but two twin beds, two plain chairs, a single bureau and a sink. As Rhona pointed out earlier, the main bathroom is a common one all the female servants share.

"It ain't much, but it's a place, free and clear." She unties her apron for the fifth time since I've met her and reties it to be once more skin tight against her wiry frame. My new coworker seems much older than the twenty-two she claims to be. Maybe the reason is her rouged cheeks and glossy lips, or maybe it's something else.

"It's nice." I set my suitcase on the chair next to the bed and wish I could collapse onto it. But the day is barely half done.

Rhona twirls a bronze curl around her fingers and leans

against the doorframe. "You sure don't say much."

"Sorry, I'm tired. It's been a long day." I force a smile. "How long have you been here?"

"Going on a year now."

"Do you like it?"

She flashes an edgy grin. "Yes, Chambers is a bore, but he's all right, I guess. The guests more than make up for his dullness."

I purse my lips and study her. Behind her powdered face, faint wear lines hint at poor choices.

"Mr. Chambers called them Crystalites," I say. "I've never heard that term before."

Rhona snorts with intentional show. "You are fresh out of school."

"I finished last fall."

"Where've you been all this time?"

I glance at my suitcase resting beside the plain second bed and decide against opening it until I have a moment's peace from my nosey-as-a-Jasper roommate. "I was taking care of my grandfather, who's been ill," I say and join her by the doorway.

"And where's he live?"

"Jasper." I force another smile. "Thanks for showing me our room, but I should probably get back to the kitchen. Mrs. Gates said she could use some help with the lunch cleanup."

Rhona rolls her eyes. "Someone always needs help, but you're new. Take my advice, and don't make yourself available for extra work. But come along. I have to show you the routine anyway."

I close the door behind me and wait impatiently for her to stop rubbing her spine against the frame like an alley cat.

"And by the way, a Crystalite is what we call a socialite from our square. They're either filthy rich, filthy important, or just

138

filthy." She snorts again.

I laugh nervously and lead the way to the kitchen. Mrs. Gates intercepts us with a frazzled plea for help and waves to the mound of dirty dishes and a new pot sputtering on the stove. Something smells burnt.

Rhona babbles about some errand she has and promises to return in an hour to run me through the evening meal routine.

My shoulders don't relax until she's gone and I'm scrubbing dishes in the torrent of Mrs. Gates's profuse thanks.

"You're a lifesaver." She dabs the perspiration on her brow with her apron. "When Bennie's not here, I go mad."

I stack another clean dish on the draining rack. "I'm here to help. Work makes the time go faster anyway."

"Time?" she gasps. "Oh no, I forgot the biscuits!" She yanks the oven door open and moans.

Over an hour later, Mrs. Gates happily hums at the state of the kitchen, and I don't protest when she offers me a seat and cup of tea. My legs still feel like lead when Rhona reappears, whistling through the kitchen door.

"On your feet, Colby! We have work to do."

Her words coincide with Chambers's appearance. I bounce to my feet, inwardly cursing her for making me look poorly when I've been the one working, not she.

He glances from Mrs. Gates's happy face to my own and gives me a half smile. Maybe he's not as dull as Rhona thinks he is.

She shows me "the routine," as she calls it, everything from where the silverware and China are to how Madame Alexis likes the table set. Then, she explains the order of the meal.

"We'll bring out the courses, silent-like." She adjusts one of my forks as if it had crossed a boundary. "Madame doesn't like the servants to chatter or linger long. It makes our job less awkward but gives us less time."

"Less time for what?" I ask.

"Less time to communicate."

"But I thought you said we stayed silent."

She winks at me. "Where's your imagination? When there's a house full of Crystalites, there are other ways to communicate."

I set down the last of the plates and square my shoulders. "Mr. Chambers made clear that I must be professional at all times. Whatever agreement you worked out is your own business, but I have no intention …"

She snorts so loudly she has to cover her mouth. "You're such a prig! But you're fresh out of school. Just don't go spoiling my fun."

"I heard the last girl's fun didn't work out well for her."

Rhona's expression darkens. "What did he tell you about Charlotte?"

"He said she made a mistake."

"Right, a mistake." She tightens her apron again. "I'm too careful for that."

"What happened to her?"

She shrugs. "One day, she disappeared—left everything in her room, which I had to clear out."

"She never came back for her things?" I ask.

Her face hardens as if to warn me not to ask more questions. "Here, let me show you where the spare linens and our trays are." After showing me a small hallway closet, Rhona dumps me off in the kitchen and excuses herself to go "powder her nose" before we serve the appetizer for the evening meal.

I fidget at the kitchen table, not sure what to do. Mr. Chambers appears to announce that Madame Alexis has arrived.

His eyes widen in shock. "Where's your uniform?"

I'm still wearing the apron Mrs. Gates let me borrow this morning. "I—I don't have one?"

He glowers. "Rhona was supposed to give you the one belonging to the last girl."

Mrs. Gates comes to my rescue. "Oh, I think she left it in the kitchen closet. Let me check. Ah, here it is."

She hands it to me, a little black number with a starchy white apron.

"Well, don't just stand there," Chambers says. "Dinner starts in five. Run to your room—or you can change in my office."

I opt for his office and avoid another run-in with Rhona. The dress is long for me, but the waist is about right. These catering maids are skinny creatures. Do they starve themselves on purpose or simply run ragged?

As I tie my apron, I glance at Mr. Chambers's desk, strewn with papers. The one on top is halfway folded, but my eyes dart to the signature. The name is meaningless to me, but the pen stroke seems vaguely familiar.

I scold myself. His affairs are none of my business.

Grabbing my dress, I drape it over my arm and then pop open the door. He and Mrs. Gates are discussing the week's menu.

I clear my throat. "Thank you for letting me use your office, Mr. Chambers. I'll hang this in the closet for now."

He nods approvingly.

Mrs. Gates clucks her tongue. "That dress is long for you, dearie. If you leave it with me tonight, I'll have it hemmed by the morning."

"Oh, it's fine. You've done enough already," I say.

"No, dearie, you've done enough. Thanks for helping me."

I blush with appreciation. At least Mr. Chambers heard that remark, too.

However, I don't relax until all the courses have been served and the dinner party retires to a different room. We begin our final task of clearing the table, and Rhona glares at me when I drop a fork on the floor.

I don't take her coldness personally. She's cross because the guests were a small, mild group, with no stunningly handsome men.

"At least there's going to be a diplomatic dinner this weekend. That ought to be fun." She's been repeating the words to herself ever since the evening started.

"Are you expecting someone?" I ask while stacking a pile of dirty plates.

She smirks. "No, that's the fun part. Thanks to the second term rule change, I get to see fresh blood all the time."

I almost lose another fork. "What rule change?"

"Oh, that's right! You've been in Jasper. The Crystal Globe University cut its program in half, effective this term. No one's sure why, but the result is that all candidates entered their internship phase this semester. As a result, our tables are often flooded with two years' worth of the smartest, most handsome fellas a girl could imagine. Several are shadowing Dome representatives for their work assignments, and so far, I've seen some killers."

"Killers?" I ask weakly.

"You really aren't that bright, are you?" She snickers. "Killers are the ones any girl would die to have."

"Right," I say and hurry to the kitchen with my tray before I drop anything else. My head is pounding. Maybe I'm just tired.

Or, maybe I'm terrified that any day, I may find myself serving one of my own classmates. Would I be able to place a soup bowl before Felix without spilling it?

Would I be able to serve Luther vanilla pudding without shaking? Would he recognize me, behind the façade?

I set the load down in the sink and press my apron to my face so Mrs. Gates thinks I'm wiping away perspiration, not tears. The thought of Luther after a day like today unhinges me.

"That's the last of them!" Rhona announces from behind me and then dumps the silverware into Mrs. Gates's sink.

But the cook isn't annoyed that suds now splatter her apron. She's studying me with a concerned look. "There, dearie, call it a day. I'll finish these."

"Don't mind if I do!" Rhona laughs and darts to the stairs. "I call the shower that actually has hot water!" And with that, she disappears.

Mrs. Gates smiles sadly. "You'll get used to her. And don't forget about your dress. Leave it outside your door after your shower, and I'll get it hemmed for you."

"Thanks," I say, determined to end my first day on a positive note. "I actually prefer cold showers."

I would give anything to be back in the stall behind my old converted-barn home, shivering under the drizzling spigot and listening to the growling mongrel outside.

When I finally crawl into bed, I retrieve the only item I packed, my notebook, and pull the covers over my head so my roommate thinks I'm sleeping. If I'm bone tired, Gath must be, too. Maybe he's wondering about me. If I could, I'd tell him tonight's verse.

Rhona,
Tight apron strings,
Rouged lips, bronze hair, brazen
words. What happened to the last girl?
Bad news.

Chapter 16

Thursday, 4.2.2150
Crystal

"You must be Sage Colby." Madame Alexis sips her morning coffee and glances at me with polite interest.

"Yes, ma'am." I gather the breakfast dishes on my tray.

"I like to meet all the staff Chambers hires," she says. "He tells me this is your first post."

"Yes, ma'am."

"I hope you'll enjoy working here. It was nice to meet you."

"Thank you, ma'am." Her words warm my heart as I carry the tray to the kitchen. I hadn't expected her to even notice me.

Bennie, a quiet girl, is helping Mrs. Gates in the kitchen with the breakfast cleanup. Rhona has already disappeared for the morning.

I rinse the dishes and set them next to Mrs. Gates's mounting pile. "Do you need any help?"

"Thanks, dearie, but Bennie and I can manage these. I do need a few things from the market and was going to ask Rhona, but she seems to have left already."

My roommate is allergic to extra work.

"I can go if you tell me what you need and where to find it."

"I need some fresh greens for tonight's salad. The rabbits got into Mr. Gates's garden again." She pauses to open a pantry cabinet. "Sam's table is on the front edge of the market—You can't miss it. He always has the freshest lettuce and spinach. If he has broccoli, get that, too. We have a running account with him, but you'll need our food registration card."

Mrs. Gates hands me a small brown envelope. "Show him this. Whatever you do, don't lose the card."

"Yes, ma'am." I find my jacket in the kitchen closet and slip the envelope next to my cube pass inside the zippered pocket.

"The market trip shouldn't take all morning, so you can still enjoy your break." She smiles but holds up a finger. "Just be back before 1100 hours. You and Rhona need to start polishing the silverware for Friday's dinner party."

"Yes, ma'am." I snatch a small basket and hurry out the door.

The morning is cool and clear. It's my first taste of freedom in a long time.

Everything looks brighter. Even the frosted dew sparkles like glass. Once past the guard house, I trace a rambling path down the road. Wandering into some grass, I pluck a wad of wildflowers and finger the delicate petals.

Their sheer, simple beauty feeds my starved soul. There were no flowers at Warren. I tuck them into my basket and press on.

I reach the fork and continue straight, though I glance at the smaller side road with renewed interest. Maybe if I have time, I can explore it and find that barn.

With quicker steps, I head toward the market where vendors

are setting out their produce and wares.

I spot a booth with a canopy overhanging a large wooden table, clustered with fresh green vegetables. An older man in a brown apron and straw hat secures a latch on the overhang.

"Are you Sam?"

He tips his hat. "Yes, miss, how can I help you?"

"Mrs. Gates sent me for some veggies." I hold out my basket.

He grins at the flowers. "You must be the new girl."

"That's right."

"Chambers runs a good place, and Mrs. Gates is one of the best cooks in Crystal. I hope you'll do well there." He smiles, but his words have an edge to them. Does he know what happened to the last girl?

"What's on your list?" he asks.

I rattle off the items. "They're for tonight."

After he helps me select a ripe assortment, I show him the card, thank him, and carefully cover the purchases with a cloth.

The market bustles with early customers. Since I have time, I weave between stalls, careful not to bump into wire chicken cages or upset a cart of potatoes.

It's all different from life in 'Prase. Our rations held little variety and included nothing as fragrant or fresh.

Past the open stall market, I reach the main street of the cube where the dirt road ends and a paved road begins. It must lead to the Dome—paved for the convenience of the representatives and Gages who enjoy the use of vehicles.

Like my cube back home, this stretch includes the office of the Gage who acts as cube enforcer. There's a table set up in front of the office building and a line forming behind it. Angry voices rise near the table, and I can't see who the men are arguing with.

"It's none of your business how many calves we have!" A man swears.

"Complete the form." A woman's level voice answers him.

"Then zero!"

Something raps on the table. I peek around the man in front of me where a Gage grips his baton. "You must report truthfully. If we have reasonable cause for suspicion, you will be audited and fined."

Next to him behind the table is a slender, brown-haired woman. *Lydia.* What is she doing there?

She's paler than I remember. I bite my lip. The line is growing longer, and my time, shorter. I make a quick decision and step behind a tall man holding a form.

"Where did you get that?" I ask him.

He grunts. "The same place I get all my summons: from the cube enforcer. You'd have to be blind to miss yours. He hands out the same form every week until you submit it. I'm tired of the litter although it does make good kindling."

"But what's it for?"

He stares at me. "Where have you been? It's the census."

I had forgotten we started a new decade this year. At Warren, there's nothing to count—other than who's breathing and who's not.

We reach the front of the line, and the man hands in his form and swears to answering truthfully.

He doesn't thank them for all the forms that have fueled his fire.

"Next!" A Gage shouts in my face. He's either the cube enforcer or assigned to help organize the census.

"Where do I get that form?" I ask. "You see, I arrived for my work orders yesterday and am wondering if I need to fill it out or if my employer will." I focus on the Gage but watch Lydia through my peripheral. She's thumbing through a stack of papers but stops mid-search and jerks at the sound of my voice.

"Gage Grayson, I think there are some spare forms inside the office. I don't have any out here."

His hand rests on his baton. "I'll be right back."

For a moment, I forget about the line behind me and the Gage who could return any minute. I forget about the careful cover Lord Osborne has crafted for me.

Standing across the table from me is someone who loves and knows the real me, despite the mask I wear.

But Lydia's eyes cloud in confusion. She recognizes my voice but not my appearance. "Do I know you, miss?"

"Yes ..." I rack my brain for something to assure her. "I once roomed with a Healer's daughter until—they moved me. I'm very much changed."

Tears swim in her eyes, but she blinks them away. "What brings you to these parts again?"

"Work assignment." I gulp. "It's complicated."

"I thought you were dead." It's a whisper. Her lips barely move.

I rearrange the cloth in my basket and lean it against the table, inches away from her forms. "Might as well have been."

"But it really is you?" Amazement flickers on her face.

"You can't say a word to anyone."

"I won't."

"Just tell me you're okay, that Jael's okay—that he's okay."

She bites her lip. "We're managing."

Managing. What has happened in Crystal since my trial?

149

The Gage returns with a ream of papers in hand. He thrusts one toward me with a grunt.

"Thank you." I lower my eyes and step aside.

Lydia motions for the next person in line to step forward. I glance back one last time. What is she even doing here? She's a Court Citizen candidate, not a census collector.

What had Rhona said? Something about a rule change and all first- and second-year candidates starting internships?

But such a despised post is no internship for a Court Citizen.

A form escapes from Lydia's pile, and the breeze blows it past me. I lunge after it, but the paper doesn't go far. It catches on a wooden post with a latched metal box at the edge of the enforcer's building.

I snatch it off the splintered wood and hand it to Lydia, who's wasted no time running over to retrieve it.

She accepts the form and coughs. "I'm here every Tuesday and Thursday. Sometimes, I set up early—around 6:30—before Grayson gets here."

My throat swells. "I'll come."

Another argument begins at the table, and she runs back to diffuse it. I hurry through the market back toward Madame Alexis's place. The fork in the road tempts me again, but there isn't time to explore it now.

After depositing the basket with Mrs. Gates, I dash to my room to change into the uniform she hemmed for me last night. Then, I channel my energy polishing silverware like my life depends on it.

Rhona mumbles about my mood but doesn't complain after I offer to shine half of her pile as well.

The work distracts me but can't make me forget the wear lines on Lydia's face and her haunting answer to my question.

Chapter 17

There's no morning break on Friday, and I get my first taste of event preparations.

Everywhere I turn, Chambers yaps at us. Add extra tables. Get out the reserve napkins and tablecloths. Set out glass bowls of pretty little candies called buttermints. Bennie and Rhona fight over each new errand to run—any chance to escape the madness.

Though I wish I could have an errand, I embrace the grunt work. Anything is better than pulling a coal cart.

"Guests will be here in an hour." Chambers's announcement startles me. I nearly spill the melted butter and herb mixture I've been basting on freshly baked bread as Mrs. Gates slides me another tray of slices to finish.

I sigh and baste faster. Bennie was supposed to return an hour ago to resume her kitchen work.

Chambers grunts behind me. "What are you doing here? Where's your uniform?"

I clutch the basting brush harder. "I—I was helping. Mrs. Gates needed …"

"Where's Bennie?" Chambers spins and searches the kitchen area, empty except for Mrs. Gates and me.

The dear lady wipes her perspiring brow. "I don't know, Mr. Chambers, but this girl is an angel. She's helped me all afternoon, after she finished her own chores."

Her words melt my thin armor. The work has helped me forget my fears but drained every ounce of energy.

Chambers actually smiles. "Good work, Sage, but you look ready to pass out. I'll finish those trays. Rhona can take the first shift, and you can report back in an hour."

A whole hour? I picture a shower and the soft quilt on my bed. "Thank you, sir."

When I reach the bathroom upstairs, Rhona is primping in front of the mirror and jumps when she sees me.

"Hullo! You're a scary sight."

"Just need a shower," I mutter and pull the curtain.

"You need more than that!" she laughs. "If you hurry, I'll add some rouge to those pale cheeks of yours. It isn't fair for only one of us to have fun this evening."

I crank on the water. The only version of fun I want is my clean bed to myself.

Rhona is gone when I finish showering, but she left her compact on the counter. How generous.

I glance at the shade and cringe. It's such a brazen red. I don't want anything drawing attention to myself.

Back in my room, I slip into my uniform and rummage through my suitcase for clean stockings. I may only have two changes of clothes, my jacket, and a uniform, but Deidra packed a

154

generous number of clean undergarments and personal items. Next time I see her, I'm giving her the biggest hug.

My hand brushes against a small, zippered case. Inside are some hair clips and another case with a mascara brush, powder, and gloss that soothes my dry lips. They are enough to brighten my face and make me look pleasant.

I set aside my black frames to apply the mascara and then, with the towel still wrapped around my damp hair, recline on my bed.

My legs and back ache. Chambers said I could have an hour. I'll just be a minute.

I jolt upright at the sound of someone pounding on the door.

"Sage? I need you downstairs. Now!" Rhona screeches from the hallway, and her heels peg each wood panel as she retreats.

I gasp. I must have fallen asleep. I rub my hair between the misshaped towel and snatch a hairclip to control my still-damp hair.

I'm halfway down the stairs when my nose itches. My glasses!

"Colby!" Chambers calls from the kitchen.

"Coming!" I hesitate for only a second. I can't lose my job over a pair of forgotten glasses.

I report at the base of the stairs. Chambers frowns at the clock but nods his approval at me. "Much better. But where are your glasses?"

He noticed? "I—One of the screws came out, and I didn't have time to fix it."

"Then fix it. I can't have a half-blind catering maid spilling coffee on guests."

"I—I'll be okay. They're mostly for long distance."

His eyes flash. "Get. Your. Glasses. Rhona can manage for

five more minutes on her own."

"Yes, sir." I dart up the stairs.

When I return, Rhona shoves a cocktail tray in my hands. "Where have you been? It's crazy out there. I can't even begin to enjoy myself."

"I'm sorry. My glasses broke."

"Forget your glasses. They're ugly anyway."

"Chambers told me I had to wear them."

She snickers. "Did he now? You're not a very good liar, Sage. I'll have to teach you a thing or two."

Color heats my cheeks. "I'm not lying."

"Oh, quit it, and get to work." She refills her coffee urn and replaces the empty creamer with a full one.

"But he said ..."

Rhona cuts me off. "Chambers hates how we maids look in glasses." She balances the tray in a hand while doing a mirror check. "I have a pair of peepers, but he won't let me wear them on the clock. He says they make me look like a secretary."

I blink. "That's the dumbest thing I've heard."

She shrugs and wipes a blotch of stray mascara from her lower lash. "Every job has its expectations. We're supposed to be scenery." She pauses to grin at me. "But I'd rather stand out than blend in. Come on. Let's spruce up the place."

"But ..."

"Oh, wait!" She glances from her tray to mine. "What are you doing with the cocktails? Here, you take the coffee." She winks. "Cocktail guys are more my style."

Rhona leads the way and pops a handful of buttermints into her pocket to "keep her breath like sugar." I sneak one just for a taste. The pretty pink thing melts on my tongue and leaves a sweet

156

minty taste.

We meet a handful of guests in the main dining area while more voices and laughter echo from the main hall.

I try to remember everything Mrs. Gates told me about evening parties. She said Madame Alexis hosts upwards of fifty guests.

An older gentleman makes eye contact and smiles.

"Coffee?" I ask.

"Yes, please. And crème."

I set the tray on a table and serve him a steaming white mug. The aroma takes me back to my first morning in the dormitory with Lydia. She'd made a fresh pot of the black brew.

Oh, Lydia.

"There you are, sir."

"Thank you, dear."

I smile and move on. *Invisible.* That's what I want to be.

My tray grows lighter with each round I make.

"Excuse me, miss, is that coffee?"

My heart crashes inside my chest. The voice is weary, but I'd recognize its deep timbre in a blizzard.

I can't let him recognize mine. Mustering all my nerve, I face him. "Yes, it is. Would you like some?" I ask in a voice shriller than my regular alto.

Luther smiles, but I can't meet his gaze. I read his lips because there's a roaring behind my ears.

"Yes, black please."

Black. Just like his gorgeous eyes.

My urn runs dry, and the cup is only half full.

I steady my hand and gulp. "I'm sorry, sir. Let me get a fresh pot for you."

"I'll start with this, thanks. I'm going to need a refill anyway."

"Yes, sir."

I place the empty urn on my tray, thankful there's nothing left to spill.

Be invisible.

"Have I seen you here before?"

I freeze in my tracks and feel the color creep up my neck. "No, I'm new. This is my first week here."

"I'm sorry to embarrass you." He sips his coffee. "I'm sure you're doing great."

"Thank you, sir." I want to run, but I'm frozen to the spot.

He sighs and cups the mug in his hands. "I know all about what being new is like. It's tough …"

"There you are, Danforth!"

I jerk my head as a tall blonde killer—to use Rhona's word—swaggers into the room. Felix's voice slices through me like a knife.

No, no, no! This can't be happening.

Rhona glares at me as she makes a dash for the kitchen with her empty cocktail tray.

"Excuse me." I snatch my own empty urn and tray. I don't start breathing again until the kitchen door closes behind me.

"There's a fresh pot ready for you, dearie." Mrs. Gates pants over a hot stove.

"Thanks."

I rinse my empty urn, wipe the spatter, and reach for the new pot when a bony hand grips my shoulders.

"The blonde one is mine!" Rhona hisses in my ear.

I shake her hand off my shoulder. "What's wrong with you? We've got work to do."

"I saw you look at him." She glares at me.

"Who didn't? He announced his entrance to the room like—like a king or something." I grasp for words.

"He's mine." She repeats. "Keep your hands off him."

I shudder. "I don't want anything to do with him."

"Liar." She mouths the word and curses me under her breath.

"No, I'm not."

She checks over her shoulder for Chambers and then steals a tube of lipstick from her pocket. She applies a generous new coat, pecks her lips together, and pops another buttermint. "Good. Don't change your mind."

Rhona snatches clean cocktail glasses from the cabinet and refills them. I escape with my fresh pot as she retightens her apron.

Luther and Felix aren't in sight, but Chambers catches me the minute I emerge. "Forget the coffee for now, and help me set out the main course."

I nod and leave my coffee on an end table. Maybe Luther will help himself, and I won't have to face him again.

As I push a cart of steaming chafers from the kitchen to the dining room, Chambers uncovers the lids. The rich aromas make my head swim—or maybe it's nerves and fatigue. But I can't remember the last time I've seen so much food in one place.

Something like panic fills me. What's wrong with me?

Sucking a deep breath, I push the cart back to the kitchen the minute Chambers unloads the last chafer.

Another cart waits, loaded with more food. My legs wobble, but I latch onto the cart rail.

Chambers appears at the door. "Leave that one until they've emptied the ones out there. Check on the plates and silverware."

I nod and grab a smaller cart with a level for dirty dishes and one with clean replacements.

The next hour, I work with Chambers, monitoring the tableware while he keeps the main courses stocked. Meanwhile, Rhona flits from room to room with her cocktails like a bee searching for nectar.

But I don't mind. Collecting dirty dishes keeps me from engaging guests and burns off my nervous energy. When we've finally cleared the main course, Chambers and I exhale in exhaustion.

"You okay? You look pale," he says.

I gulp and nod. I can't explain what I'm feeling, but at least the ground feels level for now.

"Rhona should be helping you," he mutters. "I can't pin her down tonight."

"She's got the cocktail tray."

"We've got a cocktail table. Guests can help themselves." His tone warns he'll be talking to her about her duties later.

"I'll help you set out the dessert platters, and then you can go back to serving coffee."

My heart sinks. "Should I leave it at the table? I don't want to get in anyone's way."

Chambers gives me a strange look. "You're a catering maid. You're to be visible when needed and invisible until then."

I wish I could fade into the wallpaper.

I fuss over the desserts as long as I dare before reappearing with a fresh coffee urn and fixings tray. I linger in a room of strangers. They seem safer than old friends.

I slip quietly through the dining area to the large hall and freeze. There he is.

Luther mingles in a small group by the fireplace. Perhaps the lighting is to blame, but his eyes seem even darker than I remember. Or perhaps those dark rings under his eyes are responsible.

Hard lines replace the youthful vigor of his face. How can he be so changed in such a short time?

The hall mirror mocks me. The black frames obscure my pale blue eyes, and Patrick's dye conceals my true roots. Those ridiculous facial enhancements make me look almost exotic. I'm even more changed than he.

But the mirror's reflection reveals a more fearful change in Luther, something more sinister than wear lines. The old Luther would never have engaged in intimate conversation with Felix Caesura, the Friend's only son who was partly responsible for my own exile.

Another man, taller than both Luther and Felix, joins them. I set my tray on the marble table below the mirror to keep from dropping it.

Gage Eliab tilts his head and downs a cocktail in one gulp, but his eyes flash with alertness. A man nearly my father's size, he would need more than a few drinks to dull his senses. And though he is ever the hunter, he doesn't realize his prey shares the same floor space as he.

Anyone who dares defy the ASU becomes his instant enemy, and his track record reeks with the success story of destroying my family: first with Darius, then with me.

My eyes burn. How could Luther keep company with these two? Has he forgotten me already?

As if he can read my thoughts, he glances my way and taps his cup with his fingers, raising it to request a refill.

My first instinct is to run, but that's what Portia would do.

Sage Colby will go refill his cup and then move on without a word.

I clutch the tray and hope my hands will stop shaking.

"More coffee, sir?" I keep my voice shrill and pray he won't detect the tightness in my throat.

"Yes, please." His voice rakes of exhaustion, but I keep up my guard. No Luther of mine would keep company with these two brutes.

"Really, Luther! Coffee? Lighten up, and take a real man's drink from this doll." Felix places his empty cocktail glass on a tray to his right.

It's Rhona. Her apron clings tightly to her skinny frame, and she's removed her black sweater to show off long, bare arms. She pretends not to see me as she holds a full glass out to Felix.

"Another?" She drawls her words with a curved lip.

"Thanks, doll." Felix accepts the glass with a wink.

Rhona eyes Luther. "And how about you, mister?"

"No, just coffee for me." Luther hands me his empty cup. Rhona reluctantly slinks away to serve another guest while staying as close as possible to the three men. "Felix, you said that you and Gage Eliab had some business to discuss with me?"

I take Luther's cup, careful not to let his fingers touch mine.

Felix sips from his fresh glass. "It's an idea for eliminating some paperwork."

Eliab nods and drums his fingers on the mantle. "You know those orders I need you to sign every day?"

Luther's fingers tighten as if needing something to hold. "Yes?"

"It's a waste of time—having to daily approve the *removal* of seasoned criminals."

The tightness runs up Luther's arm until it locks his jaw. "You

162

mean the *execution*."

Eliab waves his hand. "They're a burden to the state. They don't die on the satellites fast enough."

Satellite prisoners don't die fast enough? I want to scream at what I'm hearing. Shaking hard, I spill the creamer, which dribbles down the rim of Luther's cup.

But the men don't seem to notice. Luther's gaze darts between Felix and Eliab, as if he suspects they're co-conspirators in this scheme. "What do you propose, then?"

"I've drafted an amendment for a systematic thinning of the satellites," Felix says. "I want you to take a look before I submit it to the Revisionary Committee next week."

"But won't that hurt productivity?" Luther hedges. "Didn't you say before that these camps provide the labor for national initiatives?"

"Priorities change," Gage Eliab lowers his voice. "Feeding prisoners takes a back seat when that grain is needed elsewhere."

But they hardly feed us! I want to vomit. Instead, I suck down a deep breath and hand Luther his cup. "Your coffee, sir."

For a moment, the strain leaves his eyes. "Thank you, miss."

He reaches for the cup, and this time, his fingers brush mine. Like the epicenter of an earthquake, the touch sends shockwaves through me.

I quiver and hold my breath, hoping he didn't notice. But there's a question in his eyes that tells me he felt something, too.

Grabbing my tray, I turn to flee.

"Coffee's not such a bad idea." Felix's words rake over my nerves.

"Crème and sugar?" I squeak like a mouse.

He studies me through long lashes. "Anything you say, doll."

For a second, his gray eyes lock on mine. They still hold a suspicious crystal hue. The last time our eyes met, we'd fought in the archives, and I'd stabbed him.

I lower my attention to the coffee urn. Add the sugar, pour the coffee, stir in the cream, and get away. I recite the steps to keep from forgetting the order.

"There's another matter, too," Felix says.

"What's on your mind?" Eliab shifts his weight and acknowledges me. "Coffee for me, too."

I nod without looking up and add Chambers's step to my mental list. *Be invisible.*

Felix pulls a notepad from his pocket. "You remember my *See-Say-Save* initiative. It was effective at first but has lost its edge. I'd like to relaunch it with tighter guidelines and more incentives."

"Go on."

I concentrate on listening and stirring Felix's coffee while Rhona flits closer.

"We all know that certain criminals have slipped through our hands, but I don't think they've gone far. Some might be with us tonight in sheep's clothing." He writes on the paper and tears off an edge. "Making ourselves approachable to the people, all people, may be our key to discovering them."

"Your coffee." The words catch in my throat as Felix slips the paper in Rhona's apron. She winks and moves away to wait on another guest.

I skim Luther's and Eliab's faces. Did either see him do that? Do either care?

Eliab gives Felix a grim smile. "My new Gage assistant arrived. This would be a good project for you two to begin together."

Felix sips the hot brew. "What's his name?"

"Colson Crabtree. He's a Wasp transfer from Baytown, like ..." Eliab grits his teeth. "No crème for me. Just black."

Black like his eyes. Black like his heart.

I pour and set the cup on the mantle within his reach. As I do, someone brushes my back, sending hot splinters through my veins. As quickly as it came, the touch vanishes. Maybe I imagined it.

Either way, I have to get away. I can't maintain this act, not around Luther, Felix, and Eliab. The three of them together in conversation mixes as badly as water and oil. And their talk makes my blood steam.

I crash through the kitchen door, and Mrs. Gates nearly jumps out of her skin. "Dearie, you're red as a tomato!"

"I can't—Those men ..." I gulp. What's the use? She can't begin to understand.

But she knows a boiling pot when she sees one. "I'll brew more coffee. Take a minute to catch your breath."

She doesn't have to tell me twice. I slip upstairs to the bathroom and pull the stall latch shut. Sliding against the frame, I cover my face with my hands so no one can hear my angry sobs.

Chapter 18

Friday, 4.3.2150
Crystal

The night wears wearily on. It's a quarter past midnight before the last guest leaves, the last plate sets to dry, and I finally trudge up the stairs to my room.

I could use another shower, but all I want is my bed and the chance to sleep away the evening's memory. I turn on my lamp only long enough to kick off my shoes, find my nightdress and hang my uniform and apron on a peg. I pull down the old quilt on my bed, switch off the lamp and embrace the quiet darkness.

If only my mind would shut off.

The conversation among Luther, Felix, and Eliab plays over like a recording. What is Felix's motivation for this new amendment, and why is Luther working with him and Eliab in the first place? What does Felix's *See-Say-Save* initiative have to do with anything?

The door whooshes open, and I crack open an eye. The hall lighting silhouettes Rhona's tight form before she closes the door and turns the lamp back on.

"Hmm, hmm, tra-la-la!" She hums and waltzes into the room, making a bee-line for her street clothes which she'd already laid out on her bed.

I pretend to be asleep and hope she won't drag me into some dreadful recap of the night.

"Stop fooling. I know you're not sleeping!" Her uniform hits the floor with a swishing noise.

"I almost was," I mutter and roll on my side away from her.

"You're such a bore! How can you possibly sleep after an evening like that? The night is too young."

"Too young? It's past midnight, and we both have another busy day tomorrow." I pull the sheets over my head, hoping she'll get the message.

Rhona clucks her tongue. "Oh darling, some of us plan to be busy tonight."

"You can polish silverware if you want, but I'm done."

She laughs, just like the guests who had too many cocktails. "Not that kind of busy."

A zipper swooshes, and then her soft feet patter to my bedside. Why won't she go away and leave me alone?

She edges onto my bed and leans over me. "You'd be jealous if you knew who gave me his address."

Her breath reeks through the blanket and makes me cringe. She should know better than to drink on the job.

"I don't care." My eyes feel like pin cushions. "I'm exhausted. Please go away."

Again, she laughs and slaps my shoulder. "You're so dull! But I don't care. I'm sure no one slipped anything into your apron pocket."

I yank the covers down to glare at her. "I should hope not! Chambers said to be invisible."

"I wish you had been." The laugh leaves her voice. "I saw him looking at you."

"Saw who?"

"Felix." She slurs his name with uneasy familiarity.

"Who cares?" I mutter, but my heart races. Had he really been watching me? Had he seen through my disguise?

"Don't pretend with me. Any girl under fifty can't help but notice him. He's the richest, most handsome, and most privileged guy in Crystal. And tonight, he's gonna be mine."

I shiver and hug the covers to my chest. "Please tell me you're joking."

"Why should I be? Just because I'm a catering maid doesn't mean I shouldn't have my share of fun."

"But he won't mean anything by it. He'll never ask you to marry him."

Rhona laughs again, but it's coarser, harder. "And I wouldn't expect him to."

My throat tightens. Are there not enough beautiful female candidates to fill Felix's appetite, or must he prey on catering maids?

"His friend wasn't bad looking either. Maybe I'll work on him another night."

Luther. My blood heats up, and I grip the blanket. "Chambers will not approve."

"Oh, I've struck a chord." Rhona applies blood red lipstick. "You want the dark-haired one for yourself?"

Color rushes to my cheeks. "That's not what I said."

She winks and lathers another layer on her lips. "It's not what you say, honey. It's what you show, but that's all right. You can have him. I'll share the fun. Besides, he was rather gloomy, not really my type."

Rhona puckers in the mirror and then spritzes on perfume. "Wish me luck!" She grabs her coat and then stops short. "Oh, I almost forgot!" Turning her heels, she yanks at her apron and shoves her hand in the pocket.

"Can't forget his address!" She blows me a kiss and twirls out the room, forgetting to turn off the lamp.

I stare after her. How can she be this stupid? If she only knew what kind of man Felix is ... but maybe she still wouldn't care.

My gaze moves from the door to my own uniform and apron.

Apron. The pockets on the front bow outward from all the times I stuffed my hands in them. If Felix had slipped his address into Rhona's pocket, had anyone slipped something into mine?

Surely not.

But I can't shake a growing nervousness. How many people had brushed against me this evening? Too many to count.

I have to turn off the lamp anyway, so I slide out from my covers. The cold floor nips at my socked feet, and a chill runs up and down my frame.

First pocket. Empty.

Second pocket. What's this?

I grasp a small folded paper. Its jagged edges show it was torn quickly.

Hey, doll. Visit me. A scraggly address follows the words.

My heart pounds. No, no, no!!

I ball the paper up and throw it in the corner behind my suitcase.

I'm a maid, not a call girl. How dare he ... but I press pause on my churning thoughts. Felix had called both Rhona and me dolls. He only wants one-night stands. He doesn't know who I am.

I take a deep breath, switch the light off one final time, and curl into a ball with the quilt pulled to my neck. Heavy eyelids are the only escape for my trembling heart.

The next morning, Rhona stays in bed. She tells Chambers she has a cold, and Mrs. Gates confirms she's running a low fever.

"It's these late events." Mrs. Gates grumbles over breakfast. "We're all run ragged by the end of them."

Chambers arches an eye. "Rhona is used to late nights. If anyone should be tired, it's Sage." He glances my way. "You feeling all right this morning?"

I grip my hot tea mug. "Yes, only a little tired, but once I've had breakfast, I'll be fine."

"Then, eat up, dearie!" Mrs. Gates scoops more scrambled eggs onto my plate. "We've got a long day ahead of us."

The long day stretches into three with Rhona milking her cold for all it's worth. She finally appears in the kitchen Tuesday morning with a glow back in her cheeks.

But then, I'd be glowing too if I'd slept as much as she had.

"Do you have any errands for me, Mrs. Gates?" She checks herself in the mirror as Mrs. Gates finishes breakfast.

"No, Sage has offered to go this morning, but you can help me with the breakfast dishes."

Rhona puckers her face. "Oh, but I'd be more than happy ..."

"Save it." I snatch the basket off the counter and push open the kitchen door.

"Don't you want breakfast first?" Mrs. Gates asks me.

"Not hungry, but thanks," I say and shove the door closed behind me.

Truth is, I'm always hungry, but I want to see Lydia before the code enforcer arrives. That means I have to hustle.

And there's no chance I'm letting Rhona steal my first morning-errand since her *sickness*. I've been working overtime for us both. She can pull her own weight this morning and do some work for a change.

Besides, Lord Osborne will be expecting an update, and I haven't even found the barn he described to me, the one with the Translator equipment.

But I have to find Lydia first. I rush past empty stalls and the curious stares of vendors who arrived early to set up. I'll make my purchases later.

I clear the last of the booths and reach the main street. There's no light inside the enforcer's office. The bare table Lydia and the Gage had used the other day sits vacant except for dust and dew collecting on the top.

My heart sinks. Maybe I'm too early? Or maybe I'm too late, and Lydia has moved to another post.

Idling in the center of the street will only draw attention, so I return to the market and find Sam's stall. He greets me with a broad smile and asks for my list, then immediately sets about filling it without me having to say another word.

I chuckle. I've never been in a position before to have anyone want to do something for me. Though the money isn't my own, I represent it, and as a result, am treated with respect.

What if I had become a Dome representative like Madame Alexis? Would I have a nice home in a beautiful community with servants to send on errands?

Would Luther and I have been able to enjoy such a life … together?

Seeing him the other night almost made me blow my cover. I lost control over my heart rate, and everything started shaking.

I can't let him guess who I am, but at the same time, I desperately want him to see me, the real me—not as Portia Abernathy or Nevada Ingram or even Sage Colby but as the girl he used to call Cotton.

A finger taps my shoulder. "Excuse me, miss, but did you happen to drop this?"

I suck in a deep breath and whirl to face Lydia. She stares at me with a stranger's blank expression and holds out a census form. "I thought I saw you leave the street in front of my office and then found this in the dirt."

"Oh, thank you!" I accept it, too eagerly. "I must have dropped it without realizing."

"If you follow me back, I can help you with it."

"Right, but I need to finish with this vendor." I motion to Sam. He's already filled my basket halfway with the fruits and vegetables from Mrs. Gate's list.

He jerks his head toward us and glances from me to Lydia. His eyes lock on hers, and his smile vanishes. "You've no business in the market."

I gasp, but Lydia seems nonplused. "I need a word with this woman in private."

"Leave the poor girl alone—You've no right harassing her."

I blush. "It's no trouble, sir. If you wouldn't mind finishing my order, I'll be back in a moment."

He glares at Lydia but speaks to me. "If you need help, holler."

I nod and hurry after Lydia to redeem what precious minutes we have left.

"What was that about?" I whisper as we stride through the market.

"Nobody likes a census collector, but I won't waste time complaining. What are you doing here?"

"I'm a catering maid for a Dome representative. That's probably all I should tell you." I lick my lips. "But what are you doing here? I heard that all first- and second-year candidates received internships this semester, so why are you ..."

"In the streets?" She snorts. "Candidates like Jael and myself, and any others who received marks for misbehavior, received less than glowing positions."

My throat tightens. "No! This is because of me? Because you were my friend and Jael voted to keep me alive?"

Lydia grabs my arm. "We'd make the same choice a hundred times over if we had to. You were the one who showed us how wrong things here are and gave us the courage to pick up the flag."

The flag. The scene from my final Simulation class rushes over me. I had grabbed the dying soldier's flag. Jael had administered my Simulation and seen the whole thing. She must have told Lydia about it.

Brave little Jael.

"What's become of her?" I ask.

"Jael? She has a rotten internship, too. Her adviser placed her in 'Prase —in your old cube, no less—but the location has proven useful to us."

Useful? What does she mean?

Instead, I ask, "Can you get a message to her?"

Lydia's brown eyes cloud. "It's risky but can be done. Our

174

brothers—they have ways."

My mind spins. Had Lydia and Jael found the Brotherhood, too? But I don't have time for all my questions. We've nearly reached the enforcer's office, and now, light shines through the window. The Gage will be joining Lydia any moment to start the day's work.

I gulp and search Lydia's eyes. "Ask her if the brothers know where my father is."

She nods. "I'll find out what I can."

"And Luther—how is he?"

She shakes her head. "I don't see him much anymore, but he's…"

The office door opens, and Lydia's posture snaps straight like a scolding teacher. She clears her throat and places a hand on her hip. "I told you—no exceptions. Now, stop wasting my time."

I lower my head and shuffle away.

"The greedy creatures are complaining early today, huh, Collins?" The Gage's voice crackles behind me.

Lydia calls back. "Yes, I can't say that I'll miss this place once we finish our two-month assignment here."

"There will be another ungrateful cube after this one."

I pay the vendor and once again trek down the road. My damp spirits make the basket feel heavy. Lydia and Jael are both suffering lousy internships because of me.

Yet Lydia's eyes looked confident. They held a spark I hadn't seen before.

And Luther? What was she going to say about him?

My insides tighten. Last Friday, Luther spent most of the evening next to Gage Eliab and Felix. I grip the basket's handle so tightly my fingers go numb. No, he can't be one of them.

But the lonely stretch gives my mind the quiet to replay the scene. With each study, his intimacy with my two enemies seems to deepen. I remember more words, more expressions.

I reach the fork in the road. I must stop thinking of Luther as someone I can trust.

No friend of mine would share drinks with the men who wanted me dead.

Chapter 19

Tuesday, 4.7.2150
Crystal

I pick my way across potholes and washouts, overgrown weeds and wildflowers down the long, canopied lane. The cool breeze teases the treetops above and invites me deeper down the way.

Dandelions grow scattered among rocky remnants of a fence. I snatch one and blow, letting the breeze catch the seeds. They'll begin a new life somewhere else.

Maybe one day, I will, too.

The final few seeds fly beyond another stone fence, this one barely sturdier than the first. Rose-colored azalea blooms make up for its lack of grace.

Azaleas.

And there's the stone fence.

Now all I need is a mailbox … and a barn.

I lower my basket and peer further into the tree canopy. The faded paint of a once-red structure peeks out from behind it. Yes, this is the place from Osborne's Translation.

I lean in to smell the flowers and use my peripheral to search the road behind me. It's empty.

Reaching over the wall, I search the bushes for a mailbox. My nails scratch rusty metal, and I gently pull back the overgrown bush to open the latched door with the number 45 scrawled onto it.

There's one scratch of paper and only two words on it.

I'm waiting.

I ball it into a wad and stuff it in my pocket. Of all the impatient men ... It's not like I've been wasting my time. I barely sleep anymore.

Retrieving my basket, I climb over the fence toward the barn. I should have enough time to give Lord Osborne a report and return before my shift starts, as long as no stray mongrel has claimed the barn for its shelter.

The large door has fallen off its hinges, but there's enough space for me to squeeze inside with my basket. Other than the light filtering through the cracks, dust-laden blackness clouds the space.

I hesitate by the door before taking a slow next step. My boot kicks over something metal, and I bend to inspect it.

A lantern. It has a stub wick and a small, wooden matchbox secured on its side.

I strike a match, and the wick sputters to life. The flame provides enough light to intrude farther inside the barn.

The barren space includes a crumbling tack room, a caved-in loft, and several stalls. After swiping through cobwebs near the old loft, I inspect the corner stalls. Although they're as dark as the rest of the interior, no cobwebs litter the entrance.

In a back corner, a black box rests on a wooden ledge. Someone has fastened the frame to the wall.

There's a padlock on the front panel. This must be the Translator, but Lord Osborne never said anything about a key.

Setting the lamp next to my basket in the stall's center, I search the walls and ground for a key but come up empty.

The dust stings my eyes and fans my frustration. I'm wasting precious time. I retrieve my lamp and pull the crumpled paper from my pocket, but I have nothing to write with and no way to leave a message.

I wad up the paper and search for a way to attach it to the lamp. At least whoever visits this place will know I was here.

My hand brushes the bottom of the lamp, and a small, knobby piece catches my finger. I latch onto it and lift the lamp to inspect it.

The key. A slot in the lamp's base holds it in place.

I yank it out and insert it into the padlock. After a hard twist, the metal door springs open, revealing the familiar control panels of the Translator/Simulator receiver.

I flip the black switch, and the computer purrs to life. I add the parameters Lord Osborne had given me. The hay-strewn floor glows an opaque blue, and the dust creates a pixilated hue.

The room in the underground Excivis appears with its plush couch and chairs. But something is different.

A new table stands in front of the couch. On its dark countertop rests a single, white sheet.

Sage, the Translator is programmed to recognize speech patterns and keywords. To record your update, speak the word 'rabbit' and then begin. When you finish, say 'rabbit' again.

Rabbit. If he's trying to be funny, he isn't. That horrible place still holds Gath hostage, but I plan to change that when I return next month. Somehow, I will find a way.

I clear my throat and steady my voice. "Rabbit." Beyond my limited field of view, something clicks. I hope that means I'm recording.

"I arrived safely in Crystal and began my work at Madame Alexis's house," I begin. Does he even care I'm safe?

"My first catering event was yesterday. You'll be interested in some of the guests. Gage Eliab was there, along with Felix Caesura."

I hesitate. I don't want to tell him about Luther. Lord Osborne probably wouldn't be interested in a Court Citizen intern anyway.

"I overheard part of their conversation. Gage Eliab wants a Court Citizen to give him blanket permission to execute satellite prisoners and 'thin' the satellite population. Caesura ..." I pause to breathe. I must be careful to say Felix's last name instead of his first. It's better for Lord Osborne not to know my history with him.

"Caesura also wants to implement phase two of his *See-Say-Save* initiative to encourage citizens to spy on each other. His motivation seems to be ferreting out any remaining Rogue insiders—or otherwise disloyal citizens.

"Eliab liked the idea and said he wanted Caesura to work with his new Gage assistant on the project. I think he said the Gage's name was Crabtree, a Wasp transfer from Baytown."

Remembering the party scene drains me, and a long day of work looms ahead. I'm not sure if Lord Osborne cares about any of the conversations I overheard, but I hope he's pleased I was listening.

"I have to go. I have few opportunities to get out and make reports. I'll give you another update when it's safe to do so."

My voice catches. "Rabbit."

The word makes me feel small, vulnerable, worthless. I loathe that Lord Osborne chose it for my recording word as if to taunt me that I'm still a slave.

His slave.

I flick the Translator off, lock the panel, and reinsert the key underneath the lamp. Back at the cracked barn door, I puff at the light and return the lantern where I found it.

Basket in hand, I slip outside and hurry for the lane. The morning sun climbs steadily higher, and I hope I haven't wasted too much time.

Chambers corners me when I enter the kitchen. "Where have you been?" His face pinches in frustration.

I place the basket on the counter and open it to put the items away. "I went to the market to run some errands."

"Never mind. Come with me." He corrals me toward the dining room.

"What's wrong?"

"Nothing." But his tone says otherwise.

I stop short in the doorway. All the servants—Mr. and Mrs. Gates, Rhona, Bennie, and a few others—stand around the table. Their hands grip the chair backs, and their attention locks on a small party at the far end of the room.

Green uniforms form a blurry backdrop to the room, but the man front and center is Felix Caesura.

Chambers nudges me forward, and I stumble behind Mr. Gates.

Felix's eyes dart from me to Chambers. "Is that the last of them?"

"Yes, sir."

"Good. Then let's get started. You all have things to do, and I won't take much of your time."

Mrs. Gates reaches for her husband's hand, and he gives her a terse smile. The only person who doesn't appear worried is Rhona, who blushes at Felix and tightens her apron.

He doesn't even glance at her.

"Some of you may have heard of my *See-Say-Save* initiative," he begins. "Last term, I partnered with the CGA to start a program that allows candidates at the Crystal Globe to leave anonymous tips about classmates. If they have reasonable cause to suspect a peer of misplaced loyalty or infidelity to the state, they could report the behavior, and their report could never be traced back to them. The reason behind the program was recent Rogue outbreaks on campus that left several innocent people dead."

I clutch my hands behind my back. Felix doesn't mention the innocent lives lost at the hands of his Gages.

A Gage behind Felix comes into focus, and I clench my teeth to keep from gasping. It's Orbit.

He hands Felix a small scroll, and Felix continues. "With the blessing of our Commanding Gage, Gage Colson and I are extending the program beyond the university borders so that all citizens—like yourselves—can report any suspicious behavior without fear of a backlash. In fact, tips that result in the arrest of a Rogue accomplice will receive a substantial reward. It's our way of giving power to the people and ensuring that all citizens are treated equally."

I scan the solemn faces in the room and realize one prominent absence: Madame Alexis isn't here. Does she know what Felix is doing?

Felix clutches the scroll. "Last week, for example, a munitions train was robbed and derailed. All sixteen workers on the train were found dead, shot in the head. Their bodies lay in a straight line on the side of the track. They were murdered... execution style."

My hand goes to my throat. No, that isn't the Brotherhood's way. Surely, Darius wouldn't ...

"We suspect Rogues are responsible, and if so, they're growing in their numbers and brazenness. That's why we need you, our citizens, to help preserve peace and safety. We need your loyalty. Don't be a defector. Stay loyal in your service and fight against this type of violence by voicing any concerns you have."

He breaks the scroll seal and spreads it on the table. "I need each of you to sign your understanding of the program and commitment to its success. If at any time you need to make a report, simply slip the person's name and reason for suspicion into the metal box outside the enforcer's office. Does anyone have a question?"

Mr. Gates raises a shaky hand. "May we simply give the paper to Mr. Chambers to file for us? Many of us don't often get into town."

"An excellent question!" Felix flatters. "However, the answer is no. What if Mr. Chambers himself were suspect?" He chuckles as if making a joke, but his gray eyes are deadly serious. "You can't trust anyone to do your job for you."

You can't trust anyone. The words ring hollow. Felix is asking the citizens to trust him.

He smooths the document onto the table as we form a ragged line behind it. I keep my head down to avoid eye contact with Felix or Orbit.

Orbit must be the new Gath. How ironic. If only Eliab knew his new associate is even more two-faced than the last one.

My conscience stings. Calling Gath two-faced isn't right. He's one of the bravest men I know. He was simply a spy, doing his job.

Much like I'm doing mine now.

I scribble my name on the document and hand the pen to Rhona who lingers at the end of the line. No doubt she wants extra time near Felix.

She yanks it from me and winks at him. "Bet you can't guess my name."

Felix forces a tense smile and scans the document. "No, but once you sign, we'll have it for our records. Now the name above yours ..."

I turn on my heels toward the kitchen after Mrs. Gates, but I don't reach the doorway in time.

"Excuse me, miss, but I can't read your signature." Felix calls after me. His tone acts like a rope, tugging me back into the room.

I stiffen and shuffle toward him. "Sir?"

He taps the page. "Your signature—I can't read it."

"Colby, sir."

Rhona leans against the table, poised to write her own name. She glares at me for interfering. If I don't get out of her way, she's liable to stab me with the pen.

"And what is that scribbly letter in front of it?"

"That's an *S*, sir."

"And *S* stands for ..."

This is taking too much time. Why is he grilling me?

"Would you like me to rewrite my signature?" I ask. "I'm sorry it isn't neater. Penmanship isn't my strength."

"No, that's all right. I'll remember it. Thank you for your time, *S*. Colby."

He's inviting me to tell him my first name, but I won't do it.

"Good day." I bob my head and hope Orbit doesn't report

anything negative about my behavior.

Chapter 20

Thursday, 4.9.2150
Crystal

"Do you have everything you need, dearies?" Mrs. Gates flushes as she hands Rhona and me freshly bleached and ironed aprons.

I press a hand on her shoulder. "Yes, thanks to you. We don't have anything else to do but show up."

"I can't wait." Rhona primps in front of the mirror. "It's been a long time since Madame Alexis volunteered us to help cater a Dome event. This is going to be some party!"

Mrs. Gates nibbles her lower lip. "I'm just glad you girls are walking there together. After what Mr. Caesura said, I'm scared to go past the greenhouse without Mr. Gates with me. What if one of those Rogues jumps out and catches you?"

Rhona snorts. "Might be exciting. And then I'd have something to report to Mr. Felix."

"Mr. Felix?" Mrs. Gates asks.

She sighs. "I suppose *Mr. Caesura* to most people."

Mrs. Gates folds her plump arms. "What do you mean by that?"

"None of your business." Rhona flips her bronze curls and smooths her skirt.

Mrs. Gates shakes a finger in Rhona's face. "Just because good servants are hard to come by doesn't mean you can sass me."

The maid laughs and swats her hand away. "Oh, don't be grumpy! A girl only lives once. Come on, Sage, let's get this show on the road. I'm rather eager myself to meet all those filthy rich Dome representatives."

I shake my head and rub a smudge off my glasses. "We might not even see them. We're there to set up, help with catering, and be invisible."

She sweeps her hand from head to hip. "This? Invisible?"

Mrs. Gates flashes a concerned smile my way. "Good luck, dearie." She clucks her tongue at Rhona and then busies herself with the morning dishes.

The walk to the marketplace, usually a welcome diversion, feels endless with Rhona's prattling.

I breathe deeply and listen to the morning songbirds, hoping they might drown her out. At least they have something lovely to say. A chickadee flits through some of the trees, making its cheery call. When I was little, Dad had said that if I listened closely enough, I would discover the bird was flirting with me.

"Nonsense," I told him.

"Just listen," he said. "There's one long note and two short ones. The little bird is calling, 'Hey, sweetie.'"

I listened closer. The happy warbling had resembled those words.

A lump forms in my throat. "Hey, sweetie," I whisper back.

"I miss you, Dad."

Rhona stops twirling her hair next to me. "What did you say? Are you even listening to me?"

I swallow and try to smile. "Sorry, I was admiring the chickadee's song. It's beautiful, isn't it?"

She wags her head. "What are you talking about? You weren't listening. You haven't heard a word I said."

"You were probably talking about Feli—Mr. Caesura."

Her jaw tenses. "What business do you have calling him by his first name?"

I shrug and stare at the trees where the little bird has escaped from view. If only I could fly away.

"You called him that this morning."

"He and I are on a first name basis."

"I don't want to know," I mutter.

"Which brings us to the little incident from yesterday." She taps her fingers on her crossed arms.

"What?"

"That was a cute stunt you pulled with your name."

"I didn't pull any stunt. I can't help that my writing stinks."

Rhona swats at a horsefly but looks like she'd rather smack me. "Remember, he's mine."

"You can have him." A laugh dies in my throat. As much as I can't stand Rhona, I feel sorry for her. She's throwing her youth away on someone who will never love her in the true sense of the word.

"But honestly, he's only going to hurt you," I add.

"You're jealous!"

I halt as the edge of the market comes into view. "Rhona, I'm not jealous. You know deep down he's going to discard you for another pretty face some day. Don't waste your passion on him. If you want a guy, take your compatibility test and get matched."

Her expression sours into a sneer. "Compatibility test? Now let me tell you something, Miss High-and-Mighty. I already took my compatibility test—took it as soon as I could. And you know what? It matched me with some loser farmer who wanted his woman to have lots of babies, pluck chickens, and milk cows.

"No thank you, I said, but he was still my match. Poor people don't get the luxury of match options or re-matches like wealthy kids do. You know what? I had to marry the fool."

She stares at the sky. "Yes, I married him. And I ran away as soon as I could, jumped cubes in Crystal, and came here. I made up a story and landed this job.

"So, don't you tell me what's right for me or not. I'm going to squeeze what little happiness I can out of this life."

She strides angrily ahead, and I trail behind her as we pass the market and start down the paved road. Rhona is another tragedy like my sister Candace, but her story makes a rope look friendly.

The midday sun sparkles off the gold Dome ahead. Rhona finally slows enough for me to catch up. Her fury has subsided, leaving behind an insecure slip of a woman.

She fidgets with her apron. "It's so big."

I nod, remembering my first visit, but I can't tell her about that. "We'll be fine. It's one catering event. And you're really good at what you do. I'll follow your lead."

For the first time, she gives me a real smile and then puffs out her chest. "Then let's show these spoiled rich brats what steel we working girls are made of."

I grin and follow her up the marble steps to the brass-plated doors. Once inside, however, she pulls back and lets me take the lead.

I approach the round, central desk and explain Madame Alexis called for us to help with the catering event.

The middle-aged woman snivels at me. "Didn't she tell you there's a side entrance for help? Oh, never mind." She huffs and presses an intercom. "Security, I need you to pat down two maids and then show them where they're *supposed* to be."

A male Gage appears to Rhona's right. He's tall and ripped, but his face seems locked in an expressionless stare. "Follow me."

Rhona sashays after him, but I grimace. Apparently, catering maids don't receive the respect of a private security screening by a female.

She offers to strip, but at least the man has the decency to say that's not necessary. When my turn comes, I hold out my arms like a stiff mannequin and gaze at the ceiling. For once, Rhona's idle chatter serves a welcome distraction.

The last time I was here, I had worried someone might find my karambit and Taser. Although I don't miss the Taser, I'd love to have Dad's gift back. Perhaps Eliab framed it as "evidence" against me and mounted it as a trophy in his office.

I shudder at the mental image as the man's hands sweep my empty thighs.

"Sorry, miss," he mumbles. "We have to be thorough. Too many Rogues on the loose these days."

I nod, appreciative that at least he has the decency to apologize for this invasion of privacy.

He straightens and clears his throat. "Follow me."

The Gage leads us to an interior elevator. When the door opens, culinary aromas greet us. He motions to follow him through a corridor and set of double doors. The kitchen and prep area are

191

at least triple the size of the one in the Excivis, but many of the appliances and equipment look remarkably the same. Apparently, Lord Osborne only owns the best.

The Gage calls over a scrawny but attractive maid. "Isabelle, these are the catering maids from Madame Alexis's crew. Would you see they get something to eat and then show them their duties?"

I blink at his kindness, but Rhona leans on one hip, expectantly. But then, she doesn't have the dark history with Gages that I do. Aside from Gath, I've never met one this thoughtful.

Isabelle nods, gives the Gage a subtle smile, and then motions for us to sit at a narrow bar along a far wall. She slides glasses of water and two pre-wrapped sandwiches toward us.

"Eat up, and I'll be back in ten."

She doesn't have to tell me twice. Rhona picks off the burnt crust, but I nearly eat the plastic. After Warren, I never take food for granted.

For the next two hours, Isabelle, several other maids, and the two of us transform a bare circular ballroom into a candle-lit, formal dining area that rivals the elegance of the reserved space Felix had taken me in the university cafeteria that fated day.

I shuffle through a stack of name cards Isabelle handed me. She had shown Rhona and me the table layout and explained the tables are arranged by Dome profession. All the Toolers here, all the Revisionaries there, and so on.

I'm arranging the Tooler table's cards, including the one for Madame Alexis, when Rhona prances behind me. "Guess whose card I have!" She giggles then covers her mouth as if she has a secret.

I frown. "I have no idea since we don't know any Dome

192

representatives other than Madame Alexis."

Rhona makes a face. "Who cares about her name card when I have Felix's."

I frown. "But he's not …"

"A Dome representative yet?" Rhona twirls the card between her finger. "But he's as good as one, isn't he?"

I set out the last of the Tooler cards. "Okay, where's his table?"

She snorts. "Not telling you! His table's mine."

I roll my eyes. The only reason I'd care to know is so I can avoid it.

Rhona disappears toward the salad bar as I turn to the next profession in my stack. My heart flip-flops. Court Citizen.

If Felix is here, might Luther be, too?

I scan the cards. Sure enough, the last one bears his name.

He must be the favored choice for his class' Dome seat. But what—possibly awful thing—has he done to seal that deal? My stomach churns. That sandwich isn't settling well.

I drop his card in place and finish the table. I don't want to think about Luther right now and what his new circle of friends might mean.

When we finish, Rhona surveys the transformed ballroom with a wistful sigh. "It's beautiful. I'd like to eat at a place like this someday."

Eat. The word reminds me that our work is only half done.

Next, we load stainless steel carts with trays loaded with colorful fruits, lush green vegetables, steaming potatoes, and juicy pork and beef slices. Other chafers contain savory seafood ranging from lobster tail to something Rhona calls caviar.

Though it barely seems possible, the food here is even more

decadent than what we served at Alexis's event. The extravagance of it all repulses me. In Warren, my fellow inmates line barren tables devouring meager portions of mush. I shove a nagging image from my mind and focus on my work, despite the churning of my stomach.

With Rhona's help, I lift a giant punch bowl from our cart onto a table dressed in red linen. Beyond the table, a steward adjusts the lighting to a warm glow.

Rhona sighs with relief as the bowl meets the table without spilling. "There!" She plucks a pretty crystal glass from our second cart to begin decorating around the centerpiece.

But I'm staring at the punch as it sloshes and slowly settles in the bowl. My stomach splatters with it. Nausea burns my throat, and I gag it down.

"Sage ..."

A cramp rips through my abdomen, and I keel over.

Rhona rushes from the other side of the cart to me. "Sage, what's wrong? Are you okay?"

I gasp and fall against the closest wall before sliding to the floor.

"Sage!"

My vision blurs. What's wrong with me? Why does catered food have this effect on me? The aromas make my head spin. My thoughts spiral to Warren and the dirty mess hall tables, barren except for cracked bowls of soggy, tasteless pellets. The mush coats my throat, makes me gag.

Gath's bowl is already empty, but his emaciated eyes encourage me to eat.

"Sage!" Rhona shakes me back to the present.

"I'm so—orry." My words slur, and I cover my face with my

hand so she doesn't see the tears.

"What's going on here?" Isabelle's voice echoes in my ears.

"Sage isn't feeling well," Rhona says.

"But we fed you."

"I don't know what's wrong. Maybe if she just rests …"

"Get her to the kitchen, and take her to the break room. It's the door on the far left. There's a small couch. Representatives will be here any minute, and we can't have a sick catering maid."

The conversation fades in and out. Wiry arms coax me to my feet. The floor swims, and my feet drag. Someone pinches my arms on either side, pulling me along.

"Nice and easy." Soft fabric engulfs me.

"I'm sure she'll be fine." Rhona's voice catches.

"Leave her, and help me finish."

A door clicks, and the dim room blankets me. My wet eyelashes flutter. There's a yellow light from a small lamp in the corner and a skinny glass window in the door.

I curl into a fetal position, hugging my stomach. What is this pain? Why won't it go away?

Then, I recognize it. It's the phantom pains of a gnawing stomach. It's the pain I had learned to live with, the pain I had gradually forgotten after Deidra's meals repaired my malnourished body.

The rich food and savory aromas stir my memory. They paint such a raw contrast to Warren, to what Gath must still be enduring.

Am I still this vulnerable? Lord Osborne would be furious if he knew …

But he doesn't.

I break into another fit of sobs. If I feel this much pain from my psychological scars, how much pain is Gath feeling?

The yellow light darkens, and my salty eyelashes stop fighting the need to sleep and escape the horror of an upside-down society.

Chapter 21

Thursday, 4.9.2150
Crystal

Boom.

I wake in a cold sweat. Was it my barrack or the one next door?

The shot was close.

"Gath?" I whisper.

Wait, that yellow lamp … I'm not in Warren, not anymore.

I pinch the couch cushion and sit up. My head spins. Had the shot been in my dream? Yes, it was probably a nightmare.

Boom.

I fall face down into the cushion again, nearly crushing my fake glasses. Another shot and then another pierce the air.

High-pitched shouting grows closer. Doors swing open, and feet scatter like so many mice discovered in a pantry.

I tumble to my feet. Readjusting my now-crooked frames, I peek through the small window in the lounge door. White and black uniforms streak past, and one barrels into the door, throwing me backward.

"Sage, quick!" Rhona yanks my arm and drags me to my feet.

I gasp. "What's going on?"

"Someone opened fire just as dinner started. The guests dove under the tables, and we maids fled."

"Did Madame Alexis get out?"

"How should I know? The place is swarming with Dome representatives, candidates from the Globe ..."

I squeeze her arm. "Are Felix and Lu—his friend—still in there?"

Her eyes flash. "Why should you care?"

"Are they?" My heart trips over itself. Maybe Luther has sold his soul to be part of Felix's circle, but I can't let some madman shoot him.

"Yes, I was trying to shift toward Felix's table when ..."

"We have to help him—them."

She narrows her eyes. "You're crazy if you think I'm going back in there. Someone's going to get killed, and it's not going to be me."

I shove her through the door. "We have to stop the shooter."

She jerks away. "What's wrong with you? You were sick, and now, you're insane."

Three more shots fire. Rhona darts down the hall after another maid without looking back.

I race toward the swinging door separating the kitchen hallway from the ballroom. Flattening myself against the wall next to it, I squint through the small window.

The lights glare inside the room. Someone has pushed them to a blinding brilliance. Two hooded men sweep the room with weapons raised. I've never seen guns like them before. They're long like rifles, but the barrels seem to be made of some synthetic material and not wood.

But why not kill the lights?

My chest tightens. Maybe they're searching for someone.

They circle toward the Tooler table beyond the punch station and kick representatives out from hiding under the table.

I stifle a scream as one jerks Madame Alexis to her feet and grabs her chopped gray hair as one might a kitten's scruff.

"*Fraternitas Veritas!*" he screams as his companion loads a fresh magazine into the weapon.

My blood goes cold. No, this can't be happening. This isn't the Brotherhood's way.

Without thinking, I plow through the door and fly toward the lights by the punch table. The ballroom darkens as I tumble to the floor behind the table.

Cursing and more screaming pierce the room. In the remaining candlelight, the gunman's giant shadow towers above Alexis's smaller one. He still has her pinned. A pitiful groan escapes her lips as he raises the barrel.

I grab the crystal glasses next to the punch bowl and hurl them across the table at the masked man. One shatters on the wall next to Madame Alexis, and another grazes her attacker's mask.

His partner opens fire in my direction, and I dive for cover as bullets eat the wall behind me.

There's another cry, a deeper one, and more bullets, but they suddenly stop. Smoke seeps through the outer doors, which the attackers must have locked.

More screams erupt as representatives come out from under the tables to escape the smoke—which renders those closest to the doors unconscious.

Gages—It can only be a matter of time before they break through or that smoke overcomes everyone. I crawl toward the kitchen. My eyes are watering so much I can't see clearly.

A tall, dark figure topples over me, and I curl into a fetal position from the impact. If it's a gunman, I'm a goner.

Instead, a firm hand pulls me to my feet and drags me inside the kitchen door.

"Get up!" The man gasps. "Can you show us the way out?"

I blink through stinging tears. I could never miss the cadence of Luther's baritone voice.

I rub my eyes. One arm of his tux is missing, but Luther won his fight, for the same arm holds an unconscious Madame Alexis. Had he silenced the gunmen?

Then I see it. There's a handgun holstered next to his shirt. When did he learn to shoot?

"This way." I trip trying to lead him down the hallway where Rhona had retreated. With his free arm, he lifts me like a doll.

With Luther supporting us both, we reach the back elevator. I fumble to press the right button as Luther readjusts his hold on Madame Alexis.

He exhales when the door closes. "Thank you."

His words send shivers up my spine. I want to memorize every line of his face, every detail of his expression. I'm like a starving nomad seeing an oasis for the first time and hoping it's not a mirage.

"Are you okay?" His brows furrow. I look away before his warm black eyes undo me.

"You were brave in there." He sucks in air like a lifeline. "If you hadn't killed the lights and chucked those glasses, I wouldn't have had a chance to get close enough for a clean shot."

Luther pauses and glances impatiently at the levels. Three more to go. "Why did you? All the other waiters fled. What made you come back?"

I swallow and stare at my hands. They're bleeding. I must have cut them on broken glass. "She—Madame Alexis—is my employer."

"She's a good woman and lucky to have you."

I nibble my lip. "I didn't know Court Citizen candidates could shoot."

His lips form a grim line. "When you intern with the CGA, you take advantage of their shooting ranges."

His words twist my gut. *Intern with the CGA*? Is that why he's working with Eliab?

Madame Alexis moans and pulls my focus to the present. Luther adjusts her so that her head rests against his shoulder. He cradles her face.

I shouldn't be jealous of an unconscious woman old enough to be my mother, but I am.

"It's okay," he whispers. "You're going to be fine. We'll get you out of here."

Luther turns to me. "Where does this elevator take us?"

"Past the security rooms on the first floor," I say. "From there, the front entrance isn't far."

"My vehicle's around back."

I choke. "*Your* vehicle?"

"I sure hope that escort is ready to go," he mumbles.

Since when does Luther have his own vehicle?

The downstairs hallway swarms with Gages. Some other representatives who escaped from the room trickle out another elevator as Dome staff and Healers arrive.

Luther brushes off one man's attempt to check Alexis and plows through the crowd. Why is he possessive of her?

I trail him like a puppy. Who else am I going to follow? Rhona is probably halfway home by now.

There's a cluster of vehicles parked around the back, and Luther beelines for one with tall wheels and dark windows.

A man leans against the driver's side and nearly swallows the cigarette he's smoking.

"Mr. Danforth!" he sputters.

"Get lost," Luther mutters and pushes past him.

"But I'm ..."

"You're smoking on the job." Luther glares at him. "I can drive myself."

I open the back door for him, and he lays Madame Alexis down.

"Will you sit with her? We could be in for a bumpy ride."

"Sure," I say and hop inside.

Luther slams the driver's door behind him, despite the escort's protest. He twists the key, still in the ignition, and shifts to reverse.

I cling to the seat as he tears down the pavement toward the marketplace, narrowly missing Gage vehicles as they flood the pavement surrounding the Dome.

"How's she doing?"

"She's breathing okay," I say. "What happened?"

"One of the guys hit her pretty hard, but if her head's as thick as mine, it will take more than that to stop her." He chuckles. "I'll have to tell her that story sometime."

Yes, the story of when the Trader attacked us both in the old library.

Does Luther even remember I was there with him? Or has he

forgotten me?

I have to know. "Story?" I ask through trembling lips.

Luther glances in the rear-view mirror as a shadow crosses his handsome face. He sets his jaw and meets my eyes. "There was this time ... It's nothing."

My shoulders sag, and I lower my eyes to Madame Alexis so he can't see my damp lashes behind my glasses.

"Friends don't leave friends behind," he adds quietly. "She—my friend—taught me that. I don't think Madame Alexis has many friends these days. She's lucky to have a maid as loyal as you."

I press my lips together. "And she's lucky to have a friend like you."

His eyes flicker, then shift back toward the road as the wheels dig into a pothole. We must be getting close to the estate.

Luther grips the wheel and swings a hard right to avoid another rut. "You were the maid who served coffee at last week's event, weren't you?"

"Yes."

He shakes his head. "That must be it. You just seem familiar, like I've met you before. Or maybe, it's that you remind me of someone."

"Sir?"

"She's short like you."

"Poor thing."

He laughs. "No, it's a good short. What she lacks in height she makes up for in spunk ... kind of like you did tonight."

My throat tightens, choking the words I long to say. It's a good thing, too, because I don't trust my voice anymore.

But Luther is too busy watching the road to notice. "How did you come to work for Madame Alexis?"

I swallow hard. "I came from—from a place where no one will miss me."

"No one?"

My foggy head clears and remembers Lord Osborne's threat. I can't forget my cover. "Well, no one but my grandfather," I hurry to add. "He's not well, and I was taking care of him before I received my post."

"That's hard." Luther's knuckles turn white. Why is he gripping the wheel so hard?

He clears his throat. "It's hard to be apart from someone you miss, especially if you don't know how they're doing. I lie awake some nights, wondering ..."

His eyes glance back, searching my face. What is he hoping to find?

Luther catches his breath and focuses forward again. "I'm sorry. For a moment, I forgot ... Forgive me. I guess we both know what it's like to lose—miss someone, to wish for a chance to tell them ..." Then, as if to himself, he murmurs, "What I wouldn't give for this world to *blaze true* again."

My childhood rhyme. There's no mistaking his reference to it. My arms ache to touch him, to tell him that even though the world is no freer than it was then, I'm right here.

What holds me back? Is it Lord Osborne's threats? Is it the fear that I can't trust Luther anymore because of the company he keeps? Or is it my own fear that he'll reject the person I've become?

Luther pulls into Madame Alexis's driveway, putting a stop to my raging thoughts. She's still unconscious but mumbling now. She needs a medical help. I should run for Mr. Chambers at once.

But my feet hesitate, even after I jump out and make room for

Luther to reach inside for my employer.

Maybe I can give him hope. Maybe I can give myself hope that one day, things will be different.

"Maybe one day, the sun will rise to see wrong days set right," I whisper, paraphrasing a line from my same rhyme.

The effect on Luther is electric. He stares at me with confused, pleading eyes.

Color surges through my face. I've said too much. Too much is at stake if I give in to what I want. What will become of Gath if I fail?

I spin and call over my shoulder. "I'll get help."

My feet pound the pavement. Each step chides me for being a coward. Each step echoes the verses a little girl spun long ago as a desperate cry for hope. It was autumn then. It's spring now.

But that same little girl could still use some hope.

Autumn

sky, fall. Don't wake

until the rising sun

sets wrong days right and blazes true

again.

PART TWO THE
BLAZE

Chapter 22

Friday, 5.1.2150
Jasper

I stare out the train window as the sinking sun turns the clouds into pink and purple cotton balls. If only I could settle onto something soft, sleep, and stay there. The last three weeks have taxed my nerves and energy beyond the breaking point.

But now, I have an uneasy feeling that tonight's journey is going to make my day job seem like a vacation.

As the landscape blurs in the fading light, I close my eyes and remember snapshots from the day. Rhona had seemed extra grumpy at breakfast and stuffed the last biscuit in her pocket. She avoided me the way she avoids work. After the evening meal, I traded my uniform for my tweed dress and hugged Mrs. Gates goodbye. She'd probably be the only person who would miss me. Then, I had started for the Crystal station with nothing but my jacket and a light backpack.

The rhythmic train movements tempt me to sleep, but nervous energy pricks my eyes open.

Darkness descends on the horizon, meaning I'll have to navigate the Jasper outpost and find my way back to the Excivis alone in the night.

I recite the journey I had taken with Orbit a month ago and visualize it in reverse. But at that time, I had Orbit and daylight to help me.

Those woods in the dark terrify me. My only defense is an old kitchen knife I pulled from the trash, reconstructed, and sharpened. If anything, it provides a false sense of security.

But I'm a runner. I survived Warren, Orbit's training, and an attack in the Dome. Most evenings, I run a few miles after Rhona slips out for her escapades. I'm in the best shape of my life.

If only I didn't feel so alone.

After the Dome attack, Madame Alexis's household had remained quiet from parties. Although she recovered from her assault, a strain hung in the air. The woman is no fool. Someone tried to kill her, and had it not been for Luther and me, he would have succeeded.

Luther visited almost every day during her recovery, but I remained out of sight. He came to see Madame Alexis, not some catering maid.

She summoned me once to thank me for my role in saving her, and Chambers treated me with even more respect. On the other hand, Rhona grew more distant. She probably thinks I was crazy for helping rescue our employer.

The two men behind the assassination attempt committed suicide, and the Crystal Gage Administration had branded them as Rogues, members of the Brotherhood.

I refuse to believe Darius would have sent our brothers on such a mission, and yet, they spoke in the Brotherhood's name. I hope Lord Osborne will keep his promise over this weekend trip and allow me to have a Translation session with Darius. I need answers.

The train grinds to a stop at Cube 645. A few other passengers disembark with me, but most people have no interest in stopping at the Jasper trading outpost.

I keep my eyes down and walk briskly past the others. Waiting on the platform is a tall man in a trench coat and wide-brimmed hat. Although his back is to me, I can't shake the feeling he was staring at me.

Maybe I'm jittery, but Orbit had said to make sure no one follows me.

Hugging my jacket close, I slip the hood over my head, though my dark hair matches the sky. Sometimes, I forget I'm not a cotton-top anymore.

I retrace my steps behind the hostel and follow the tracks as Orbit and I had done a month ago. But the journey is much longer on foot. What had Orbit said? Twelve miles?

I pick up my pace. I'll need to jog part of the way if I want to complete the journey in less than three hours. Despite my protesting feet and exhausted body, I tighten the straps on my backpack and begin.

Distant howls and forest screeches disturb the dusky woods. The moon cracks only a sliver of a smile. I'm drenched in sweat from the adrenaline surging inside me.

Why does the otherwise quiet forest seem so loud tonight, as if it has to tattle on my errand? Rocks crunch somewhere behind me, and I whirl. But no one is there.

The screeching forest quiets. Animals know when a predator lurks.

Blood pounds in my ears. Do they see me as a predator, or do they sense something or someone else?

Finally, the decrepit wooden station appears like a deformed shadow alongside the tracks. I pant in relief and rush toward it. I'm well into the early morning hours, but the longest part of my journey is now behind me.

I count off a dozen paces behind the station to identify the thick oak. An urgency makes me climb it as quickly as I dare.

I reach the nook well above the ground and freeze. Leaves crackle on the forest floor. Could it be a bear? If so, this tree is no hiding place.

A mongrel? A bobcat?

A hunter?

Animals with fangs and claws seem more inviting than a man, for that could mean only one thing: that someone has followed me.

A hushed silence falls. There are no more sounds except for a cicada's song. Seconds stretch to minutes.

I slump in the oak's arms, too exhausted to move. The rest of my trip will wait for daylight.

Curling inside my jacket, I shiver myself to sleep.

Songbirds wake me as cold dew coats my stiff limbs. I shake off a hazy head and remember my errand.

Shifting my weight, I reach into the oak's wooden crevice to retrieve the box stuffed inside. I squint to read the small compass, but the morning is still too dark.

Foggy clouds hug the sky, leaving no trace of moonlight. I slip the box back into its hole and grip the compass tightly.

Though my body wants to rest longer, my mind won't let it. The next hour drags until the blackness turns a shifty gray and then a dull blue.

I can read the compass now. It's time to move on. I climb down and point the compass west-northwest.

No mysterious hunter dogs my steps this morning. I wonder if I imagined one last night, or if something were stalking me.

Well after dawn breaks, I reach the training arena and hurry to the tunnel entrance. I hope to find Deidra. I need a cup of hot tea, breakfast, and a real bed.

But the woman in the kitchen is not Deidra. She surveys my damp hair and soiled clothes with uneasiness.

"Where's Deidra?" I hope her name will at least convince this woman I'm not a trespasser.

She studies me with slanted eyes. "Deidra? You know her?"

"Yes, she helped prepare me for my assignment."

"Wait here." She vanishes without offering me as much as a cup of water. But I don't feel the need to be polite. I help myself to a tall glass of milk and two boiled eggs in the fridge.

I've just finished the milk when Deidra appears. Her eyes swell with relief, but she stands rigidly in the doorway.

"I'll get her cleaned up," she tells the other woman who grunts her good-riddance.

Sliding off my chair, I pop an egg in my mouth and trail Deidra. Not until she closes the door to my old room does she drop her stiff façade.

"You're okay!" She squeezes my shoulders in sisterly fashion. "We heard about the Dome attack, and you didn't respond to the mailbox communication."

That stupid mailbox.

"Yes, I'm fine. It's hard finding time to get away from work."
I slump onto the edge of the bed, wanting nothing more than to curl up and sleep.

Deidra studies me with a knowing gaze. "Something else is bothering you."

I fall backward onto the bed, not caring I probably have oak leaves still in my hair. "I'm exhausted, Deidra. I worked all day yesterday and spent all night trying to get here."

"You can't hide behind fatigue. There's a strain in your eyes."

I prop myself upright. "Strain? Where would you like me to start? Because I could …"

She holds up a hand. "Tell your complaints to a hot bath and save the report for Lord Osborne. But I know heartbroken eyes when I see them."

I wince. Who is this woman, and how can she read me so well?

She sits next to me and picks foliage out of my hair. "Oh, don't pretend with me. A woman who's had her heart broken can always recognize the same wound in another."

Deidra pauses. "Did you see your special friend?"

My shoulders sag. "I did. He and I—we both helped save Madame Alexis from the Dome attack. The two of us working together felt like old times. I wanted to tell him who I was …"

"But you didn't."

My throat constricts. "No, because I don't know if I can trust him. What if he's changed? What if he doesn't feel the same way about me anymore?"

She sighs and runs her fingers through my hair. "Fear. It's the enemy of love. The two can't coexist."

"You don't know our story," I mumble.

"Then tell me."

I start as far back as I can remember. I tell her about the whistling neighbor boy, our three-legged races, and how he called me Cotton. I tell her what his brother did to mine and what happened to my family. I tell her how we met on the train to Crystal, how he taught me to run again, and how he ultimately sent me to the satellite.

When I finish, I'm crying. Telling someone about Luther relieves the pent-up pressure inside me. Is this what having an older sister or mother to talk to feels like?

She wipes tears off my cheek. "He cares, Sage. He may not know what you've been through, but at the same time, you don't know what he's had to sacrifice in losing you. You don't know how many lonely nights he's cried himself to sleep, wondering if he'll ever see you again."

I blink. "Really?"

"Let me tell you a story—of someone who's been on the other side." She starts to braid my hair to give her fingers something to do.

"I was a young girl once, too," she says, "and I loved a simple boy. My family lived in Beryl, right on the stubby peg of the southernmost peninsula. It was a small fishing community. The ocean provided our livelihood.

"Each night, Abel and I watched the sun set over the water and dreamed of our future together. He was helping my father trap lobsters when the ships came.

"We'd never seen anything like them—long, fierce freighters. They were a twisted combination of cargo and battle ships. They hugged our coastline to avoid a southern gale but caught on a sandbar.

"Men began jumping like black ants overboard, and even a

215

fool could tell they were prisoners, desperate to escape. The few who made it to the shore pleaded with us to hide them. They said they were wrongly imprisoned on satellites and were being used as slaves."

She closes her eyes. "At first, we thought they were mad, but their horrific stories were too graphic, too raw to be the railings of madmen. We gave them what food we could before they took off for the next closest key.

"But in doing so, we sealed our fate. Their taskmasters came searching for them. At first, we denied seeing any escaped sailors, but these men knew their business. They cruelly plied the truth from another villager.

"Abel warned that we were all in danger, but no one in the village believed him. Everyone else thought the ships would leave once the tide changed, and we'd never see them again."

Her eyes moisten. "I believed him, but I was still a teenager in my father's house. After dinner, as was our custom, he came by for our sunset date. But that night, he took me to a small lagoon. He waded waist deep, pulled me in after him, and told me to take a deep breath."

She laughs. "I'd follow him anywhere. Having lived by the water our whole lives, I think we were both part fish. But that dive made me think my lungs would burst. He tugged me deeper until we surfaced in an underwater cave. It was a perfect hideout, a perfect place for two teenage lovers."

She blushes. "But Abel didn't touch me. He said he had to look my father in the eye without feeling ashamed. He told me to wait there until he came for me. He promised I would be safe there, that no one would find me if—if the worst happened. And if nothing happened and the ship left at dawn, he would bring me back home."

She lowers her hands to her lap and stares at them. "Trouble is, he never came back."

I hug my waist. "What happened?"

"When I finally bucked up the courage to swim out on my own, the sun didn't greet me. Billowing smoke did. The crew had torched our homes and killed anyone who stood in their way. Many were missing, though. I guess they imprisoned them to replace the runaways."

"I'm sorry," I say softly. "Did you find Abel?"

"No, he must have been among those taken." Her words are barely above a whisper. "But I did find my family—or what was left of them."

She quickly wipes her face with her hand. "Anyway, I was the only survivor and too stricken with grief to try living. I probably would have killed myself if he hadn't arrived."

"He?"

"Anton—Lord Osborne. He has a nose for tragedy. He knows exactly where to find people who are willing to do anything for revenge."

I shiver. But I'm not working for revenge, right? I'm working for Gath, for Darius, and for the Brotherhood.

"I became one of his best spies. The things I agreed to do …" She suddenly stands and brushes her skirt. "We need to get you cleaned up. Lord Osborne will want to speak with you." Deidra turns to the bathroom and yanks on the hot water.

I follow her, but my mind is reeling. "I'm so sorry, Deidra. But why have you told me this?"

Her brown eyes hold back tears. "Because, Sage, I don't want fear to destroy your future the way hate destroyed mine."

Chapter 23

The blue light of the Translator gives Lord Osborne's smile an eerie glow. The man has done nothing to ease my growing concerns. No sooner did I arrive in the meeting room than he programmed the Translation—said he didn't want to keep Darius "waiting" any longer.

Since when does he care about Darius's or my interests more than his?

My tired eyes strain to focus on the figments of my brother's face that gradually grow clearer.

He wears a beard now. It's a reddish hue and speckled with gray. Strange how it ages him and makes him resemble Dad.

I wish he wouldn't hide secrets from me like Dad did. I wish he would tell me where our father is.

"Portia!" He forces a half grin. "You're looking well."

"Her name is Sage." Lord Osborne corrects him.

"She's Portia to me. Sister, what can you tell me about

Crystal? Any news?"

"There was an attack in the Dome," I say, "but I guess you already know about that."

Darius frowns. "I've heard about the incident. What else can you tell me about it?"

"I was going to ask you the same thing." I cross my arms. "Two gunmen attempted to assassinate my employer, Madame Alexis, and spoke in the name of the Brotherhood."

My brother jerks in his seat. "What?"

"Yes, they shouted *Fraternitas Veritas*. Please tell me we weren't responsible?" I try to keep my tone level, but it sounds accusing to my own ears.

"Of course not," Darius insists. "I wouldn't jeopardize precious lives on a pointless mission like that."

To my left, Lord Osborne shifts in his seat. I turn my attention to him. "Do you know who's behind the attack?"

He chuckles softly. "It sounds like your Brotherhood has a secret admirer. After all, imitation is the sincerest form of flattery."

"But these attackers are giving us a bad reputation," I argue. "We're not cold-blooded killers, and we certainly wouldn't go after the only Dome representative I know who actually cares about the ASU's values."

Lord Osborne laughs louder this time. "The ASU doesn't have values. Most leaders don't. Corruption is how they stay in power. Your Brotherhood might not be as pure as you'd like to think. Or has Darius not told you his Baytown stories?"

Darius glares at him. "Revolutions run on blood, and frankly, it's time someone other than the citizens donated."

Lord Osborne holds up his hands. "Quite right, but I don't understand why your little sister is squeamish about an

220

assassination."

"It's about the target." I blurt back. "Madame Alexis seems to care about the people ..."

"You are naïve." He clucks his tongue. "You can't trust anyone in the Dome to care for anyone but himself."

"Don't you think some people want to do the right thing?"

He inspects his fingers. "No, I place all my bets on pain, because it's the one stimuli that people always respond to the same way."

I shudder, remembering Deidra's story. I can't waste this opportunity to talk to Darius by arguing with my employer.

"Let me tell you what else I learned," I say and recount again the conversations I overheard at Alexis's party. When I finish, I ask, "Do you have any idea why Felix and Eliab would want to execute prisoners?"

Darius taps his fingers together. "Unfortunately, no. The Dome knows we've hacked into their system, so they're being very careful in their transmissions. The best we can do is guess their next move, and what you just told me doesn't make sense. They're thinning the prisoners in the satellites, and yet they need the manpower to meet their quotas. We need to find out why and the timeline if those prisoners—most of whom are probably innocent—stand a chance."

His tired voice makes the burden on my shoulders feel heavier. "I'll keep my ears open, but at the end of the day, I'm a catering maid."

"You're the closest thing we have to an insider, Portia."

"But what are you planning to do?" I ask.

"He doesn't have a plan." Osborne smirks. "Has your Pelagic Project failed, too?"

Darius's jaw tightens. "Take care of yourself, Portia. If you learn something, let me know."

Too soon, his face disintegrates into the pixelated space. I'm left staring at the wall, wondering how a meeting can leave me this dissatisfied.

Lord Osborne rises to pour himself a glass of brandy. "I don't suppose you know anything about his project?"

"I don't even know what pelagic means," I admit.

He chuckles and smiles patronizingly at me. "Education these days is such a waste. Pelagic has to do with the open sea or ocean."

I frown. "I don't understand."

He sips his now-full glass. "Your brother is a Tooler—as was your father, if I'm not mistaken."

My stomach tightens. I hate how he refers to Dad in the past tense.

"Your brother also majored in Coastal Defense, and rumors say he's capable of making anything. I'd like to know what seaworthy project he's undertaking."

Osborne is fishing—and trying to get me to spy on my own brother. Well, I won't do it even though I wish Darius wouldn't keep secrets from me.

My silence seems to agitate Osborne who raps his fingers in frustration. "It doesn't much matter," he mumbles to himself. "He doesn't have a plan anyway."

"Why do you keep saying that?" I demand.

He returns to his seat and studies me. "Your Brotherhood is a band of rebels whose ideals can't take shape into real action."

I bristle. "Then would you rather no one challenge the Dome's abuses?"

He smirks at me. "I don't deny you're a well-meaning bunch,

222

but at the end of the day, you'll fizzle like all the other revolutionaries who have gone before you."

"I bet that's what England thought, too."

"England?"

"Haven't you heard of the Revolutionary War?"

"My dear girl, your brother is no George Washington."

I narrow my eyes. "I didn't say he was, but a spark is all you need to set a fire going."

Lord Osborne sets down his glass and leans forward. "Sage, I love your optimism, but your Brotherhood is trying to light a match in a rainforest. It's never going to catch. You'd need a giant conflagration to start the kind of change you want to see."

An impossible thought strikes me, but I dismiss it to focus on the antagonist before me. "Then what would you suggest? That we sit back and do nothing?"

He leans in his seat and crosses his legs. "Stop fighting against a brick wall, and learn how to scale it."

My head is too sleep-deprived to appreciate metaphors.

"Take me, for example," he continues. "I've learned to thrive in these times. As I said before, the key is all about knowing what people want and finding ways to solve their problems."

"You don't take sides?"

"I work for the highest bidder." He swigs the last of his glass. "You might be surprised at all the clients who have come to me for services."

A knot grows in my stomach. I can't trust this man. He would sell his soul—and mine, too—if they would buy something he wanted.

"But enough about your brother and his problems. Let's talk about my fee."

223

I tense. "Fee? But I'm already working for you at Madame Alexis's estate."

"That's earning your keep." He jumps to his feet and pecks at a keyboard in the wall. The image of a map appears.

I don't have to be an expert at geography to recognize the layout of Warren Satellite.

"As you reported, Gage Eliab wants routine satellite executions. Your brother thinks there's a larger motivation for this new order, but I think he's missing the obvious one."

I shift my weight uneasily.

"Come now, you don't have to search long to find a reason Eliab wants to destroy the Brotherhood. There are the obvious political reasons, but there are personal ones, too. Your brother has cost him good men, and at one time, his own rank. Plus, there's the Baytown uprising."

"What happened at Baytown?" I ask.

A half-grin curls his lips. "You should ask him sometime."

I sigh. Why can't he answer my question?

"And then, there's his vendetta against you. Orbit uncovered the details about how you planted that virus. He tells me that you and another Rogue insider pulled off the stunt. He also tells me that the timing matches the dismissal of a high-ranking Gage, the one he replaced on Eliab's staff."

A nagging fear pricks my skin. Has he discovered that Gath was our insider?

Lord Osborne studies me. "Tell me more about your accomplice."

"He was—one of the Brotherhood's runners," I say. "I think he escaped."

"What about the Gage?"

I shrug. "There was a Gage who stood trial about the same time I did, but that's all I know."

"Is it?" His piercing eyes accuse me. "Then let me tell you a little more about him." Something in his voice warns I may not want to hear his story.

"I think I told you about this man before—his name is Gath Aden, but you would only have heard of him as Gage Gath. You see, Gages only go by their first names. It's a shallow attempt to conceal their identities to protect kin who might suffer by the people's hands if others guessed their relations to a Gage."

I moisten my dry lips and swallow, waiting for him to continue.

"But let me back up the story," Lord Osborne says. "After your brother's trial and sentencing, Gage Eliab was demoted and sent to work as the prisoner transport agent for Baytown. That's where he met Wasp Gath. The two were brutal in their methods. Your brother can tell you more about what they did to prisoners if you'd really like to know."

I feel like someone is squeezing my heart. Surely Gath doesn't belong in the same sentence as Eliab.

"About that same time, I began my underground work. It became both my livelihood and the means to protect my family from the Dome's cruel reach. You see, western life is rough. If you think the east coast suffered from the Apocalyptic conditions, then imagine the destruction out west as ten times worse.

"Still, some of us, those wanting a freer life, attempted it. I found a lucrative livelihood in black market running—finding ways to get people the resources they wanted."

His jaw tightens at the memory. "But I was young and naïve. A clever Wasp—Gath Aden—discovered I was the source

225

supplying some of the unruly civilians with personal weapons. His moles found my underworld, and one day when I was gone, destroyed everything and everyone I loved."

His body trembles with rage. "My wife was pregnant with our first child. But that didn't matter to them."

"I'm sorry." For the first time, I actually do feel sorry for this man. "When did all this happen?"

"Seven years ago—Right before the Baytown satellite uprising." He flexes his jaw. "But time doesn't make a man forget some things. I haven't forgotten Gath and Eliab, and I suspect Eliab won't forget your brother and you."

He redirects his attention to the digital map and uses his fingers to focus on the Warren compound.

The mere layout of the place makes me shiver as if I'm still trapped inside. "What does this have to do with me?"

"It has to do with your assignment tomorrow."

I jump to my feet. "You're not sending me back there."

He glares at me. "Yes, I am."

"I won't go."

"Yes, you will. You're paying the fee for my services to your brother, remember? Now sit down, and listen."

His words slam against my heart. I'm trapped—have been trapped—ever since I stepped into the Excivis.

Lord Osborne pecks at his keyboard. Two identity badges flash on the screen. One is Eliab's, and the other is Gath's.

"Through another mole, I'm sending word of your disappearance from Warren—along with your prisoner number and picture— to CGA headquarters. If my theory is right, Gage Eliab will come to Warren to investigate."

I flinch. "Why would you do that? Do you want him to

recapture me?"

"You can't see beyond your own nose, can you?" he taunts. "If Gage Eliab comes to Warren, I'll have my opportunity for revenge. And you'll have the opportunity for yours."

I shudder. "I don't want revenge. I just don't want him to ever find me."

"If you don't want revenge on Gage Eliab, then perhaps Gage Gath will help motivate you."

"What?" My voice catches, and I glance away from his picture with pretend disinterest.

"Do you recognize him from your time at Crystal?"

I swallow the lump in my throat. I'm tired of lying but can't betray Gath to this man. "No."

"Look closer. You told me there was a Gage who stood trial about the time you did. Orbit confirmed my suspicions that it was indeed Gage Gath. Apparently, he failed a major mission."

"So?" I stare at the screen and Gath's picture. He was healthy and strong then.

"He was the Gage sent to catch your Brotherhood's runner, and his botched mission killed your father."

Chapter 24

Saturday, 5.2.2150
Excivis

Blood rushes to my face, and the room swirls as Lord Osborne's words echo off the walls.

I rub my temples to focus my spinning thoughts. "Darius didn't say Dad was dead."

Lord Osborne arches his brow with mock pity. "Fool girl, you're only hearing what you want to hear. Your brother didn't have to use so many words to tell you. Everything about his body language expressed your loss."

"I don't believe you."

He wags his head and laughs. "Do I have to present his body to convince you? That seems a little extreme but doable. Perhaps Darius has his reasons for not telling you about the casualties from the explosion."

Casualties, plural? Oh, God, please not Foxworth too.

I gulp. I have no right to ask Washington's God for anything. He isn't mine yet. I don't even know how to begin. And surely, he would be annoyed with someone who only thinks of him when her world is falling apart.

I swallow. The silent weight on my chest makes breathing almost impossible.

Lord Osborne taps impatiently on the screen. "Do you recognize him from the Warren prison camp?"

"There are several barracks." I wheeze the words. "By the end of our work, we all look dark as coal."

"He's there. He must be—if he's still alive," he mutters. "You might even have been placed on the same prison train. Memorize his picture, because I want you to keep an eye out for him when you go to Warren tomorrow."

Another man's face flashes on the screen. It's the lead pipeliner from Baytown who caused Gath so much grief.

What's left of my stomach twists into knots.

Lord Osborne narrows his eyes. "You recognize this man, yes?"

"Yes, sir. He and some of his crew—they were assigned to our—my—barrack."

"Our?" He pounces.

"My friend," I say as calmly as possible. "He and I looked out for each other. He's probably dead now."

"Most likely. Focus on what matters." He circles Rig's image with his index finger. "This man is your mission tomorrow. You will help him escape."

"Escape?" I sputter. "The escape your last runner planned, the one for me, left him frying in a Wasp's chair."

"Then you'll have to do a better job, won't you?"

The Translator screen retracts into the ceiling as Lord Osborne switches off the computer and then excuses himself. I remain in my seat and stare blankly as the last of the screen disappears.

Did Darius know everything he would ask of me? Did he know this man was constantly throwing me into the arms of danger? This latest impossible plan requires me to rescue a prisoner I don't even like.

Yet, it might give me a chance to keep my vow and rescue Gath, too. I promised I would go back for him.

Just not this way. I lean against the couch cushions, wishing they could swallow me and take me someplace, any place, but Warren at first light tomorrow. I'm such a coward.

An escape—That's what I need. I plant my focus on the dark shelves behind where the screen had been. They're bookshelves, lined with rows of hardback and leather-bound editions.

A starved ache for learning and a sudden longing possess me. I haven't touched a book since my term in Crystal. Maybe I can't run from my problems, but I can try to forget about them for a few hours.

I quietly approach the shelves and run my fingers down embellished spines and embossed titles. A new hunger shoves away the fatigue and fear.

A thick, black leathery book hides in a far corner. Five silver letters shimmer on the spine. B-I-B-L-E.

I had seen the title in the archives. I pull the book from its dusty perch and open the cover.

Someone had written a personal message in faded, slanted

writing. I squint my eyes to read.

My sweet Cassandra,

For graduation, this is my gift to you. You'll soon move on to start your new life with Antonio, and since you can't take me with you, please take my grandmother's Bible. I can't find any more like it. They've probably been confiscated. Promise me you'll always hide these words in your heart.

I pause and reread the name, Antonio. That's Osborne's first name. Was Cassandra his young wife? Though I can't stand her husband, I feel sorry for her and her tragic death—if only revenging her hadn't consumed the man. Maybe at one point, he hadn't been heartless.

But there's no use wasting time wishing for what-ifs. I continue reading.

Our world is a warped place, but here, you can find unchanging truth. And the truth will always set you free. (John 8:32)

Your loving mother

I read the last lines over again.

Truth. A pang slices at my heart. Dad had said that lies can protect me, but only the truth can free us.

His voice whispers in my memory.

I carefully fold the page to the contents and scan for the title John. There are four of them? Someone must have liked the sound of his own name.

But wait, most of the titles—the table of contents calls them books—are names. Perhaps they indicate authorship.

At least someone had the decency to add tabs with the different book titles so that I can easily find my way.

I stop at the first book called John and find chapter eight, verse thirty-two.

And ye shall know the truth, and the truth shall make you free.

Yes, this is the place. I skim through the chapter, but the words read like riddles. There's a story about a woman caught in adultery, and a man named Jesus who saves her from stoning. He tells her to go and sin no more.

Then people called the Pharisees argue with him over his authority. Jesus tells them he is from above and they are from below ... None of that makes sense. He calls those who "continue in his word" his disciples, and then there's the verse about truth.

But the Pharisees don't understand it. I don't understand it.

Frowning, I read on. There's an argument about bondage and freedom. Now those are words I understand.

But it's all phrased in such a confusing way. The Pharisees become more upset, and my headache drills deeper into my skull.

Why do ye not understand my speech? even because ye cannot hear my word.

Jesus' question pierces my heart. No, I don't understand.

But that doesn't mean I don't want to.

"Miss Colby?"

I shove the book on the shelf and spin. Patrick, the hairdresser, stands with arms folded.

"Lord Osborne said I might find you here and that you need some attention."

I hurry away from the bookshelves and toward him. "That's good of you to ask, but I think ..."

The frown on his face stops me. "It doesn't matter what you think. I'm seeing your roots, and they don't match your disguise. Come with me. I have work to do."

I resent being called *work*, but Patrick is a genius at what he does. I've caught Rhona glancing jealously at my tresses.

I hesitate. "Is it—just my hair?" I might bolt if he comes at me with another needle.

He rolls his eyes. "Your injections are good for at least another five months. Now come along."

I trail him like a mongrel with its tail between its legs.

I will never get used to the dye's smell, but when that treatment is done, he trims up the stray ends, and I relax. In fact, I doze intermittently, so he flicks me with the edge of his scissors when he needs me to move my head.

After applying a fresh tint to my eyebrows as well, he surveys me with the pride of an artist.

"You might be minced meat tomorrow, but at least you'll look like a reckoning force."

"Thanks?"

He sweeps the hair on the floor. "You'd better hurry, or you'll be late for dinner. And Lord Osborne does not appreciate tardiness."

He doesn't have to tell me twice.

Chapter 25

Sunday, 5.3.2150
Excivis

The stiff gray uniform fits snugly. That's a change. Maybe some meat is finally starting to stick to my bones.

The last spy who wore it had to be on her deathbed because anyone smaller than me can't last long.

Unless she was a child.

I swallow and force away the thought.

Deidra watches me with folded arms as I pin on the nametag. Her starchy navy sleeves scratch against her trim suit—a uniform I've never seen her wear before. She unfolds her arms and shakes her head. "You won't get past inspection if you don't dress to code." She clucks her tongue and undoes the pin. "Here, I'll do it."

"I've never had to pretend to be a Wasp before," I apologize.

"But you lived among them long enough to notice how they dress, didn't you?"

"I avoided eye contact. Any prisoner who wants to live does."

"Yes, but any smart girl doesn't miss details—like which side of the uniform the nametag goes on." She finishes and reaches for a beret on the bed. "Here, I'll twist your hair back, and then we'll add the cap."

I sit obediently on the bed next to her as her nimble fingers work on my hair. Thanks to Deidra, every strand will be in place.

Good, because every fiber of courage within me is falling to pieces.

"Can't you go for me?" I whisper. "You're the expert spy. I don't think I can do this. If I return to Warren, I may never leave again."

She jabs a pin into my scalp. "No one can do your job for you. Lord Osborne selected you for a reason."

"Maybe he's trying to get rid of me. This is a suicide mission, you know."

"Not if you do it right."

"But the last runner who tried ..."

"He made a mistake. You'll be a smart girl, and you won't."

Deidra displays none of the sisterly sympathy I desperately want. She hands me a belt and holster to slide on it.

I inspect the black plastic. "A holster? That means ..."

"You're a Wasp, remember? A side arm is standard carry."

My heart thumps. Though Orbit had taught me how to use one, I never dreamed of carrying a real gun. The fact I'm acting as a fraud somewhat spoils the glow.

Keeping the barrel pointed down, she offers me the handgun. "Yes, it's loaded. Don't aim at anything you're not willing to destroy."

The smooth metal barrel slides cleanly into the holster with a satisfying click.

"Don't forget your glasses." She hands me a different pair of frames. They're black, cat-eye frames that give my face a snarky twist.

Deidra winks. "You look like a vixen in those. Now let's give those Warren Wasps a taste of their own medicine."

I blink. "I thought you said ..."

"I said no one can do your job for you, and no one can do mine but me." She smirks and hands me a black tote that holds a folder of the plagiarized orders. "It's showtime, Wasp Sybil. And if I'm responsible for your escort, you will be on time."

I gasp in delight and relief. "Really? You mean ..."

She straightens and frowns at me. "That's no way for a Wasp to talk. Think terse. Think thankless. Talk little, and say much."

I clear my throat and try to sound stern. "Let's be off!"

She groans and rolls her eyes. "Talk as little as possible. Let your orders speak for you."

In my defense, it is 0400 hours, and I haven't had a trace of coffee.

We emerge from the drainage pipe as a revving sound breaks the pre-dawn silence. To my left, square headlights emerge like eyes in a wild forest. There must be a secret storage garage to house Osborne's larger equipment.

My dull brain kicks into gear. Right, we need a large vehicle to transport the pipeliner crew and steal its leader. Even in the darkness, I recognize the CGA's trademark Merlin Falcon on the driver's door. Apparently, my employer thrives on operation details.

But if that's the case, why is he so foolish to send in someone like me to complete the mission? Lord Osborne doesn't know the lead pipeliner—Rig—like I do. How can a wispy girl like me command a nasty like him?

A silent man climbs in beside me as Deidra takes the wheel. I wonder if he's mute, or if he has merely mastered the "talk as little as possible" rule.

I sit between them, trying not to let the leathery seat grow too comfortable, but the adrenaline pumping in my veins thwarts any chance of sleep.

The drive stretches into a silent hour. It seems strange that we take such a roundabout trip when the Excivis lies concealed close to the coal mines.

Deformed shadows from the forest blur outside my window. Crooked trees and frost-bitten shrubs herald the approach of Warren. It has a way of deadening anything within its reach.

Too soon, the tires stop at the guardhouse. Deidra hands the Wasp our papers with an air of icy indifference.

Oh, why can't she play my part? But there's no use wishing.

I steel my eyes and ignore the guard. He is Deidra's concern, not mine.

Mine is Wasp Harris.

The clock in the truck reads 0507. The prisoners will be in their bunks until the 0530 execution shot heralds the new day.

That gives me less than half an hour with Harris. I hope I won't need that much time.

The man beside me hops out and holds the door. My boots dig into the gravel as I leave Deidra and him behind.

I have to come out of this alive. Deidra and that nameless mercenary are depending on me.

Pinching the black tote under my arm, I march up the Wasp station's steps and yank open Harris's office door.

He's reclining in his desk chair with his boots atop a table and sipping from a black mug. His eyes widen at my appearance. Boots hit the floor, and he chokes on his coffee.

Rage surges through me. All these months, he's been drinking coffee while we rabbits starve.

I chide myself. I can't think of myself as a rabbit anymore.

But Peppermint is. Her cage sits on the adjacent wall, and her terrified bunny eyes shrink into her shiny coat as I kick the door closed.

"I'm Wasp Sybil. Here are my orders." I slap the folder on his desk. As he glances at the orders, his scowl sends a surge of panic through me.

I mask it with a glower to match his and the hardest tone I can muster. "I expect that pipeliner crew loaded and ready to go by 0600 hours."

He flicks the file back at me, and the papers scatter on the ground. "Load them yourself."

I resist the instinct to retrieve them but instead crush the closest paper with my boot until it's soiled and torn on the rough wooden floor.

"Sign and submit the orders before my tires leave the lot, or you'll have more than one transport agent at your jugular."

Harris scratches his chair on the floor and presses his wrists into his table, leaning toward me with a taunting laugh. "I said, load them yourself." His lip curls to a snarl. "See if you leave the barrack in one piece."

Peppermint scampers in circles inside her cage, terrified of our rising voices.

Talk little. Say much.

I take a deep breath and then spin. *Pretend it's a drill.* As Orbit instructed, I smoothly draw the handgun, aim, and fire.

Peppermint falls limp, and the cage goes silent. Blood

splotches her once spotless white coat. Harris roars in rage, but I re-holster my weapon. "Now, about that pipeliner crew?"

He mutters obscenities and marches out the door.

I dart to the cage, unlatch the hinge, and open my black tote. I've never killed something before unless I'd planned to eat it, but today, Peppermint might be my key to surviving.

"Coming?" Harris yells from outside.

I join him and hope he doesn't notice the bulge in my bag.

He strides toward my old barrack with such fury I can barely keep up with him. "Since you're so clever with a gun, you can do the honors this morning."

He unlocks the chains on the door. They fall to the side like clattering dead men's bones.

The noise rouses only a few of the prisoners. Most are too lost in sleep, the one place they can retreat from the hunger and misery of their lives.

With each step farther inside, the more my dread increases.

To my horror, Harris stops at my old bunk. How can he possibly know?

I tell myself that he doesn't, that this is a horrible coincidence.

Sunken deep inside himself sleeps Gath, a shadow of his previous self. Relief and guilt battle inside me. Yes, he's alive, but how he has suffered! And what have I done for him? Nothing. Guilt threatens to break my fragile facade.

Harris smirks and taps his side. "Hey, trigger-happy, today's number is 86. That's the wheezing fellow on the second bunk. Why don't you wake up the place?"

Rising nausea burns my throat. No, he can't expect me to execute someone. A rabbit is game, but a man ...

"What's your problem, princess? Is killing a criminal beneath you?"

I cross my arms. "I'm not here to do your dirty work. I'm here to collect my pipeline crew."

He gnashes his teeth. "Fine."

Dear, God …

The shot rings in my ears like a condemning mob. Could I have done something to save that man's life?

At least his misery is over. His death was mercifully free from the fear that now rakes through the barracks. Prisoners bolt out of their beds to form a haggard inspection line.

Harris strides to the center. I trail behind, long enough to watch Gath limp to his place. He ignores the gore plastered on the wall above him and doesn't even lift his gaze to mine.

He knows better than to stare a Wasp in the face.

"Rise and shine, my pets!" Harris calls. "I have a special surprise for you. We have the honor today of Wasp Sybil's presence. She's here to whip you pipeline gents into shape for your next assignment. You can thank her for missing breakfast."

Hate burns inside their eyes. I square my shoulders, trying to look braver than I feel.

Harris retreats to the entrance. I start after him, determined not to be made a fool, but he holds up a hand. "Did I mention your other option? You can eat her for breakfast."

He laughs, exaggerates a bow, and slams the door behind him, leaving me alone in the center of the cold floor.

I'm an island, surrounded by starving piranha.

The women keep their eyes down, but the men, one by one, raise theirs to inspect me. Revolt and insubordination mean automatic execution, but Harris had invited them to dine at my expense.

I clutch the tote at my side and focus on Gath. Finally, his eyes meet mine.

Without thinking, I remove my glasses. He has to see my heart in my eyes—despite all my outward changes.

A faint grin spreads across his lips, but it vanishes an instant later when Rig swaggers toward me.

The pipeliner isn't as thick as he used to be. Living at Warren has created hollows in his cheeks. His sun-bleached hair lies matted and long around his ears.

"What do you say, men?" he circles me like a shark. "Shall we eat this Waspy for breakfast?"

Jeering echoes off the concrete walls.

I reseat my cat-eyes and stuff my hand into the tote.

Rig stiffens. Maybe he thinks I have a gun. I do, but I have something more powerful yet.

I fling the dead rabbit at his feet. "How about you eat Peppermint for breakfast?"

The room erupts into cheers as confusion conquers Rig's face. "How did you …"

His surprise sparks a crazy idea. But I can't miss this opportunity for a truce, a way to save Gath, and a chance to ignite a revolution. I move past him to Gath's side.

"What? You don't recognize Rabbit 12017?" I ask Rig and squeeze Gath's arm. His lips tremble, but no sound comes out.

Rig shakes himself. "But how did you …"

"There's no time for that. Listen closely. I'm here to help you—that's you, Rig—escape. My orders are to transfer your pipeline crew. There will be an accident on the way that will allow you to get away."

"What about the rest of us?" The voice is thick with hope.

I shake my head. "If you all escaped, my cover would be blown, and I could never help another prisoner. But what if you pipeliners lay the detonating cord—the groundwork to setting you and a bunch of other satellite prisoners free?"

"We're listening," Rig says.

"After you escape, your crew will continue the journey to Baytown. You men will stop at other satellite camps on the way where you can set in motion the plans for one giant ..."

I pause for breath. *You'd need a giant conflagration to start the kind of change you want to see.* That's what Lord Osborne had said. Maybe for once, he's right.

"One giant conflagration," I finish.

The men frown at me. "Confla—what?"

"Conflagration—fire." I shiver. This is a crazy idea.

"So you want to set the satellites on fire?" Rig asks. "But what are you going to use for fuel?"

"The Warren mines are full of coal dust and firedamp. Someone just has to create a spark in the right place to set off a chain reaction. There will have to be other explosive sources at the other satellites. Can you manage that?"

The pipeliners exchange glances, then nod. "But when? If this is going to have an impact, it has to be synchronized. Otherwise, our efforts will look like isolated riots, and we'll get ourselves killed."

I swallow. I'm making this plan up as I go.

My gaze darts to Gath. He can't last much longer than a month, and I have another full month before returning to Jasper. Will that give the prisoners enough time to prepare?

But if the date isn't soon, this dream of revolution will burn out—and Eliab and Felix might pass their satellite execution amendment.

"How long is the trip to Baytown?" I ask.

Rig rubs his chin. "It took us three weeks to get here, what with all the new lines and repairs we had to do."

"I'll give you until the first Sunday of June," I say.

"It's never going to work," a sullen man mutters. "Besides, no one's going to volunteer to set the first fire. There's no way he'll survive."

"We might as well die fighting," another says.

"Are you volunteering?" Rig leers. The man goes silent.

"We have to band together as brothers, or we'll die like rabbits," I argue. "First, that means we stop fighting with each other."

Rig stares at the rabbit and then at me. "I told you the day you delivered that rabbit would be the day I'd leave the traitor alone. I suppose you're right."

He pauses and narrows his eyes at Gath. "I still have good cause to hate you, but I'm willing to move on."

Rig picks the rabbit from the floor and hurls its body under a bunk for someone to skin later. "I say we follow Waspy. If she can kill Harris's pet, surely we can light a match to this place. What do you say, men?"

The barrack cheers. Who cares if Harris hears? He probably thinks they're devouring me.

I slap my arms to my side. "I want a straight line."

The pipeline crew scurries into place.

I glare at them. "Don't look happy about it. Now, march!"

They scrape their feet down the long aisle toward the door. I fall in line at the rear but stop in front of Gath.

"Come with me," I whisper. "I can get you out now. I'll make up something."

He shakes his head. "My place is here. With the pipeliners leaving, who else will make sure the prisoners make preparations for next month? When the time comes, who will strike that spark? I will. It's the least I can do—and maybe my last chance—to do right by you."

What does he mean? Could Lord Osborne be right about him and my father?

I can't believe it. I won't.

I cling to his arm. "Find the trap door in the mine—the one by the seam you closed. I'll send food."

"No fear, sister. I'm not very hungry anymore."

"Promise me you'll go there. Promise me ..."

He uncurls my fingers from his arm and kisses my forehead. "*Fraternitas Veritas.*"

Chapter 26

Sunday, 5.3.2150
Warren Satellite

Harris chokes on his coffee and stares as if I'm a phantom.

I retrieve the torn order from the floor and fling it at him. "I want it signed and submitted—yesterday."

He tumbles out of his chair and staggers to his feet. I can't give him any time to recover.

I yank the door handle to leave. "I could slap you with insubordination paperwork up to the rafters."

He sputters, but his tongue trips over itself.

"Have another rabbit ready for me next month, and I'll reconsider. I like target practice."

His face flushes. "You'll be back?"

"Weren't you listening? I'm the new transport agent." I snatch a peppermint candy from a goblet by the door. "Till next month, my pet."

My guard escort stands erect by the passenger door and opens it for me before circling around back and lowering the rear door, locking the prisoners inside.

Deidra starts the engine without a glance my way.

We don't say a word till Warren disappears behind us.

"Do you have the coordinates for the pipeliner's drop-off point?" I ask.

"Affirmative. It's where I'm dropping you off, too."

I blink. "But I thought …"

"Change of plans. You don't have time to transfer the rest of the pipeliners to the prisoner train if you're going to catch your own ride to Crystal today. Lord Osborne gave me a new script. Wasp Sybil was injured during the prisoner escape. That's what the transcript will read. She'll request and be granted a month's leave by the CGA until her assignment next month."

I'm more than happy to retire my Wasp cap until then.

"Okay," I say, lowering the soiled tote to the floor and stretching my tired limbs. My adrenaline has withered like a desert stream.

"I was right," she adds. "You were the girl for the job."

"I'm tired, Deidra."

She winks at me. "Me, too. But you're alive. We all are, thanks to you. Don't get sloppy now."

I nod as she presses the brakes. This must be our stop—and my last chance to tell Deidra about Gath. "Deidra, there's something I need you to do for me."

"What's that?" She shifts to park, and the guard beside me hops out.

I squeeze her arm. "I have a friend in Warren, and he's starving to death. I promised I'd get food to him somehow. He knows about the trap door at the end of the long hallway. Could you …"

248

"Yes." She clasps her hand over mine. "Now, go."

As I climb out the truck's cab, the guard tugs the rear door upright and then trains his weapon, ready to shoot any deserters.

I don't tell him he won't need it today.

The pipeliners blink at the sudden brightness and then freeze on the hard flooring of their transport prison.

"Rig," I call inside. "This is our exit."

He scrambles to his feet as the others stare sadly after him. Rig thumps his fist on his chest in a parting gesture. "I won't forget you. Next month will be your turn. We'll show the world we pipeliner rats are made for more than dying."

The guard clutches his weapon tighter. He must think this speech a diversion, the pipeliner's way of stalling for time before helping his men escape.

But the other men don't move as the door once again locks them in place. The man returns to the truck's cab, and Deidra shifts to drive.

Rig follows me into the woods. I recognize them as the ones outside Orbit's training arena.

We'll reach the Excivis within half an hour. I don't have much time to talk to the pipeliner alone.

"Why do you hate him so much?" I keep my voice low.

He stops. "What? You mean Gath?"

I don't slow down. "Keep walking. And you must promise to call him Phil."

"Why is he important to you?"

"I've lost count of how many times he's saved my life. He's one of the few friends I have."

Rig snorts. "You have a strange choice in friends. Maybe you wouldn't call him that if you knew what he's done."

I square my shoulders and block his path. Perhaps Rig can elaborate on what Osborne told me. "What has he done?"

The question wrenches my gut. Part of me doesn't want to hear, but the other part demands the truth.

His jaw tightens. "I'll tell you what I know, which I'm sure isn't all. But you'll get a picture of the man he is."

"The man he was."

Rig waves his hand. "Doesn't matter. You can't wash that kind of blood off your hands."

I gulp and continue walking, slower this time.

He falls into step beside me. "When I arrived in Baytown— never mind how—Wasp Gath was in command."

Wasp Gath. The title doesn't fit. The idea of him being an equal with the likes of Harris doesn't settle well.

"Not long afterward, Eliab arrived as the new prisoner transport agent—the same role you played today. Only, he had a boulder-sized chip on his shoulder. I pieced together pretty quick that it had something to do with one of our prisoners. I think if Eliab could have killed the guy outright, he would have."

My breath catches. "What was the prisoner's name?"

"I don't know his real name or remember his number, but he went by Abe."

Darius.

"Go on," I say. "What did Eliab do to him?"

"In his role, he couldn't touch him. He was an agent. He couldn't kill unless in self-defense. His job was to move in new prisoners and transfer out specialized crews." Rig pauses. "But Eliab soon chummed up with the one person who could kill him, and that would be your Phil."

"No, that doesn't make sense," I mutter.

250

"How's that?" Rig demands.

I can't tell him that Darius and Gath are best friends, that Gath has risked his life for him and me—not to mention our other brothers.

"Never mind. We're almost to the Excivis. Tell me what you know."

Rig scowls. "Then stop interrupting. Now, where was I?"

"You were saying that Eliab and Gath worked together."

"Yeah, they worked together all right. Back then, Wasps didn't receive the daily execution orders like Harris does, so they had to be more creative. They established individual quotas. See, Baytown is different than Warren. In Warren, your mining roles depend on each other, so for the most part, you're working toward the same quotas.

"In Baytown, it's every man for himself. The shipyard welders and laborers work independently at our stations.

"So, if a Wasp had it out for a man, he could sabotage his equipment to prevent him from making his quota. Not making quota more than three times was grounds for elimination. I watched Gath take a cutting torch to a prisoner."

"Stop!" I lean against a tree, hugging my waist and wanting to erase the image now seared in my memory.

"You asked. Should I go on?"

"No—Not about that anyway." I swallow. "Were you there for the Baytown uprising? Tell me about that instead."

Rig offers a hand to help steady me. I refuse and stagger forward.

He laughs. "I'll tell you about the uprising. It's the one time we prisoners had a chance to give those Wasps a taste of their own medicine.

251

"You see, even if our equipment weren't sabotaged by a Wasp, a man could still miss quota because of illness. Abe pieced together that it was the fumes making many of us sick. He called it Fume Fever. Our workspaces were poorly ventilated. Sure, there was what appeared to be a vent in the ceilings, but those things led to nowhere. Besides, our spaces were crowded, and the weaker men succumbed the fastest.

"For this reason, the Wasps assigned to guard us didn't actually stay in our workspaces. They had cozy, air-conditioned offices on the outer edges of the factory. They would inspect us and our quotas a few times a day but otherwise, leave us in our misery."

A grin creeps across his face. "Well, Abe, he was a clever one. He cut and routed a ventilation tube from our ceiling to the regular air ventilation system used in the Wasp offices. While he did this, the rest of us worked extra hard to meet his quota. We didn't understand his plan at first. All he told us was that he would make sure we wouldn't die because of Fume Fever.

"But when Wasps started dropping like flying insects ..." Rig snorts at his own pun. "We put two and two together. Now, it was the Wasps, not the prisoners, complaining of nausea, fever, and chills. The guard count dropped until a mere skeletal force was guarding us.

"And that's when we sprung the revolt. We slipped out of the factory to the offices where the weakened guards were trying to work. We knocked them off first. Then, armed with their own weapons, we took out the healthier Wasps at the barracks."

We've nearly reached the hidden entrance to the Excivis. I retie my boots to stall for time.

Rig leans against a tree. "That's when Wasp Gath and some

252

of the other head honchos appeared, but with our numbers, we captured them, too.

"We had our fun with Gath's colleagues, just so he knew what he had coming. But then somewhere, an alarm sounded. Even more than revenge, we wanted our freedom. We took some cheap shots at Gath and then bound him hand and foot. A few of us set the barracks on fire, and we tossed him inside to burn."

"Then how did he escape?" I ask.

Rig swears. "I guess if you're the devil, you can find a way."

I bite my lip. How had he escaped?

"What about—about this Abe? What happened to him?"

"I don't know. He disappeared. The rest of us, on the other hand, didn't get very far before Eliab and reinforcements arrived. They probably would have executed all of us if they didn't need us to keep slaving for them.

"Anyway, not long after that, we heard that Eliab and Gath shipped out to Crystal. Go figure, they were both promoted for quelling the revolt."

We reach the door, and I hesitate. "Rig, I helped you escape today. Can you promise me something?"

He narrows his eyes. "That depends. You may have helped me, but you weren't the only one. I've heard of the guy who's fronting you. I owe him as much as I owe you."

"He might ask you about Gath—might ask if you know where he is."

"And why shouldn't I tell him?"

"Because I'm asking you not to."

Rig runs a hand through his hair. "Listen, you're a nice kid, but I can't promise that."

My lip quivers, and I slowly enter the concrete drainage pipe.

At the end of it, I place my fingerprint onto the scanner by the door, like Orbit taught me. The door cracks open, revealing the long hallway inside.

I feel a hand on my shoulder. "Why would you want to protect him anyway? Don't you see? He deserves what he gets."

I shake my head. "The Gath I know isn't the same man you described to me. I don't know what happened or when it happened, but my friend is different now."

"Your friend?" His tone drips with scorn. "Maybe you wouldn't call him that if he were responsible for the deaths of people you cared about."

His words echo in the tunnel and in my mind. What if Lord Osborne is telling the truth? What if Gath killed my father? If he did, will I hate him as much as Rig does?

My throat constricts. No, Dad can't be dead. And I refuse to believe Gath would have killed him.

Lord Osborne is gone. No one says where, and I don't ask. His absence might buy Gath a few more days of safety.

Although I work for him, Lord Osborne is hardly on my side. Some days, I think he's as dangerous as Eliab.

Rig doesn't complain except about the food. I grin and tell him about my rations when I first arrived. His expression suggests he plans to bribe the cook into giving him an extra portion later. If he does, he'll be too busy puking his dinner in the next hour to wonder what I'm doing.

I excuse myself and follow an impulse to visit Lord Osborne's library. Its quiet solitude invites a chance to think.

And try to untangle the mystery of that book.

I pull the Bible off the shelf and settle on the sofa. Gently, I flip open the worn cover, hoping for answers, but the subtitles don't make sense. I'm not about to puzzle over that truth passage again.

There's an index in the back, but it won't help if I don't know what I'm looking for.

I skim the alphabetical listings. Most names are foreign to me, and most of the words blur until I reach "P." One nearly jumps off the page.

Prisoner. Ah, here's a word I understand.

Let's see what this book, this Bible, has to say about people like Gath and me.

*the poor, and despiseth not his **p** ... Ps 69:33*

*sighing of the **p** come before thee ... Ps 79:11*

*The Lord looseth the **p** ... Ps 146:7*

I stop on the last line. Isn't *looseth* an old word meaning to free? *Freedom* and *prisoner* don't belong in the same sentence. Clumsily, I shift through pages until I find the book of Psalms.

With a sudden hunger, I start reading Psalm 146 at the beginning.

1 Praise ye the Lord. Praise the Lord, O my soul.

2 While I live will I praise the Lord: I will sing praises unto my God while I have any being.

3 Put not your trust in princes, nor in the son of man, in whom there is no help.

4 His breath goeth forth, he returneth to his earth; in that very day his thoughts perish.

5 Happy is he that hath the God of Jacob for his help, whose hope is in the Lord his God:

6 Which made heaven, and earth, the sea, and all that therein is: which keepeth truth for ever:

7 Which executeth judgment for the oppressed: which giveth food to the hungry. The Lord looseth the prisoners ...

Tears blur my eyes. Why am I crying? I must be tired. Or maybe, it's these words.

Who is this Lord who can help a prisoner? Who is the God of Jacob? Did he really create the heaven and earth? Is that fabled place called heaven real after all?

What does it mean to keep truth? I would give anything just to find out what is truth, let alone hold on to it.

He executes *judgment for the oppressed*—people like me. He gives *food to the hungry*—that's people like Rig and Gath.

He looses the prisoners. Can this God really set us free? And if so, how?

I read the rest of the short chapter. There are more wonderful words, but no instruction guide. There are only two commands in the whole chapter. The first is to praise the Lord.

But how can I praise him when I don't even know him?

The second command is implied. It says not to trust in princes or in other men. The flip side is that I should trust in this Lord.

Trust. I don't trust anyone these days. Everyone I've trusted has let me down—or disappeared from my life.

Wearily, I close the book and shelve it. I have a train to catch.

Chapter 27

Monday, 5.4.2150
Crystal

It has to be 0200 hours when I reach Madame Alexis's home. Through bloodshot eyes, I rinse off the sweat and dirt of my journey with a cold, quick shower and then crawl into bed. I'm shivering but too tired to search for the hair dryer Rhona likely stole from the bathroom again.

Her side of the room seems unusually quiet. I hope she's sleeping deeply and not out on one of her after-hour escapades.

I set the alarm on the stand, knowing that if I don't, I'll miss breakfast.

Underneath all my blankets, I curl up and close my eyes. But I can't stop trembling. Maybe it's just the cold, or maybe it's the strain from the tall shadow that dogged my steps from the Jasper outpost all the way to Crystal.

I pass out from exhaustion, but my dreams are anything but peaceful.

My alarm chirps what seems but minutes later. How can I operate on four hours of sleep? But I don't have a choice.

Eyes puffy, I sleep-walk to the bathroom and splash water on my face. Back in my room, I twist my hair into a bun and retrieve my glasses. At least they will help hide my bloodshot eyes.

Rhona's bed is already made, and her side of the room is unusually tidy. I never heard her leave this morning.

But then, I barely heard my alarm go off.

A fog seems to hang over my head and all the kitchen at breakfast. The other servants don't chatter as they usually do. Although Mrs. Gates greets me with a motherly squeeze, her eyes look red, too.

That's when my fuzzy brain registers someone is missing, but I wait until Mrs. Gates starts to clear the breakfast dishes before asking for details.

"What's going on?" I trail behind her into the kitchen. "Where's Rhona?"

Her lips tremble as fresh tears gush from her eyes. "Oh, dearie, if only we knew."

"What? You mean she just disappeared—like the other catering maid?"

"I'm afraid so. It happened yesterday. She never came down to breakfast, and when Mr. Chambers asked me to fetch her, she wasn't in her room. All her things were still there, except her small handbag. She hasn't been seen since, and no one knows when she left."

My heart drops. Though she's catty and a pill sometimes, I

was starting to like her.

"I'm sure she's all right," I say, but my words sound hollow to my ears. What if she went out with the wrong guy? What if …

"It's been a nightmare, what with you being gone too." She wipes her eyes. "But there, I shouldn't complain. How's your grandfather, dearie?"

My foggy brain kicks into gear. "Oh, he's doing as well as can be expected. It was just a really long trip."

She sighs. "And it's going to be a longer day."

I slip into my apron and begin to set out breakfast for Madame Alexis. Chambers is kind enough to help me.

He carries a steaming tray of sausage. "We'll be looking for another catering maid. Can you recommend anyone?"

I nearly spill the orange juice glass. "You don't think Rhona will come back?"

Chambers stiffens. "Even if she does, I'll have to let her go. Her behavior is not becoming. She's pulled stunts like this before, but she's always returned in the morning. Oh yes, I know about her nightly antics. If good maids weren't hard to come by, I would have dismissed her long ago."

I fumble folding the napkin. "If I think of anyone, I'll let you know."

"If only girls nowadays didn't have to live secret lives," he mumbles.

I glance up. "Sir?"

He flushes as if he hadn't meant me to hear him. "If I could find another dependable girl like you, maybe I would sleep better at night. There's a big event a week from this Saturday, and if we're still shorthanded …"

"We'll manage," I say softly. "And maybe you'll find

259

someone else."

But the only applicants prove undesirable. One didn't bring any references, and the second smelled like a cocktail bar.

The Friday before the event, Chambers drafts Bennie into part-time catering service, and she grudgingly accepts my training.

"I'd rather be in the kitchen," she mutters as we replace the dining room linens.

"We'd all rather be somewhere else, Bennie," I say.

"Yes, but catering maids never last long anymore," she says. "I don't want to disappear too."

"Pretend you're invisible, and whatever you do, don't flirt."

She snorts. "Me? Flirt? I'm not pretty like you and Rhona."

"Every girl has her own charm, Bennie. Just don't try to test yours on houseguests. I think that was Rhona's mistake."

But I should have saved my breath. The morning of the banquet, Bennie complains of a head cold and refuses to set foot outside the kitchen. Chambers colors purple at her insubordination, but Mrs. Gates protests she needs help in the kitchen anyway.

That leaves me. Chambers promises to do double duty between welcoming guests and refilling glasses, but I know I'll be bearing the brunt of the catering work alone.

Still, when Mrs. Gates thrusts a basket in my hand for a last-minute errand to the market, I don't object.

I haven't had a chance to contact Lydia since returning to Jasper. As I start down the dirt road, I do the math and realize she can have only a week or so left at her current station, if her post there hasn't already expired. Didn't she say something about a two-month assignment? What if she's moved somewhere else?

A pang of guilt makes me quicken my step. My reason for wanting to see her is purely selfish. I haven't even considered how worried she might be about my long absence.

After depositing my shopping basket and Mrs. Gates's list with Sam, I hurry toward the enforcer's office.

There are two people standing behind the table outside and badgering the people in line, but Lydia is not one of them.

My heart sinks. I missed my last chance to find out if anyone's heard about my father.

I trudge to the vendor's booth where my nearly finished basket waits. The man's efficiency chides my own ineptness.

But is it my fault? How can I serve two masters and still find time for what matters most?

Hot tears burn my eyes, but I blink them back. Feeling sorry for myself won't accomplish anything.

The vendor hands me the full basket. "That's the last of your order, miss. I've wrapped the meat as tightly as possible to keep it cool, but you'll need to hurry to keep it from spoiling. Today is unusually warm for April."

I had forgotten my coat and not even missed it. Breaking the sixties did make for a warm day.

"Thanks, I'll hurry." I hand him the purchase card. "I appreciate you getting my order done so fast."

He nods but presses his lips into a frown. "I don't want you hanging around the market longer than you need to. That enforcer has been looking for you. I don't want any trouble for a nice girl like you."

His words prick my ears. "Enforcer?"

Surely Eliab can't have found me here.

He returns the card and scowls. "I knew that census collector was trouble the first time she followed you to my stall."

I shake with relief. "What did she say?"

The vendor misinterprets my shivering. "Like I said, if you hurry, she never has to know you were here."

"What did she say? I—I need to know."

He crosses his arms. "She said to tell you that she's been promoted—ain't that nice—and now works inside the enforcer's office. She said to tell you that you must go inside to see her—about your outstanding business."

I gulp down the hope I feel. "Thank you for telling me. Like you said, I should hurry."

"I won't tell on you."

His gruff loyalty warms me, but now, I have to deceive him, too.

I pretend to start for the road toward Madame Alexis's community but circle back and nearly run to the enforcer's office.

Two grim-faced men out front block my entrance. "State your business."

"Court Citizen Collins has requested to see me." I plaster on a worried frown. "I—uh—I have something outstanding that I owe her."

One of the brutes grunts. "It's about time you show up. Are you the one she's been looking for?"

I blush and stammer nonsense.

"Make it fast." The second pushes me toward the door.

I fall against it and twist the knob. The interior reminds me a little of Harris's office, except that there are two metal desks that contrast with the rough wooden floor. Beyond the desk is a holding cell, which for the moment, is mercifully empty. There's one small window near the door, but a dark, dirty curtain drapes over it.

The first desk is vacant. Behind the second, Lydia jolts straight, and her brown eyes widen. The relief of recognition on her face fades into a glowering mask.

"Don't just stand there. Shut that door."

I stagger inside and slam the door behind me. "I'm sorry I'm late." I raise my voice so the men outside can hear.

She all but shouts, "I don't want excuses!" And then she winks at me and beckons me toward her.

I want to hug her and cry, but instead, I fall into the seat across from her. "I'm sorry it's taken me this long to come back. You have no idea …"

"Don't apologize. We don't have much time." She lowers her voice. "I've heard snippets from our brothers—and Luther …"

"You talked to Luther?" I interrupt.

"Of course," she says. "He's the one who helped me find Red and join the Brotherhood."

"The Brotherhood?" My breath catches. "Is he …?" Maybe I've been wrong about why Luther's been spending so much time with Eliab and Felix.

She sighs. "He might as well be. He's helped us in many ways, but he's also worried about the direction the Brotherhood is taking—with these recent atrocities done in our name. Jael assures me we're not behind them, but I don't have any good explanations for Luther."

I smile softly. Luther has always had a strong sense of justice and order. It's why he believed in following the established process for reaching the Dome and making changes. If only everyone played by the rules.

Lydia's soft brown eyes look strained. "I'm only going to be at this post for another two weeks, and then, who knows where I'll be sent."

Her words remind me how short our time is. "Have you heard

anything from Jael?"

"She's doing well."

I move my lips but can't speak the words. *And my father?*

Lydia shakes her head, bobbing the high bun on her head. I miss the way she used to wear her wavy hair in long tresses. But then, I miss a great many things these days.

"There's no word on your father," she whispers, "but Jael found Foxworth."

"If Fox survived the blast, then maybe ..."

The door bangs open. "Is this girl giving you trouble?" the enforcer demands.

Lydia's face transforms into a scowl, and she stares at me with strange eyes. "You have two weeks. Now, get out!"

She glances at the enforcer. "No problems here. Just another beggar."

He grunts. "You're too generous with them."

Lydia laughs, a raucous laugh I would never have thought her capable of. "No, Grayson, I just have a longer fuse than you do."

I clutch my basket and dart past him and down the street. I don't stop running until I reach the fork in the road.

Sweat soaks the back of my shirt. I should visit the abandoned barn to make a report to Lord Osborne, but my basket has grown warm, too warm for comfort. If the meat spoils because I dilly-dallied, Chambers and Mrs. Gates won't be happy.

With the banquet tonight, I can't afford any missteps. I need to guard my cover and keep my connection with Lydia. She's given me a spark of hope that my father might be alive.

Chapter 28

Saturday, 5.16.2150
Crystal

"Dearie, you are a vision." Mrs. Gates gushes as I tie on the clean apron she pressed for me. How this woman finds time to mother me warms my heart. She says it's her small way to repay me for running myself ragged on her errands.

I glance in the hallway mirror. My own tall bun reminds me of Lydia's, except that I've curled some short strands to frame my face.

She clucks her tongue. "Don't let any of those men get dicey with you, or I'll come out waving my frying pan." She chuckles. "And then Chambers will be furious, and I'll lose my place."

Mrs. Gates would make quite the picture, waving a cast-iron skillet at Felix.

I tuck one of the longer curls behind my ear. "I hope that won't be necessary."

The first pot of coffee finishes, and I retrieve the chilled cream canister. My tray now complete, I have no reason to dawdle any longer. "Wish me luck."

She smiles and then turns to help a grumbling Bennie put the finishing touches on the main course: oven-baked flounder topped with a shrimp cream sauce. The aroma would make most people's mouths water, but it tightens the knots in my stomach.

Three coffee pots later, there's still no sign of Felix, Eliab, or Luther. I start to relax and fall into a rhythm.

Chambers meets me as my current canister goes dry. "Check the cocktail bar, and then help me set out the main course."

"Yes, sir." I discard my tray and set another pot brewing. Chambers hands me a clean tray of shot glasses and two more chilled bottles.

"Wait." He pops open one of the bottles and pours himself a shot glass.

I blink in surprise. I've never seen Chambers drink on the night of a party. He always scolded Rhona about her bad habit.

"Is everything okay, sir?" I ask.

He downs the glass in one swig and takes a deep breath. "I need something to steady my nerves. This night has me on edge."

Chambers straightens his collar and starts adding Mrs. Gates's steaming trays to a serving cart.

All that food ... I take a deep breath and square my shoulders, determined not to let my starvation scars undo me tonight.

I pass the bowl of buttermint candies on my way to the cocktail bar and stop short. Without hesitating, I snatch a handful as I'd seen Rhona do before and pop one in my mouth while dumping the rest in my apron pocket. If I feel woozy, maybe the candy will keep my gag reflex at bay.

I've no sooner set down the fresh bottles and glasses at the cocktail bar when someone's hot breath comes on the back of my neck.

"I see Rhona's taught you a thing or two, but I won't tell."

My skin pricks, and I catch my breath. I'd know Felix's voice anywhere. I wave my hand toward the table, inviting him to help himself.

I keep my eyes low. "I don't know what you mean."

He nudges me. "Don't you? One of those bottles is partly empty. Aren't you girls starting a little early tonight?"

I blush. "I didn't take any."

"You don't have to lie to me. I'll keep your secret. Besides, I prefer my catering maids a little tipsy."

My face feels as flushed as a crimson rose. "Excuse me. I have to set out the main course."

But as I turn, he catches my arm. "Now where are your manners? I'd like a glass before you go. It's much more enjoyable to watch a pretty girl pour your drink."

His breath already smells, but I've seen Felix hold his liquor. He's not a drunk flirt. He's a calculating killer.

He motions to his preference, and I try to steady my shaking hands. But it's no use.

I hand him the glass with trembling fingers.

He takes a sip and grins at me. "Do I make you nervous?"

He has no idea.

I cap the bottle and then brush my skirt to give my nervous energy an outlet. "Is there anything else I can get you?"

"That depends on how late you want to stay up tonight and if you have as much spunk as the last girl."

My heart races. What does he know about Rhona? Will he tell me?

"I'm sorry, but my coworker no longer works here."

He studies me with sharp gray eyes. "She served her purpose, but you're ten times prettier. Besides, after this night's done, you might be looking for some company."

I curtsy and spin, retreating to the kitchen while sucking down several buttermints to fight the sour aftertaste of Felix's encounter.

She served her purpose ... after this night's done, you might be looking for some company.

What does he mean? Is there a reason Chambers is on edge?

The serving carts wait in the kitchen, each one loaded with covered metal trays, steaming with fragrant aromas. Beyond them, Mrs. Gates slices something—cheese?—on a cutting board while Bennie feverishly spreads something else.

Odd. The guests already finished the hors-d'oeuvres.

I reach for the first cart to push it out the door when Chambers steps in my path. He's pale, and his left eye twitches.

"What is it?" I ask.

"We're delaying dinner."

"Sir?"

"Madame Alexis is not feeling well, and the most notable houseguests haven't arrived yet." He pivots on his heels and reaches for the cheese tray. "Is this ready?"

Mrs. Gates huffs. "It's not pretty, and it's the last of the cheese."

"It's fine." He jerks a thumb at me. "Take this out and then offer guests more coffee. I've got to get back out front to wait for her to arrive."

"Her?"

Chambers's eyes flash at me. "Get going."

I sigh. "Yes, sir."

Bennie catches my eye. "I'll start the coffee again for you."

268

"Thanks." Maybe she feels guilty for deserting me out front, or maybe she needs something else to relieve the tension we're all feeling.

The cheese and crackers vanish within minutes of my setting out the tray. But then, we must have forty guests. How can we be this underprepared for such a crowd?

I'm dizzy from the demand for coffee and frowning faces of the hungry guests. Felix's is among them. He and another man I've never seen before are talking in a small sitting area, composed of a few leather chairs and a coffee table, lined with four full shot glasses.

His companion is a short, light-complexioned man, maybe in his mid-forties. He wears metal-rimmed glasses and a steel expression to match it.

Such a small man has never looked so dangerous.

Felix waves me over, and my stomach flip flops. I swallow and offer a terse smile. "Coffee, sir?"

Felix crosses his arms and raps his fingers across his starchy sportscoat. "Where's the host?"

I hesitate but decide to tell what I know. "She isn't feeling well. That's what the steward said."

"But she will be down?"

My skin crawls as his companion stares at me for an answer. I focus on Felix, who strangely seems the less terrifying of the two.

"I think so," I say. "But I heard we're still waiting for some notable houseguests to arrive."

The companion's eyes dart to Felix. "Juliana is late."

"She'll be here," Felix mutters. Something like fear burns on his face.

The man parts his lips to reveal crooked—or are those

broken?—teeth. "Coffee for me then."

My heart rate drops. What is it about this man that makes me want to run?

"Black coffee," he says.

I nod and rest my tray on the coffee table to pour his cup. I hand him the steaming mug, which he accepts without acknowledging me. He's studying Felix with piercing eyes.

"You're not drying up on me, are you, Caesura?"

I reach for my tray. I've got to get away. If Felix stares hard enough, he could recognize me, and his friend scares me. He reminds me of the Trader but concealed in a gentleman's garb.

"On the contrary, I've never felt more—thirsty."

I stare at the shot glasses—the four full ones that have been resting on the table all along. Something is out of place.

Felix's companion laughs, but there's a withering glint in his eyes. "Good. I've made promises about you. I'd like you to live up to them."

I withdraw from their seating area. Bennie, clutching two fresh champagne bottles, nearly collides with me at the kitchen entrance.

She shoves the bottles into my chest and grabs my tray. "Here, take these. Someone complained the bar is dry."

"But my coffee …"

"I'll start a new pot. Now shoo!"

The coward. Doesn't she realize I'd like to hide in the kitchen for a change? But I go through the motions. Fill new glasses held out to me by tipsy hands. Place the new bottles in the ice buckets.

The ice is melting. Bennie didn't even think we'd need fresh ice.

I carefully remove the bucket with the least ice but still

270

manage to knock over the dwindling stack of shot glasses.

I need a third hand to keep one from smashing on the floor.

Someone else beats me to it. "Looks like you could use some help out here." It's Luther's mellow baritone voice. But his unexpected appearance disorients me. He's like a gust of wind in a stagnant room. It's a welcome presence, but it blows over the precarious stack of cards.

I study his thick hand, which holds the fragile glass so gently, and in a flash, realize what's wrong.

What's wrong with Felix, what's wrong with his friend, what's wrong with those four shot glasses on the table.

Without thinking, I drop the ice bucket and reach for the glass in his hand.

The next thirty seconds unfold like chaos in slow motion.

The bucket bounces off the floor, sending ice water spattering over my clothes and the floor. Luther drops the glass in my hand and steps back to avoid getting spattered himself.

"I'm—I'm sorry." I stammer and squeeze the glass. "But it's different."

He stares at me as if I were a ghost.

Oh no! I'd forgotten my shrill catering voice and spoken, not like Sage Colby, but like Portia Abernathy.

I blush and fall to my knees, mopping the floor with my apron and keenly conscious of all the gawking eyes on me, the clumsy catering maid.

At that moment, Chambers enters the hallway with several dark figures behind him.

He clears his throat and announces, "Ladies and gentleman, it is my privilege to present to you the Friend of our one united nation, Juliana Caesura, and her escort, Commanding Gage Eliab."

She's less than a stone's throw away, and she's staring at the spectacle, at me.

Those keen eyes hold disdain and something else—fear.

I reach for the table to help me stand and find Luther's hand instead. He helps me to my feet with all the dignity of a Court Citizen and all the tenderness of an admirer.

His hungry eyes search my face for answers, for affirmation.

I offer an apologetic, gaping mouth and rush for the closest exit.

Chapter 29

Saturday, 5.16.2150
Crystal

Chambers finds me crying in the kitchen by the back door. I wouldn't have stopped there, except someone had deadbolted it, and my hands were shaking too hard to undo it.

I can never escape my prisons. When will I be free from all the falseness?

"What's wrong with her?" He demands of Mrs. Gates and Bennie, who have been badgering me with questions since I crumpled to the floor.

Mrs. Gates starts blubbering herself. "I don't know, but it's too much—all these houseguests and just her. And some of those men—they're beastly."

Chambers's nostrils flare, and he shoves Bennie toward the door. "Get out there and—do something!"

She pinches her lips, snatches the coffee pot and tray, and shoves past him in what might be the boldest move of her life.

I gasp for air and try to control my breathing. "Something's wrong."

Chambers swears, not once but twice. "Tell me something I don't know."

I hold out the shot glass. "This—there's a different one out there."

He stares. "Talk sense, Sage."

I suck down a deep breath. "There's a substitute—not one of ours. And it's filled with—with something. I don't know who it's for."

His face registers my fear. "Where?"

"In the sitting area …"

He pulls me to my feet. "Show me." He claims a food cart and motions for me to take another. There's still work to do.

We've just passed through the hallway to the dining room when a woman's scream pierces the mansion.

Was that Bennie? I grip the railing on my cart to steady myself.

Not Chambers. He abandons the cart and races past the buffet area to the ballroom. Taking a deep breath, I release the cart and rush after him.

When I reach the entrance to the ballroom, I can't see. The guests huddle tightly together, each craning for a better view.

I wait at the doorway between the dining room and ballroom, not willing to shove past people to confirm my fear.

A broad-shouldered man with grizzled hair beelines to the front hallway, shouting orders.

I shrink farther against the wall as Gage Eliab whirls to form a one-man barricade to the exit.

He barks into his handheld radio and then folds his arms, surveying the scene. With a grim scowl, he clears his throat and bellows, "Ladies and gentlemen, remain where you are, and remain calm. There's been a murder. The Friend has been poisoned."

My throat goes dry as the crowd surges in confusion. Some fall backward, but others charge toward Eliab, demanding answers.

But no one gets past him, and within seconds, the front door bursts open as other enforcers arrive. Orbit—Gage Colson—leads the entourage.

How could back-up reach the estate so soon?

At their entrance, the crowd retreats to the edges of the room, giving me a clear shot of the fateful sitting area.

Felix cradles Juliana's head in his lap, but it's the Friend's eyes that unhinge me. They are wide open and rigid, staring straight ahead with a look of betrayal and terror.

I'm absorbed in the scene and don't see Luther until he steps in front of me and spins us both inside the privacy of the empty dining room. He smothers me in a fierce embrace.

"It is you!" He hugs the breath right out of me.

"Yes," I gasp. "I'm sorry I deceived you, but I ..."

Luther pulls back but doesn't release me. His eyes reveal an inward struggle of deep emotion and confusion. "But what are you doing here? Why didn't you tell me ...?"

He glances toward the doorway where Eliab's loud voice attempts to regain control. A horrified expression crosses his face. "Did you do this?"

I shake my head, ashamed he would think me a murderer. "No—no, I didn't! I swear. I was going to try to stop it."

He drops his hands to his side. "You knew?"

I desperately want him to touch me again. He has to believe

I'm not to blame. "I thought something might be wrong. The shot glasses ..."

Chambers rounds the corner and nearly collides into us. He stares at Luther and squares his shoulders. "Court Citizen Danforth, what is the meaning of this?"

"The Friend's been poisoned," he says. "I saw Port—this maid—by the bar not long ago."

Blood rushes to my cheeks. *No, no, no! Luther, you have to trust me. I can explain.*

But my words tangle on my tongue. "I didn't ..."

Chambers reaches for me as if to protect me. "The girl's not to blame. She's an overworked and exhausted employee."

I melt against his fatherly grasp. He's trying to shield me.

Luther's eyes don't leave my face as if to discern what's true and what's not. "She told me that she suspected something was wrong. Not doing anything to stop a crime is as bad as perpetrating it."

Chambers gives me a disapproving glare, but then, he can't understand what's happened between Luther and me. "She had just reported a discrepancy with the shot glasses, that one didn't match our collection. I was on my way to investigate when we heard the scream."

"We're too late," Luther mutters. Does he blame himself as well as me?

He shifts his attention to Chambers. "And where is the host? Where's Madame Alexis?"

Chambers hesitates. "She's in her room. She's not feeling well."

I step away from Chambers, bridging the gap between the two men. "Will she come down now?"

"I—It depends," Chambers says. He studies Luther hard as if deciding what to say in his presence.

"What do you mean?" I ask. "The Friend's been murdered in her own home. Some people might even think she's behind her death."

Luther casts a furtive look at the doorway as if worried someone might appear any minute. "I warned her she needed to get away, but she said her duty was here—that she had to block Felix's revision to the satellite laws."

"What revision?" I ask.

He shakes his head. "He worked with Eliab to write an amendment to the Codex rules about prisoner terms."

"How so?" I whisper, fearing I might already know the answer.

"To cut them short—but not by releasing the prisoners. His solution is permanent—early execution. Alexis's blocking vote has been one of the few standing in his way, and she rallied a committee to propose an alternative that would require approval on a case-by-case basis by the Court Citizen system before any satellite could implement his policy."

Luther runs his fingers through his dark hair. "But now, what does it matter? The Friend's been murdered in Alexis's house. Felix can easily discredit her authority and loyalty."

Chambers places a hand on my shoulder and pulls me toward the kitchen. "That's just what those enforcers want—to pin the assassination on her," he says.

I plant my feet to stall for time. Chambers doesn't want me talking with Luther. "Maybe that's what someone planned all along," I say. "Remember the attempt on Madame Alexis's life a few weeks ago? Someone wants her silenced. What better way to dispose of her than blame her for the assassination?"

Luther's face hardens. "If you're right—and I think you are—then the real murderers are …"

An enforcer rounds the corner and immediately salutes Luther. The gesture sends goosebumps down my arms. Enforcers only salute superiors. Does he consider Luther such, because he's working with Eliab?

"Court Citizen Danforth, Commanding Gage Eliab requests your presence." The man jerks his arm to his side and narrows his eyes at Chambers and me. "All household members and employees must report to the ballroom immediately."

Chambers nods his head. "I'll round up the kitchen staff."

The enforcer gives him a hard look. "Anyone who attempts to leave the house will be shot."

"Understood," Chambers says.

"And Court Citizen Danforth, Gage Eliab needs you for the announcement."

"Tell him I'll be right there."

The enforcer clicks his heels and disappears.

"What about Madame Alexis?" I whisper. "She still hasn't come down yet?"

Chambers clears his throat. "You might as well know the truth: I locked her in her room."

"You what?" Luther and I ask in unison.

"It was the only way to protect her. She can't poison someone if she isn't present."

My thoughts blur. Did Chambers know Juliana was going to be murdered? But how?

Luther rubs his cheeks, drawing my attention to the dark rings under his eyes. "It won't matter. Since someone staged the murder here, that person wants to frame Alexis. She has to get away."

Chambers opens his jaw to say something but studies Luther with clear distrust. "Well, now, if you'll excuse us …"

Luther grabs his arm. "You have to get her out of here. I can buy you some time."

"And why would you do that? You work for Gage Eliab. Or are you trying to frame the whole household?"

Luther glares at him. "Alexis is my mentor. I may work for Gage Eliab, but right now, I'm your only chance of helping her."

Chambers puffs out steam. "Fine. There's a back door from her wing of the house. It's an unlikely exit that will take you through the greenhouse and down past the Gates's cottage out back."

"Then you're going with her?" I ask.

He grins at me. "No, you are."

"But I …"

"It's time to hang up your apron, Sage." He presses the key to her room in my palm.

"What?" My jaw nearly unhinges.

"You really should check that mailbox more often," he mutters, "but I'll return the message. Now, go!"

How does he know about the mailbox? Lord Osborne, Orbit, and Darius are the only others aware of its purpose. One of them must have told him. But who?

I stare at the key. "But where do I go—where do I take her?"

"She knows," Chambers says. "You have to help her escape." With that, he rushes toward the kitchen, calling for Mrs. Gates.

Luther spins me toward him. He pokes my glasses above my forehead and stares into my eyes. "You're so changed, but I'd know your voice—and your eyes—anywhere. Is that why you kept your head down?"

I nod softly. His touch sends shockwaves through me. "Oh, Luther, you have no idea," I murmur.

He tugs me to his chest. "I want to understand, but I just found you—and now I'm about to lose you again."

"I …" but Luther stops my words with a kiss that deepens with every borrowed second.

He finally releases me. There's so much I want to say but no words—or breath to say them.

Luther's breath warms my skin. "You taste like mint candy."

I blush deeper. "I'll explain someday."

He brushes a stray curl behind my ear, and then his expression turns serious. "Do you know where Lydia's working?"

"Yes."

He tugs my glasses back onto my nose. "Find Lydia as early as you can tomorrow morning, and I'll have a message waiting for you—and hopefully, a way out of Crystal. I can't lose you again."

My head pounds as Luther and I emerge into the main ballroom. He strides to the center, calling all attention toward himself and Gage Eliab while I slink up the staircase.

Eliab leans toward him and presses something into his hand. I reach the top of the stairs and don't dare look back to see what happens next.

I rarely enter this part of the house, but Rhona made sure I received the full tour. Regardless, I can't miss the banging coming from Madame Alexis's door.

Jamming the key into the lock, I twist it open. She lunges toward me, and it's all I can do to keep her from darting around me. She's trim and a head taller than I am.

Her eyes flash. "What is the meaning of this?"

"Shh!" I press a finger to my lips. "We have to get out of here."

"I'm not going anywhere until ..."

"Yes, you are. You're coming with me right now if you want to live." I glance over my shoulder. I don't have time for a catfight.

"Of all the impertinent ..."

"The Friend's been murdered in your house, and someone is trying to frame you. You either come with me or you rot in Gage Eliab's prison."

Alexis's hand flies to her mouth. "Dear, God!"

I grab her free hand. "Chambers said you know the way out. I'm here to help you."

She allows me to pull her into the hallway. "You're the girl who helped rescue me from the Dome attack, aren't you?"

"Yes, ma'am."

Voices echo from the stairs, and I yank her arm like she's a dog on a leash. "Which way?"

She moistens her lips and casts an anxious glance behind us. "But running makes me look guilty."

"Running saves your life."

Running. The word reminds me of Luther. He's the one who taught me how to run in the first place. Ever since then, I've been doing nothing else.

She swallows. "This way."

I release her hand and follow her through the weaving hallways until we reach a door. Opening it reveals a narrow, metal stairwell into the greenhouse Mr. Gates calls his pride and joy.

I hesitate. "The enforcer said that if they catch anyone escaping, they'll shoot to kill."

"No one knows about this exit—no one but the servants and

281

me."

The spiraling steps are ominously dark and silent, but what choice do we have?

"I'll go first," I say. "If something happens, don't stop for me."

She shakes her head and juts out her chin. "You didn't leave me behind. I'm not leaving you."

There's no time to argue. I start down the metal stairwell, but each step sends clanging tremors up and down the railing. I'm shivering when we reach the bottom.

"All clear?" Alexis asks from behind me.

"Not so fast." A taut figure appears next to an arbor.

"Rhona!" I clutch the bottom rail. "What are you doing here? Where've you been?"

She sashays toward us, but her hand firmly grips a handheld radio. It's like the one the Gage held earlier.

"I've been on official business." She curls her lip. "Turns out, that *See-Say-Save* program of Mr. Caesura's comes with a fair share of perks."

Madame Alexis narrows her eyes. "There's nothing to report from my household."

"Isn't there?" Rhona laughs, then waves her hand in a spiral toward the stairwell. "Then what do you call this? Don't tell me you two decided to go for a stroll while there's a house party underway.

"Oh, and surely you've heard the horrible news about the Friend!" She arches her penciled brows. "I hear the house is under lockdown, so I can't imagine what you two would be doing here—unless you have something to hide."

I step toward her. "What does it matter to you?"

She raises the handheld to her mouth, finger poised to press the push-to-talk button. "Really, Sage, I thought you were smarter than to get mixed up in treason."

"Wait, Rhona!" I take another step closer.

She backs into a glass table by the arbor. "Stay where you are, Sage. If you do exactly what I say, I'll pretend you weren't here."

I freeze, knowing every delay costs us precious time. Behind me, Madame Alexis breathes heavily. She must be as terrified as I am.

I level my voice. "Rhona, someone's trying to frame Madame Alexis. We have to help her."

Rhona sneers. "I don't care about that, Sage. I care about a little bit more happiness before my past catches up."

"But you have to listen ..."

From behind, Madame Alexis pushes me aside, and I stagger into a patch of tomatoes. A familiar zapping sequence fills the air, and Rhona shrieks.

I jump to my feet as Madame Alexis tosses her Taser among some shrubs. It must have been a single cartridge version, not like my old one.

"Come on!" She darts through the greenhouse aisle. I jump over Rhona's unconscious body and race after her to the exit. We crouch inside the doorway, checking for enforcers.

"They're bound to be watching the grounds," she says softly. "But the woods are just beyond. Stay close."

I grin in the dark. This woman has spunk. I want to think that if I'd ever reached the Dome, I would have been her kind of representative.

Like possums in the night, we slink across the dewy grass. In our haste, we both forgot coats. Though the night is not freezing yet, the temperature must be in the low forties.

We reach the cover of the forest, and Alexis picks up the pace. Her long strides are hard to match, and she streaks with familiar ease over the crunchy floor of leaves and twigs.

Shouts ring out behind us. Our small lead time will soon vaporize.

"Quick!" Alexis glances to check that I'm still with her.

I pant and ignore the cramp in my side. I haven't run in a week, but adrenaline compensates for the difference.

She plunges into a clearing, and we land ankle deep in a stream. The icy water pricks my skin, but Alexis waves me on. We run along with the current, and I stagger after her. The loose pebbles and uneven stream bed make speed difficult.

Something howls in the distance. Do the Gages have tracker dogs? I silently bless Alexis. At least the water will cover our scent.

A quarter mile down, we cross to the other side and re-enter the forest's blanket of darkness. Still, Alexis races onward as if each step gives her more energy, as if the distance lets her shed a burden from her shoulders. Her breathing comes regulated and clean.

Ahead, a silvery lake glistens in the moonlight. We break through the trees and slide down a sandy hill onto a narrow beach.

Tucked inside the ledge is a rowboat. We splash toward it, yanking it from the dry ground into the water.

There's only one oar, and Alexis claims it. I scramble inside before she leaves me behind.

This wiry woman amazes me. Her gray hair now streaks wildly across her face, etched with a fierce determination.

We glide silently across the lonely lake. A mournful loon calls to its mate, while a fish snaps the surface for a fly.

I close my eyes and remember another lake, much smaller than this one, where my brother Darius once rowed for me in his homemade boat. We'd fished in secret and shared our fears and dreams.

Now, he seems far away. I can only hope I'm running in the direction that will one day bring us both home.

Chapter 30

Saturday, 5.16.2150
Crystal

Alexis banks the boat on a grassy beach, and I stumble over the side. The freezing, shallow water seeps into my black dress boots, the pair Mrs. Gates had given me after more closely inspecting the leathery brown pair Lord Osborne had provided.

The stillness of the lake helps quiet my pounding chest, and for the first time, I think about how impractical our predicament is.

I'm in my black uniform, having yanked the apron off during our flight in the woods. Alexis wears an elegant sequined dress with a high-cut skirt that has at least allowed her to run easily.

But we're hardly prepared for a hike up the hill that looms more like a mountain above the embankment.

Wind sweeps across the lake, heralding a freezing drizzle. It's light but heavy enough to seep through my dress and chill my core.

Alexis secures the boat to a post on a small beach, using an old rope from the boat. She yanks a tight knot and jerks her head toward the grassy ridge. "This way."

Shivering in my soppy shoes, I follow her. I grow more nervous as I calculate our mounting problems, but she doesn't seem aware of them. She becomes nimbler and more energized as the night drags on.

I climb close behind her, careful not to slip in the mud beginning to form. "Have you been this way before?"

"Shh! Don't talk till we reach the cabin."

Cabin. She knows these woods. That's a relief anyway. If only this cabin can have a fireplace and fuzzy blanket, I'll be content.

We leave the grassy banks surrounding the lake and enter another phase of the forest. A night owl hoots, and something scampers in the bushes nearby.

Alexis doesn't seem concerned or even notice that I jump at every sound. Maybe these parts aren't known for mongrels, but my father's warning to never hike unarmed in the woods rings in my memory. And unless she has a spare Taser, we're completely weaponless.

She stops and peers into the darkness. "There it is," she whispers.

I stare into the forest's blindfold. There's a jagged outcropping ahead. Is that what she means?

Distant howling echoes across the lake. Could the trackers have picked up our scent on the other side of the river? And if they scour the mountainside, what's to keep them from tracing us here?

The rain comes harder and though we're drenched, I breathe easier. It will help cover our tracks and blur our scent.

The rock outcropping looms before us and cuts a semi-circle in the landscape, but the forest has grown around it, mostly concealing it from view.

Alexis waves me around the front and down a gentler path to

leveler ground on the protected side. There, half-built inside the rock and half made of wood sits the cabin.

Alexis fumbles with a combination lock—at least that's what I assume it is. She takes forever getting the right pattern. Thanks to the rain, neither of us can see very well.

Finally, she exhales in relief and twists the metal handle. I follow her inside. Though the rain can't reach us here, droplets continue to fall from my hair and the hem of my dress.

"Close the door, and wait here."

I latch the door, plummeting the interior into an eerie darkness. There's one window, but it's covered.

I reach to remove my glasses and realize with a start they're not there. I must have lost them in the woods.

Lamplight flickers to life, illuminating the single-room cabin. There are both an L-shaped kitchen and a sitting area complete with a couch, twin bed, bookcase and table for two.

Alexis sets the lamp on the table and crouches by the bed and pulls out a drawer. Clever.

"Here." She tosses a folded brown dress at me and grabs a silver one for herself. "We can wear these tonight and hope your dress dries by tomorrow."

"This dress?" There's little chance it will dry by morning.

"Yes, you'll need it tomorrow to buy our tickets out of here." She chuckles as I unfold the dress she gave me. It's at least two inches longer than me. "I'm afraid you won't be able to wear any of mine."

Questions swarm in my head, but I'm too tired to ask any of them. "Are we safe here?"

"As safe as anywhere."

Small consolation.

"Hurry now." She nods at the dress. "You can have the couch. And there's tap water from the sink if you're thirsty, but you'll have to help yourself in the dark. I'm blowing out the lamp in a minute."

"But the window is covered," I protest as I slip out of my dress and into the brown one before draping my uniform over the table to dry.

She shakes her head. "Doesn't matter. Light still gets through. I probably should have gone without the window, but on summer days, it's beautiful to look out."

This must be her retreat. I like this woman more and more.

Except when she blows out the light and I trip on a stool while trying to find a glass. The water must be from a spring because it's fresh and freezing, but it tastes good on my parched throat.

More carefully, I make my way to the couch, feeling along the edges of the room. I fall onto the fabric cushion, yank a scratchy throw blanket on top of me, and pass out.

A firm hand shakes me awake. "Get up!"

My eyes burn from not enough sleep. A small glow from the lamp silhouettes Alexis, or the woman I assume is Alexis.

But her hair is now blonde with short ringlets framing her face, more youthful and less lined with wear.

I elbow myself upright and squint to focus my eyes. "Madame Alexis?"

She cocks her head and laughs. "I fooled you. That's good. Oh, and you can drop the *Madame*. After last night, we should be on a first name basis."

"But how …"

"It's just a wig and some cosmetic contouring." She grabs something from the back of the couch. It's a fuzzy, gray sweater, probably three sizes too big for me. Next to it is a mass of gray curls.

"Get dressed." She nods toward my black uniform, still draped over the table. "Then I need to help you with the wig and your make-up."

I push off my blanket and shiver as the chilly air pricks my skin. "Make-up?"

"Yes, you're going to make a delightful granny."

My dress isn't dry and putting it on makes me even colder. "Can we start a fire? My dress is still damp."

She frowns and hands me the sweater. "Can't risk someone seeing the smoke."

The gray sweater would feel wonderful if soggy synthetic fabric didn't separate it from my skin.

Alexis motions me to sit on the couch facing her. I coat myself with the other blanket as she balances a makeup pallet in one hand.

"Close your eyes." She doesn't have to tell me twice.

"How do you have all this here?" I ask.

She presses something that feels like a pencil to my forehead. "This place is my retreat."

"But the makeup and the wigs …"

She chuckles. "They're my disguises. I like to wander in the marketplace, and some people and enforcers would recognize me in plainclothes. I invented a few personas to conceal my identity but never imagined those outings would prepare me for escaping one day."

"I'm going to be an old woman?"

"Yes, now hold still." Powder brushes my cheeks, and I don't dare breathe. Then, she runs her fingers along my cheeks and around my lips before applying more powder.

I cough and suck in a fresh breath as soon as she pauses.

"Not bad. Open your eyes, and see for yourself." She holds a small mirror out to me, and I stare at an aged version of myself.

Creases etch my forehead, and she's created lines around my mouth to make my cheeks seem saggy. White powder plasters the effect in place.

"Oh, I almost forgot the wig." Alexis grabs the gob of gray curls from the top of the couch and tucks my black hair inside the hair piece.

Now, I really look old. "Am I supposed to be your mother?"

"Yes, dear," she laughs. "Your name is Mrs. Leonora Wembley, and I'm your loving daughter Jasmine."

I grin. "I don't suppose my loving daughter made me breakfast?"

"Breakfast is to go." She nods toward two brown bags by the front door. "It's dry cereal, I'm afraid. Help me fill our canteens, and then we'll leave. We have to make the early train."

"Where are we going?" I grab a canteen from the cabinet and turn on the faucet. At least the pipes didn't freeze last night.

For the first time, Alexis's shoulders tremble. "I have a brother in Chrysolite. I think he might help me."

"You think?" I ask.

She sighs. "I haven't seen him since my draft, more years ago than I care to count. We've communicated by letters over the years."

"When was your last letter to him?" I ask.

Her shoulders slump. "A year ago. He wasn't well at the time, but I couldn't get away to visit him."

"Your brother's house will be the first place Gage Eliab will search for you," I say. "Going to see him will be exactly what he will expect."

Alexis's eyes moisten. "But where else can I go? I have no other family, no friends."

I cap my canteen and start filling hers. "Yes, you do—that is, if you promise not to betray them."

"Who do you mean?" She pulls some granola bars from a kitchen drawer and stuffs them inside a small backpack.

There's no reason I shouldn't tell her. After all, she can't report me now.

"The Brotherhood." I hand her the now-full canteen.

She stiffens and narrows her eyes at me. "I would never accept help from the people who tried to assassinate me and murdered innocent rail workers."

I shake my head. "The Brotherhood wasn't behind those attacks—That's what someone wants you to believe."

Her eyes flash. "I don't care what you've heard, but I won't help a terrorist group."

Blood rushes to my face. "Terrorist group? We're not the ones who strap innocent people into torture machines, starve prisoners on satellites, execute them for personal amusement, and use our nation's soil to appease a global dictator."

She flinches as if I'd slapped her. "How on earth do you know all that?"

I glare at her. "I've experienced your *corrective* equipment and been nearly worked to death on a satellite—before coming here."

"Then you're an escaped prisoner?"

293

I spank the cap on her canteen and slide it to her. "Does it matter? We've both been prisoners, just in different settings."

Her eyes snap at me again. Oh, this woman is proud. "I am a Dome representative, not a prisoner."

I cross my arms. "The Dome is a prison, of sorts. And since you've disagreed with some rather important people, now your colleagues are trying to knock you off."

"I'll fight back."

"You won't win—not that way."

"Then what do you suggest?" she demands.

My thoughts race. Would Darius approve of what I'm about to say? But he isn't here to consult. "Join the Brotherhood," I say. "We can help you, and you can help us."

Her fingers clench around the canteen. "You're a Rogue. Is that it? And you've been spying on me by working in my home?"

"No—it's not like that ..."

Her expression tenses. "Let me guess. You're behind the Friend's assassination. You framed me?"

I shake my head. "You've got this all backward. I had nothing to do with her murder. I was there trying to glean intel for the Brotherhood, and twice, I've risked my neck to save your skin. I thought you were a friend of the people. I guess I was a fool."

"I am a friend of justice," Alexis says, "not a band of Rogues."

I adjust my wig. "You're something of a Rogue yourself, now."

Alexis chokes then sputters to contradict me, but I hold up a hand. "Yes, I am a Rogue and a member of the Brotherhood. You might have even heard of me. I'm Portia Abernathy ..."

Her eyes widen. "You're Abernathy? But your brother ..."

"I know. He's the leader of the Brotherhood."

She steps backward as if to distance the space between us.

I step toward her, losing my patience. "Look, you have two choices. You can go back to your home, be imprisoned, and likely executed. Or, you can trust me. I'll help you any way I can, and I believe my brothers will do the same. We just want a better world, a place where we can actually be free."

"Everyone is a master to someone," she says, but her tone is softer.

"Yes, but we'd prefer to choose."

She slings her backpack on her shoulder and scans the simple room. There's a wistfulness to her expression. Perhaps she yearns for freedom, too.

"I'll go with you," she says at last. "I don't have much of a choice, and maybe, we can help each other." She hands me a maroon purse to complete my outfit.

"Good." I grin. The thing is hideous, but maybe I'm not supposed to have any sense of style at my age.

"Let's go." She slings on her backpack. "We need to catch the early train."

I adjust the sweater and paw at the purse. Inside is a pair of gloves to help hide my young hands and another pair of fake, black glasses. I can't get away from those things.

I shove them up my nose and wink at her. "Don't be hasty, Jasmine darling. There's somewhere we need to go first."

Chapter 31

Sunday, 5.17.2150
Crystal

The fake IDs Alexis made seem to burn a hole in my pocket as I wait at the enforcer's station. Lydia is finishing with another person, and I've already annoyed the Gage by insisting I talk with a woman.

Although he tries to ignore me, I play with the clasp on my purse so that it makes a short popping sound. He keeps mumbling, "Eccentric old hag." He probably thinks I'm too deaf to hear him.

Lydia waves away the woman across from her. The woman sulks toward the door, and Lydia massages her temples. She must be exhausted from the strain of this role.

"Make it quick," the Gage snaps at me. "We're short today."

"Short? Why, son, you are a good deal taller than I am." I rasp my voice in my throat the way I've heard older people do.

He scowls. "Short *staffed.*"

My chest tightens. I wonder if the staffing problem has to do with the Friend's assassination. As far as I can tell, though, no one has made her death public knowledge.

But I'm not about to waste precious time asking this Gage questions that might compromise my cover. I shuffle into the seat, and Lydia studies me with tired eyes. They soften as they rest on my face, but I realize the sympathy is from pity and not recognition. I do look like a ridiculous, perhaps not quite altogether, old woman.

"And what are you here for today?" she asks.

I attempt my best impersonation of Mrs. Gates's motherly vernacular. "Well, dearie, I think there's a problem with my daughter's passport."

She sighs. "Problem?"

"Something about the expiration date." I slip the two fake passports from my purse and grasp them tightly in my hands, knowing Lydia's trained eye will recognize them as frauds. Alexis thinks she is clever, but her versions are children's playthings compared to Lord Osborne's professional imitations.

"Let me see," Lydia says.

I slap them onto the table but keep my gloved thumb pressed on top of them. "My sweet Jasmine thinks her friend Mr. Luther will help us."

Lydia's eyes widen. "Does she? And who is your friend that he can help?"

"He's a good man, studying to be someone important." I cough and choose my words carefully. I want Lydia to recognize me without drawing the attention of the Gage. "Mr. Luther—He gave her a message and told us to come see you. He said you might be able to help us."

Lydia pales, but she nods her head as if my request were routine enough. "Yes, Mr. Luther said I might be expecting someone. But I hardly expected you. May I see those passports?"

I remove my thumb and let her take them. I hold my breath, not because I think Lydia will betray me, but because I don't know what Luther has told her. But one look at the passports, and she'll know I'm not a grandma.

Lydia scans them without even raising an eyebrow and pushes them across the desk toward me. Then, she reaches into a drawer and hands me an envelope. "I'm sorry, but I don't have any more time to give you. Everyone's short today—even the trains are."

She stands and circles her desk to offer me a hand. I take it and wobble to my feet.

Lydia grips my arm and mutters, "Ticket stations are down. You have to catch the train at 0900, or you won't get out. Luther's waiting ..."

Heavy boots clomp behind me. "You've bothered my colleague long enough." The Gage yanks me from Lydia's arm and shoves me toward the door.

I crane my neck to look at Lydia. She slaps her hands together as if wiping away dirt and narrows her eyes. "Now don't test my patience! Next time, I won't let you off this easy."

The Gage snorts, and I hobble out the door, probably quicker than any old lady should be allowed.

Alexis—or, Jasmine—rushes toward me from where she'd been waiting by a vendor's booth in the marketplace. "Mother! Are you all right?"

I grab her arm and point toward the tracks. "We have to hurry. If we don't catch the 0900 train, we're not getting away."

She gasps, "But I don't have tickets! Someone told me the ticketmaster is closed."

I'm still clutching the envelope Lydia gave me. "I have the

tickets."

Arms linked together, we hustle toward the train that steams on the tracks. A few passengers idle on the platform, most keeping their eyes low to avoid the Gages who patrol the place.

"Do you still have our passports?" Alexis hisses in my ear as we fall into a line to board the train.

"Yes, but they're no good," I whisper. "Any Gage will be able to tell they're fake."

"But I ..."

I shake my head and open the envelope. Inside are two tickets. The date of purchase was yesterday night.

Luther must have ordered them shortly after the Friend was killed. My heart swells that he was already planning then how he could help me.

We're five passengers away from the conductor. He's inspecting each ticket and passport with painful detail.

My throat goes dry. There's no way he won't suspect our passports. They're not even quite the right size.

Someone taps my shoulder. "Excuse me, ma'am, but I think you dropped this." Luther's tone is etched with urgency.

Behind me, Alexis lets out a little gasp, but I ignore her and focus on Luther. He gives me two passports and a smile that melts my insides.

"Why—young man—how did you know ..." I stammer. My throat is so tight I don't have to pretend to rasp anymore.

Luther doesn't answer but cuts us in line as we reach the conductor.

"Well, Mr. Danforth!" The conductor taps his cap. The man can't be more than twenty-two. "It's a pleasure having you travel with us today."

"Thanks, Mason." Luther hands him his ticket and passport. The man doesn't even look at them.

Instead, he colors. "Why—I didn't think you'd remember me, sir."

"Not remember a classmate?" Luther chuckles.

Mason cracks an embarrassed smile. "Well, it's just, you're important now, and I ..."

"And you make sure my travels are safe and on time. I can't thank you enough for that."

"Thank you, sir." He returns his travel documents.

Luther takes my hand. "This lady took a nasty fall on the platform, and I promised her daughter I'd see them safely on board."

"Well, well!" Mason clucks his tongue at me. "I'm sorry, ma'am. These old planks aren't what they should be."

"You're too kind," I murmur, holding out our documents.

Luther takes them and dexterously moves the tickets to be on top for the conductor to see first.

Mason snaps the ticket in half and slides his finger inside the passports to inspect them.

"You and Clara still going strong?" Luther asks, moving me past him so I can reach the car railing.

Mason flushes. "You remember, Dirk, don't you?"

Luther grunts. "It's hard to forget someone as roguish as that one."

I hold my breath as Mason lowers his eyes, but he doesn't seem to be focusing on the passports anymore. He perfunctorily flips them open and closed.

"Dirk and she ran away together last month."

"Scoundrel," Luther scowls. He holds out his hand for the

passports and ticket stubs.

Mason presses them inside his palm. "Yeah."

Luther passes them to Alexis. "Keep your chin up, Mason. You'll find the right one. And when you do, never let go."

He grips the back of my arm and follows me up the steps. "I made that mistake once. Next time, I'm not letting her out of my sight—no matter how big the risk."

It's a good thing Luther's holding my arm, or I might have melted.

Mason clears his throat. "Thanks, Danforth. Safe travels to you."

"I appreciate it."

"All aboard!" He calls roughly to the next passenger.

Though he's behind me, Luther guides me through the hallway and into a dining car where he directs me to a booth.

The aroma of soup and sandwiches from behind the service counter remind me how empty my stomach is. My granola bar for breakfast was anything but filling.

Luther leans close and blows on my curls. "You doing all right there, Granny?"

I slant my eyes at him. "How did you spot us so easily?"

He winks. "There aren't many people as short as you, and most old ladies don't have a pinched waistline."

I poke him in the gut. "Mind your manners, Sonny. Is that any way to treat your elders?"

He plants a kiss on my forehead, then grimaces. "Wow, that's a lot of powder."

I swipe a napkin and dab the white dust off his lips. "You can thank my sweet daughter for that."

Alexis presses her fist to her lips to keep from laughing.

"Aren't you two adorable? It's like you've known each other all your lives."

If only she knew.

Luther blushes and straightens. At least the passengers around us seem too busy with their own orders to wonder why a handsome Court Citizen is flirting with a small, old lady.

A clear plastic covers the table, and displayed beneath it is the menu. I tap it with my gloved finger and study it until my face feels less hot.

Coffee. The word blurs on the menu. For a split second, I think of the percolator in Lydia's and my room and the conversations we'd shared over steaming mugs. I miss those times.

Now, she's slaving as a census worker, and I'm on my third—or fourth—name since Luther deposited Gath and me in that train car.

I turn from the menu to my purse. What had happened to our passports after we had boarded?

"Mother, did you lose something?" Alexis asks.

I frown. "Our passports, dear?"

"I have them—and the ones from Mr. ..."

"Call me Luther," he says.

"That will be Mr. Luther to you." I shake a dusty finger at Alexis.

She rolls her eyes and inspects Luther's passports. She bites her lip to keep from laughing and slides one across the table to me.

"I believe that one is yours, Ms. Aimee Cotton."

It's my turn to roll my eyes. "Really?" I mouth at Luther.

He grins and holds up his hands. "What? Aimee's a pretty name, and I figured I'd trip and call you Cotton anyway."

I stare at a modified version of my picture. My hair appears a

303

dark brown, and I'm wearing blue-rimmed glasses. It's a plausible look for Sage Colby but nothing like my disguise today.

He lowers his voice. "Don't let anyone see the pictures until we've been able to adjust your appearances."

"You mean …?"

My question goes unfinished as a waiter appears to take our orders. Luther rambles off his order and nudges me to go next.

"I'd like coffee and a chicken sandwich," I say, though I glance nervously at Alexis. She had conveniently forgotten to put a wallet in my purse.

As soon as the waiter leaves, I prop my elbows on the table and stare at her. "I assume you're picking up the tab today, Jasmine dear?"

"Aimee, have you already forgotten? It's Amelia."

Aimee and Amelia alliterate. Luther would think that's clever.

"But yes, I've got the tab covered." She leans back in her booth, adjusting her blonde curls and looking almost relaxed.

My muscles only start to un-tense when the waiter delivers my steaming coffee mug and a cool pitcher of cream.

I stir in the cream and a pack of sugar, watching the white milk swirl in the dark coffee.

Luther tenses and edges out of the booth. "Well, ma'am, I'm glad you're feeling better, but business calls me away."

The dining door opens, and a trio of Gages enters. Luther strides to greet them, only partially blocking my view.

No one could miss the menacing Gage in the middle. I want to slide under the table. What is Eliab doing on this train?

I flash my eyes at Alexis and shake my head, warning her not to look behind. Her back is to the door, which is a blessing.

I sip my coffee. If Eliab fully enters the car, he'll see everyone and immediately suspect two women sitting by themselves. Even if one is wearing a white wig.

But the dining car is full, which is our only hope of cover, and more people have entered now that the train has started moving.

Alexis perches on her seat and smiles at a stranger beside us. I bury my nose in my coffee cup, unable to handle the suspense any longer and not wanting to make conversation with anyone.

"Excuse me, do you need a place to sit?" she asks. "My mother and I can make room. We don't need the full booth."

"That's very nice of you," a woman's voice replies. "There isn't any place else to sit."

I slant my eyes to briefly observe the older couple. Alexis bothers with some mild pleasantries while I pretend to be off-color in my corner.

"Don't bother about my mother." Alexis reaches to pat my hand, and I pull back. "She's a little cross until her coffee kicks in."

I want to make a face at her, but that might appear immature—something a teenager would do.

Wait, I'm not even a teenager anymore. I was nineteen when I started at the Crystal Globe, but my birthday was in February. It's May now.

I passed into my second decade sometime during my sentence at Warren. There was no cake or celebration. I hadn't even remembered the day.

Who cares about a birthday when you didn't get breakfast?

Twenty. The word sinks in while Alexis continues her idle chatter. I suddenly feel old, not because of years, but because of my experiences.

Most twenty-somethings don't contour creases into their

foreheads and wear gray wigs for a chance to grow old someday.

Despite Luther's attempt to intercept Eliab, the Gages move further into the dining car. Luther positions himself at Eliab's side.

He looks too comfortable there like he belongs next to him.

A sinking feeling in my gut makes me wonder if he does. Had Luther not been talking with Felix and Eliab at that first dinner event? Yet his actions confirm he still cares about me. If only I could talk to him under normal circumstances and not as a fugitive, maybe I could make sense of things.

Luther and his party stride toward the bar but remain standing. Eliab's two companions don't order but watch the room, their eyes sweeping over the occupants like a lighthouse searching for lost ships.

The bar's proximity to our booth both makes me nervous and provides a chance to catch snippets of their conversation.

"You know I don't drink," Luther says.

"Man, after last night, I'd think you'd change your mind."

"I think better when my head's clear."

There's a pause. Eliab must be draining his glass. "You'll think sharper with this poison in your blood."

I shiver. How can Luther tolerate his company?

"Any word on the perpetrators?" Luther asks.

"No, but Alexis and that girl can't get far. This is the last train from Crystal until the new Friend is instated, and there were no ticket sales this morning."

"When is Mr. Caesura planning to make his announcement?"

Felix. He must have gotten his wish, but imagining him as the new Friend makes me shiver.

"Tonight. He and the Rosh agent were meeting this morning."

Rosh agent. The man with Felix at dinner wasn't just a Dome

official. He was a messenger from our nation's landlord, as Darius would say.

But I know only the Rosh League by name, the name famous for destroying the past civilization and enslaving my own.

"Do you think he'll be upping the terms?" Luther asks.

"That's none of our business. We do our jobs."

"Right. Then why are we headed south?"

"Alexis's family lives in Chrysolite, but I won't need much time there to determine if they know anything about her whereabouts."

I hope Alexis is too busy in her conversation with the couple to eavesdrop, or she might lose control knowing her brother is Eliab's next target.

"And what then?"

"We'll be visiting one of the testing facilities for some new— compliance methods. Your role is to observe and report to the panel what I need you to say."

There's a strained silence. Is Eliab referring to the panel that's considering the satellite-thinning program or something else?

"I'm also getting some leads about Warren having problems with escaped prisoners and missing workers," Eliab continues.

"Is that anything new?" Luther asks. "The Wasps always seem to have a hard time keeping control."

"Careful," Eliab warns. "You've never been to a satellite, have you? You can't begin to understand what life there is like. Those posts can drive an enforcer mad."

"I see." Luther's voice is so low I can barely hear.

"If the panel listens to reason, I won't need to waste your time. But if it doesn't, you'll have to trail along when I visit that satellite—and investigate the prisoner discrepancies. Alexis's naïve sense of justice requires more of a paper trail, but you can take care of a few signatures for me. Isn't that right, Danforth?"

Luther laughs nervously but doesn't reply.

"If the reports are true, some of the prisoners in question might interest you."

Someone grabs my free hand resting on the table. "Hello, Mother? Are you listening?" Alexis's brow furrows. She must want to put some distance between Eliab and us. "Hurry up and finish your sandwich. I want to catch some sleep in a passenger car."

I swallow and carefully wrap the sandwich in a napkin. "My teeth are hurting me, Amelia. We can go now. I'll nibble on this later."

The couple who joined us scoots to the side so we can leave. I don't look behind me to see if anyone is watching.

Someone always seems to be.

Chapter 32

Sunday, 5.17.2150
Crystal

I lean against the cool window pane, feeling the train vibrations and wishing I could sleep. But Eliab's words play over in my mind ... *some of the prisoners in question might interest you.*

He specifically referred to Warren and escaped prisoners. But then, Lord Osborne had said he would leave a paper trail for him to find.

Oh, Luther. I miss him already. If he hadn't shown up when he did, Alexis and I might never have passed the conductor's inspection. Luther was watching out for me when I least expected.

And that kiss back at Alexis's home. I touch my lips gently, remembering it. Yes, he still cares for me.

When will I see him again? So far, he and Eliab's troupe haven't bothered with our passenger car. Luther is either keeping him busy in the dining car or making sure to choose a different passenger car than we did.

Considering the circumstances, I shouldn't want to meet

him—not with his current company. But since when does my heart take cues from my head?

A pang of guilt squeezes my chest. How can I think about my own hopeless romance when other people I love are suffering, dying—maybe already dead?

Gath had looked so gaunt, and yet, he'd refused to come with me. Will he be able to survive until I return next month?

More guilt sweeps over me. So much depends on Gath for my feeble plan to even catch fire. With his tunneling experience, he doubtless knows areas in the mines where the air is too dangerous to work, unstable areas where he can easily provoke an explosion. He's also the one who will rally other prisoners to the plan while ensuring they keep silent about it.

How many people will have to die to make my plan work? And will Gath be one of them?

The tiny hope for love I had entertained moments before fizzles inside my breast. I can't let myself love yet. I may not even be able to live with myself if more people I care about suffer because of me.

I choke down a sob. The cost of freedom is so high.

Alexis nudges my shoulder. "Wake up, granny. This is our stop."

If only I had been sleeping.

The train crawls toward the platform. I frown as I recognize it as the capital cube of Chrysoprase and fumble for the ticket stub in my purse. This isn't my home cube. Why would Luther send us here?

Maybe there wasn't an available train going directly to my old cube, and Luther decided to get us as close as he could. This destination would draw less suspicion than someone traveling to a remote, poor one.

Alexis rises from her seat and takes my arm to escort me toward the exit. She's either really good at this acting thing or worried about how silent I've been.

The steam sprays my face. As it fades to reveal the platform and cube beyond, I grip her arm tighter.

This place holds nightmarish memories. Eleven years ago, I had watched Darius graduate here and listened to him refuse his draft. Two days later, I returned for his trial. I lost my brother and best friend that day—and made an enemy of Gage Eliab. I bit him, and he nearly broke my back. And now, he's just a few train cars away and likely still hunting for me.

Eight months ago, I graduated here, was drafted here. I had thought that taking the draft would ultimately save my family and bring Darius home. How wrong I had been.

Alexis's grip tightens as we disembark with other passengers. I take a deep breath and tug her toward the ticket office.

"What now?" she asks.

"We're not home," I whisper. "Not yet."

She glances nervously to her left and then leans closer to my ear. "I think we should come back later—when there are fewer people here. I feel like someone's looking for us."

I follow her gaze to a stout woman standing in the platform's center with her back toward me. She pivots on her heels, scanning the crowd.

My breath catches. With shoulders squared, she seems to be fighting against her mousy timidity. Her dark, thick hair falls to her shoulders. I'd never seen it down like that before, but I'd recognize those opaque plastic glasses and smooth, sweet face anywhere.

"Wait here," I say to Alexis and then shuffle toward the woman.

She seems to sense me and instantly locks eyes with me. I wait until I'm within speaking distance and then drop my passport while pretending to be too stiff to retrieve it.

Her crisp uniform matches the one Lydia wears. It must be the standard attire of an interning candidate.

"You dropped this, ma'am?" Jael's searching eyes squint behind her glasses. Patrick's alterations and Alexis's makeup job have her fooled.

"I'm so clumsy," I say. "Thank you."

She hesitates. "You're welcome."

I sigh and stuff the passport into my purse. I had hoped she would look at the picture and recognize Luther's doctored photo.

If I could, I'd just give her a bear hug. But the platform swarms with Gages and other official personnel.

"You don't happen to know of any good bakeries around here?" I ask. "I have this craving for red velvet cupcakes."

Jael's eyes widen, and a relieved smile breaks on her lips. "Not here, but I know a confectionary in Cube 1519. Shall I take you there? That train leaves in fifteen."

She reaches into her pocket and flashes three tickets. Then, she shoves them inside her coat and lowers her voice. "Where's— your friend?"

I don't answer but wave over Alexis who retreated to a bench near the ticket counter. She's been watching me with a horrified expression. Could she really think I'd betray her after all we've been through?

When she reaches my side, I squeeze her arm reassuringly. "Daughter, this kind lady is going to help us catch the next train."

312

Jael extends her hand to shake Alexis's. "I'm Jael Bennett, assistant to the cube officer at Cube 1519. Your—uh, mother—and I go way back."

If the cube officer hasn't changed, Jael's post must be as unpleasant as Lydia's. That man is as ornery as they come.

"Let's wait off to the side." Jael nods toward wooden benches at the far end of the platform. Most of the seats are taken, but Jael finds one for Alexis not far from where we claim two.

The train we disembarked chugs away. Luther didn't get off, buying us some time while Eliab pursues a rabbit trail to Chrysolite. When he discovers Alexis isn't at her brother's, there's no telling where he'll go next.

But hopefully, we'll be safely stowed away somewhere by the Brotherhood and too far off his radar to locate.

"I can't believe it's you," Jael whispers. "I thought you were dead."

"How did you know we were coming?" I ask.

"Lydia messaged me on the wire. Luther told her it was urgent but said chances were slim you'd actually make the train."

"Wire? What do you mean?"

Her lips part in a sly grin. "You're not the only girl on board with this revolution."

Revolution. Chills run down my spine, yet there isn't a better word to describe the desperate attempts of a threadbare band of brothers. And sisters.

Jael folds her arms and stares into the distance as if she weren't really talking to me. "After you disappeared, I figured I had two choices: live as a pawn like Felix or risk everything like you did to make a difference."

Jael sucks in a deep breath. "I chose to put on my big girl boots and brave up."

"You've always been brave, Jael."

She shakes her head. "No, I haven't. I didn't realize what a coward I was until I met you."

Now it's my turn to disagree. "We all have to fight our inner cowards. Some rounds go better than others."

I pause. "But you mentioned a wire. What's that about?"

"That's your brother's handiwork and a credit to your father, too. Darius created his own Morse code line, and our brothers ran it through the tunnels your father engineered."

"Dad …" I swallow. "What's the word on my father?"

Jael's brow creases. "I've never met him, only heard of him. I also heard he was in the explosion."

"So was Foxworth," I say. "Have you met him?"

She blushes. "Yes, Fox and I work together. He's the one who helped connect me with our brothers when I was first assigned to the cube enforcer's office."

Fox? I bite my lip to keep from smiling too broadly at her rosy cheeks.

"He didn't trust me at first." She laughs softly. "But Lydia confirmed my story about voting in your favor at the trial. After she talked to Darius, he talked to Fox."

My head swirls. Lydia and Jael both stepped up to the plate when I got shipped away. "But how?" I frown. "How did Lydia find Darius?"

"Luther pointed her in the right direction," Jael says.

A distant whistle blows, though I can't yet see the train that will take me to the place I once called home.

"But Luther doesn't know Darius is still alive," I say.

She scans the platform as if searching for something. Though she seems satisfied not to find it, she sits straighter as the train nears. "I'm sorry, what were you saying?"

"I was saying that as far as Luther knows, Darius died on a satellite," I repeat. "I never had the chance to tell him my brother is still alive."

"Well, he knows now," Jael says. "When Lydia first connected them on the wire, they messaged all the time—though not as much anymore."

The questions cross my mind too quickly for me to process them. I stare at Jael with eyes that plead for answers.

She flashes a sympathetic smile. "I'll try to explain, but we don't have much time before the train gets here. I need to distance myself from you as well … don't want anyone thinking we're more than acquaintances."

I nod and wait for her to continue.

Jael rises and pretends to pick at some lint on her uniform. "Luther told Lydia you had met a man called Red on one of your outings. The next trip to Cube 1776, Lydia hopped on the train with the other Trippers to find him."

Lydia had hated the idea of those outings and refused to go while we were roommates, and yet, she had gone in the end to find Red.

"Yes, she told me that much," I say.

"Once she convinced Red that she was your friend, he connected her to Darius. She then brought Luther and me into the loop." Jael pauses to grin. "You should have heard her trying to make Luther believe your brother is still alive. I guess you three had been pretty close growing up."

"Yes," I murmur softly. "We were like a three-strand cord—an unbreakable friendship."

"Red set up a secret wire connection for Lydia to use, and she arranged for Darius and Luther to message each other," she explains. "Once Luther realized he was messaging his old friend, he immediately told him that he'd changed your satellite sentence location at the last minute. He said you and Gath went to a place called Warren instead of Baytown. Darius promised he knew someone who could help break you out."

She pauses as a shadow crosses her face. "But as time passed, Luther became increasingly angry with Darius, because it was taking him so long to rescue you. Darius insisted he was doing everything he could, but that his—underground contact—was blocking him.

"Then, about that time, Luther received his internship assignment with Felix and that awful Gage Eliab, making any wire communications with Darius limited. I think your time at Warren, along with the recent attacks done by Brotherhood imposters, put a real strain on their friendship."

The image of Darius and Luther arguing about me reminds me of Luther's childhood pledge to Darius—that he would take care of me if anything happened to my brother. Now, they're both trying to take care of me but don't understand each other's methods.

"Has Luther talked to Darius since I arrived in Crystal?" I ask.

Jael shifts her attention to the platform. "The first time was last night. He sent word on the wire that he'd found you and was arranging for your transport to 'Prase. We haven't heard anything from him since."

I smile softly. "He helped smuggle Alexis and me onto the train this morning, and he's actually still on it, riding undercover with Gage Eliab."

316

Jael sighs. "Poor guy. Working with that Gage has to be one tough job."

My heart swells. How did a girl like me get lucky to have friends like these? And to think that a few months ago, I didn't think true friends existed. Again, I'd been so wrong.

Since I've been gone, Luther has been helping unite my friends, my family—and feverishly trying to find me. Though he's arranged for my safety, he's still in danger.

Jael changes her tone. "When our train arrives in your old cube, don't go to your family's house. It's been watched ever since I've started working for the enforcer's office. Instead, go to your neighbor's house."

"Neighbor? Dad and I never talked with our neighbors."

She wrinkles her nose. "Then now is a good time to start."

I gape at her. "But which one?"

"The closest one," she says, impatiently, and then walks away.

I stare after her. Jael is still full of surprises, many of which I am only beginning to understand.

Chapter 33

Sunday, 5.17.2150
Chrysoprase

I don't remember much about my neighbor, except his grizzled face, which hasn't changed. It remains twisted with suspicion. "Can I help you?"

Alexis nudges me to start talking. I stammer to explain. "We're—we're looking for someone."

His lips part, revealing cracked teeth and one gold crown. "Everybody's looking for somebody."

Jael had disappeared inside the cube enforcer's office as soon as the train pulled into Cube 1519. She provided no further directions.

We should have waited for her before coming here. This man is going to think we're crazy, that we don't know what we're talking about.

He'd be about right.

"Well?" He gnaws on something, probably chewing tobacco, inside his cheek and then wads it up in the other one.

I blow out a breath. "I'm looking for my father." It's practically the same line I used during the only other conversation I'd had with this man on that desperate night so long ago.

He squints at me. "Ain't you a little old to find your pappy? I'm guessing he's crossed on yonder."

His words strike too close to what might be the truth. I shift my gaze over my shoulder, very much doubting I can say anything to convince this man to help us. Does Jael even know what she's talking about? At this rate, I'd have better luck if I went looking for that old quarry on my own and left Alexis behind.

"You'll have to forgive her." Alexis's words and impatient tone return my focus to my former neighbor. "We've had a long journey, and a friend told us that one of her old neighbors might be able to help us—give us a place to rest until she gets off work. We're sorry to have bothered you."

Alexis links her arm inside mine and steers me away.

"Wait!" The man hollers after us. "I—I am expectin' some company. My friend told me some—neighbors—might call. Maybe that's you."

Alexis pauses and guides me to the door, still maintaining her iron-like grip on my arm. I suspect it has less to do with my appearance and more with annoyance. "Would you tell your friend that Ms. Cotton and her companion have arrived?"

The man's eyes flash. He nods vigorously and beckons us inside.

Cotton. I had wanted to hear Luther call me that again. Now, thanks to him, it seems the nickname has become another alias.

The one-room house is cramped and dusty, with a cluttered counter, dirty dishes, and other signs of bachelorhood.

He makes room for us on a tattered couch. I wince, worried

that Alexis will scorn such an offer.

Instead, her face softens. "Thank you for having us. We've had a very long journey, and your place feels ... inviting." She finishes with a gracious smile.

The man grins bashfully. "That's the nicest thing someone's said about this place. Can I get you some coffee?"

Alexis catches my eye, and I give a subtle shake of my wig, remembering the "poor-folks" molasses-like version Red had served.

"Just water would be wonderful." She offers another smile.

"You bet." He turns to the small sink, and Alexis distracts herself with a stenciled picture on the wall. I guess she'd rather not know where her cup comes from.

"There you go ..." He hands us each a cup, but his voice trails off. He instantly straightens, and I follow his example.

"What?" I whisper, but he spins and disappears into a small closet or possibly a pantry.

Alexis holds up a finger, and only then do I hear the faint series of taps.

A memory stirs. During my first outing with the Trippers, Red had made a similar noise on that panel in his kitchen, the one he had covered with his kitchen apron. Perhaps this is the Morse Code system Jael had mentioned.

Our host appears moments later, his expression tight. "Follow me."

I jolt upright, faster even than Alexis. The man's eyes widen.

Oh, right. Alexis is supposed to grip my arm and yank me around. Well, I'm done playing. This man is either our friend or not, and regardless, the twitching of his mouth suggests that something is wrong.

He leads us out back to a woodshed. Because I'm short, I'm the only one who doesn't have to duck under the doorway.

The interior reveals wood storage as well as a thick workshop counter and bench. The wood-paneled floor is covered with woodchips and a healthy layer of dirt.

As soon as he shuts the door, the man falls to his knees and slides his hand across the floor's messy surface. There's a small click, and a narrow panel pops open.

It's a secret entrance, a tunnel perhaps? He must have designed a hidden latch, practically invisible to the eye and concealed by the wood chippings. I study this man with new curiosity and wonder what an interesting personality my former neighbor might be.

He stands over the entrance. "Hurry. A busybody told the cube enforcer that two strangers, not from these parts, came this way. They're searching houses."

"Where does it lead?" I ask, jumping down.

"Go left at every fork." His gnarly hand pushes the panel closed almost before Alexis slides all the way inside.

"But …"

"Shh!"

There's a scraping noise, and sawdust falls through the cracks. He must be covering up the panel with the wood chips again. I fumble deeper inside the tunnel, covering my mouth to keep from choking.

My boot kicks a metal, oblong object. I drop to my knees and grope for what I hope is a flashlight.

My hands brush against the cool metal and feel for the switch. The light filters through the dusty space, and I retreat deeper into the tunnel, hoping for cleaner air. Behind me, Alexis tumbles forward to catch up.

I'm not waiting to hear if someone finds my neighbor in the woodshed. If enforcement discovers this tunnel, I plan to be far enough ahead of them to have a decent chance of escape.

Training the light low, I maneuver comfortably through the single-file space. Alexis follows silently, except for the occasional grunt when her head hits the ceiling.

My height is a definite advantage in confined spaces.

I walk past the first fork before I realize it's there. It's nothing but a hole in the rocky, clay wall.

"Left," I whisper. Even I have to crouch this time.

"Are you sure this is the way? It's awfully small." Her eyes flash fear and her expression borders on panic. She's probably never experienced this type of confined space. After my work in the mines, though, this place feels like a playground.

"He said left at every fork. If it's a dead end, we'll come back here." I plunge ahead, not giving her time to think. We can't go back, so there's no point catering to her fear, though I do feel sorry for her.

It's not a dead end, and we continue through the catacomb-like tunnels. The Egyptian visual makes me think of Jael. She had been fascinated with the text on Egypt during our trip to the archives.

Was she in trouble for not intercepting the two "strangers" at the station?

I wonder why I didn't think of this problem sooner ... probably my lack of sleep. Anyone visiting a cube—whether for school, work, or family—had to present passports. With the exception of my Tripping outings, I'd always done so.

But for Alexis and me, checking in with the cube enforcer

would have been pointless. Luther's passport pictures don't match our current disguises, and Luther wasn't here to help us bluff through inspection.

Behind me, Alexis's breathing comes heavier.

"Are you all right back there?" I call.

"I—I don't like tight places." Her voice quivers. "Just keep talking to me."

"Okay, why don't you tell me how you know Luther."

"As long as you promise to tell me how you know him."

"Deal."

She takes a trembling breath. "In the Dome, I'm on the committee for welcoming our interns. Part of the process involves assigning them mentors from our existing Dome representatives. I only get to mentor one, and I want that one to count.

"Most of the candidates are cocky and full of their own self-importance. When I introduce myself as a Tooler, I explain the hard, manual work and sweat that goes into my profession. I also talk about traits like honesty, integrity, and a strong work ethic. Most of the candidates turn up their noses at me, except the ones in my own profession. However, a mentor must be from a different profession, because the role is to provide objectivity."

Alexis's breathing has become more regulated. Good. She's forgetting her surroundings and focusing on the story.

Her voice even takes on a lighter tone. "Only one candidate outside the Tooler profession came up to me after my speech. He thanked me for my challenge and said he would be honored to learn from me. I was doubly shocked because he was both a man and an elite Court Citizen candidate. Most of the candidates I mentor are women because many men are chauvinists."

"Let me guess," I say with a smile. "That man was Luther."

"Yes, and what a fine young man he is." There's no missing the admiration in her voice. "After two months mentoring him, I began to realize he was also mentoring me. About that time, Felix Caesura, as part of his Revisionary internship, introduced a proposed change to the Codex. At first, I found the motion innocent enough. Most representatives don't waste too much time with satellite laws.

"But our Ethics Committee raised a red flag, and I looked closer at the amendment. Buried beneath flowery language was a new rule that would allow Wasps–with no oversight—to perform a *cleaning*. That's just a nice term for executing in mass prisoners who have served over three months or have proven unruly. In other words, Wasps could overrule the prisoners' sentences."

I shiver. "That's awful."

"Awful. Inhumane. Unlawful." Her voice rises to a shrill cry. "It was all those things and more. I led a counter-initiative to block it. Shortly after that, the attempt on my life occurred. Thanks to you and Luther, the assassins were unsuccessful."

"What happened to the proposal?" I ask.

"A few other representatives and I worked with the Ethics Committee to revise the counter-initiative. Our version would require a Court Citizen to personally inspect the satellite conditions and prisoners to determine if a large-scale *cleaning*—I hate that word—was appropriate. At least it would require a limited form of checks and balances."

"Check and balances?" I ask. "I haven't heard that expression before."

"Only Revisionary candidates completing their training would know it. And they would only spurn it." Alexis spits the final words, then continues. "It's a term from the last civilization, and the Crystal Globe doesn't teach the concept anymore."

I pause at another left turn and hope Alexis won't notice that the walls are even tighter. "What does it mean?"

"Back then, there were three branches of government, and each one was accountable to the other. If one branch became corrupt, the other two were still able to 'check' its power."

"Sounds like a smart idea," I say. "Is that essentially what our Dome does now?"

She hesitates. "The Friend oversees the Dome, but representatives do have limited power, mostly when we band together in a committee. But then there are threats, and many representatives aren't willing to risk their personal safety even for something they think is right or wrong."

"Threats?"

"Ours is an imperfect system, Portia, but then, aren't all governments?" She sighs. "Luther warned me that I needed to let some other representatives stand up for the counter-initiative, but I didn't listen. I wasn't sure anyone else would fight for it—and I wasn't about to let him try. Gage Eliab scrutinizes him because he's at the top of his class. I fear he may even try to abuse his role as Court Citizen to serve his purposes."

My heart twists as I think back to the conversation I overheard on the train. I hate that my enemy now wields influence over Luther.

"But how do you know Luther?" she asks. "I saw the way he looks at you. Not many handsome men look at old ladies that way."

I chuckle and wipe some of the powder off my perspiring forehead. Then, I dive into my story.

After what feels like an hour, the tunnel suddenly widens. I've been so focused on retelling my own memories that I hadn't noticed the transformation of the walls from clay to solid rock.

"I think we're here." I step into a stone room, much like the one where I had last seen my father. If my hunch is right, we've reached the stone quarry cave.

"Finally." Alexis slumps to the floor and places her head between her knees.

I squat beside her. And here I'd thought that all the talking had helped. "You okay?"

She keeps her head low. "Yes, I'm a little dizzy—probably dehydrated. Give me a minute."

"I'll be around the corner," I say. "I want to see what's ahead."

Alexis reaches for my wrist. "No, don't leave me."

I pat her hand and press the light against it. "Here, you can hold the flashlight."

She accepts it like a lifeline. Maybe I should have let her carry it sooner.

I slip my wrist free. "Listen, there's a faint light ahead. I'm going to check it out. Relax, and I'll be right back."

She nods. "I just need a minute."

"And that's all I'll need to see what's ahead." I try not to seem eager to leave her, but as I round the corner, I'm almost sure we're in the same cave where Foxworth brought me before. If we are, maybe Foxworth—even Darius—aren't far away.

My boot slips and sends a stream of pebbles pouring down the rocky floor before me.

I skid, arms flailing in an attempt to keep my balance, and tumble forward until the floor levels out. My shoulder slams into a rock wall, and I wince at the pain, though nothing feels broken.

"Osborne hasn't given you any training in stealth." The wry voice echoes in the cavernous room.

I shake off a daze and squint in the dim light. A long, wiry man strides toward me. He's carrying a lantern, which casts shadowy fingers across his cheek.

Wait, those aren't shadows. The side of his face illuminated by the lantern is a melted scar of skin, stretched tautly around his clear blue eye.

"Foxworth?" I whisper.

He snickers. "Yeah, the fire from that tunnel explosion couldn't catch all of me anyway. I was too fast for it."

My throat goes dry as his whole frame comes into focus. Only the left side of his face is burned, as is his hand holding the lantern. His right side appears normal.

I look away. "I'm sorry."

"Don't be." He steps closer, forcing me to make eye contact. "I'm as fast as ever, and I recovered quickly, thanks to our network of Healers."

He winks. "Besides, Jael says the scars give me *presence*, whatever that means."

Jael? She had called him Fox. I grin, thinking what a strange match these two make. Yet, they seem to complement each other. She isn't the timid, uncertain candidate I had met months ago, and Foxworth is more approachable, despite his scars.

"The tunnel explosion." I gulp. "You made it out safely, but Darius said Dad was with you. What happened to him?"

He hedges. "Didn't Darius tell you?"

"Tell me what?" I demand.

A noise behind us pulls my attention away from his uncertain eyes. "Portia? Where are you?"

Alexis. I groan as guilt sweeps over me. I had told her I would only be gone a minute. "That's my companion," I say. "She's not a fan of confined spaces."

"You mean the Dome representative you helped steal away?" Foxworth follows as I retrace my steps.

"Yes, Madame Alexis."

He frowns. "Have you talked to Darius?"

"No, there wasn't any time or way for me to communicate with him. The assassination happened so fast, and I had to get Alexis out of Crystal."

He lowers his voice. "This is a big problem—the kind of thing you need to clear with Darius first. What if one of those Crystal Gages picks up your scent and traces you here? Someone already tipped off the cube enforcer that two strangers disembarked. If they put two and two together, they could trace you to Husk's. He won't talk, but you'll have his blood on your hands."

I stop abruptly. "What was I supposed to do? Chambers threw Alexis and me together."

"Who is Chambers?" he demands.

I gape at him. "I assumed he was one of us after the way he acted."

"We don't have any insiders left inside Crystal—except for Lydia and Luther."

His words sink in. If Chambers isn't part of the Brotherhood but knew about the mailbox, then the only other option is that he's another agent for Lord Osborne. But since when does my employer care about a Dome representative?

Alexis's voice calls out to us again. It's closer, louder.

I can't think about Osborne right now. "I had no choice but to help her escape. Felix staged the Friend's assassination to frame her, and as far as I know, she's the only level-headed representative in the Dome. She might even help us. I couldn't let him kill her."

Foxworth's eyes widen. "Wait, the Friend is dead?"

"You haven't heard? Her son Felix—at least I think he's to blame—poisoned her last night. There hasn't been an announcement yet, but I thought you might have known."

He shakes his head. "You are—or were—our best intel, but bringing her here is a huge risk. I'm just worried Darius isn't going to approve."

I sigh. "Then wait till he hears what else I've set in motion."

There's a mix of respect and worry on Foxworth's face. "I'm afraid to ask."

"There you are!" Alexis's flashlight beam glares in my eyes.

I wince and step out of the light. "I'm sorry. I found one of our brothers. We were about to come back for you."

"Our brothers?" The edge in her voice makes me groan. Either she's tired and angry with me for leaving her, or bringing her here was not the best move on my part.

"Yes, our brothers," I say firmly. "We're offering you shelter and protection. We only ask that you keep our confidence."

I hold my breath and watch as she and Foxworth size the other up. Foxworth might be angry with me for speaking on behalf of the Brotherhood, and Alexis could very well stab me in the back.

She slowly extends a hand for Foxworth to shake. "I'm sorry. You'll have to forgive me. I haven't slept much. This girl saved my life, and I owe you—and your Brotherhood—a debt of gratitude."

Foxworth nods, approvingly. "Welcome to our refuge. We don't turn away those in trouble. We're pretty used to living with it."

Chapter 34

Sunday, 5.17.2150
Chrysoprase

Foxworth serves wild potato stew that helps thaw Alexis's and my frayed nerves. She seems much more relaxed around the fire, which casts a gentle glow off the cave room's wall.

I can't tell if it's the darkness or confined space that bothers Alexis more. Maybe it's both.

She's no sooner finished her bowl than she slouches lower against the cave wall, and her eyelids flutter to stay awake.

Foxworth has barely spoken since leading us here and feeding us. He probably doesn't know what to do with Alexis, and I can't blame him. But now, I'm in the awkward spot of convincing the Brotherhood to help her or figuring out how to move her to the Excivis for shelter.

I frown. Was that what Chambers thought I would do all along? But what interest does Lord Osborne have in Alexis? Why would he want to protect her?

Or does he simply want to use her, the same way he's using

me, to get something he wants? I shiver, despite the warm coals. My eyelids feel gritty and scratchy, thanks to all the excess powder clumping on my face. I yank the wig off and use it to wipe off some of the make-up. What I really need is a shower and sleep.

If Foxworth doesn't want to talk, I should follow Alexis's example and get some shut-eye. But as I close my eyes, he shifts toward me.

I blink. He's shaking his head—What is that supposed to mean?

Foxworth disappears outside the room, returning moments later with a blanket.

I sigh. He's a thoughtful one. Maybe that's why Jael likes him.

Without a sound, he slips toward Alexis, gently placing the blanket around her shoulders. Unconsciously, she snuggles into it. She's already asleep.

Okay, where's my blanket?

He holds a finger to his lips and motions me to follow him. I force my stiff limbs into service and crawl after him into the main tunnel.

As pins and needles prick my left leg, I hobble to lean against a wall. "What is it?"

"We need to go." He nods toward a dark pathway. "There's a meeting tonight. As soon as Lydia relayed that you were coming, Darius called us together, and I'm supposed to bring you."

"Darius?" I whisper. "You mean, he's here?"

Foxworth gives me a wry smile. "Not here. We have about a five-mile jog to the meeting place where he and the others will be waiting."

My heart sinks. Five miles and jog do not belong together in any sentence right now. "Five miles? I can barely keep my eyes open."

He winks. "You're out of practice, then?"

I rub my tingling leg. "I ran through a forest last night and walked for hours to get back to Crystal to catch a train this morning, wondering at every turn how we would even survive. I overdosed on adrenaline the last 24 hours, so I'm a little shot right now."

With his scarred face, Foxworth doesn't change expressions much, but his eyes seem to soften. "I know you're tired, but this is important. You need to update Darius and the others about the Friend and any other news that might help us brace for the transition of power—and we need to talk about the Dome representative."

"Others?" I repeat. "Who else is coming?"

"As many as can make it," he says. "Seeing that they had a whole day's notice, I expect our meeting will be a good-sized group."

I wrinkle my nose. "Wait, how did you know I'd actually reach 'Prase in one piece?"

His skin stretches to a half-grin. "You managed to escape Warren, didn't you?"

I snort. "Barely."

"Barely counts." He stuffs his hand into his pocket and pulls out a small flashlight.

I glance over my shoulder. "What about Alexis?"

"She'll still be asleep when we get back."

"But what if she wakes up?"

He shakes his head. "She won't—not after what I put in her stew."

I roll my eyes. "Great. You drugged her?"

"Yep."

"Then I sure hope you put an extra dose of energy in mine." I follow him down another dark, narrow tunnel.

Dad spent most of my growing up years building these tunnels without telling me. Alexis may find them suffocating, but I find them inviting as if a missing piece of me is somehow close.

I want to ask Foxworth about Dad, now that we're alone, but he wasn't kidding when he said jog. It's all I can do to breathe, not trip, and keep his flashlight in view.

We wind through the tunnels and then emerge into a depressed meadow. The night wind slaps my face and makes me run faster to stay close to Foxworth. We're in mongrel territory, though those beasts almost seem friendly compared to the Gages hunting for Alexis and me.

Despite the cold, I break a sweat. I'm tempted to throw off the gray sweater but can't leave it behind for someone to find and trace me. Besides, I'll probably be freezing again once my blood has a chance to settle.

We enter a rocky outcropping and plunge into another hole in the ground. This one is even a tight squeeze for me, but if Foxworth can fit, I can, too.

Light gleams at the end of the tunnel, and Foxworth quickens his pace. As the light grows closer, the walls broaden until we reach a rock-like doorframe.

Foxworth plunges ahead without pausing, but I no longer need his light. I press my hands to my knees, panting like a dog and trying to catch my breath.

But the sight before me takes what little I have left away.

A dozen or so men and a few women form a jagged semi-circle in the dome-shaped room. They're seated on stone slabs in a jigsaw pattern, whispering softly among themselves. Each has his own lantern, which collectively fills the space with a soft aura.

As Foxworth descends to the floor, they all stand. Many hands go straight to their sidearms but relax as they recognize him.

One man at the front of the group glances past him toward where I hesitate at the entrance above. The lantern's glow glints off his coppery brown hair. My brother's eyes light up, and he darts toward me. Even though I look nothing like the Portia he once knew, I'm the girl Foxworth brought and by default his sister.

A surge of energy propels me forward, and we meet halfway on the rocky stairway to the floor. His strong arms enfold me, and I lean into his chest, feeling the closest to home I have in a long time.

"I'm sorry for what's happened to you," Darius whispers. "I couldn't protect you like I'd wanted."

I nod, not wanting to spoil the moment. "But you didn't leave me alone. I had Gath."

"Gath." Darius pulls back to search my eyes. "How is he?"

"He's still at Warren." I gulp.

"But he's alive?"

"I hope so."

The space behind us has grown still as if the others don't want to spoil our reunion. Darius wraps an arm around my shoulder and leads me down the rest of the stone steps to the floor. "Brothers and sisters," he begins, "I'm honored for you to finally meet Portia, my sister and a credit to us all." His voice echoes off the walls and is soon swallowed by their cheers.

Yes, cheers. I blink in surprise and scan the faces. Standing heads above the others is Red, my old friend from Cube 1776.

He steps forward and greets me with his own bear hug. "I

knew you were something special. I'm proud of how brave and strong you've become."

His embrace feels so much like Dad's. "What do you mean?"

Red grins. "What? Didn't you notice that tall shadow trailing your steps?"

I gasp. "You mean—You've been following me?"

He nods. "Anytime you traveled between Crystal and Jasper, I followed to make sure you arrived safely. It's the least I could do—for Darius and for your dad."

"Dad?" I whisper.

He gives me a cryptic smile. "I'm sure that wherever he is, he's right proud of you, too."

Before I can ask him more, his smile tightens with regret. "Wish we could have kept you out of that hellhole."

A woman half his size steps from behind him and cuts my conversation with Red short. She's no longer wearing her uniform but corduroy pants and a thick sweater.

"Portia!" Jael cries and wraps her arms around me. I squeeze her tightly. Goodness, this is like some crazy family reunion—except Dad's still missing.

She readjusts her glasses. "You made it. I was worried after that nosy-Rosie reported two strangers had left the train. Thankfully, she has a reputation for being a gossip, and I was able to discredit her story and convince the enforcer she had only seen two women, already registered in our cube."

The only other member I recognize is Husk, my old neighbor. I'm relieved he's here and not spending the night in the cube enforcer's cage.

Darius motions for everyone to quiet down. I'm only too happy to fall onto a cool stone nearby. Foxworth claims a spot possessively close to Jael.

"Thanks for making the trip," Darius begins. "I want to give Portia time to fill us in on events in Crystal, but first, is there anything you haven't been able to share on the wire?"

Close to my right, Red clears his throat. "Randolph couldn't be here today—too busy running his tavern to get away—but messaged me about something strange a recent lodger from the coast reported. The man said someone had seen a black iron 'boat' emerge from under the water's surface by the port. A small company of men had disembarked, but their uniforms didn't match the Dome members. They spoke with an accent, too."

"Sounds like a submarine, just like that message we intercepted suggested," Darius says. "When was this?"

"A few days ago," Red replies. "Who do you think they are?"

Darius frowns. "The message we picked up didn't say."

"Could be a Rosh representative," I say.

Darius arches an eyebrow and turns to me. "Why do you say that?"

"There was a strange man talking with Felix Caesura at Alexis's house party," I explain.

"When was the party?"

"Last night—when the Friend was assassinated."

Murmurs fill the room, and Darius's own eyes grow wide. "Assassinated?"

"Yes, her son Felix and his Gage escort tried to pin the murder on Alexis, which is why I had to help her escape."

"Maybe you should start at the beginning," Darius says quietly.

The coals of the fire inside the cave room glow dimmer when I finish. No one bothered to stir them, and my story starting at Warren to the present took well over an hour. I didn't leave anything out—including the pipeliner's mission to lay the groundwork for a chain-reaction rebellion across the satellites.

Red puffs out a breath and shakes his head. "So, the plan is to coordinate synchronized explosions across the satellites?"

I purse my lips and nod. Even to my own ears, the plan sounds impossible.

Though I had tried not to focus on Darius while retelling my story, I couldn't miss his body language. He grew increasingly more rigid as the creases in his face deepened.

Is he angry because so many lives are at stake? Or is he angry because I gave an order without asking him first?

"There's no way to communicate among the rebels inside the satellites," he says at last. "What if they can't find explosive materials at some of the camps? Having only one or two explosions is going to look like a minor rebellion, easily subdued. The Wasps will kill everyone involved—and then some just for fun."

I swallow and wish my throat didn't feel like sandpaper. "Prisoners are resourceful. They'll find a way if it means a chance to live. They already know the plan. They just have to find a way to make it work."

Darius grunts. "Easier said than done."

Red shifts his weight and stares at my brother. "It's no more difficult than the stunt you pulled at Baytown years ago."

Darius rises to poke the coals. "That was different. Baytown was only one satellite, and I'd mapped out the plan a hundred times before actually presenting it to the other inmates. And then we hashed it out some more. This plan only has a date and a goal but no details. You're placing a lot of weight on the ability of prisoners you've never even met, living in circumstances you can't even imagine."

I stiffen my upper lip. "I survived in Warren for three months. I think I can imagine."

Darius gives me a half smile. "Portia, Warren is a playground compared to Baytown."

"Then tell me about Baytown." I cross my arms. "And is Red referring to what people call the Baytown Uprising?"

My brother nods but focuses his attention on the coals, now glowing a deeper red.

I probe, despite the rigidness in his jaw. "And is Baytown where you met Gath? Someone said he was a Wasp there. Is that true?"

Darius slowly spins and sits with legs akimbo on the dirty rock floor. "I guess it's my turn to tell a story." He scans the rest of the group who have remained so quiet I had almost forgotten them. "Some of you have a long journey ahead of you. If you need to leave, go ahead."

The others shake their heads. Foxworth reads their expressions and seems to answer for them all. "We need to know what our plan is, and if we're mobilizing to support the satellite uprising. Though we can't communicate with those planning the explosions, we can stand ready to rescue them afterward and arrange homes for them to hideout until the worst of the Dome's wrath passes."

"But if the plan works, do we even need to worry about the

Dome?" Darius asks. "It sounds like Portia expects the new Friend—presumably Juliana's son—to try to escape somewhere with what's left of his loyal Gages." The skepticism in his voice borders on sarcastic.

I wince and respond in a shaking voice. "That's the best-case scenario, yes. Once word of the destroyed satellites spreads and word leaks out how the Dome has been treating prisoners, I hope most of the citizens will finally revolt against the few enforcers who stand over them. Even though the Gages in the squares have many advantages, they're outnumbered if the citizens actually band together."

Foxworth exchanges a look with Jael, who gives an affirmative shake of her head. "We know plans don't often go the way we want, but this domino effect is certainly possible. Either way, if we're backing this plan, we need to get busy making preparations. People need to be ready to spread the word of the explosions and the truth about the satellites. We'll also need to mobilize teams after the explosions to evacuate the surviving prisoners."

Surviving prisoners. I shudder, but Foxworth is right. Many will die in this plan I've set in motion. But perhaps many will become free because of it. Is the risk worth the sacrifice?

I hold my breath as we all wait for Darius's response. He tosses a stick into the waning fire and wipes his hands. "Yes, nothing worth doing is cheap. This is a big gamble, and it could cost us everything."

He pauses, and his eyes soften. "But living in Baytown is hell. If someone told me I had a chance at freedom or to go down fighting, my every drop of sweat and blood would burn to find a way."

Though Darius's expression is still hard, I read approval in his gaze. "Yes, we'll move forward with Portia's plan."

"Fail or win, we have to try," Red agrees.

"It will be our version of crossing the Rubicon," Jael adds. Her words meet with puzzled faces. Even I haven't heard that expression.

She blushes sheepishly. "It's a long story, but *crossing the Rubicon* basically means no turning back. When Julius Caesar ordered his army to cross the Rubicon River, he essentially committed high treason and declared war against the ruling Roman Senate. And we're about ready to start a head-on insurrection against the Dome and Friend. There's no hiding after we blow satellites off the map."

I can't help but smile. Darius is grinning, too.

He stands and motions to dismiss the assembly. "Then let's get ready to cross the Rubicon."

Chapter 35

Monday, 5.18.2150
Chrysoprase

Even though most of the assembly has left for their return journey, my core friends remain. We still have to settle the matter of protecting Alexis, and I'm determined to hear Darius's Baytown story before budging.

The five of us huddle closer to the last heat from the dying coals. Though the cave is surprisingly well insulated, the night's chill has started gnawing through my clothes.

We can't sit here forever and freeze to death, so I break the silence. "It's time for your story, Darius. Tell me what happened at Baytown. I don't know what to believe about Gath."

Darius sets his jaw. "All you need to know about Gath is that he's the truest friend you could want."

I sigh. "I know that, Darius. But I have to know the truth—about Gath, about Dad."

He cringes. "Okay, I'll tell you about Baytown, but you're going to wish I hadn't."

I hug my knees to my chest and shift my gaze to Jael, who's pressed against Foxworth's side to help stay warm. I wish ... but what does it matter?

Red scoots a little closer, and his shoulder brushes mine. Before I can protest, he takes off his own jacket and wraps it around my sweater.

He gives me a lopsided smile and pats my shoulder. The gesture warms me but fills me with a sad ache. Dad would have done the same thing. Does he know where my father is, and why will no one tell me?

Darius begins his tale. "When I arrived in Baytown, Gath was the head Wasp and the worst of the worst. You've lived in Warren so you can use your imagination. Let's just say we all hated him. As soon as I arrived, I began scoping my options. Baytown is primarily a shipyard. Capable slaves learned to weld or assemble vessels—everything from submarines to ships. Strong slaves broke their backs carrying freight or the rich materials mined at the other satellites. Everyone else did a myriad of other thankless tasks until they were worked to death."

He closes his eyes as if remembering. "There was one prisoner named Christopher who didn't spend his every waking breath cursing Gath or spinning a million ways to get even. Christopher was even younger than I was, maybe eighteen or nineteen. He was the son of a rich man from one of the southern squares. He wasn't there for any crime but for refusing to keep quiet about his religion.

"Gath tried to break that boy, but that boy broke Gath. Even when Gath was working him over, he'd cry out ..." Darius's voice trails off. He blinks away the moisture in his eyes. "We had to listen to his screams at night."

My own throat constricts. "What did the boy say?"

344

Darius swallows hard. "I forgive you because Jesus forgave me."

My heart beats wildly. Jesus is the name from that black book. He's the man who saved the woman from being stoned to death. But what could this boy have done that needed forgiving?

"Did Christopher ever explain what he meant?" I whisper.

Darius snorts. "Plenty of times. After all, he was in prison for sharing his beliefs, and no satellite was going to shut him up."

I glance over at Jael. Her eyes look as wide as my own must be.

"He said that a book called the Bible—one the first Friend of the ASU banned not long after starting his term—holds the answers to the problems our world faces. He said it's the story of a world broken because of man's disobedience to the God who created him. However, God still loved his creation, but because he was also a just God, required that there be a penalty for the disobedience."

Darius sighs. "I'm sorry, but I've heard this story too many times, and it still sounds like a crazy fairy tale."

"Go on," Jael encourages. "It doesn't sound crazy to me."

My brother rubs his head. "If you say so. As Christopher told the story, the solution to this problem was that God sent his own Son to bear the punishment that men should have received."

I frown. "Had his Son done something wrong?"

"No, that's the strange part," Darius says. "His Son was perfect, sinless as Christopher would say. And only a guiltless substitute could pay the price."

"So what happened to the Son?" Jael asks.

"He sacrificed himself—or I should say, let the people of earth kill him. In those days, the Romans—I guess that would include the Julius Caesar Jael mentioned—would crucify criminals. And because the Romans were in control at the time, that's how this Son called Jesus died."

His words take me back to that graveyard—the one with the cross in the center. Could this be the reason why?

"What's crucify?" Foxworth asks.

"It's when someone gets nailed to a cross," I blurt out before Darius can respond. "It was a horrible way to die."

Darius nods. "That's right. Anyway, Jesus let himself be executed."

Red shrugs. "So he died. What could the Dome possibly have against a kid who wanted to believe a nice story about mankind's so-called redemption?"

My brother holds up a hand. "I'm getting there. Apparently, Christopher said Jesus didn't stay dead. He came back to life three days later. Since he had power over death and had paid for humanity's crimes, he now could extend forgiveness to any person who simply believed in him—believed that his sacrifice was enough to save them. Essentially, he mended the broken relationship between God and his creation."

Red sucks in a deep breath. "It's a nice story all right, but if that were the case, we wouldn't be in this mess."

"It would seem that way," Darius agrees, "but according to Christopher, Jesus didn't demand that all humanity accept his offer. He gave them a choice. Some accept him, and some reject him. Either way, men and women have to live with the earthly consequences of their disobedience—but those who believe can experience a perfect place called heaven with him for eternity— what Christopher called life after death."

Foxworth opens his mouth to speak, but Darius cuts him off.

"I know. It's a crazy story, but that's how Christopher told it. And for some reason, the Friend decided that anyone who continued to spread the story after he banned the book that told it should be silenced."

Jael shivers. "Well, every Friend since must have done a good job of that, because I've never heard about Jesus."

I pull Red's jacket tighter around my shoulders. "What happened to Christopher?"

"It was the night before I led the inmates in a revolt. Have you heard that story?"

"Yes, pieces of it anyway," I say.

Darius nods. "Anyway, Gath carried his limp body to our cell. The kid was barely breathing, but it was Gath who looked like a cadaver. His dark face was ghastly white, and his eyes were haunted.

"No Wasp ever sets foot inside our cell, but Gath did that night. He walked the whole way in and laid what was left of Christopher in his bunk as gingerly as a mother might lay a baby in a cradle. All of us had a chance to jump him, but no one moved. We just watched him. After he slid the cell door shut, Gath kept wiping his hands on his uniform. I'm pretty sure he was choking sobs as he disappeared down the hallway."

Darius drops his voice so low I can barely hear him. "Christopher died the next morning. For the other inmates, his death lit the match we'd been dying to set. In one hour, we had destroyed the communications, wiped out half the Gage force, and set most of the place on fire."

"What happened to Gath in all that?" I want to hear Darius's version of Rig's account.

"The inmates caught him and were planning to pummel him

347

to bits, but I reached him before they got too far. He was still a bloody mess. I made up a lie on the spot about backup being spotted in the distance and that they had better run for it. I promised to finish off Gath and join them."

My brother squeezes his hands as if remembering the scene. "I pointed a handgun at his head—It was too merciful a death but at least it would serve justice.

"Gath didn't try to stop me, though I guessed he still could have. Instead, he looked me square in the face with the most tortured eyes. And he said, 'Can you ever forgive me?'"

Darius rushes on and squints as a tear charges past his lashes. "He had Christopher's eyes. I mean—They were still Gath's silver eyes, but they shone like Christopher's had. And I instantly knew he was different, and that if I killed him, I'd be killing a piece of Christopher.

"So I dropped the gun and untied him. And we ran out of the hellhole together. We've been brothers ever since, and though I can't explain why, I think Gath is a better man than I will ever be."

I bite my lip but can't stop the tears like my brother could. No wonder Gath didn't prevent the pipeliner from attacking him. He must still think himself worthy of his blows.

Foxworth stands. "It's getting late—or I should say early. If we don't head back soon, Alexis will be awake before we get there."

I wipe my tired, puffy eyes and try to focus. "Darius, what should we do about Alexis? I think she will help us, but we're taking a chance on her. For some reason, I think Lord Osborne wants her."

A shadow crosses Darius's face. "If the price were right, Osborne would make a deal with anyone. There's no telling why he might want her."

"So will you protect her?" I press him for an answer.

"If she wants our protection," he agrees. "But if she wants to go free, we'll let her go. We'll just have to be very careful so she can't find us again."

His words drive home the risk. By bringing in Alexis, I've exposed my brothers to possible danger. If Alexis wants no part with us, then she could reveal us to outsiders.

But Felix seems to want her dead. I hope she'll realize we aren't the ones trying to harm her.

I give Darius a sad smile. "I have to go back to Lord Osborne and find a way to check on Gath—and see if there's anything he needs from me to help our plan along."

"I hate to see you go back there," Darius grumbles. "But more than likely, Osborne is expecting you—and maybe Alexis, too. If you don't show, then he'll think you were either captured or tried to escape him. But with a man like Osborne, he'd find you again. Your best option is to say you helped Alexis escape to her brother and then came in by yourself."

My head pounds from fatigue. "I need to get at least a few hours of sleep before making that journey."

Foxworth stands. "Yes, we need to return to Alexis."

He hugs Jael goodbye, and Darius squeezes my shoulder. "I can't wait for the day when we can quit saying goodbye."

I smile tiredly. "Me too. And I can't wait for the day when I can finally be myself again."

Darius ruffles my hair. "There's blonde roots under that dark dye. Osborne can only hide the real you for so long."

"I hope so." I sigh. "Sometimes, I forget what being Portia feels like."

He wraps me in his arms. "It feels like this."

For a moment, I feel safe and loved. Even though Darius may not agree or approve of my rash decision to set this fireball plan in motion, he's still my brother and has my back. After all, that's what brothers do.

The stress lines on Alexis's forehead slowly soften as Foxworth and I take turns explaining her choice over a breakfast of stale crackers and jerky. The early morning light doesn't touch this place of the cave, which likely only adds to Alexis's nerves.

She nibbles on a cracker as her sharp gaze darts between us two. "So you'll let me go, no strings attached?"

Foxworth nods. "Yes, we just ask you don't lead anyone else back here. That said, we'll have to give you a drug to help blur your memory, but it's no guarantee you won't remember."

She frowns. "That sounds like strings attached."

I rub my temples. Two hours' sleep didn't put a dent in the exhaustion I feel. "Look, Alexis, we have to protect the lives of our brothers. I brought you here and put everyone in danger. I did it because I wanted to help you. And so far, you've escaped Felix's Gages."

"I appreciate what you've done," she says slowly, "but there have been several recent attacks that cost many innocent rail workers their lives. I heard your Brotherhood is responsible, and I can't condone pointless acts of terror."

I narrow my eyes. "The Brotherhood isn't brutal. It's not our way."

Alexis gives me a hard stare. "You were working for me when

those attacks happened, so you can't speak to their source." She turns to Foxworth. "What do you have to say?"

I bite my lip to hold back more hot words, but my stomach drops. I've had these same doubts myself. Am I too naive and idealistic? Would Darius give brutal orders if he had a good enough reason? But what reason can there be to murder innocent civilian workers?

Foxworth gnaws on a piece of jerky before answering. "Are you referring to the Lapis line massacre—the one where the attackers spray-painted *Fraternitas Veritas* in red on the cargo cars and left the bodies lined up, execution style?"

Alexis stiffens. "That was one of the incidents, yes."

He continues to chew. "That wasn't us. We never use red spray paint, only green."

I blink. Is he being serious?

Alexis glares at him. "Excuse me?"

Her scowl makes Foxworth choke. "I'm sorry. That was a bad joke. We honestly had nothing to do with that incident, but I get that you don't want to take my word for it. The Brotherhood has marked its actions with our motto in the past. Portia here will remember the spotlights at Crystal."

I nod. Wow, that seems like years ago.

He pounds his chest to clear his airways, then reaches for his canteen. "And while our actions have caused the deaths of innocent people, those deaths have been unfortunate side effects. We've never directly targeted civilians—only Gages."

"And Dome representatives like me," she accuses.

Foxworth shakes his head. "You're wrong there, too. We've stolen your intel and hacked into your meetings, but we've never plotted against individuals. Our target is more of an ideology, and if you had to put a face with it, then it would be the Friend."

"Then who tried to kill me?" she demands.

"Isn't it obvious?" I ask. "You opposed Felix's initiative in the Dome. I'd wager he and Eliab were behind your assassination attempt. After what I overheard at your party, I'm confident Felix also wanted to pin the Friend's death on you—which would give him a convenient excuse to dispose of you."

Arms crossed, she shifts her weight and frowns at me. "But he just said that the Friend would have been the Brotherhood's target. How do I know you all weren't behind her assassination?"

My shoulders droop, and I sigh again. We're going in circles and are no closer to gaining Alexis's trust than when we started.

But Foxworth is sharper than I am. "Why would we assassinate the Friend now? Portia knew that Felix wanted his mother's position. Why would we trade one tyrant for perhaps a worse one?"

Alexis uncrosses her arms. "You have a point there. Felix is an arrogant fool and will be ten times worse than his mother. But even if we assume Felix had her killed, what reason could he have for staging those massacres and mimicking your group?"

"Now that is a good question," Foxworth says. "I wish I knew the answer."

Maybe it wasn't Felix. I open my mouth to speak the words but gulp them down. All I have is a suspicion and no solid proof—and not a clue what could motivate Lord Osborne to do such random acts of terror. But that man is as mysterious as people come.

Just thinking of him makes sweat bead on my neck. I hate that my unwritten contract with the man has no end date. Whenever I become useless to him, he'll probably find a way to discard me like so much dirt a person might sweep into the garbage.

Alexis takes a deep breath. "Thanks for your patience with me. I just—well, I lost my home, my livelihood, and my future all in one day. Eliab probably has his henchmen on my trail."

She picks at a piece of jerky. "So, what I'm trying to say is that I'm an outlaw now, like you. I suppose you all can't be any worse than some of the sleazy characters in the Dome."

Foxworth snorts. "Is that supposed to be a compliment?"

Alexis blushes. "I'm sorry. A suit doesn't make a man a gentleman, and dirty jeans don't make him a commoner."

"I agree," I say. "A man with the heart of a prince might wear a miner's helmet." A pang wracks my heart. After Darius's story, I have no doubt that Gath's dark past no longer defines him.

Alexis squares her shoulders. "Okay, I want to stay. There's no life for me back in Crystal. But I have one request."

"Ask away," Foxworth says.

"Tell me what I can do to help."

Chapter 36

Monday, 5.18.2150
Chrysoprase

I twist my dyed black hair inside a knitted gray cap and grudgingly accept yet another pair of plastic glasses that Foxworth hands me. My former neighbor Husk had arrived half an hour before to escort Alexis to a temporary hiding location and also deliver my train ticket to Jasper. Now, it's my turn to leave for the long walk to the familiar 'Prase station.

Though the little sleep I managed wasn't nearly enough, it helped clear some cobwebs in my mind and reminded me that Darius never answered my burning question.

Foxworth studies me with an approving nod. "You look ready to go."

I slide the glasses on my nose and purse my lips. "Can you tell me why Darius skirted my question about Dad?"

He shoves his hands in his pockets. "What do you mean?"

I cross my arms. "When I asked about Gath and Dad, he told the story of Baytown but never talked about Dad. I was tired and

355

forgot to bring up the subject again."

He rubs his hand over the burnt skin on his face. "That wasn't the first time you'd asked him, was it?"

I frown. "No."

"And what did he tell you the first time?"

"He told me Dad was dead."

"Then believe him." He doesn't look at me directly.

"I can't," I say. "I think Darius is keeping Dad a secret from me—just like the Pelagic Project, whatever that is."

Foxworth's eyes widen. "How did you hear about that?"

"Osborne has mentioned it twice," I say. "Obviously, Darius doesn't think I need to know about it, and I'm okay with that. But I'm not okay with him deceiving me about Dad."

He shifts his gaze to the small, dark green bag he's letting me borrow for my trip back to the Excivis. "You'd better get started for that station. And you'll want to top off your canteen."

"I already did." I snap.

He flinches but doesn't respond.

I snatch the bag and sling it over my shoulder. "I guess since you're eager to get rid of me, I'll get out of your way."

He stiffens. "You don't want to miss your train. That Osborne character doesn't seem like a patient man."

"He isn't a lot of things, but at least I don't expect him to be. My brothers, on the other hand, I expect to tell me the truth." Even as I speak the words, I know they are unfair. Foxworth has been kind to me, and though he won't tell me about my dad either, it's not fair of me to lash out at him.

"Portia, I'm sorry." He sighs. "But Darius has your best interests at heart."

I suck down the words ready to spew off my tongue. Foxworth

356

is only following Darius's orders.

And for some reason, he wants him to lie to me.

Eight, maybe nine hours later, I sink deeper into the sofa in Lord Osborne's library, feeling sick to my stomach. Will this day never end?

The yellow lamp's nauseating glow doesn't help, but it's the scowl on Lord Osborne's face that causes my stomach to churn.

My "debriefing" has progressively turned into an interrogation.

He sits with legs crossed and hands gripping a crystal glass. "Where is Alexis?"

"I already told you," I say, trying to ignore the pit in my stomach. "I helped her escape the party, and we hid in her mountain cabin until she felt we could safely leave. She didn't say where she planned to go, but she did talk about a brother. My guess is she went to stay with him."

"You both took separate trains out of Crystal?" he asks.

He must know there was only one train that left the Crystal station. He's trying to trap me with a trick question. "No, we heard the trains at the central Crystal station stopped running the day after the Friend's assassination. We had to hitch rides to the next closest station."

Lord Osborne sips his glass. "And what train did Alexis take?"

"I didn't see," I say. "My train left before hers, and I wasn't with her when she bought the ticket."

A subtle smile tugs at his lips. Does he guess I'm lying to him and finds it amusing?

"You have three weeks before your next scheduled mission at Warren," he says at last. "I'll have to find a way for you to earn your keep between now and then. Chambers did a nice job saving his position but wrecked any chance of your usefulness back in Crystal."

I flinch at his choice of the word *usefulness*. All I am is a tool to him, and he'll have no reason to keep me once I'm no longer an asset.

"I didn't realize Chambers was one of us," I say to help quiet my nerves.

He shrugs. "There was no point in telling you. You'd either figure it out on your own or find out eventually."

An awkward silence stretches to a full minute. Though I'm not supposed to speak unless spoken to, I can't bear the strain. "At least you still have Orbit on the inside."

Lord Osborne's eyes flash. "Orbit's mission is no concern of yours." His anger fades to a humorous smile. "Not yet."

What is that supposed to mean?

He sets down his empty glass and stands. "Report to Deidra. She'll find something you can do to be useful."

I rise too eagerly. "Yes, sir."

I've nearly reached the doorway when he clears his throat. "I know you're lying, Sage Colby."

I mask my feelings with a shocked expression. "Sir?"

"You know where Alexis is," he accuses.

"I honestly have no idea," I say, and for once, it's the truth. Foxworth didn't tell me where Husk was taking her.

"I hope for your sake that you don't because I will find out." He strides past me and opens the door. "I know you lied to me about Gath Aden. You knew all along where he was, didn't you?"

His words set my heart racing. Did Rig tell him about Gath? And if he did, what's to keep Lord Osborne from harming him? But I have to pretend I don't know anything.

I curl my lip. "You flatter me. I wish I were as resourceful as you say. Then maybe I wouldn't have to keep proving myself."

"Deliver them both to me, and you won't have to." He studies me with cold eyes. "Either that, or you can spend the next three weeks scrubbing dishes with Deidra."

I nod in acknowledgment and slip past him. "I'll go find her and see how I can help."

Voices drift through the kitchen doors. One is Deidra's, but she's not alone. That other pesky woman is with her.

"You're feeding a runaway, aren't you?" the woman accuses.

"I don't know what you're talking about," Deidra says dryly.

"Don't you? Then why are you packing the dinner leftovers in old plastic boxes?"

There's no response, only clanging pots and pans, followed by the rush of water in the sink.

"If I tell Lord Osborne, you'll be in trouble," the woman hisses.

"You're a pest, Bertha!" Deidra swears. "If you must know, I'm feeding a stray kitten. There, are you happy? We waste so much food as it is, and the poor thing lost its mother."

There's a skeptical pause. "Do you mean a whole litter? Because no one kitten could possibly eat all that food."

I shove through the doors and approach the women with a smile. "Excuse me, but Lord Osborne sent me to help in the kitchen."

Deidra's grin spreads across her face like butter slathered on fresh bread. The other woman grunts and points at the sink. "Get to work on those." She shakes a warning finger at Deidra. "It had better be a cute kitten, and I want to see it."

"Where are you going?" Deidra demands.

"I'm done for the day." She hangs her apron on a wooden peg and marches for the door.

Deidra moves her hands to her hips. "No, you're not. We've got all of dinner to clean up."

"You've got the little miss to help." She sneers. "Besides, if I'm going to keep your secret, you owe me."

Deidra glares at her. "Fine, go knock yourself out for all I care."

The woman mutters and shoves through the double doors.

As soon as she's gone, Deidra rushes to me and wraps me in her arms. "You're back early! After I heard about the Friend and Alexis, I was worried."

I hug her like a sister. "Yes, things got a little dicey, as Mrs. Gates might say."

She pulls back. "Mrs. Gates?"

"The cook at Alexis's estate," I explain. "She was a sweet woman who tried to watch out for me."

Deidra grins. "I'm glad someone was doing that job."

I laugh lightly and study her closer. There's something different—more youthful—about her. It's almost like a glow, like her former tropical beauty is back.

Maybe it's her hair. She's wearing it braided and not in that ugly, tight bun.

"You got a kitten?" I say to help conceal the curious thoughts

360

swirling in my head.

Her smile fades, and her gaze darts toward the double doors as if she expects Bertha to be listening in. "Yes, he's a sweet, black one. He's emaciated and happens to live in the coal mines."

I gape at her, wondering if I heard her right. "You mean— How long ..."

"I discovered him shortly after your last visit, but my small attempts have done little to put any meat on his bones." Despite the strain in her eye, Deidra's cheeks glow. "But I think his coloring has improved."

My heart flutters. "Can I—Will you take me to see him?"

She nods tersely. "We've got chores first."

I roll my sleeves and attack the dishes while Deidra bags the leftovers in a small brown sack and then mops the floor. Neither of us speaks for the next hour, but we complete the kitchen chores in record time.

I wonder why she's acting as excited as I am to go see this "kitten." I'm the one who's been worrying about Gath ever since I left Warren. Deidra was only doing me a favor by finding him and slipping him food like I'd asked her to.

When I've put away the last dish, Deidra flips off the light and snatches the sack. Silently, she peeks out the doorway and then motions for me to follow her.

I sense her urgency. The time must be approaching eight o'clock, and the prisoners will be leaving the mines in half an hour or as soon as daylight dies. We don't have much time to meet Gath.

We slip down a dark hallway. At first, I don't recognize it, and then I remember it as one Orbit had led me down. She yanks open a door and retrieves a flashlight on the other side.

We need it, too, because the passage inside the mine is

completely dark. I tremble as the smell and dank walls flood my mind with awful memories, but Deidra confidently leads the way.

Finally, she slows. Her light reveals something ahead in our path. It's long and sinewy and stretches across the tunnel floor. We would have tripped over it if she hadn't …

I gasp. That's not part of the floor. That's a body—a body naturally as coal black as the walls themselves. He must have fallen asleep waiting for us.

Waiting for her.

Deidra drops to her knees and cradles the man's head in her arms. His eyes flicker open, and a smile plays across his lips.

I've never seen Gath smile that way before.

Deidra goes to pieces, kissing his forehead, cheeks, lips. I blink and pinch myself to make sure I'm seeing this right.

Her brown cheeks blush crimson when she remembers I'm standing right behind her. Gath pulls himself upright and curls an arm around Deidra. When he sees me, his smile broadens. It's a comrade's smile now.

"You sent me an angel." His voice sounds like himself, even though he looks nearly as starved as I remember.

"But Gath, I—I don't understand …" I stammer.

Deidra tugs me down to join them on the rocky floor. "Sage, you know this man as Gath. I know him as Abel."

I stare from one to the other as her words sink in. Abel? Her lost teenage love?

"He was taken by that ship as I suspected," she says. "But he survived."

"On hate." Gath glances at Deidra. "I guess we both did."

I shake my head in disbelief. "But Darius said you were a Wasp."

"I became one." He swallows and gazes sadly at Deidra. "One of the Wasps in command saw my potential. He taught me to be cruel to my fellow prisoners. I did whatever he asked if it meant a chance to be free.

"But I didn't realize that what I thought was freedom was in fact a worse kind of captivity than a slave ship."

Deidra opens the bag and hands him the food containers. He can't talk and eat, so I wait impatiently for him to finish.

He thanks Deidra with a kiss. I frown, still trying to absorb the emotions I'm feeling.

Gath guzzles a small water jar and wipes his mouth. "Long story short, I earned my supposed freedom, and this other Wasp sent me to a training camp for Wasps in the Black Tundra. You either leave that place crueler than the icy winter or you never leave.

"I survived and became a notorious Wasps, earning my dark reputation at Baytown. But my hatred was eating me inside out. I took pleasure in torturing prisoners—the very kind I had once been. And then I met a prisoner named Christopher."

His breath catches, and he winces.

"Darius told me about Christopher," I whisper.

Gath studies me with pained eyes. "I was a monster to that boy, but he—he showed me how to find real freedom. Jesus gave me the forgiveness my hate-eaten soul craved and then a second chance at life when your brother rescued me. The rest is history."

He pats Deidra's hand and then rises to a hunched position. "I have to get going to join the others marching to Warren."

"Stay with us," Deidra pleads. "You don't have to go back to that hell-pit."

Gath shakes his head and looks past her to me. "Yes, I do. I have to make sure all the prisoners know the plan for VW-Day. I don't want anyone getting left behind in the mines when they go up in flames."

"VW-Day?" I force a grin.

"Victory in Warren Day. That's what we're calling it, anyway."

My throat is dry. He's choosing Warren over Deidra to honor his commitment to my plan—my crazy plan which might get us all killed.

I lower my eyes. "You don't have to do this. You can leave now and have your life back."

"Portia Abernathy." His stern voice makes me jolt and stare into his eyes, now ablaze. "We started something, and we're going to finish it. Your plan has given the prisoners hope they can be free, too. And it's given me time to tell them what real freedom looks like."

Is he talking about freedom from the satellite—or the freedom that Christopher showed him?

I want to ask him more about the story that changed him, but now isn't the time. Instead, I ask, "What's your plan—for VW Day? How can we help?"

He shifts his weight. "It has to be a time when prisoners aren't in the mines. You know we don't get a meal at noon, but the water line forms around that time. My plan is to start the fire then. That way, if something goes wrong, the prisoners outside won't be blamed."

Deidra stiffens. "And who's starting the fire? Firedamp and coal dust will ignite in seconds. That person won't be able to run fast enough."

Gath offers a terse smile. "Leave that to me."

She glares at me. "Was this your idea? I just found him after all these years, and now you're planning him to run a suicide mission?"

My gut twists. I don't want Gath's blood on my hands. I never meant for him to die.

"Beatrice." Gath's words hold warmth and a warning.

I blink. That must be Deidra's real name.

"We both have jobs to do." He turns to me. "I'm at Warren for a reason, and you're working with Osborne for a reason."

"But he wants you dead," I protest. "I've been trying to hide your whereabouts from him, but he's searching for you. He knows you're at Warren."

"Let him find me," Gath says, "but I'm not going to let down my brothers and sisters. We've started this plan, and we're going to finish it. If we back out, we bow to wicked men and their tyranny. No, Portia, get your fire back. We finish this."

"But you just said hate nearly destroyed you!" I cry.

He reaches to grip my shoulder. "I'm not talking about hate. I'm talking about fire—a cause—doing what's right. I'm not fighting because I hate people. I'm fighting because I love them."

Gath's eyes seem to penetrate my empty soul. "Why are you fighting, Portia?"

I squint at his intensity. All the reasons in my head sound foolish compared to his. "I—I don't know anymore."

He shakes me. "Figure it out fast. We have a revolution to win."

Chapter 37

Sunday, 6.7.2150

Jasper

The transport truck bounces noisily along the dirt road and down a path that will lead to victory or defeat—and probably death, even in the best-case scenario.

Deidra drives silently beside me. Her black hair, like mine, is pinned inside a cap, and we both wear official ASU uniforms, but mine is that of a Wasp. Hers is the navy-blue suit of my driver.

On the other side of me sits our armed escort. His silent company suits my mood.

The last three weeks have been some of the most confusing of my life.

The romance of Deidra and Gath—Beatrice and Abel—still makes my head spin. No wonder she glows. The man she loves and had presumed dead is alive. That would make anyone giddy.

But Gath's insistence on remaining in Warren put a strain on their newly-found relationship. She couldn't understand why he chose a slave camp over her company when she could sneak him out and start life over.

And as Gath gradually regained strength from our food provisions, he also became more aloof to her affections and more focused on the chain-reaction plan I set in motion. As a result, Deidra had grown colder toward me, as if I were competing with her happiness.

Am I?

When I had first met Gath, he seemed a cold, heartless Gage. He even administered my own corrective treatment, which left me void of a personality for an entire month.

But he also countered the treatment with an antibiotic that ensured I would recover. He looked out for me on two Tripper outings, rescued me from a Trader, and sacrificed his own well-being in the satellite camp to keep my spirits up and my body alive.

He could have avoided the satellite in the first place by escaping that train. Only, he didn't. He had chosen to stay by my side. Is that love? Or is that brotherly comradery?

I stare out the windshield at the cloudless day. Gath has never treated me with anything but respect. He could have taken advantage of me numerous times when we had to share a bunk out of necessity in the prisoner barracks.

But that was a survival situation. He was protecting me from the other prisoners. I never saw him as a threat to my own virtue. He's never treated me like anything but a sister.

So now, why does Deidra treat me this way? Haven't I told her about Luther? The memory of his kiss lingers on my lips and sends goosebumps up my skin. He's saved my life more times than one. He's given me tough love when I needed it: training me how to run and how to survive for a future neither of us could have imagined. He even sentenced me to a satellite to protect me from

Eliab and had our destination switched to Warren where I had a greater chance of survival than at Baytown.

Luther has made clear that he loves me. Gath's actions have spoken love as well, but it's a different kind of love, a brotherly love that's willing to lay down his life for a friend.

I close my eyes. I love them both, just in different ways.

Deidra jerks the wheel to avoid a rut, and I blink to focus on what I'm supposed to do.

This mission seems much fuzzier than the last, and Lord Osborne evaded all my attempts for more details. The folder in my lap contains another transport order, this time for three able-bodied men who are needed to replace some recent casualties on an adjoining pipelining crew.

At least, that's what the order says. In reality, they're the three lucky prisoners handpicked by Lord Osborne to rescue.

"Won't three men look suspicious?" I had asked.

"Just bring them to me," he snapped. "You did fine last time. Repeat that performance, and you have nothing to worry about."

But his tone made me uneasy. Last time, my mission was clear: to rescue one pipeliner: Rig. This time, he had simply told me to rescue "three men."

My gut warns that these three men can't all have struck bargains with Lord Osborne, but who am I to question him?

Besides, I need to get in that satellite today. If all goes well with Gath, I plan to transport more than three men to freedom.

For the first time since receiving my orders, I glance at the list of numbers on the transport list.

Number 12018 leaps off the page.

I squint and check again. My fingers grip the paper. Is this a coincidence, or does Osborne know Gath's number is on his list?

Surely, he knows.

The vehicle winds the familiar road leading to Warren. This late in the spring, snow still clings to the ground but in smaller quantities. The semi-melted slush reveals arms and legs of frozen prisoners. Their limbs, rigid from death, seem to point me to go back and avoid the road ahead.

I shiver. Perhaps later this day, my body will join theirs.

No, I can't think that way. And I can't let my brothers and sisters down.

Though I don't understand all that Gath believes, I agree his reason to fight is the best one I can figure. If I fight because I love my family and friends, then I'm fighting for a good reason. Having a home and someone to love are the rewards if I succeed—and survive.

The truck reaches the gate, and Deidra shows her papers. The Warren guard opens the gate, and we enter the forbidding courtyard.

"It's all you from here." She parks the truck and offers me a tense half-smile. "You got this."

"Thanks," I say and scoot toward the door after the armed escort. I give her one last searching look. "Whatever happens, thanks for everything. I hope we both get our happy endings."

Deidra moistens her lips. "Yes, I hope so. That's the plan." She clears her throat. "Remember, you're Wasp Sybil now."

"Right." I wipe the smile off my face. "Talk little. Let my orders speak for me."

She hesitates as if to say something else and then nods toward the passenger door. "Go get 'em, Waspy."

A growing dread grips my chest as I mount the stairs to Harris's office. Even though I know the prisoners are still in their bunks, the early-morning courtyard is eerily silent. To the right of the stairs is another armed vehicle, a four-seater like the one Luther and I had used to help Alexis escape the Dome after the failed assassination attempt.

How did Harris manage to get one of those for his own personal use?

I set my jaw and yank open the door. Like last time, Harris reclines with his feet on his desk, but instead of surprised or annoyed, he seems pleased.

"Wasp Sybil, right on time." He removes his boots from the desk and then stretches his back to extend his full height—so much taller than I am.

His unhurriedness alarms me. Even more does the smirk on his face.

I deepen the scowl on my own and slap the folder on his desk. "I'm here for the three pipeliner replacements."

"Yes, that." He yawns. "I already received my copy of the orders. Wouldn't you prefer some more practice first? I have another rabbit."

I glance to his cage where what could be Peppermint's twin gnaws on pellets. Harris crosses his arms and studies me. "What? Is Licorice not as plump as Peppermint? Can't you bulls-eye a smaller critter?"

I point at him and then slam my hand on the folder. "I don't have time for nonsense today. Tell me where to find the transfers."

"That's it, then. You'd prefer a bigger target?" A wicked grin spreads across his lips. "I have the chore for you."

Before I can move, Harris leaps across the room and shoves open the door. "Follow me, Wasp Sybil."

I glare at him. "I have a job to do."

He makes a mocking bow. "Don't we all."

I don't know whether to feel relieved or worried when he directs me toward my old barrack—Gath's barrack—as he had done last time. Perhaps I can bluff my way out with the prisoners again.

The long, narrow building is darker than I remember, but Harris strides confidently forward, past the rows of inmates unconscious from exhaustion.

He stops intentionally at Gath's bunk, unholsters his sidearm, and lowers it.

No, no, no! Not again ...

"What are you doing?" I demand through gritted teeth.

He smirks. "That's right. I did say you could do the honors."

I gaze at the sleeping occupant, all but masked in the darkness. But I can never forget this bunk.

My throat constricts. "What honors?"

"Wake up call." He slides his gun back in the holster and points to the one on my hip.

"I don't ..."

"Consider it your morning target practice." He leers at me. "Oh, come on! This one's much bigger than Licorice."

He's trapped me, and he knows it. If I don't shoot the prisoner, I blow my cover. No Wasp would think twice about killing an inmate.

But I can't shoot Gath.

372

The whole mission hangs on the next second.

In one trembling breath, I reach for my handgun, draw, and fire.

Chapter 38

Sunday, 6.7.2150

Jasper

Harris curses and clutches his chest. He gasps and staggers against the frame behind him.

It was a bad shot, and not even the close-range handgun round will keep him down for long. If I don't finish him with a shot to the head, he'll alert his comrades.

But firing a second shot will also warn the other Wasps there's trouble since Harris only fires one execution round per day.

It will also make me a murderer.

There's scuffling behind me. No doubt all the prisoners are popping out from their beds and gaping at me.

I aim again and focus the sites between Harris's anger-ridden eyes.

Someone yanks me from behind and hurls me to the ground. The round goes off, ricocheting off the concrete walls and planting itself in some unfortunate prisoner's skin. The man howls in pain. My own head reels from colliding with Gath's bunk on my way to the floor.

My vision blurs. Are there three men or six towering over me?

One jerks me to my feet and pins my arms. "Fool," he whispers in my ear.

I blink. *Orbit*. I'd know his voice anywhere.

The other two men come into focus. Eliab stands with his gun drawn. His black eyes peer at me as if second-guessing himself.

The second man steps forward and swipes the fake glasses off my face. *Oh, God, what is Luther doing here?* For a split second, I see the pain and fear in his eyes, but he masks them with blank indifference. "You were right, Gage Eliab. Someone did a face job on her, but this is Portia Abernathy."

My heart pounds. How has Eliab found me? Why is Luther here? Unless Alexis's counter-initiative passed …

Orbit pushes me toward Eliab for closer inspection. He yanks my hair to find a hint of blonde at the nape of my neck.

Eliab nods in satisfaction. "Good work. Luther, call back-up for Commanding Wasp Harris. Orbit, give her to me, and collect her fellow criminal."

Eliab's fingers press deep into my skin as he replaces his manacle grip with Orbit's. He whispers threats down my neck, but I fix my gaze on Gath's bunk.

And the terrified stranger who occupies it.

Orbit steps back and glowers at the bleeding Harris. "Where is Gath Aden—your prisoner number 12018?"

Harris grimaces. "Don't know."

The prisoner slinks into the shadows with the other cowering inmates as Luther returns with three other Wasps who carry Harris away.

Eliab spins me toward him, and his gnarled face glares down

at me. "Where is your accomplice?"

"I came here for Gath, too." I try to control my breathing. "His number was on my list to transport."

Eliab frowns and wags his head to Orbit. "Question the prisoners." Meanwhile, Eliab locks my wrists in cuffs.

Orbit returns minutes later. "One man says he never left the mine last night. He said men don't come back all the time, so he didn't see the harm in taking over his bunk."

My head spins. What happened to Gath? Hadn't he been meeting Deidra for food right before the march out of the mines? She didn't say anything had been out of the ordinary. What could have happened to him?

Maybe he stayed behind intentionally to prepare to ignite the firedamp. I have no doubt he's found what he needs. Or maybe ... I shudder. The only other reason is someone stopped him from returning to camp and captured him. Though Deidra insisted no one knew other than the cantankerous kitchen woman about her "kitten," what if Lord Osborne had learned about her evening errand? What if he had discovered Gath?

After all, there can only be one man behind the tip that led Eliab to find me today: the man who wants his revenge on the two Gages responsible for murdering his family.

My employer, Lord—no, I'm done calling him that. Osborne didn't send me on a mission today. He strung me to a hook and cast me inside Warren as bait.

I exhale in anger, but the only way to survive this round and still give my plan a hope of success is to play along. If I don't, Orbit will lead him to Osborne anyway, and there will be no reason to keep me around.

"I know where he is," I say.

Orbit slaps me. "Don't listen to her. She's lying."

I glare at him. "There's only one man who has the resources to rescue prisoners."

Eliab arches his eyebrow. "And who's that?"

"The same man who broke me out."

"Why should we believe you?" Luther asks. He glances at my bruised wrists, and his eyes twitch.

It's subtle, but I don't need more to believe he's playing his part—for me.

I focus on Eliab. He's the one I have to convince to let me live. Because Orbit trained me, I know he'd probably consider a bullet to the head a merciful finish to my miserable life.

I glance from Orbit to Eliab. "Because Osborne sent me here."

Orbit's eyes widen. "Are you referring to *the* Antonio Osborne?"

My trainer is such an actor, and although I'm blind to the script, I play along. "Yes—He runs an underground network."

The Commanding Gage furrows his brow. "I know him. In fact, I owe him a visit."

Now it's my turn to look shocked. "A visit for what?"

Eliab crosses his arms as a smooth, cocky expression settles on his face. "He promised to find me a missing person, and he's past his deadline."

A missing person. Surely, he isn't talking about me. Is he referring to Alexis?

Eliab nods toward Orbit, who grips my arm. "Sir," Orbit says, "but we haven't received word where to meet him."

"We don't need an invitation when we have his spy in our custody."

Orbit shakes his head. "Maybe that's what he wants—for us

378

to walk right into his hands."

I marvel at Orbit who pretends to be the devil's advocate when he wants nothing better than for Eliab to play right into Osborne's plan.

Eliab snorts. "I put the scoundrel out of business once before, and I can clean house again. If he wants to start working for the CGA, he's going to have to play by our rules and deliver on time."

My head reels. Osborne is working for the CGA? But he told me he wants revenge on Gath and Eliab, so why would he partner with the very man responsible for his family's death?

Orbit tightens his grip, and I wince. Does he have to act this cruel? It's probably his fault I'm in this predicament.

No, it's Osborne's fault. He's the one who set me up to fail.

"He's an opportunist, sir," Orbit says. "I don't trust him."

"I don't trust him either. But now I have two things he wants: his spy and his contract. If he doesn't deliver and meet my terms, he'll have more to worry about than staying in business."

Two Wasps appear to whip the prisoners out of their bunks. There will be no breakfast this morning again, thanks to me.

My own stomach twists at their starving figures. They must hate me for causing them even more trouble. Some glare at me, but others glance my way with desperate hope.

I give them the slightest nod. Our plan must go on, with or without Gath.

Orbit pushes me toward the door while Eliab barks orders to a Wasp behind me. "Tell Harris's second in command I'll need to borrow the equipment we delivered."

The Wasp hesitates for a moment. "Yes, sir." He strides past his companion who's corralling the inmates toward the courtyard.

"One more thing," Eliab calls after him.

The Wasp stiffens but dutifully acknowledges Eliab. "Sir?"

He smirks my direction. "I'll also need half a dozen prisoners, including this one."

As the inmates begin their morning march from the courtyard to the mine, I shrink inside myself, feeling more like the rabbit Harris used to call me than a confident runner for Osborne.

I choke in horror as we pass the transporter truck and find Osborne's armed escort lying in a heap on the ground. Probably shot. I don't see Deidra's body and hope she somehow escaped.

A Wasp climbs in the cab, while several others inspect the back and then load crates and a handful of inmates inside. I recognize a few from the barracks. Their terrified eyes hold the silent question I understand all too well: Is the mission still on? And if it is, what is freedom going to cost us?

I stagger toward the vehicle that should have been a tell-tale sign to me earlier that something was wrong. Orbit shoves me in the back, and Luther climbs in on the other side of me. After Wasps finish loading the transport truck, Eliab takes the passenger seat next to a Wasp in the front seat of my vehicle.

There's a self-assured smirk on his face. I worry it has to do with the transport truck, the unlucky prisoners loaded inside, and those crates. What is his plan for turning the tables on Osborne's trap?

He has to know that entering the mines in search of Gath is dangerous, but for some reason, he's confident he can play a better hand.

Being squished next to Luther makes me feel safer than I am.

He leans into my shoulder. His strength and presence offer a much-needed calm.

The armored vehicle winds down the road toward the mine. I've never driven the path before and am surprised at how short a ride it is. Marching it morning and night as a prisoner made it feel like several miles.

The vehicle stops a couple hundred feet from the mine's gaping mouth, and the Wasps from the transporter jump out with weapons ready. They order the prisoners to unload the crates.

As Orbit tugs me out behind him, he stares into my eyes and offers a silent apology as he unlocks my cuffs.

My pulse quickens. Why does he look pained?

A Wasp unclasps the crates. There are three of them: two larger ones and one small one. The Wasps herd the five selected prisoners and me into a line, while another one removes black vests from the larger crates.

The man shoves them into our hands and orders us to wear them.

They're heavy and fibrous, but through the mesh, I feel wires and something like a control box or …

"Zip it!" A Wasp steps in front of me, holding something in his hand. It's a miniature combination lock.

Hands sweating, I fumble for the vest's zipper, which starts on both ends and meets in the middle of my chest. The Wasp loops the lock in place and slides his thumb over the three combination numbers, giving me no chance to guess what their unlocked sequence might be.

But the vest is much too big for me. That's good. I can squeeze out of it when no one's looking.

Luther offers a reassuring glance. Maybe he knows the

combination. Maybe he can get me out of this thing.

After the Wasps padlock our vests in place, Orbit opens the smaller crate. Inside are thin black boxes, wide enough to hold maybe one or two tablets.

He lifts the lid on the box and moves toward me. Then, he removes a crystal, translucent collar.

I tense. Although I've never seen a collar like this before, I recognize the color and the floating corpuscles inside.

Orbit opens the latch and moves toward my neck, but I jump backward. A Wasp immediately pounces and takes out my legs from underneath me. I fall to the ground as he strikes at me with his whip.

I roll so that it misses my face and hits the jacket, which buzzes at the impact. Eliab curses at him to stop, and Orbit yanks me to my feet.

Again, he reaches to strap the collar around my neck, but I block him with my arms and sink the heel of my hand into his chin.

Orbit curses and slugs at me. I stagger onto the ground to avoid his wild blow.

"Enough!" Eliab roars from behind him. "I'll choke her myself."

"No, you won't!" Luther jumps in front of him to shield me. "Our Ethics Committee hasn't approved these collars for use on people."

Eliab scowls. "She's not a person. She's a prisoner."

"I don't care." Luther shakes his head. "I understand the vests—Tasers don't kill people, but these collars are untested."

"Tasers?" Eliab's scowl twists into a grin. "You think those are rigged with Tasers?"

He laughs and slaps Luther's shoulder. "Son, I know you're

trained to judge the law, but right now, I am the law. And you won't interfere with my methods."

Eliab steps around Luther and looms over me. "Get up."

I glare at him and slowly rise. "I agreed to take you to the hidden entrance, but I won't do it if you put that thing on my neck. I know what it is."

"You think you know." He plays with the latch. "But it needs more testing, and you're the perfect subject."

I back away from him. "No, you're wrong, and you'll never find the entrance without me."

Orbit rubs his chin, but his bleeding lip curls with subtle admiration.

"You're in no position to bargain with me." Eliab leers. "Perhaps I should demonstrate the vest you're wearing." He motions to a Wasp who pushes a woman forward.

My chests twists at her terror. Please, no …

Eliab returns the collar to its box and removes two palm-sized remotes from one of the larger crates. He leaves one on the crate and snatches the other in his hand.

"Take her over there—at least 300 yards away." Eliab waves toward an empty patch of dirt away from the mine's entrance.

The woman wails as the Wasp reaches for her.

"What kind of monster are you?" I scream at him.

"Shut up!" Eliab shouts. "Or I'll press your button instead."

"Do it." I dare him. "You kill her, and you might as well press mine, too. I won't take one step into that cave to help you find what you're looking for."

For what feels like a minute, we stare down each other as the woman continues to scream. The Wasp hesitates, staring anxiously at Eliab for his order.

Eliab shakes in fury. "Put her back in line, and get a spare vest!" He jabs a finger in my face. "I'll kill you myself if you make one more demand."

The woman whimpers and rejoins the others in line while the Wasp retrieves another black vest, shouts a number to Eliab, and then runs toward the opening with it.

As he reaches the ditch, Eliab presses the button. A whistling noise sounds from inside all our vests as if synchronized. The next instant, the vest in his hand explodes, incinerating him.

The female prisoner shrieks, and the other Wasps stare at each other in horror. Orbit steps in front of Luther who looks ready to lunge for Eliab's jugular. Does he suspect Luther's threadbare loyalty?

Eliab yanks my wrists and twists them once more behind my back, cuffing my hands in place. I'm too stunned to protest.

His bristled jaw scratches my ear. "Life is cheap, Abernathy. And yours is much cheaper than one subordinate Wasp."

Chapter 39

Sunday, 6.17.2150
Warren Satellite

I lead the way inside the mines with Orbit and Eliab on either side of me. Luther falls in line behind me. Knowing he has my back is the one comfort I have left.

The other five prisoners trail behind him, followed by the remaining five Wasps who carry a small pack and lantern. They seem to have shrunk inside themselves after the needless death of their comrade. Eliab has a talent for making people hate him.

At least the collars had returned to their crates and remained with the vehicles—Luther saw to that himself. After the demonstration, he hadn't asked for permission from Eliab before taking charge of the crates and closing them.

Despite his scowl, Eliab didn't stop him. The vest demonstration alone had been enough to convince all us prisoners to cooperate.

Besides, Eliab still holds his remote, collateral to keep me in line. He made clear I'm "unlucky number six" and that his finger is itching to press my button.

The only reason he doesn't press it is that for the moment, he needs me. Osborne must not have given him the rendezvous location to meet about the so-called "missing person." I'm the only one who can lead him into Osborne's secret domain.

Rather, I'm the only one who pretends to know the way. Orbit knows better than I do, but he can't tell without blowing his cover.

I decide to take the long route to where Deidra was feeding Gath. That location leads through the dark, rarely used hallway that will take us back toward the kitchen and give Orbit any number of opportunities to alert Osborne to our presence.

The thought terrifies me, though. The five other prisoners and I will simply become the human shields to protect Eliab—or the explosives to help him escape—if Osborne and Eliab can't come to terms.

I stop at the covert entrance. "This is it. There's a hidden latch here in the wall that opens the door. We'll enter a dark hallway and then come out by the kitchen."

For the first time, uncertainty crosses Eliab's face. "And where do you suggest we find Osborne—and Gath?"

"Lord Osborne has a favorite library," I say, "but that's too nice a place for a prisoner."

I rack my brain. Although Osborne may have a prison chamber somewhere, I've never seen it. I was prisoner enough in my comfortable room.

There's movement to my left. Orbit plucks something off the floor. It's an old coal mining pick. Had it belonged to Gath? With his other hand, he pries a rock off the wall and flips it thoughtfully in his hand.

Flips it.

"There is a small outdoor arena," I say slowly. "It's where Osborne trains his agents and is heavily concealed in the woods at the back exit of the Excivis."

"Excivis?" Eliab demands.

"It's what Osborne calls his underground apartments," I say. "Anyway, we could use the arena as a staging area, and move inside the Excivis from there."

"And lose the element of surprise?" Eliab scoffs. "I may be walking in here blind, but I'm not a fool."

"Sir, we could leave the extra prisoners there while we scope out the place," Orbit suggests.

Eliab narrows his eyes at Orbit. "I didn't bring them along because I wanted baggage. I brought them for collateral damage." He waves the other Wasps toward him. "Each one of you, take a prisoner and split up inside. Use cuffs or whatever you have in your day bags to bind, gag and hide them out of sight."

"Where do we go from there, sir?" one of the Wasps asks.

Eliab frowns at me. "You said there's an arena in the woods?"

"Yes," I say.

"Yes, *sir!*" Orbit butts me in the gut with the blunt end of the pick. I cough and stagger backward into someone. Luther's strong hands catch me before I tumble into the coal wall.

A growl surges through his throat as if he plans to rip Orbit's head off his shoulders.

Despite the throbbing in my stomach, I push away from him and gasp loudly, hoping both actions distract attention away from Luther.

"Yes, sir!" I cough again and lean against the cave's wall for support.

"Idiot!" Luther rants at Orbit and steps in front of me. "We need her to show us the way. You slugging her around is only costing us time."

"Danforth's right." Eliab's harsh tongue lashes into Orbit. "Save your rage. You'll have plenty of time later for sport." He turns to talk again to the Wasps. "Once you've secured your prisoner, wait in this arena."

Orbit pretends to sulk, and my head is too blurry to figure out what beating me up will accomplish.

I clench my fists inside my cuffs. Maybe he's getting even for when I punched him—or he's reminding me to fight.

"We need a map," Eliab mutters and motions for one of the Wasps to place his lantern on the dusty ground. He unlatches my cuffs. "Draw, Abernathy."

"With what—sir?" I stretch my fingers to help bring back the circulation.

Orbit shoves the pick in my face but thankfully doesn't hit me. "Use this."

I grip the wooden handle and use the dull metal blade to scratch on the rocky floor. "We're here. Once we pass through this entrance, there's a long hallway that opens by the kitchen. If you go left, the hallway extends until you reach an exit door. Open it, and you'll be inside a drainage pipe that leads to the arena."

"What's down the other end of the hall?" Eliab asks.

"That leads you to other hallways. Some lead to corridors, but the widest one takes you to the center of the Excivis."

"How do we get to Osborne's library?" Orbit grumbles. Like he doesn't know.

"You have to take the same hallway. Once you reach the main opening, there's a side hallway and a staircase that spirals downward. That will lead us to the library."

The Wasps huddle close. One mutters, "Where do we hide the prisoners?"

My gut twists. They're asking me to select these poor people's graves. "There are different levels in the central room—You'll see them at the end of the main hallway. Or, you can go down some of the smaller corridors to the rooms. Be sure to count your turns, though, because getting lost in the place is easy."

Eliab straightens. "Use your judgment."

"And then you'll meet us at the arena?" the Wasp asks.

"You ask as many questions as a schoolboy," Orbit spats. "Do your job and wait for the next order."

I grin in the dim light. *Don't ask questions.* How many times had Orbit drilled that into my brain?

"Just be ready." Eliab yanks the coal pick out of my hand. "We'll either come out with Gath or be prepared for the place to explode."

Eliab doesn't know that Osborne is playing him like a fiddle. If Osborne has his way, neither Gath nor Eliab will leave alive.

And who am I fooling? I'm the one wearing a detonator vest.

I'll be the first to go up in smoke.

Smoke. The planned mine explosion. We only have a few hours until noon and only one chance to coordinate our explosion with the other satellites, assuming the pipeliners delivered the message.

But someone has to ignite a firedamp pocket and catch enough coal dust on fire. The terrified expressions on the prisoners' faces reveal a desperate desire to survive. No wonder Gath feels he has to be the one.

A new resolve fills me. I can't let him. He's done nothing but suffer for my sake. If I can manage to save him from Osborne, he deserves a second chance, a life with Deidra.

If I can get hold of Eliab's detonator, I can set off more than a spark inside that mine—with or without knowing where to find firedamp.

I chance a look at Luther, and my chest constricts. The stormy fire in his own eyes makes me realize he's on a rescue mission of his own, a rescue mission aimed at saving me.

It's a mission he has to lose. But first, I have to find a way to tell him that I love him, that I wish things could have been different, and that I hope he'll find room in his heart to forgive me.

I step back to let the Wasps more closely inspect the map I've drawn. It's rough, but they're well-trained. They'll be able to find their way.

Luther's hand brushes against mine, reassuring me he's right there.

I turn my head toward him and blow words under my breath. "Rescue the prisoners."

He dares to squeeze my hand. Good. He heard me.

Luther puts some distance between us and addresses Gage Eliab. "Should I go with you or wait in the outdoor arena?"

Eliab frowns, almost as if he had forgotten about Luther. "Wait in the arena, and stay out of sight."

Orbit trips the trap door and pushes it open to reveal the dark hallway.

"Up front, Abernathy." Eliab yanks at my hands to cuff them again. He latches them tighter than before. There's no hope of squeezing out. "Orbit, come with me. The rest of you know where to go once the hallway ends."

I lead the way, and despite our numbers, we move with stealthy silence. We reach the main hallway which breaks off into the smaller corridors. Just beyond is the kitchen entrance.

Without a word, the Wasps disperse with prisoners in tow toward the right.

Luther nods at Eliab and takes a left toward the back exit. My throat goes dry as he disappears down the hall. I never said any of the things I'd wanted to say.

Now, I'll have to carry all those unsaid longings to the grave.

The dark, silent library holds no trace of Osborne, and although we had approached his sacred space without seeing another person, there is no doubt the master knows we're here.

Eliab examines the Simulation interface with interest, but his fidgety fingers betray his anxiety. "Find Osborne," he snaps at me. "Bring him here. If you're not back in ten minutes, I'm pressing this button."

If only I could get out of the cuffs, I could be rid of the vest and care less if he pushes that blasted button.

Orbit scowls. "I don't trust her. Should I go with her?"

Eliab considers for a moment, then nods. "Yes, but in that case, I expect you both back in five."

My escort shoves me through the library's entrance. We retrace our steps up the staircase, both having the same location in mind: the dining room.

"Can you get me out of these?" I mutter and twist my neck to indicate my cuffs. I jump up the last step onto the upper hallway landing while struggling not to trip.

"No, I can't blow my cover yet."

"Blow your cover?" I shoot back. "You're going to blow a

whole lot more than that if this vest goes off."

"Eliab won't press that button until he has what he wants." Orbit cranes to peer through doorways and other levels. "And right now, you've hung two juicy pieces of bait in front of him. Unlucky for him, we don't have either of them—but that doesn't matter now. You got him here, and Osborne will be pleased."

"What do you mean?" I demand. "Osborne has Gath."

He shakes his head and glares at me. "No, he doesn't. And if you don't want Osborne pressing that button himself, you'd better come clean with him about Gath. The pipeliner told him he was in Warren, which is why his number was on your orders today. You've known about him all along, haven't you?"

I gulp. "Yes."

Orbit swears under his breath. "That's what Osborne figured. What he doesn't know is why you're bent on protecting him. He's a monster, Sage. Didn't Osborne tell you what he and Eliab did to his family? I heard he's responsible for your dad's death, too."

"I've heard all that, but he's different now," I insist, trying to keep up. "He's saved my life so many times. I can't let Osborne kill him."

"Then I can't help you." Orbit snorts. "You've lied to Osborne. He might tell me to detonate your vest myself."

I wince. After all we've been through together, would he really press that button?

A servant darts across the hallway ahead of us, and Orbit tackles him. The man relaxes when he recognizes his employer's spy. The man mumbles something I can't understand, and Orbit yanks me the other direction. "He's at the piano. If we hurry, we can catch him and get back to the library before Eliab gets anxious."

I pant after him. The landing to the piano level is ahead of us, and classical music drifts through the hallway.

Orbit stops and studies me a moment. His eye twitches. "Let me do the talking. Maybe I can get you out of this alive if you just tell me where Gath is."

"I—I don't know," I stammer. "I saw his number on the transport orders and had hoped to help him escape."

Orbit's face twists in confusion as the music suddenly stops. "If you don't have him, then who does?"

It's a question neither of us can answer.

Osborne appears at the edge of the landing above us. He's dressed in starchy beige pants and a black crew-neck shirt.

"What's the meaning of this?" His gaze darts from my black vest to Orbit.

"Gage Eliab is here—just as you wanted, but not according to plan," Orbit says in a low voice.

What does that mean?

Orbit continues, "We took him to the library—He's waiting for you."

This news doesn't seem to surprise Osborne. Had he known Eliab would be at Warren today?

My employer's sharp eyes focus on me. "What are you doing in that ridiculous vest? Where are the prisoners you were to bring me?"

I swallow. "Eliab was waiting at Warren—He ambushed me. He's threatening to blow me up if ..."

"We have to get back to the library," Orbit cuts me off. "Otherwise, he might suspect me. Right now, he doesn't know I work for you."

Osborne nods at Orbit. "Lead the way." He takes the stairs by two to join us, then snatches my arm with a vice-like grip as Orbit turns away.

"You have some explaining to do."

I jerk away from him, but he doesn't let go. "Today's been a nightmare, and now it's my fault? I walked into a trap—or was that what you had planned all along?" I demand.

He releases my arm. "Play this out, and I'll give you another chance."

I glower at him and flush with anger. "Another chance for what? To get myself killed? No, thank you. I want out."

"Out of that vest? I'll consider it if you behave."

"That's not what I meant."

We reach the stairs to the library again. Osborne slaps a hand on my back and pushes me downward.

The brute knows what I meant. He has to.

But maybe he never intends to relinquish his hold on me.

Chapter 40

Sunday, 6.7.2150
Excivis

The air in the library vibrates with tension. The curt introduction between Eliab and Osborne had ended in strained silence.

Now, Osborne makes an attempt at hospitality—as if a moccasin could ever make friends with a mongrel.

He pours three crystal glasses of brandy and offers one to Eliab who stiffly refuses. The Gage stands with his back against the mantle where an antique clock ticks the time away. He keeps one hand poised on his shooting hip and the other at the pocket of his jacket with the detonator.

I form a triangle between the two and wiggle nervously on the sofa, while Orbit waits like a statue at the doorway.

"She said you had Gath—and you're overdue to deliver Alexis," Eliab says at last. Though he's a good head taller than Osborne, he seems smaller in his presence.

"Did she say that?" Osborne tips his glass toward me and

chuckles—though his eyes glint at me in suspicion. "She's quite the two-faced thing. Thanks to her, I have neither at the moment."

"You're lying," Eliab accuses and shifts his gaze toward me.

"No, she's the one who's lying. Go ahead. Ask her where Gage Gath and Madame Alexis are."

Eliab doesn't need to ask. He shoots daggers with his eyes.

"I don't know," I say. "I was as surprised as you not to find Gath in his bunk, but you heard the prisoner. He said Gath didn't come out of the mines, so I assumed Osborne had taken him." I add under my breath. "I know he's been looking for him."

Osborne laughs again, a deep guttural sound. "Isn't she a witch? I save her life, and she rewards me with disloyalty."

Eliab jerks his head to Osborne. "Why do you want Gath?"

Osborne's fake smile morphs into a sneer. "The same reason I want you, Gage Eliab. Or have you forgotten what you did to my family? I believe you Gages like to call it *sport*."

Eliab narrows his eyes. "Are you threatening me? If you want to do business with the new Friend, you had better watch how you treat his Commanding Gage."

"Oh, I'll do business with him—with or without you."

"I think not." Eliab flashes the detonator. "I press this button, and we all get to meet our families again."

His words rake across my conscience. Who has Eliab lost? I think of Candace and Mom, maybe even Dad. Do families truly reunite in death? Is there an eternity like Christopher believed, or do we cease to exist?

I glance to the bookshelves beyond Eliab where the black book rests, right where I left it. Does it hold the answers?

A scowl contorts Osborne's face. "No, Gage Eliab, we disabled the detonator in her vest before returning here."

I blink. What is Osborne saying? They did no such thing ...

Eliab jerks toward Orbit as the implication of Osborne's words register. Osborne just exposed Orbit. The double agent now aims his handgun, the same semi-automatic he used to train me, at Eliab's chest.

The Gage shakes in rage. He has nowhere to run but slams his thumb against a button on the detonator. I cringe and close my eyes as the whistle goes off in my vest.

An explosion makes the walls shake. I blink and feel my chest. The vest is still there—and so am I.

"Hah!" Eliab points a finger at Osborne. "You're bluffing. She nearly jumped out of her skin."

"What was that?" Osborne looks at Orbit for an answer as concrete dust falls from the ceiling.

"Ah, didn't your spy tell you?" Eliab glowers at Orbit who continues to hold his weapon ready. "I planted several prisoners with vests like hers throughout your little domain. As I press these buttons, they explode—and your sacred fortress along with it."

The explosion makes my stomach lurch. I can only hope Luther rescued the prisoner before the vest detonated.

"You arrogant fool." Osborne steps toward Eliab. "If that explosion reaches the coal mines, the dust will set off an explosion none of us will survive."

Had the miners heard the explosion? The clock on the mantle reads a quarter past 1000 hours. If the Wasps heard the blast, will they evacuate the mines early?

"Besides, your precious Friend needs you like a cat needs a mouse. He has the Rosh League at his back. And with a rising star like Gage Colson, he won't miss you for long."

Osborne snaps his fingers. Eliab detects the signal a split-second too late. Orbit's handgun round shatters Eliab's wrist before he can press another button. The detonator flies out of his hand as he curses and returns fire with his shooting hand.

I dive to the floor for cover as a rapid succession of bullets discharge above my head. They tear through Eliab's chest and forehead, and he collapses to the ground, a gory corpse.

I want to tear my eyes away from the carnage, but I can't help but stare. The man who dogged my steps—is gone. Hate consumed him in life and death. The ugly aftermath makes me want to vomit.

Yet, I am just as capable of hate. I can't let it destroy me the same way.

Gath is right. Loving people is the only reason to live.

The click of an empty magazine snaps me to the present. As Orbit reloads behind me, I inchworm to reach the detonator remote and roll to my side to grab it with my cuffed wrists. I curl to my knees and slide the remote into my back pocket while Osborne talks with Orbit. "Who else came with you?"

Orbit slams a fresh magazine in his handgun. "There are five prisoners and five Wasps—plus one other man who accompanied Eliab."

Osborne paces in front of him in an uncommon display of nerves. "Eliminate them all. We can't have anyone knowing about our presence here."

"I can take care of the Wasps and Eliab's other man—They're waiting in the arena—but the prisoners are hiding somewhere inside." Orbit seats his handgun in its holster.

My employer strides toward the wall and pushes a button. "My men here will find the prisoners. They'll be easy enough to silence. You take care of the others.

"Then, return to Warren with the story that Wasp Sybil was a

398

spy and led you into an ambush. You alone escaped. Be convincing. You'll need the Commanding Wasp to back your story if the CGA investigates.

"Leave the bodies in the arena, and I'll have my men stage them inside the mine to make the deaths appear to be a prisoner ambush."

"Understood," Orbit says and then glances at me. "What about her?"

Osborne's jaw tenses. "She only did half her job right, and she lied to me. I don't tolerate insubordination."

Orbit draws his gun again and aims at my head. I'm still kneeling, hands cuffed, in execution position.

Please. I move my lips, but no sound comes out.

He lowers his gun, eyes still trained on me. "Sir, if I take her alive to Harris and execute her there, he won't question my loyalty or story."

Horror displaces my temporary relief. Better to die now than be humiliated in front of Harris.

Osborne nods slowly. "Brilliant." He crouches on the floor and snatches my chin between his fingers. "Or better yet, let Harris have his own way with her." He pauses to flash his teeth. "Unless, my dear, you want to finish the job you started."

I flinch but stay quiet.

"Where is Gath? Tell me, and I'll make sure Orbit gives you a merciful shot to the head."

The pressure on my jaw makes talking hard. "I don't know."

He releases me and wipes his hands on his pants as if wiping away dirt. "Have it your way. Harris will enjoy skinning a rabbit."

I swallow hard as Orbit yanks me to my feet. "I'll send word once I reach Crystal."

"Perfect," Osborne says. He gives me a mock bow. "Goodbye, Sage."

"What will you tell my brother?" I demand.

"I'll tell him you died in a gunfight and let him think you're a hero." His laughter echoes up the stairway and chases me into the hall.

Orbit's grim countenance matches his mission. He shoves me through the exit door, out the drainage pipe, and into the blinding daylight.

I won't survive to reach Warren. As soon as I see Luther, I'm screaming for him to run. I won't let Orbit kill him.

He jabs the gun barrel in my back to march ahead of him into the clearing. There are those blasted tires and that grueling course.

And then there are the Wasps, their bodies fallen in the grass like dead mongrels. My eyes widen as I pass the first. Who could have done this?

Orbit tugs me with him into the shadows. His body pulses with adrenaline. He's now on full alert because someone has beaten us here, someone who would be a good enough shot to surprise all five Wasps with a fatal round.

"Drop the gun."

Though I can't see him, Luther's voice sends a shockwave of hope and a surge of pride through me.

"I said drop the gun."

Orbit lowers it from my back and reluctantly drops it at his feet.

"Now let her go."

Orbit wraps an arm around my waist and pulls me against his chest. "If I let her go, you'll kill me."

"No, I won't."

He snorts. "Don't waste words with me. She's wearing a detonator vest. You fire at me, and you kill her, too."

There's no response. Orbit edges back toward the drainage pipe. Inside, the exit door remains unlatched from moments before.

"Stop, Orbit!" I cry. "I'll tell him not to shoot you. But please, get me out of these cuffs, and let me go."

He swears under his breath. "And who are you to tell him what to do?"

I swallow hard and steady my voice. "I'm the girl he loves."

Chapter 41

Sunday, 6.7.2150
Jasper

Orbit tenses at first and then relaxes his grip. "Wondered why he kept reaching for you in the mines."

I laugh nervously. "I was worried he'd give himself away."

He still holds me close to him. "Tell him yourself. Then, I'll let you go... wasn't going to let Harris skin you anyway."

"Thanks for that."

I clear my throat and call out. "Luther, don't shoot! He's going to let me go."

"He's my friend," Orbit mutters in my ear. "Tell him that, too."

"You call this friendship?"

"I'm letting you live, right?"

I roll my eyes before calling out again. "And Luther, he's my friend—saved my life."

There's no response from the woods, but Luther must have heard me.

Orbit's scratchy chin presses against my neck. "Good call. Never make a boyfriend jealous. Now, hold still."

He unlocks my cuffs, and I shake my wrists in relief. "Can you get this vest off, too?"

"Yeah, don't want someone accidentally pushing that button." He thumbs through the numbers on the vest. "Let's see if I remember right. Four, seven ..."

A barrel appears from the cracked doorway behind Orbit. I shriek but not fast enough. A shot slices the air and buries itself in Orbit's shoulder. He curses and drags me to the ground.

A wiry man steps halfway out from behind the ajar door. "I should kill you now." Osborne spats, raising his weapon to Orbit's face.

"Get down!" Orbit hisses through the pain. "There's a marksman out there. He said that if I released her, I could go."

Osborne's eyes narrow, but he retreats completely behind the door. "Who's out there?" he asks from behind it.

"It's another double agent—Eliab's assistant." Orbit grits his teeth in pain. "He must be working for the Brotherhood. He killed all the Wasps."

"Send Portia out—now!" Luther bellows from somewhere in the woods. He can't have a good view of either of us now that we're tucked inside the pipe.

"Keep the girl in front of you, and very slowly crawl inside." Osborne's tone is lethal.

I struggle to free myself from Orbit's single-handed grip. Osborne is only going to kill me. Inside or outside doesn't matter.

I shove Orbit in the chest, pushing him into Osborne's line of sight and buying a few seconds for my escape.

Bullets eat the ground behind me as I dart across the arena and leap behind one of the giant tires.

Osborne doesn't dare pursue with Luther's sights on the exit.

A shrill whistle sounds from inside my vest. On reflex, I cover my ears while bracing myself. A dull boom immediately follows, rolling the ground beneath my feet.

I feel my chest and arms. It must have been another vest.

I jerk the detonator out of my back pocket. Had I accidentally bumped it? I'm still trying to process what happened when my vest rings with the high-pitch alarm a second time.

And I'm not pressing any buttons.

Wait, there were two detonators in that crate. Eliab only took one. Who has the second?

I don't wait for the boom before frantically fingering the combination lock on my vest. Orbit entered the first two numbers, but I don't know which of the six I need to break the lock.

One.

The lock won't budge. The whistle goes off again.

Two.

Sweat trickles between my fingers as another boom rocks the earth in the distance.

Three.

I jerk at the lock as if force will make a difference and then scroll to the next number.

Four.

A bullet grazes the tire by my head, and I fall flat on the ground, still trying to pry off the vest. Panic freezes my brain. What number am I on?

There's no return fire from the woods, and another terror grips me. Is Luther hurt? Surely Osborne can't have hit him?

Replace panic with praise.

The thought blindsides me. Where had it come from?

Praise ... There had only been two commands that I'd read in the Bible. The first was to praise the Lord.

The second had been to trust ... in the Lord and not in men.

"Help me, God," I whisper. "I—I trust you can."

I take a deep breath. The trembling in my fingers subsides enough so I can scroll past five to six. The lock releases, and I squirm out of the vest and kick it away from me.

My heart pounds a blessing as I guerrilla-crawl from one tire to the next to increase my distance from the vest.

"*Fraternitas Veritas*." The words drip with disdain.

I twist onto my back as Osborne steps around the tire behind me, his revolver pointed at my forehead. I had been focused on ridding myself of the vest and hadn't noticed him creeping towards me.

The laughter in his throat rumbles like a bad joke. "What a catchy little slogan you have there. Your Brotherhood has served its purpose, though not the one you wanted. It's provided a perfect cover for my own operations and even given me a platform."

I narrow my eyes. "What—what do you mean?"

"I made your Brotherhood look more capable than it really is. That drove Gage Eliab's own underlings to me. When I promised I could help them find you, I got the contract I wanted—and my revenge to boot."

"Wait, you were behind those rail incidents?"

A slow smirk creeps across his cheeks. "Classic, wasn't it? If your group weren't so predictable, I would have had a harder time convincing Eliab the Rogue threat was on the rise."

"But why?" I dig my nails into the dirt. "What good has any of that done you?"

"A world of good. Gage Eliab is history, and now, my own spy stands to replace him. Once I find and deliver Madame Alexis ..."

"You'll never find her," I cut him off.

He snorts and adjusts his grip. "Yes, I will. When I do, I'll close my first contract with the CGA and pave the groundwork for future projects—projects that will pay handsomely."

"I thought you hated the CGA."

"So?" he demands. "If I can profit from them, I'll squeeze them dry and then move on—Why think small when the world is much bigger than one land mass?"

I glare at him. "And what's the point? What good will all the wealth in the world do you?"

He arches his brow as if my question is absurd. "It'll buy me even more power."

"Power? Do you think that will bring you happiness? Life is meaningless if you make it about yourself."

His eyes burn. "I don't have anyone left to share it with. You have to replace the emptiness with something."

"Then replace it with something that matters—and people matter."

"You and your ideals. That's your problem. Your Brotherhood is nothing but a fairy tale—a fool's attempt to create false hope."

I slide my hand into my back pocket. "You can't fault us for offering people hope."

"No, I don't." He steps closer and adjusts his finger on the trigger. "But I won't let rebel idealists ruin the hard-earned life I've built for myself. I gave you a fair chance, but you've outlived your *usefulness*."

That word sets off an alarm in my head. I yank the detonator from my pocket and slam my finger onto number six.

Chapter 42

Sunday, 6.7.2150
Excivis

A whistle screeches, and I lunge behind the last tire as Osborne fires. A bullet sears through my thigh as the vest explosion rocks the arena. Osborne's fiery silhouette flails and falls to the ground, but a chain reaction of booms from the direction of the mine drown his screams.

I bury my head in my arms, too jarred to think clearly.

Seconds later, someone tugs me from my hiding place and sweeps me into his arms. I flutter singed lashes as the cool shade of the tree canopy offers relief to the scorched arena.

Luther smells of gunpowder and sweat. I bury my head in his neck.

"We're getting out of this, Cotton," he promises. "But you're hurt?" He sets me down by a tree and traces his finger around the bloody patch on my pant leg. Behind us, black smoke pools over the mines.

"I'll be okay, but what happened?"

"My magazine ran dry," Luther mutters.

"Who was setting off those other vests?"

"How'd you know it was the vests?" Luther pulls a knife from his pocket and cuts away the bloody fabric on my leg.

I wince but don't complain. "Because mine kept whistling every time one was about to explode. It must have been linked to the others somehow."

He nods slowly. "That makes sense. I hadn't thought about that when I gave the second detonator to Gath."

"Gath?" I blink.

He seems not to hear me. "Now, hold still. This will hurt a bit."

I ball my fists as he probes the gunshot wound in my leg. All the while my mind reels. How had Luther found Gath?

"This could be worse," he says, taking the fabric he had torn off and wrapping it around my thigh in a make-shift tourniquet. "The bullet exited out the other side, so that's good. But you have some muscle tearing, and you're losing blood. We've got to get you to an expert Healer. I can't do much more, especially without supplies."

I catch my breath from the pain. "But Gath? You found him?"

His hand brushes my cheek. "Yes, I was searching for the prisoners and found him in one of the rooms. He was groggy, like he'd been drugged, but after I dunked his head under the sink a couple times, he came around."

"But how ... ?" I press my eyes closed to fight a searing headache and the fire throbbing in my thigh.

"Shh! Don't talk." Luther gingerly scoops me into his arms. "It was someone named Beatrice. He said she was trying to protect him from a suicide mission, that she didn't understand why he had to be the one to set off an explosion."

"Beatrice," I whisper. "Oh, Deidra, what did you do?"

"Huh?"

I sigh. "Beatrice is one of Osborne's agents who goes by Deidra. But go on."

"It took me a few minutes to realize he was talking about blowing the mine," Luther says. "At first, I thought he was crazy, and then, I realized he was serious. I know Gath well enough not to ask questions but to trust him. By this time, I'd rescued all but one of the prisoners and stripped their vests, using the combination code I read on the crate. Gath and I found all but the one ..." He sucks down a deep breath.

"I heard the explosion," I say softly.

"Anyway, I gave Gath the vests and the spare detonator. He was going to place them in the mines and plant one in Osborne's underground."

"And where's Deidra?" I ask.

"I don't know—I never met her," Luther says. "After all this, I'm not sure I want to."

"She's pretty fierce," I grin. "Guess I can't blame her for wanting to save her man."

"Her man?" Luther asks.

"That's a long story."

"We've got a long road ahead." Luther gives me an endearing smile. "How do we get out of here anyway?"

"If we can find one of Osborne's vehicles, that would be our best option. There's a camouflage canopy garage on the other side of the drainage pipe. The transport truck is gone, but there might be something else we can use."

He hesitates. "I don't want to leave you."

"I'll slow you down," I say. "Don't worry. I'm not going anywhere."

"Be right back." He sets me down carefully again and takes off running.

The roar of a fire rages from the mountain behind us. Warren won't be able to fill quotas anytime soon.

Despite the destruction, I smile. At least we've plugged one flow to the Rosh League's supply chain. If the other satellite explosions succeed, we might dam the resources they've been banking on.

How will that Rosh agent react? How will this affect Felix's rule? All these questions, I can't answer.

A truck engine revs in the distance, and I claw at the tree and use my one good leg to hobble to my feet.

Luther runs toward me and catches me in his arms. "I told you to stay put."

"I didn't get far." I laugh. "Remember those three-legged races from our childhood? I'm ready for one."

"You're not racing anytime soon." Despite my protests, he lifts me into his arms again and rushes toward the idling vehicle. It's a four-seater with high tires. Driving through brush won't be a problem for this machine.

After sliding me into the back seat to keep my leg elevated, he circles around and jumps into the driver's. "You're going to have to navigate. I don't know my way around this place."

Black smoke billows above the mine and spreads like a volcanic cloud above us. Was Gath able to evacuate the prisoners before the explosion?

"We have to find Gath and Deidra," I say. "I only know the long way to Warren, but most of it has a fairly decent road."

I motion for him to turn around. The uneven earth rocks the vehicle, and every pit and pothole make me wince.

As soon as the earth levels, Luther accelerates despite the smoke clouding his vision. His knuckles grow white from gripping the wheel, and I hold onto the seat to keep from falling out of it.

Despite the low visibility, I recognize the familiar fork in the road. "Left or right?" Luther asks.

I hesitate. Left takes us to the Warren compound, which is also covered in smoke. Right leads to the still-exploding mine.

"Right," I say. "Gath might still be in the mines."

Luther accelerates again, only to slam on the brakes moments later to avoid hitting someone in the road. The prisoner slams his fist against Luther's door and screams.

My blood curdles. Luther wears his Crystal uniform. The man might mistake him for a guard and try to ...

Luther's window cracks as the man throws a rock against it. Luther steps on the gas and swerves away to keep from running over the man.

"Are you okay?" He calls over his shoulder.

I gasp. "They think you're one of them. I should drive."

"You're the one wearing a Wasp uniform."

He has a point. "But some of them might recognize me as a former prisoner."

He shakes his head. "You can't drive with a bullet hole in your leg."

More prisoners run from the smoke, their emaciated silhouettes looking like dead people awakening from a graveyard. More rocks fly at the vehicle as we press closer to the blaze.

Suddenly, Luther yanks the wheel, and we spin full circle. "We have to turn around. Visibility is awful, and these prisoners are going to eat us alive if they manage to stop us."

My mouth goes dry. My crazy plan has worked, and now, we're in as much danger from the people we rescued than from their former captors.

I want to roll down the window and scream at them and tell them they're free. But I can't reason with starved rioters.

The vehicle's engine groans as Luther maneuvers up the sandy incline toward the compound. The tires dig into the dirt, but we skid down the trail.

"Hold on!" Luther cries. He jerks the wheel sideways, and the vehicle claws its way out of the sand, hugging the landscape at a verticle line that runs perpendicular to the path.

"Warren's the other way!" I shout above another explosion.

His lips form a grim line. "We're getting out of here. I can't see with all this smoke, and if we meet a horde of prisoners, we're never getting through."

I hug my seat and stare out the smokey back window. Darius said he would organize local members of the Brotherhood to help. Maybe once the fires die down, they'll be able to come in and do some good.

The tires finally find level ground. It's the road that will lead to the Jasper station, the place where seven months ago, my satellite train journey ended. Now, Warren burns, a giant conflagration that will give our brothers a much-needed victory against the ruling Dome and its misuse of civilian prisoners. Perhaps it will be but the first of a chain-reaction fire, the signal that revolution and change are coming to this blood-weary land.

Still, there's a cost. I can only hope Gath and Deidra aren't part of it.

I twist away from the rear window. Luther's body relaxes a

little as the distance between us and Warren increases. He glances over his shoulder to check on me.

His smile scatters the worry choking my heart and helps the road ahead seem brighter. "We're going to make it, Cotton."

Cotton. Whatever happens, I can finally be myself again. That's all he wants me to be.

I scoot forward on my seat and squeeze his shoulder. "Yes, we are."

He returns his attention to the road, and I follow his gaze. The only way to live is forward.

Notes

[i] "North Bridge Questions." NPS.gov.

[ii] "Bedford Flag." Revolutionary-war-and-beyond.com.

About the Author

Kristen Hogrefe is a multi-published novelist and teacher who challenges young adults and the young at heart to think truthfully and live daringly.

Her publishing journey began in 2010 with the first book in her young adult (YA) suspense trilogy *Wings of the Dawn*. She completed the trilogy in the fall of 2014, and in 2016, contracted with Write Integrity Press for a new YA dystopian trilogy: The Rogues.

Kristen also has the heart of an educator and mentor. She teaches secondary language arts for Alpha Omega Academy and served in youth ministry for many years. Through Word Weavers International, she encourages aspiring writers and acts as president for an online writing group. She enjoys speaking events that allow her to connect with readers and other writers.

A lifelong Florida resident, Kristen loves adventuring outdoors and running with friends. Connect with her online at KristenHogrefe.com.

Acknowledgments

Ralph Waldo Emerson said, "Cultivate the habit of being grateful for every good thing that comes to you, and to give thanks continuously. And because all things have contributed to your advancement, you should include all things in your gratitude." If I were to spell out "all things" and all the people who made a difference during the writing of this book, you would have another whole book to read. Instead, I'll be brief, though this list is by no means exhaustive.

As always, my family, especially my parents, remain a constant encouragement to me, and words can't express my appreciation for them. I also want to say a special thanks to my friend Devon Curtis and to my fellow writing comrade Ashley Jones for their advice and insight on the rough draft.

I want to give my heartfelt thanks to graphic artist Kelli Sorg (Make It Snappy) for designing yet another fabulous cover!

Once again, I'm grateful to my editor Marji Laine and her team for helping make this book the best it can be.

Most of all, I'm thankful to my Savior Jesus Christ for His presence in my life and for giving me the stewardship of writing. My desire is that He would be pleased with my stories, and that in some small way, they would make a difference in a reader's life.

Discussion Questions

1. Portia struggles with her identity in many ways throughout this book. She's forced to answer to a prisoner number, not a name; Wasp Harris refers to her and the other prisoners as "rabbits," nothing more than animals; and she juggles fake identities to stay safe. To add insult to injury, Lord Osborne changes her appearance—from the color of her hair to dermal implants.

Have you ever struggled with your identity being tied to your appearance or with unkind words someone has said? If so, visit KristenHogrefe.com and search for the blog post "Unchanging Identity in Christ." Consider these verses in the Bible: Genesis 1:27, I Corinthians 3:16, and Matthew 6:19-21. How does the biblical definition of our identity go below skin level?

2. When Portia and Madame Alexis escape to Chrysoprase by train, Jael meets them at the station and tells them to seek shelter at Portia's neighbor's house. Portia balks at the idea, protesting that she and her dad never talked with their neighbors. Jael's reply cuts to the chase: "Then now is a good time to start."

In our culture, most of us rarely see the people who live next door because we're so busy with our own lives. Some say that social media and online networking have replaced our desire (and perhaps our ability) to personally connect with others around us.

If someone asked you how well you know your neighbors, what would you say? Have you replaced personal connections with social media? If so, what can you do to change that?

3. Madame Alexis explains to Portia about the United States' system of "checks and balances" among the three branches of

government. In this system, the three branches are accountable to each other to keep one from dominating and abusing power.

The United States Constitution spells out the Separation of Power in Articles 1, 2, and 3. Can you name the three branches of government and their primary functions? How do these separate branches both complement and restrain the other? What potential pitfalls could occur with a breakdown of any one branch?

4. As Portia uncovers Gath's story and true identity, she realizes that everything she's heard about his sordid past is true—yet she can't reconcile such brutality with the character of the man who has risked his life for her. The only explanation for Gath's radical transformation is the power of God to give second chances.

The Bible tells the story of the extreme conversion of a man named Saul, who went from persecuting Christians to proclaiming the very Gospel he originally set out to destroy. You can read his true story in Acts 9.

Have you ever felt as though you've done something unforgiveable? The stories of Gath and Saul provide a different perspective. How can you apply that to your own life story?

5. Though Portia's psychological scars from the satellite run deep, she isn't the only character who struggles with fear. In fact, Portia helps Madame Alexis overcome her anxiety of confined spaces by keeping her engaged in conversation as they travel through the underground tunnel.

Do you have an unresolved fear? What can you do to overcome it? How can you help others face their own giants? Check out these Bible verses to give you more insight and encouragement: Isaiah 43:1-2, Isaiah 41:10, Psalm 118:6, 2 Timothy 1:7, and I John 4:18.

Book One of The Rogues

**A Revisionary
rewrites the rules.**

**A Rogue breaks
them.**

Which one is she?

Nineteen-year-old
Portia Abernathy plans
to earn a Dome seat
and rewrite the Codex
rules to rescue her
exiled brother. Her
journey demands
answers from the past
civilization, but
uncovering the truth
means breaking the
rules she set out to
rewrite.

Where will the world be in 2149? If citizens forget their past,
they will be lost in an identity crisis. That's exactly the state of
the American Socialists United (ASU). This dystopian story
opens in Cube 1519, a ghetto where the only use for obsolete cell
phones is to throw them like rocks at mongrels. Portia and her
father survive like many other citizens, with no electricity or
technology and no expectation for a better life.

Yet Portia remembers her brother Darius—before he was taken
from her. Now that's she's graduated, she determines to get him
back. She thinks earning a Dome seat as a Revisionary candidate

will be her ticket to rewriting the Codex and reversing his sentence. However, when she receives her draft and arrives at the Crystal Globe University for training, she discovers the world is very different outside her cube and that prisoners like Darius aren't the only ones trapped by the system.

Written for young adults, *THE REVISIONARY* offers a suspenseful plot, flashbacks to America's Revolutionary era, and rediscovery of the founding values needed to rebuild Portia's unraveling world. "In school, teens hear that if they don't learn from history's lessons, they're destined to repeat them," author Kristen Hogrefe says. "Portia lives in a world where leaders wield ignorance to control citizens. Only when Portia sets out to rescue her brother does she realize the lie she's been living and determines to break free."

Blockbuster novels like *The Hunger Games*, *Divergent*, and *The Giver* popularized the dystopian YA genre. *THE REVISIONARY* builds a dystopia of a different kind—one that looks backward to find wisdom to move forward to offer an underlying message of heritage and hope.

Also From Write Integrity

Action and Adventure

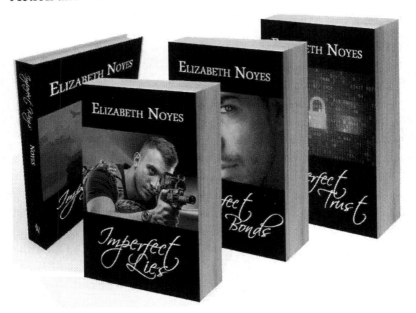

The Imperfect Series brings the action from a cattle ranch in Idaho to military-like operations all over the world. The author has a unique perspective and insight and creates vivid pictures of both!

Book 1 – *IMPERFECT WINGS*

Evil stalks TJ McKendrick.
Three years after burying her father, TJ visits Honduras where he died. While there, she witnesses a murder and is forced to flee.

The last thing Garrett Cameron needs is another woman interrupting his life, but when the feisty vixen that blew his mission two years ago shows up at his ranch running for her life, what can he do?

Only faith in God and trust in each other can overcome the deadly odds they face.

The Bird Face Series follows young Wendy Robichaud through the most desperate of situations, high school with all of its trauma and drama.

Book 1 – *8 NOTES TO A NOBODY*

"Funny how you can live your days as a clueless little kid, believing you look just fine ... until someone knocks you in the heart with it."

Wendy Robichaud doesn't care one bit about being popular like good-looking classmates Tookie and the Sticks—until Brainiac bully John-Monster schemes against her, and someone leaves anonymous sticky-note messages all over school. Even her best friend, Jennifer, is hiding something and pulling away. But the spring program, abandoned puppies, and high school track team tryouts don't leave much time to play detective. And the more Wendy discovers about the people around her, the more there is to learn.

When secrets and failed dreams kick off the summer after eighth grade, who will be around to support her as high school starts in the fall?

**Thank you
for reading our books!**

**Look for other books
published by**

Write Integrity Press
www.WriteIntegrity.com

Made in the USA
Middletown, DE
07 August 2019